PRAISE FOR
THE THIRD RULE OF TEN

*"Tenzing 'Ten' Norbu may be the most interesting
PI in modern crime fiction. The Third Rule of Ten,
the third book in the series, is beautifully written
and intricately plotted, but as always, it's the heart
and soul of Ten that carry the greatest appeal,
drawing the reader on a spiritual journey that is as
satisfying as the climax. I loved this book."*

—Robert Ferrigno,
New York Times best-selling author of the Assassin trilogy

"The Third Rule of Ten *will grab you by the throat
and not let go. In Tenzing Norbu, Gay Hendricks
and Tinker Lindsay have created a Buddhist action hero
(yes, there is such a thing) who is sympathetic, moral,
and self-reflective. Crackling with wit, superbly
drawn characters, and a blistering plot,*
The Third Rule of Ten *will keep you going until
you take a deep, meditative breath on the last page."*

—Diane Mott Davidson,
New York Times best-selling author of *The Whole Enchilada*

"I loved it!"

—Jack Kornfield,
author of *A Path with Heart*

D0280866

THE
THIRD RULE
OF TEN

ALSO BY GAY HENDRICKS
AND TINKER LINDSAY

The First Rule of Ten

The Second Rule of Ten

The Broken Rules of Ten (e-book only)

Available from Hay House
Please visit:

Hay House UK: **www.hayhouse.co.uk**
Hay House USA: **www.hayhouse.com®**
Hay House Australia: **www.hayhouse.com.au**
Hay House South Africa: **www.hayhouse.co.za**
Hay House India: **www.hayhouse.co.in**

THE THIRD RULE OF TEN

A TENZING NORBU MYSTERY

GAY HENDRICKS & TINKER LINDSAY

HAY HOUSE

Carlsbad, California • New York City • London • Sydney
Johannesburg • Vancouver • Hong Kong • New Delhi

First published and distributed in the United Kingdom by:
Hay House UK Ltd, Astley House, 33 Notting Hill Gate, London W11 3JQ
Tel: +44 (0)20 3675 2450; Fax: +44 (0)20 3675 2451
www.hayhouse.co.uk

Published and distributed in the United States of America by:
Hay House Inc., PO Box 5100, Carlsbad, CA 92018-5100
Tel: (1) 760 431 7695 or (800) 654 5126
Fax: (1) 760 431 6948 or (800) 650 5115
www.hayhouse.com

Published and distributed in Australia by:
Hay House Australia Ltd, 18/36 Ralph St, Alexandria NSW 2015
Tel: (61) 2 9669 4299; Fax: (61) 2 9669 4144
www.hayhouse.com.au

Published and distributed in the Republic of South Africa by:
Hay House SA (Pty) Ltd, PO Box 990, Witkoppen 2068
Tel/Fax: (27) 11 467 8904
www.hayhouse.co.za

Published and distributed in India by:
Hay House Publishers India, Muskaan Complex, Plot No.3, B-2,
Vasant Kunj, New Delhi 110 070
Tel: (91) 11 4176 1620; Fax: (91) 11 4176 1630
www.hayhouse.co.in

Distributed in Canada by:
Raincoast, 9050 Shaughnessy St, Vancouver BC V6P 6E5
Tel: (1) 604 323 7100; Fax: (1) 604 323 2600

Copyright © 2014 by Gay Hendricks and Tinker Lindsay

Photo of Gay Hendricks: Mikki Willis
Photo of Tinker Lindsay: Cameron Keys

A catalogue record for this book is available from the British Library.

ISBN: 978-1-78180-271-7

Printed and bound in Great Britain by TJ International Ltd

MIX
Paper from
responsible sources
FSC
www.fsc.org   **FSC® C013056**

What have I done?
The cell phone in my pocket vibrated. I glanced at the screen and saw it was Bill Bohannon, my ex-partner. In that moment, it felt like light years since we'd been Detective II's in LAPD's elite Robbery/Homicide division. Now Bill was a Detective III, and I was about to become one of his cases.

"Hey," I said.

Bill's voice was thick with sleep. "I thought I told you to stay out of trouble. Your buddy Mike said something triggered the security system. Everything okay?"

I looked at the two still bodies.

"Not exactly," I said. "I got two men down, one more wounded and at large."

Bill woke up fast. "Two men down. How down?"

"As down as they can get," I said.

Bill groaned.

"The kills were righteous," I said, but I wondered if that was true.

A siren wailed in the distance, drawing closer. My night was about to get even more complicated.

"Bill, I hate to ask, but—"

"I'm on my way," he barked. "Don't say a word to anyone until I get there."

Don't say a word. More secrets to keep. Mere days ago I had made myself a new rule: to be mindful of the darker side of secrets. To keep current with the truth, not just within myself, but also with those affected by my actions. And now I had manifested one of the worst truths I could ever have imagined.

The two lifeless bodies lay sprawled on the ground like a pair of indefensible reproaches. As I studied them, an ice cold wave rolled through my insides. I shivered.

What have I done?

CHAPTER 1

TWO DAYS EARLIER

"Ayúdame." The high-pitched voice was edged with stress and close, as if the owner's mouth hovered an inch from my ear. *"Ayúdame."*

My eyes snapped open, but my body knew better than to move. The muted light pressing through the bedroom window announced it was almost dawn. My eyes shifted right. The space by my side of the bed, where a woman in distress—a woman in distress who spoke Spanish—should be standing, was empty. I lifted my head and quick-scanned the rest of the bedroom. Empty. I rolled onto my left side, facing Heather. As usual, sometime during the night she had inched to the rim of the mattress and manufactured a rumpled bunker of bedclothes, within which her breath rose and fell in the steady rhythm signifying deep sleep. Her sloped silhouette was beautiful. I reached across the bed to trace my fingers along her curved side, but pulled my arm back. In the months we had been officially together, I'd learned at least one very important lesson: Never, ever wake up a forensic medical examiner on her one day off.

At my feet, the feline puddle of fur and whiskers called Tank was equally still, so it wasn't his *meow* I'd heard. Finally, I checked the small monitor on my wall, which was connected to a series of small cameras outside—my electronic eyeballs on any intrusive dangers. Nothing. No one else was here, inside or out. I was hearing things, experiencing

3

some kind of auditory hallucination. Great: one more item to add to my list of worrisome new behaviors.

Sunday or not, sleep was no longer an option. I slipped out of bed and pulled on a baggy pair of sweatpants and a long-sleeved, cotton T-shirt. Tank lifted his head. His green eyes narrowed in the soft light, observing me as I dressed. His whiskers twitched—the equivalent of a cat shrug. He curled like a cashew, tucked his nose between his paws, and went back to sleep.

I tiptoed into the living room, grabbed the plaid blanket Heather had recently added to the sectional sofa, wrapped it around my shoulders, and padded through the kitchen and outside to the deck, careful to deactivate the Guard-on system first. After several months of living with this ridiculously expensive and hypervigilant organism of panoramic cameras and outdoor sensors, digital alerts and interconnected alarms, I was finally getting used to the thing. I still didn't know whether to thank or curse my late client Julius Rosen for bequeathing me such a high-tech, über-expensive security system. It arrived with a handwritten note in Julius's tiny, crabbed writing—one more symptom of his advanced Parkinson's. "For my friend Tenzing Norbu," the note read. "I deeply regret putting you on the radar of certain people and hope this will give you the protection you need and deserve."

When "certain people" include Mexican drug lords, four miniscule outdoor cameras and two indoor digital screens don't exactly add up to safety, but in the end I appreciated the gesture. At $6,000 a pop, there was no way I would have paid for a Guard-on system myself. In any case, apart from a few startled raccoons, one terrified jogger, and several accidental triggers by me, nothing had yet proved cause for alarm. So to speak.

I shivered and pulled my blanket tighter. The canyon was draped in its own blanket, this one of thick mist—the southern California June gloom had arrived early this year.

A coyote chuckled. Another replied. Soon a jumble of feral wails and eerie shrieks filled the dawn air, like a chorus of frightened women.

Ayúdame.

I rubbed my arms and did a brisk stomping dance to shake off my mood. I had a big day ahead of me. No reason to start out, as my mother, Valerie, used to put it, "on a bummer."

A warm body brushed against my ankles.

"Hey, Tank. Change your mind?"

I bent down, enveloped 17 pounds of sleepy cat in a wool blanket, and hauled the dense bundle up to my chest.

The coyote cries faded into silence. The mist thinned. Watery early morning sunshine barely pierced the layers of fog and darkness. Topanga Canyon seemed especially secretive today, as if unconsciously crossing her arms tight, holding any private thoughts deep in her shadowy folds.

She's hiding things. Just like me.

I should meditate, I thought. *It's been a few days.*

I should contact Yeshe and Lobsang. Ditto.

Even as I noticed these thoughts, I knew I wouldn't take the actions. I also knew it hadn't been days. It had been weeks, enough weeks to qualify as months. This was my new method of justification, ever since I'd returned from India: When in doubt, deflect. Avoid. Hedge the truth. Some might call it dissembling. I preferred to think of it as being mindful of my need for privacy, for allowing the time and space to figure things out for myself. I had ceased writing Yeshe and Lobsang letters. Technology, combined with their move back to Dharamshala, made snail mail redundant. But my retreat from communication had little to do with computer networks. When I had written them letters in the past, the simple act of putting pen to paper meant I was willing to connect with my feelings and listen to my heart. Not now. I preferred not to look closely at anything uncomfortable right now. Grief takes on its own form of healing—everybody says so.

Only in my case, I wasn't sure the grieving had even started.

I'd returned from Dharamshala in December a changed man, with a new label to add to my growing arsenal of personal identifications: Tenzing Norbu, ex-Tibetan lama, ex-LAPD cop, licensed private investigator—and now, orphan.

My father was dead, his body gone. I had been able to sit with him, chant with him, to the end. I helped prepare his remains and transfer them to the ceremonial palanquin. I helped carry his corpse to the hastily constructed "fire house," helped place him inside the cremation *stupa*, close it up, whitewash it, and decorate it with bright swabs of paint and brilliant prayer flags. I had joined my best friends, Lama Yeshe and Lama Lobsang, in reciting prayers and performing rituals. I participated in the grand and strangely moving Buddhist ceremony of praise, release, and incineration. I watched my father ignite and transform into a tower of flames. I observed the lamas break open the fire house to retrieve his burned relics, and watched the ritual master—my old tutor Lama Sonam, bent with age himself—sift through Apa's ashes for significant signs.

My father was dead, his body gone. Before I left Dharamshala, I met with Lama Sonam privately, so he could share with me the evidence left in the remains: evidence, he assured me, that proved my father was a highly realized man. With shining eyes, Lama Sonam spoke of the special orb-like formation, associated with a refined mind, discovered in my father's bone fragments and the small footprint, pressed into the sand mandala created for the ceremony, that faced southwest, indicating where my father would be reborn. Other proof I saw with my own eyes: the rainbow that arched across the sky the hour he left his body; the weird pliability of his shrunken bones and muscles—untouched by *rigor mortis* after death—that allowed the monastery's resident healer, Lama Tashi, to manipulate my father's limbs into lotus position before his cremation. All of us witnessed the dark smoke from the incineration rising straight up in the air and hovering there in an unwavering column, while all around it the prayer flags snapped and swayed. It was as if in one final, stubborn act my father's smoldering residue ignored the laws of nature, choosing instead to aim for his own higher purpose. (Now, *that* was the father I knew.) Whether any of these things made Apa a venerated being, I couldn't say. I was certainly not the right person to ask.

My father was dead, his body gone. We had made our peace. But there were still some things I hadn't dared ask him before he left his body, and he hadn't chosen to disclose. I didn't push; a man deserves his privacy. But I had yet to completely dispel the smoky darkness his passing left in my heart. The secrets imbedded there.

The sun was finally up. Tank bolted from my arms and darted inside. Either his stomach or his bladder was making its needs known. Come to think of it . . .

I stepped off the deck for a quick pee, promised my own growling stomach I would make it very happy, very soon, then returned to the kitchen to deal with the rest of my essential morning tasks. Namely: feed cat, feed cat, and feed cat.

Back in the bedroom, I tried to change into my jeans and T-shirt quietly, but Heather hears like a hawk sees.

"Where're you off to?" Her voice was muffled with sleep, and sounded slightly irritated. I crossed to the bed and kissed her lightly on the forehead. Framed with a tangle of blonde hair, her face glowed in the pale light, ridiculously flawless.

"Sorry. Work. Remember? I told you last night. I have another appointment with Mac Gannon. And you have no right to look like this on five hours of sleep."

Heather's lips formed a little pout. "Oh, right. Your new best friend. Some people get to have all the fun." She licked her index finger and touched the back of my hand, making a sound like hot oil hitting a skillet: *Sssttt!* "Hotshot. Okay then. Have fun. Keep me posted."

As was often the case with Heather these days, I couldn't tell if she was fine with me going, upset, or somewhere in between. As was often the case with me these days, I chose not to investigate.

Heather and I weren't living together yet, but we probably spent four nights a week sharing a bed. Weekdays, I went to her condominium in Santa Monica. Weekends, she stayed with me. But our full schedules meant we rarely had time to really talk or better yet, not talk and just be.

Time to get ready. I ran a brush over my cropped lawn of black hair. Not much more I could do there. This being Mac Gannon, I made a last-minute decision to swank up a little and grabbed the black cashmere blazer Heather had given me for my 31st birthday. I decided not to accessorize, however. My Wilson Combat Supergrade would remain locked in the closet safe for the time being. The only imminent danger at the moment was the result of my rampant imagination.

"Heather?"

"Mmm."

"You speak Spanish, right?"

"Enough to get by."

"What does ayúdame mean?"

She met my eyes; hers were a little troubled.

"Ayúdame means *Help me.*"

A small chill snaked up my spine. I shrugged it off. So someone was asking for help—it was probably my own troubled psyche.

"I'll call you later," I said. "If you go out, don't forget to—"

"Reset the Guard-on. Got it." She rolled away and buried her head in the pillow. Okay, upset. But hopefully not the kind of upset a few hours of deep sleep wouldn't make right.

I hustled out the kitchen door, passing a contented Tank nose-deep in a bowl of canned mixed grill. The air was still chilly, and I pulled on my blazer. Now I was warm but also uncomfortable, sideswiped by a cascade of unpleasant thoughts about the night Heather had given me the jacket. There'd been tension in the air the whole evening, and the off-center feeling still lingered, as if captured in the seams of the garment. My mind started to scamper down a familiar misery tunnel. I yanked it back like restraining a leashed dog. Whatever my girlfriend problems were, there was no way I could solve them right now. I hurried over to my loaner car, a smart little Tesla Model S. It was Sunday morning. I was apparently a hotshot. I had people to see, places to go.

Secrets to keep.

Chapter 2

I was really zipping down Topanga Canyon. The Tesla was cruising at 70 miles per hour with an unnerving absence of engine noise. These all-electric sports cars are deceptively meek-looking, considering the power they contain—like that proverbial soft-spoken guy next door who harbors a cache of AK-47s under his bed and winds up unleashing a firestorm at the local mall.

I whizzed past the Buddha wall, where a hand-stenciled mural of the seated Sakyamuni has watched over Topanga Canyon Boulevard for decades. The delicate painted icon, one hand cupping a bright blue earth in place of the usual begging bowl, seemed to raise his eyebrow at me. I checked my speedometer. Whoa, pushing 80. I eased off the accelerator.

My Mustang was getting a weekend overhaul at the shop in Santa Monica, and I'd decided on an impulse to cross the street, slip the salesman a little cash incentive, and request a weekend "test-drive" of this merry little Tesla. I told the dealership I drove a lot for my work, which was the truth, and might be in the market for this car, which wasn't. A silver Tesla Model S is almost as unusual as a bright yellow '65 Shelby Mustang 350, and just as terrible a choice for surveillance. No, my next "work" car, and hopefully not for a while, would probably be another secondhand, drab Toyota, the only elegant thing about it the smoked glass finish I would give its windows.

So far, so good: the main canyon artery, often clogged, was almost empty. The high hum from the electric motor created a jaunty duet with the whistling wind. Within minutes, I pulled into Pat's Topanga Grill, my mouth already watering.

With its rustic wood-slatted siding, the building looked more like a saloon than a coffee shop, although this saloon was flanked by asphalt on one side and California sycamores on the other. A pair of matching wooden sharks, nose-to-nose on the swinging double-door entrance, hinted further at Pat's unique take on dining decor. Inside, designer surfboards floated overhead, and local artwork, most notably Pat's, crowded the walls. As always, my eye went to the resurrected road sign hung near the kitchen area: "Topanga," the reflective letters proclaimed, and underneath, "pop 3342 elev 720." The population had probably tripled by now—which still made my community barely a hamlet by L.A. standards. I assumed the elevation hadn't changed.

I nodded to Pat, his mustache drooping under bristling brows as he stood guard by the kitchen. I received a gruff nod in return and considered that a triumph. Something about him reminded me of my childhood nemesis at the monastery, the grim kitchen monk, Lama Dorje. Both men had an uncanny way of knowing exactly when somebody was about to do something wrong and would pounce on hapless perps with an eagerness that bordered on glee. Luckily, I didn't have mandatory kitchen duty as part of my life anymore, though Tank might disagree.

I circumvented a couple of shaggy dogs and helped myself to a cup of excellent fresh-brewed coffee. I claimed a small, rickety wooden table for two in the corner, leaving the long counter and bigger tables free. The local brunch crowd would start drifting in soon, some grabbing seats outside facing the trees, where their welcomed dogs could explore, others lugging their fat Sunday papers indoors for spreading out and passing around. Topanga residents considered Pat's the next best thing to home sweet home, a place you could gather and chill for hours. But woe to the city visitor who arrived here expecting and demanding fast, courteous service. I'd seen more than one of them scurry off unfed after being politely ignored, if not publicly humiliated, by the man himself.

I leaned back in my chair, content. In a few hours, some skinny guitarist, barely awake and still scratching his balls, would set up a mike and start strumming and singing '60s hits, which qualified as brunch entertainment. I would be long gone by then.

I'd been introduced to Pat's years ago by one of its most celebrated regulars, Zimmy Backus, an ex-rocker of some fame himself. Zimmy and I were deep in real estate negotiations at the time. I was a rookie cop on a limited budget and desperate to rent Zimmy's beautiful Zen-like Topanga Canyon getaway. Zimmy was in the throes of a bad divorce from a Japanese wild woman who'd left him for a bass player with a bigger coke habit than both of them combined. For some reason, Zimmy decided almost immediately he liked me, so he gave me a good deal. A fellow vegetarian, he'd hauled me to Pat's and treated us both to his usual, a Veggie Club sandwich. We toasted our long-term rental agreement with thick chocolate malts.

I bought the house from Zimmy six years later. By then I had graduated to LAPD Detective I, Burglary/Homicide, so my income was bordering on respectable. Plus, my late mother's trust had come through, and I could finally afford the down payment. Zimmy and I had returned to his favorite eatery for one final soy bacon blowout. It was the only time I've ever seen Pat get a little misty.

I closed my eyes, picturing Zimmy's scruffy smile, and sent him some loving-kindness: *May you be safe and protected. May you be healthy and strong. May you live with ease. May you be free.*

I'd taken a break from Pat's for a while—couldn't afford the long waits, and there are only so many veggie burritos you can stomach—but lately I'd made a point of coming here a lot. I liked the total absence of LAPD cops, for one.

For another, I had never brought Heather here. She didn't even know Pat's Topanga Grill existed.

My favorite grumpy waitress, Patrice, her left eyebrow sprouting a freshly planted row of studs, swung by with her pencil and pad.

"The usual?"

I smiled. "What else?"

She wheeled away, and my smile faded. There wasn't anything usual about my "usual."

It was too warm inside for the cashmere blazer, and I slipped it off with a feeling of relief. Heather had made a huge effort for my birthday. She'd booked us "our" table at "our" place, the Inn of the Seventh Ray, and had preordered an exquisite, six-course vegan taster menu, wine pairings included. She'd turned heads crossing the outdoor court-yard in her red silk dress and glossy high-heeled boots. But Heather doesn't miss much, and she could tell I wasn't all there. I'd unwrapped and put on the cashmere blazer, smil-ing hard. It itched a little around the collar, but I resisted scratching. The silence grew. So did the tension.

Heather had drained her wineglass and set it down with a clunk.

"Is it your father?"

"Is what my father?"

"You know. Ten, when you left for India, we were fine. More than fine. Amazing. But ever since you got back . . ."

"I'm just tired," I said. "Work's been nonstop, in case you haven't noticed."

She stood up.

"I'm sorry," I said. "Heather . . ." But it was too late. She'd fled to the restroom. She did that a lot. When she got back, I could tell from her puffy, red-rimmed eyes that she'd been crying, though she reassured me she hadn't and she understood and everything was fine.

Everything wasn't fine, and we both knew it. But how could I put into words what I could barely feel? Everything seemed up for reinterpretation somehow: what I did, what I thought, how I felt.

Who I was with.

In the heady days after we'd pledged to be spiritual and romantic partners, Heather and I had floated through time in a bliss-bubble of early love and mutual infatuation. We barely ate and slept even less. We sat together, morning and evening, in deep meditation, which often led to a more physical version of linking up, and called or texted incessantly in the hours between. When Heather dropped me off at LAX on my way to India to spend time with my ill father, we reassured each other the separation would only make us stronger. I left love-struck. I was gone for six weeks. I returned a stranger.

We never could seem to find our earlier rhythm. I had expected to be gone for only two weeks, but I was wrong. Communication had been spotty—and unsatisfactory. The time difference alone made staying connected a challenge. And now that Heather had finally been hired full-time as a deputy medical examiner for the county coroner's office, she was on call 24/7. I myself had returned to a long list of new clients clamoring for my help.

The trip had scarred us both, but neither of us knew how to broach the subject. Heather grew busier and busier, and I grew more and more withdrawn.

I sipped my coffee, my heart a little heavy. So much loss lately.

Seemingly mere moments after I landed back on American soil—although in fact two months had passed—another father figure made an abrupt exit, a client in a missing persons case. Julius Rosen's questionable behavior had let me down in the end, but I still considered him a mentor of sorts. So when his quavering phone call asked me to meet him at Cedars-Sinai Medical Center, I didn't hesitate. "I feel lousy," Julius said. "I think this may be it." We met outside, and I accompanied him into the emergency room, trailing behind his wheelchair as

Julius, canes waving, mumbled, "No extreme measures! No extreme measures!" to anyone who crossed his path.

Within 48 hours, the pneumonia had filled both lungs, easily swatting aside any and all non-extreme measures. Parkinson's disease had rendered his frozen vocal chords almost useless by this time, but somehow I could still understand him. On day three, Julius opened his eyes and motioned me close. It was the eve of our Tibetan New Year, Losar, 2012—the Year of the Male Water Dragon; a year, our pundits predicted, of mixed blessings and great contradictions.

"'M n't g'ing t'gt b'tr, 'm I?" he mumbled.

I touched his arm. "No, Julius. You're not going to get better." One of the hardest truths I'd ever told.

He shuddered. Water leaked from the corners of his eyes, a brief acknowledgment of a lost life, lost in more ways than one. He glanced at the framed photograph of his late wife, Dorothy—the only personal item he'd brought from home—nodded once as if satisfied, lay down, and closed his eyes.

He died as our new year dawned, a man, too, of great contradictions—and left me a Guard-on security system and $100,000 tax-free to remember him by. The Guard-on unit was set up for all to see. The money was my little secret. I told myself that as long as my ex-partner Bill Bohannon was struggling to pay the bills—Detective-III pay notwithstanding, he still had twin girls going tc an expensive preschool—it wasn't fair to tell him of my good fortune. I told myself that Heather didn't need to know every single detail of my financial life. I told myself it was nobody else's concern—so much easier than exploring why the money felt strangely shameful.

Two fathers' lives ended, and immediately the withholding of little truths, here and there, began.

Meanwhile, my private investigator business had taken off. Somehow, I'd become the go-to guy for heavy spenders in Los Angeles. They all talk to each other, I guess. After I'd landed a notorious Hollywood producer and a billionaire philanthropist as my first two clients, not to mention rubbed shoulders with a young, heartthrob megastar, word of my work swelled from a trio to a chorus, guaranteeing a steady stream of well-paying customers. Everyone loved the idea of a Tibetan ex-monk who promised high-quality service coupled with absolute confidentiality. Buddhism was sexy: who knew?

Beautiful girlfriend, booming business, fat bank account: I should be feeling liberated on all fronts. Instead, I felt trapped, caught in a snare of my own making.

Patrice set my plate in front of me.

"Hunter omelet, whole wheat," she drawled. I stared down at the bulging omelet, inhaling the gamy scent of bacon, sausage, and thick-sliced ham, with a few grilled mushrooms thrown in for luck. I had become a hunter overnight. After not eating a morsel of animal flesh in decades, I suddenly couldn't get enough of it.

I also couldn't bring myself to admit this to my adamantly vegan girlfriend.

I took a big forkful of omelet, washing it down with a slug of hot coffee, followed by another bite and another. I could feel the rich animal protein entering my bloodstream like a drug, and for a moment I was tempted to throw back my head and howl.

A man deserves his privacy. My recent stay at the monastery had reminded me again how precious privacy can be. The total lack of it had been one of the factors that drove me away from the monastic life to begin with. But as my tutor, Lama Sonam, once told me, after catching me fibbing about some escapade or other, practicing noble speech and action requires constant vigilance, and there's a fine line between privacy and secrecy. One creates healthy boundaries, he said; the other, unhealthy walls. One liberates; the other isolates. One is about honoring one's self; the other

17

dishonors one's connection to others. And a withheld truth, even a seemingly inconsequential one, has a nasty way of multiplying, eventually leading to a stampede of secrets and lies that trample any hope for inner ease.

Noble speech and noble action: I was a long way from either.

I took a deep breath, then let it out slowly. If my life up until now had taught me anything, it was that nothing ever stayed put, and change was not only possible, it was inevitable. True for the Buddha 2,600 years ago. True for me this morning. Julius Rosen himself said it to me once, although from him the message was laced with irony: The key to living a good life? Tell the truth.

I felt the intention bubble up inside, forming a new rule: *I will practice more transparency and keep current with the truth, both with myself and with those close to me.*

I'd better, before this tendency to hedge became a habit, and the habit became an addiction.

I glanced at my watch. I'd make it to Mac Gannon's estate with a few minutes to spare. Maybe I'd get to see my favorite redhead first—well, third-favorite redhead, after Bill's carrot-topped twin toddlers, Lola and Maude. I sopped up the last smear of bacon grease with a corner of toast. My phone buzzed.

Heather, she of the emotional-Geiger-counter intuition.

"Hey," I said.

"Hey. Sorry I was grumpy earlier."

"You? Grumpy?"

"Ten . . ." Heather sighed. "Are you at Mac Gannon's place yet? I just left the house."

"Nope. I stopped for a quick coffee and breakfast."

"Where? Maybe I can join you. I'm famished."

I pushed my grease-streaked plate away and waved at Patrice, tucking a twenty under my water glass. "Just paying the check now," I said. "Maybe next time. Listen, I'd better get going."

Heather said nothing, and my stomach muscles tightened. This was ridiculous. Where was my bold intention now? I was terrified to talk to my girlfriend. Terrified to tell her . . . what? That I ate meat? That I couldn't bring myself to meditate? That I had lots of money in the bank and little to no idea who I was without my father looming in the background?

"Heather, listen. I really do have to go. But I promise you we will talk soon. Really talk. Okay? Promise."

"Okay," Heather said, her voice quiet. We simultaneously took deep in-and-out breaths, and I could feel a slight current of relief pass back and forth. "Love you."

"Love you, too."

I climbed back into the Tesla a little lighter of heart. It wasn't exactly the noble truth, but it was a start.

Chapter 3

I texted Mac: ON MY WAY. Soon I had turned onto Pacific Coast Highway and was headed south in the direction of the actor's estate. Mac Gannon had found fame playing action heroes in blockbuster movies, and he'd done well enough at it to own several large chunks of Malibu on both sides of the PCH. There weren't a lot of action film screenings at Dorje Yidam, the monastery where I grew up, as in none, and I rarely went to the movies as a working cop in Los Angeles. I don't own a television. In fact, I still hadn't seen a single Mac Gannon movie, one secret I was definitely keeping to myself. But I'd researched the man thoroughly, of course, the first time he hired me, and had discovered that among other notable awards, he'd managed to win two DUI's plus an aggravated assault, later reduced to a misdemeanor, on an officer of the peace. His generous support of the Los Angeles Police Protective League was almost as legendary as his blackout binges. The story inside the stories was easy to decipher. Drunk Mac was a racist nightmare. Sober Mac—the one I met—was a charitable charmer.

I'd been contacted by Gannon in January on a missing persons job. As was often the case, the misper was a family member, his 16-year-old daughter, Maggie. It had sounded fairly straightforward, and it was—resolved within 24 hours, with little fuss. After I'd made the usual rounds of social media snooping, best-friend interviewing, and judicious asking around, the tip-off was provided by her best friend, a gentle modern dancer with a shock of neon pink hair by the name of Mickey Noona. He let it slip that Maggie, like him, had recently discovered she preferred smooching members of her own gender, one in particular.

One confession led to another, and it soon emerged that Maggie had been walked in on by her stepmother, Penelope, while goofing around, so to speak, with a classmate, Annie. Maggie had fled rather than face her ultra-conservative Catholic father's self-righteous ranting about sin and hell. The stepmother neglected to tell Mac what had happened, maybe for the same reason.

In fact, the only person in that household who seemed completely unafraid of Mac was his other daughter, an intrepid nine-year-old redhead by the name of Melissa. She was clearly the light of all their lives, a blast of energy that rocketed through the airless celebrity existence daily—and usually on roller blades.

I'd found Maggie hiding out in the Brentwood home of her smug mother, one more example of a joint-custody parent delighted to harbor a disgruntled child while keeping an ex in the dark. I'd returned Maggie to her father pissed off, but safe and sound. Case solved. Necessary follow-up sweaty conversations between family members? Not my business. But the whole incident had stayed off of YouTube, the nightly news, and TMZ. Mac had deeply appreciated my discretion, and now, according to his call late last night, a "mystery" friend of his urgently needed my services.

I was getting tired of celebrity mispers, lucrative though they might be. Missing-persons cases are, in their own way, intensely affecting, eliciting from clients bursts of raw anger and grief caused by love gone wrong. Easy physically—as far as actual footwork goes—but hard on everyone's emotional machinery. Just last month, retrieving a film director's sullen son from a head shop in Hollywood and returning him to his exhausted parents for the third time in as many months, I found myself wishing I'd been trained as a family therapist as well as a homicide detective. The Buddha got it right again: life is suffering.

To which I would add, especially life with an entitled, rebellious adolescent.

People who hire a private investigator more often than not have issues that are no more solvable by a detective than by a dogcatcher. Take "domestic surveillance," a fancy term for tracking down wayward spouses and snapping pictures of them doing the things wayward spouses do. The problem isn't getting proof. The proof reflects the problem. My last sales call, just yesterday, had turned into an unsales call, as I successfully talked a would-be client out of hiring me. The studio executive was seeking domestic surveillance. The target? His wife. I'd blurted out, "You don't need a private detective. Spend your money on couples counseling." *Click.*

Mac Gannon's new "mystery" case wasn't spouse spying. I'd clarified that with him last night.

I drove through Malibu proper and turned north onto the narrow private road that led to Mac's main entrance. As I climbed the hill, a clunky black Ford passenger van with tinted windows trundled toward me. I moved slightly right to let it pass. I didn't catch the logo on its side.

I pulled up at Mac's gate, a massive, 30-by-15-foot bas-relief sculpture of a blue ocean wave cresting across a yellow-orange background. After several exposures, I still couldn't decide if it was a work of art or a garish monstrosity.

I lowered my window and pushed the intercom button.

A voice crackled. "Name?"

"Tenzing Norbu. I have a ten o'clock appointment with Mr. Gannon."

"Sorry, son, I don't see anything here for a Ten at ten. I do, however, see an appointment for an Eleven at eleven."

"Um."

"I'm just playing with you! Get your butt up here, Norbu! I've missed you something awful!"

Mac Gannon: Mr. Charm.

The gate swung open, and I entered a sensory banquet

of beauty. Lush tropical plants and flowering shrubs lined both sides of the driveway and spilled over the rolling hills of the estate. The last time I was here, I'd spotted a lizard the emerald color of my favorite goddess, Green Tara. This time, a majestic African Grey parrot squawked in greeting from a palmetto tree as I passed. The main house lay ahead on my right, a sprawling one-story, adobe-style hacienda with jutting wings. Several smaller buildings, each with its own architectural stamp, dotted the grounds nearby.

Up the hill, the tip of a steeple marked Mac's personal Catholic chapel, used by him for daily private prayer and mostly hidden behind a scrubby phalanx of bushes. After I'd returned the wayward Maggie, Mac had insisted on bringing the whole family, plus me and a hastily robed priest-in-residence, into the chapel for an improvised group blessing. At least I assumed it was a blessing—the words were in Latin. For all I know the priest might have been begging their God to convert this Buddhist heathen before it was too late.

I parked the Tesla along the circular gravel driveway, taking note of a gleaming black Mercedes S-Class sedan and a couple of lesser cars, the kind that peons like me tend to drive. I stretched, stealing a moment to drink in the beautiful surroundings. Maintaining paradise was no doubt an expensive megahassle, but that didn't mean I couldn't appreciate its wonders.

"Ten! Ten!"

A skinny twig of a girl barreled up to me on roller blades, wheels flashing. She skidded to a halt.

"Melissa!"

"Daddy said you were coming! Did you bring Tank?"

On my last visit here, Melissa had wheedled out of me the fact that I had a Persian Blue pet with green eyes, along with a vague promise that someday she and he would meet. I could now see that Melissa was going to hold me to that promise—for the rest of my life, if need be.

I smacked my forehead.

"Not this time, Melissa," I said. "Sorry. I'm here for work, and Tank doesn't travel unless it's for play. He loves to play. Just like someone else I know. . . ."

"Me!" Melissa's grin illuminated her freckled face. Her hair had been wrestled into a single long, thick braid, but numerous wisps had made their escape. The red-gold strands glowed like live wires in the sunlight. The child was irresistible, her innate magnetism a direct inheritance from a charismatic father.

"Is your dad inside?"

I gestured toward Mac's office, a spectacular Balinese-style structure with pagodas and a lot of burnished wood. Mac had told me to meet him there.

Melissa's face abruptly clenched into a fierce scowl. She usually cycled through several weather systems per minute. "They're taking pictures," she said. "I'm not allowed."

She started to gnaw on a thumbnail. I saw that the other nails were bitten to the quick, and my heart broke a little. Nine was too young to be doing that.

A voice boomed out behind us. "You wearin' Ten out again, Missy?"

Melissa pirouetted on her blades, shrieking with joy as she narrowly escaped her father's mock lunge. She took off up the driveway, a blur of wheels and elbows.

I smiled. "She's a bright light, isn't she?"

"That she is," Mac said. "Missy will either grow up to be the President of the United States, or the leader of some vast criminal enterprise. I don't think there's any middle ground with her. Good to see you again, Ten."

I needn't have bothered with my blazer. Mac was wearing jeans, cowboy boots, and a blue denim shirt, tails untucked to hide a thickening waist.

"Likewise," I smiled. On an impulse, I glanced at Mac's hands. His fingernails were chewed down even farther than Melissa's. Kids inherit the bad along with the good.

"That your Tesla?" Mac squinted.

"No. Loaner."

As he strolled over to take a look—anything else in Southern California was a serious breach of etiquette—I was once again reminded how short Mac was, several inches south of my five foot ten. His personality was anything but small, however, and somehow over the months he'd elongated in my imagination.

Mac straightened up and shot me a loose, happy grin. He looked great, years younger than his actual 49. I squinted at his tan, glowing face: what had happened to the spider web of wrinkles caused by his lifelong two-pack-a-day habit? Then I realized: Mac was wearing make-up.

"How's Maggie doing," I asked, as he ambled back to my side.

"Beats the shit out of me," he answered. The vein on his left temple started to throb.

I said nothing.

"This is her mother's month, which means I'm persona non grata. Unless and until they need something from me, of course. You'd think, after that last stunt she pulled . . ." Mac patted his upper left pocket, where a pack of cigarettes should be. "Goddammit, I'd kill for a smoke." He caught my look and shrugged. "Don't mind me. Time to put on a new patch."

"How's that going for you?" He'd been trying to stop smoking the last time I was here.

"Ask me in a week. Quitting's a bitch. Hell, I'll probably die from the little fuckers either way. They say smoking takes ten years off your life, but they don't tell you the really nasty part—it takes it out of the middle. Half the time I wake up feeling like an old man." He sent a clump of gravel flying with the tip of his boot.

"Sounds rough," I said.

He seemed to remember himself, and just like that, he was as amiable as a laughing Buddha.

"No worries," he said. "Follow me, my friend. They're inside."

"They?"

"In my office. Won't take long. Let's go."

He ushered me into his office, and I paused to appreciate the wild, exotic feel of the room: the carved wooden totem sculptures lining the walls, the dark tropical-hardwood floor polished to a high gloss.

"I love this space," I said.

"Want to know a secret?"

"Sure," I said. *There's not a metal nail in the whole building.*

"There's not a metal nail in the whole building."

"Amazing," I said, as I had the first time he told me, and the second. Mac had his patter down.

"Mac!" a husky voice called out. "You didn't tell me your man was good-looking! Come over here, honey. I do believe you're my first encounter with a Tibetan holy man."

A forty-something woman in a tight black skirt and a bright pink jacket, topped by a gleaming helmet of light brown hair, flashed a toothy smile at me, like a piranha about to meet a very tasty minnow. She was perched on a stool, a hand towel draped around her neck. Her calves were muscular, her feet arched inside very high heels. She looked vaguely familiar. A large pair of sunglasses hung from her blouse. She tipped her face, as a young black girl applied a final coat of what looked like tan shellac to the woman's cheeks. As I watched, the woman scratched her forearm a few times. Her nails were curved claws, the same pink as her jacket.

A poker-faced man, buttoned inside a pinstriped suit, stood guard to her left. His dark brown hair was slicked back, and I was guessing he was somewhere in his thirties. Not a grin in sight—his stare was unblinking. I thought for a moment he might be the woman's bodyguard, but a closer look at his well-cut clothes changed my mind. With my new breed of clients, I had become somewhat of an expert on these things. Security guys don't usually troop around in spotless $3,000 suits.

Mac took my elbow and ushered me over.

"This is Tenzing Norbu, Bets. Ten, this is my high school sweetheart, Bets McMurtry."

"That's State Representative McMurtry to you, Gannon." She reached out from under the towel, took my hand, and gave it a squeeze.

That's why she was familiar. Assemblywoman Elizabeth "Bets" McMurtry was up for reelection this November, representing some area north of here. I knew this because of a recent spread in the Sunday *L. A. Times* that Heather had read out loud to me. Heather was a political junkie, as well as a diehard liberal, and she made sure I kept up with such things. According to the article, three years ago, McMurtry, a recently widowed, self-made businesswoman, had come out of seemingly nowhere to run for office. She was a highly unlikely, highly conservative challenger for her district's seat. Within a few months, the dark horse had created a horse race, and by summer, polls showed she was not only a sure bet to win her party's nomination but likely to unseat the Democratic incumbent. Sure enough, come November, she'd beaten her opponent handily and was expected to win reelection by a landslide this year. Heather had shown me a photograph of McMurtry standing by an American flag: same pink jacket, same toothy smile. Heather positively loathed the Bets McMurtrys of this world: pro-life, anti-everything-else women, she said, who should know better.

Heather had read on, her voice tight with disapproval. Bets McMurtry was now not only the new darling of the Tea Party crowd but also the recipient of a large infusion of cash from a Super PAC called New Americans for Freedom.

"The actual identities of these New Americans stay safely anonymous, of course," Heather had grumbled, tossing the paper aside. "Fucking SCOTUS and their Citizens

United fiasco." The 2010 decision by the Supreme Court to remove the ban on corporate donors had infuriated Heather at the time: she told me more than once that she had predicted the resulting flood of PAC money committed to extreme political agendas while hiding behind generic patriotic names.

Whoever these new Americans were, they were desperately hoping Bets McMurtry could breathe life into the Republican Party and, who knows, maybe even claim the governor's seat in 2016.

I sighed inside. Heather was not going to be pleased if Assemblywoman Elizabeth "Bets" McMurtry was, in fact, my mystery client. Oh, well. Add that to the pile, Norbu.

Bets canted her head to one side, studying me. She had not let go of my hand. Her hazel irises were ringed with gold. Her eyes bored into mine. "He'll do," she said to Mac. She blinked the slow, sexy blink of a sleepy tigress. I pulled my hand away.

I haven't been around many politicians, but I've been around plenty of con artists. They love to project a peculiar brand of sexual essence to their audience, even if it's an audience of one, the cop who's busting them. Good detectives can smell a con a mile away, and my detective sniffer concluded that Bets McMurtry most definitely exuded that raw scent.

She flashed another smile. "Look at this boy! I could eat him up. He makes me feel forty again."

I noticed that the man in the suit didn't soften his thin-lipped expression. His gaze tried to be menacing, but I got the sense that he was working a little too hard at it.

Bets followed my glance and waved a hand at him. "Tenzing, this is my main man, Mark Goodhue. I run for office. He runs my life."

Goodhue's grip was quick and not quite hard enough. I made a mental note to find out what the official label is for "running my life." Campaign manager? P.R. person? Boy-toy?

Goodhue glanced at his watch. "Shall we get going here?" He scooped up Bets's sunglasses, motioned, and a photographer stepped forward as the make-up girl scurried over to Mac and gave his forehead a quick dusting.

I never cease to be amazed by the tendency of the super-rich to insist on absolute promptness from others, while having no problem making everybody else wait. My teeth clenched. I aimed a couple of deep breaths at the tight muscles, wiggling my jaw back and forth. Better.

"Mind giving me some direction?" Mac said to Goodhue. His voice was affable, but his gaze was sharp, as he sized Goodhue up. For Mac, any male was competition.

Goodhue shrugged. "All you need to do is put your arm around Assemblywoman McMurtry and act natural. These are for our website. No biggy."

"Okay," Mac said, his voice tightening. "So, am I supposed to play it like Bets and I have stayed good buddies over the years? Or is this some kind of spontaneous surprise reunion?"

Having to ask questions like that is one of many reasons I would never make it in the acting profession. Halfway in and my head would explode.

Goodhue's shrug was curt. "You're good buddies. 'This is my good buddy, Bets.' That's what people will want to think, so that's the way to play it."

Twenty minutes later, the photographs had been snapped; the photographer and make-up girl had packed up and gone.

Mac and Bets exchanged a wordless glance.

"Mark," Bets said. "Can you give us a few minutes, please?"

Goodhue's mouth pursed with disapproval, but he picked up his leather computer bag and walked out, his spine rigid.

Mac's eyes flashed. "That pal of yours has a broom permanently jammed up his you-know-what. You should hire *him* to clean your house."

Rather than laugh, Bets teared up.

"Ah, shit, Bets," Mac said. "Don't mind me. Just trying to lighten things up around here." Mac motioned us both to a rattan loveseat and armchair around a glass coffee table at the far end of the room. Bets lowered herself onto the loveseat. She scratched her other arm, caught me noticing, and folded her hands in her lap. I took the armchair. Mac wheeled a high-backed, chrome-and-leather desk chair across the floor, positioning it next to Bets. He plopped onto the seat and spun around a few times before coming to a halt, facing frontward.

I waited.

Mac and Bets exchanged a second silent glance, and my pulse quickened. I had absolutely no idea what was coming next. I liked the feeling.

Bets straightened her shoulders. Any whiff of con artistry had fled the premises. She looked genuinely worried, and for the first time, I found her appealing.

"I guess I should start at the beginning," she said, her cat eyes troubled.

CHAPTER 4

Bets reached to her right and patted Mac's hand. "We go back a ways, don't we, Mac?"

She turned to me. "Mac tells me you're a long way from home."

"You could say that," I told her.

She nodded. "Fish out of water. Me, too. Never felt like I fit in, even when I was little. Only child, boo-hoo, and all that. And then, when I was about fifteen, I experienced the trauma of downsizing—long before it was popular, mind you. In my case, I wound up on the wrong side of Beverly Hills. I guess you could say I was one of the original kids-from-a-broken-home—at least that's how it felt to me. My parents got divorced when nobody else's parents did. My father split, and my mother had to work when nobody else's mother did. Mom went from Beverly Hills matron to overworked real-estate agent. I went from living in a mansion to living in a two-bedroom bungalow in the flats, just in time for high school. But you know what? I was finally okay. At school I had Mac, and at home I had Clara."

"Clara?" I said.

"Clara Fuentes. Our housekeeper, from Guatemala. She came to live with us right after my father left. She was so young—more like an older sister, really. Her English was broken, and my Spanish was worse, but she still let me know I was special. She loved me, and that attention was the anchor that kept me from floating away."

Bets glanced at Mac. "And as for Mac here, well, let's just say having Mac Gannon for your first boyfriend meant even the bitchiest bitches overlooked any other issues."

"Damn straight," Mac said.

"We were that ninth-grade couple everyone else wanted to be," Bets said. "Then my mother up and married her real estate-developer boss, and my life blew up one more time. We moved to Antelope Valley, and I was the odd kid out all over again, only this time with a broken heart." Bets nudged Mac. "I'm dry as a prairie dog's fart, Mac. You got anything to drink?"

"Bets," Mac warned.

"I'm talking about iced tea. Cool your *cojones*, will you?" Bets may have been born in Beverly Hills, but her years in Antelope Valley had given her the down-home drawl of a homegrown Texan.

Mac pressed an intercom. "Mrs. O'Malley, can you bring us three iced teas, please?"

I glanced at my watch. I was an hour into this visit and still no closer to knowing why I was here.

"So," I said. "Antelope Valley?"

Bets swallowed. "Well, I got into a bit of hot water there. All of a sudden, I had way too much time on my hands, not to mention money. Clara tried her best to rein me in, but I was a hell-raiser, no two ways about it. Damn near died once or twice. Until I was rescued yet again."

"Another boyfriend?"

"Not exactly. More like a best friend for life." Her hazel eyes flashed. "I found Jesus, Mr. Norbu. Or maybe I should say, He found me."

There was a quiet knock at the door.

The name "Mrs. O'Malley" had conjured up a tiny, grey-haired Irish lady in a plaid dress and sensible shoes. Let's just say my mind conjured wrong. Mrs. O'Malley was a young, stunning ash blonde with world-class architecture. Piercing turquoise eyes winked from behind wire-rimmed glasses. She balanced three tall glasses and a pitcher of amber liquid on a rattan tray that matched the furniture.

She nodded to Bets and arched her eyebrows at me.

"This is Tenzing Norbu," Mac said to her. "And you remember my friend, Bets."

I pushed to my feet.

"Constance O'Malley," she said, "and please, sit down!" Mac was beaming like a proud father. At least I got the Irish part right. I could hear faint traces of Dublin lilt.

She set the tray down on the coffee table, filled the glasses, and exited. We each claimed a frosty glass. I took a long, grateful pull and tasted mint and lemongrass.

"She's new," Bets said. "You boning her?"

I spluttered into my glass.

"None of your damn business," Mac answered.

"Thought so," Bets said, and blotted her mouth daintily with a linen napkin.

I had just about reached my limit of small talk.

"Ms. McMurtry, why am I here?" I asked.

She set her glass down. Cleared her throat.

"It's Clara," she said, her voice low. "She's gone."

Not what I expected.

"Ah," I said. "Have you submitted a missing persons report to your local police?"

Bets raised her hand to halt me. "No police report," she said. "Nobody can know."

Mac put in his own two bits. "Useless fucks. I wouldn't let the local cops clean my gutters."

"Nevertheless . . . ," I said.

"No police report," she repeated.

"Right. Well . . ."

"I just need you to find her for me."

It's always best to get the money part done first, especially when you charge as much as I do. "Did Mac tell you my fees? I book my time in three-day increments. I charge five thousand a day and require half up front."

"I'm paying," Mac said. "We need to keep this off her books." He frowned. As an early client, he'd paid me by the day. "You think it'll take three days? You found Maggie in one."

"One is ideal," I said, "but I charge for three." My voice was firm. I'd been practicing. "We'll hope for the best, but if I haven't found Clara within seventy-two hours, we'll need to use another approach." I didn't want to spell it out. Three out of every four people who disappear are found within the first 12 hours. It's the one out of four that causes the gut to clench. I hoped Clara Fuentes didn't land in that category. Most of them either stayed lost or were found without a pulse.

Bets's mouth thinned. "Mr. Norbu—"

"Ten, please."

"Ten, this is very delicate, understand? No one can know about this. No one."

Mac jumped in again. "I told you, Bets. He's the best."

"Yeah, well, sometimes the best isn't good enough," she snapped. "Look at the Meg Whitman fiasco. Spends a hundred sixty million of her own dough on 'the best,' and one disgruntled maid later, Looney-tunes Brown gets elected anyway." Her face had turned a dull red. "The goddamned mainstream media is already sharpening its claws over me. They'd love nothing more than a nice juicy reason to pounce."

I took out a small notebook and pen. I was still old-school when it came to the early stages of an investigation, and I'd learned under Bill's tutelage that this straightforward action tended to calm people down.

I started with what I thought was a simple question.

"How long has your housekeeper been missing?"

Wrong question.

"I don't know!" Bets wailed. "I've been fundraising up and down the state, and I gave her last week off. But then she didn't show up for work on Friday. And I've been calling and calling, and she doesn't answer! That's not like her! She's always been . . . been there for . . ." Her words dissolved into harsh sobs. I stared at Bets in fascination. Tears were literally shooting horizontally from her eyes. How was that even possible?

She honked into her napkin. Mac shifted in his seat and looked away, as if embarrassed.

I tried again. "Where does she live?"

"With me. In Antelope Valley." Bets sniffed, on firmer ground again. "And here, when I'm here; I still have my Mom's bungalow. Clara's been with me my whole life, Ten. She's like a sister to me. We even wear the same size clothes." Her eyes started to well up again.

"Where does she usually go on her days off?" I asked hastily.

Bets shook her head. "I don't know," she whispered.

"Okay," I said. "No matter. Let's start with the basics. I'm going to need her full name, driver's license if she has one, date of birth, social security number . . ." My voice trailed off as my eyes registered Bets. She was shaking her head *no,* over and over again.

I made another stab.

"Green card?"

No.

"Credit card?"

No.

"Bank account?"

"I pay her in cash," Bets whispered. "Just like my mother did."

I sat back. "Ms. McMurtry, are you telling me Clara is an illegal? That technically, she doesn't exist? Are you saying all you have for me is a name?"

She nodded, miserable.

"Do you even know if Clara Fuentes *is* her name?"

She shook her head, more miserable.

"Do you have a recent photograph of her?" Bets looked down. "Any photograph of her?"

Her embarrassed silence was answer enough. I sat back in my chair. Now what?

"Don't forget about Sofia," Mac piped up.

Bets brightened. I picked up my pen. "Who's Sofia?"

Now it was Mac's turn.

"See, we were lookin' for some new help earlier in the year. The wife pulled a groin muscle riding her horse, got laid up in bed, and damned if our housekeeper didn't up and quit right around the same time." He shot Bets a look. "And no, I wasn't boning her, thank you very much." He downed the rest of his iced tea and poured himself another one.

"I remembered how great Clara was, and I called Bets, out of the blue. We hadn't talked in years, but so what? I asked if she had any recommendations. Well, it turns out Clara had—sorry, *has*—a half-sister or half-niece or some sort of relation who'd just come here from . . . Nicaragua, was it?"

"Guatemala," Bets said. "And they're cousins."

"Whatever. Anyway, she'd just started working for some fancy-schmancy maid service."

"Mark pulled some strings," Bets added.

"Whatever," Mac said again. "Long and short of it is, we signed up with them, and now she's here four days a week, plus Sundays. No driving to the bus stop necessary— all the maids get dropped off, picked up, even bring their own organic cleaning products. It costs a fucking fortune, but it keeps the wife *muy* happy."

I recalled the black van laboring down Mac's driveway—and wondered.

"What's the name of the service?"

"No idea," Mac said. "Not my bailiwick. Bets?"

She shrugged. "Mark knows," she said.

"Okay, well, is she here at your house now?" I asked Mac.

"Is who here?"

"Sofia," I said, trying to stay calm. "Clara's cousin." I took a deep inhale. The man had the attention span of a gnat.

"Lemme see." Mac used his cell phone this time. "Hey. We need to know if that new Mexican—sorry, Nicaraguan—cleaning gal, Sofia, is still here. Can you check?" He frowned. "Then call Penelope on her cell. Thanks. Oh, and sweetheart, can you wire seventy-five hundred into Tenzing Norbu's account? We've got his information on file. Thanks, darlin'."

So much for "Mrs. O'Malley," I thought.

A second thought plucked my brain. I turned my attention back to Bets McMurtry.

"Ms. McMurtry?"

"Gawd almighty, son. You've seen me covered in snot. I think we've graduated to 'Bets.'"

"Bets, you mentioned you've tried calling Clara. Does she have a cell phone?"

"Smart!" she said, tapping her temple with a pink talon. "Yes, I replaced her ancient flip-phone for Christmas. Bought her an iPhone. I was sick to death of never getting through."

For the first time, a butterfly of hope fluttered inside.

"Do you have that number?"

Bets had already whipped out her phone and was scrolling through her contacts list.

"Here it is: 661-478-1319."

I wrote it down. "661. Do you live in Lancaster, by any chance?"

"That's right. You know it?"

"I do." I smiled; I knew Lancaster well. I made a mental note to call my very first client, John D, later. He'd probably have some choice words about Bets McMurtry's political leanings.

Bets scowled as she clicked through a long series of text messages. "Uh-oh. I'm in deep doo-doo. Late for a ladies' prayer brunch and Mark's got himself in a royal snit. You need anything else?"

"Not for now. I'll be in touch soon."

"Okay, but only through Mac, okay? No direct e-mails. No calls. No texts. Don't want any goddamned reporters catching wind of this."

"Okay."

She fished a small mirror out of her purse and checked her face. "I look like warmed-over roadkill," she muttered. "I wouldn't vote for me if I was the last politician alive."

She stood, tugged her jacket into place with a sharp jerk, and flashed me her piranha smile. I stood as well. As she pushed by, she paused, then encircled my wrist with her thumb and forefinger. "I was sick a while back, Ten. Really, really sick. My husband's dead. We never had kids. That woman spooned food into me as I lay in my bed. She mopped up after me. Changed my sheets." She squeezed my wrist, a single, decisive clamp. "Find her."

She trotted out the door, her high heels clicking.

Mac had walk-wheeled his chair back to his desk and was at his computer, checking e-mail.

"I guess I'll go see about Sofia then," I said. Mac waved me away, already on to the next thing.

I stepped outside, blinking in the bright sunlight. As I headed up the driveway toward the main house, I heard the brisk *clip-clop* of iron on asphalt. I spun around. Penelope Gannon loomed over me, attached to a snorting black beast the size of a two-story building. I'm not fond of horseback riding. If the gods had wanted us to gallop, they'd have given us hooves.

I shielded my eyes, looking up.

"Hello, Mr. Norbu." Penelope's voice was cool. I may not be a fan of horseback riding, but Penelope Gannon was even less a fan of mine. I'd already poked my nose once into private family business, and one time was plenty. She swung off her steed and landed with a wince. She rubbed her groin area. "Still healing," she said, catching my look. "I understand you need to talk to Sofia. She should be in the master bathroom. It's grout-cleaning day."

I took a step toward the house. She handed me the reins with a look that would freeze water. "I'll just go inside and check."

I could understand not wanting me inside, but I wondered why Penelope hadn't already sent Mac or Mrs. O'Malley into the master bedroom to get Sofia. Then I pictured Mrs. O'Malley and stopped wondering.

Penelope tugged off her black riding helmet as she strode into the house, slightly favoring her right leg. She was lithe and athletic, with the same fine, red hair as Melissa, pulled back in a ponytail secured with a plain rubber band. I had never once seen her dressed in anything but a white polo shirt, jodhpurs, and tall brown riding boots.

Now what? I reached out one hand and gave the horse's nose a tentative pat. He jerked away, spraying spittle and yanking the reins loose. I scrambled to reclaim them and tightened my grip.

"Um. No. Okay? No. Just . . . stay still." He took a step closer, lowered his massive cranium, and started to nibble at my hair. I ducked away, still clutching the reins.

Cats. Cats are the right size for a pet.

The front door opened, and Penelope hurried back to me, her limp more evident. Melissa stood in the doorway, her fingers in her mouth.

"She's gone!" Penelope said. "I don't understand it! Sofia's pickup time is always five." She worked her mouth. "I'd better call the agency. This is completely unacceptable." Tiny beads of sweat, like dew, appeared on her upper lip. She must really care about keeping her grout clean.

I shoved the reins at her before she got any wild ideas about taking off again.

"Will you let me know when you reach Sofia?"

"Of course," Penelope said, but she was a million miles away, her eyes darting from palm tree to palm tree, as if Sofia might be crouched behind a spray of fronds.

I waved good-bye to Melissa, still alone in the doorway, but her eyes were glued to her mother. I made a wide arc around Penelope's horse and slid into the Tesla, grateful for seat belts, steering wheels, and brakes. I realized I still

41

didn't know the name of the agency, but Penelope and her horse had disappeared. So had Melissa. I buckled up. Before I took off, I flipped open my notebook to check my notes. Or should I say note.

I had a cell phone number. Not much on its own. But a cell phone number plus a SIM card, plus a built-in GPS, plus an ex-partner still on the force? With any luck, I would locate Clara Fuentes before nightfall.

CHAPTER 5

"No can do, pal."

"Ha, ha, ha. You're kidding, Bill, right?" I had him on speaker and directed my dismay to the phone resting in my lap as I wound my electricity-fueled way up Topanga to my house.

"Ten, need I remind you what I do these days? I'm D-Three. You know what that means, right? That I'm responsible for making sure mooks like you and I used to be stay on the straight and narrow?"

"Don't call me that. It's politically incorrect. Besides, I'm from Tibet."

"Jesus. Mook, not gook. Didn't you see *Goodfellas?*" Bill sighed. "No, of course you didn't. Who do you need to ping, anyway?"

I gave him the shorthand on the trace, leaving out certain key details, such as who, what, and why. "The phone contract's under my client's name, but she can't go the cell phone-carrier route to trace it, for reasons of acute paranoia— I mean, privacy. Otherwise, what I have to work with is a bunch of blanks."

"I don't envy you," Bill said. "Even with NamUs expanding its national database, we've had a helluva time tracking down unregistered aliens reported missing. I can think of maybe one success story out of hundreds, and she wasn't even missing, just shacked up with a new boyfriend. I mean, think about it—where do you even start? Half of them have no ID, and the half that do trace back to someone who's deceased, or living in another state, happily ignorant that his or her personal information has been hijacked. Needle in a haystack, Ten. That's what you've got going on."

"Nobody said being a gumshoe was easy."

I waited. I knew Bill well.

"Ah, crap. Give me the fucking number. I'll see what I can do."

"Thanks," I said, but he had already rung off. I texted him Clara's number and added a smiley-face emoticon, guaranteed to make him mad all over again, in that best-of-friends way. Bill and I saw each other rarely these days, but once a partner, always a partner.

I thought about what he'd said. If NamUs, the National Missing and Unidentified Persons System, had problems tracking down illegals, my own chance of success seemed pretty slim. Everything hung on the cell phone.

I was grateful for his help. I always had my recovering hacker, Mike, data jockey extraordinaire, on call as a backup plan, but as Bill pointed out, tracing someone else's cell phone was illegal for anyone but the cops. I hated to knowingly ask Mike to break the law. I had kept him out of prison as a juvenile; I didn't want to send him there as an adult.

As I pulled up to my house, I pressed a random button on my phone. Once I reached my front door, the little genies inside the system would have already authenticated me and lowered their guns. I mentally bowed down to the genius of Mike.

"It's simple," he'd said, after setting up the personalized feature for me. Mike's phone was connected to my Guard-on breach alerts, and I'd woken him up several afternoons—Mike sleeps all day and works all night—by accidentally setting off the alarm. By the time I made it inside my house, it was too late to disarm the system. "All I had to do," he went on, ignoring the growing glaze coating my eyes, "was assign your wireless network a static IP address and set up a Guard-on network item to ping the IP every five seconds. That way, when you're close, you return the ping, and the system can check the MAC and initiate a bunch of macros, alerting the house you're home. Easy-peasy."

Welcome to Mike's brain—and my world.

Tank met me at the door, his tail swishing. I reached down to pet him. He sniffed my hand and stalked away.

"It's horse," I said. "And if it helps, I don't like them any more than you do."

I washed my hands and made peace with a tuna-water offering. I was hungry myself and decided on peanut butter on toast. Only I couldn't find the peanut butter, and my bread had broken out in suspicious little green splotches. I settled on a banana. As I peeled the fruit, I noticed a small yellow Post-it had fallen on the floor by the counter. I picked it up.

"Dr. K. M F 6!!!" was inked on it, in Heather's looping, little-girl script. A small daisy was doodled next to the time.

Who was Dr. K.? More to the point, why did he deserve a daisy?

My cell phone buzzed.

"Found it," Bill said. "I can get you within three hundred and twenty-eight feet."

"That was fast," I said.

Police used to rely on cell-tower triangulation to track down the geographic location of a phone. It wasn't an exact science, but at least it gave us a general sense of locality and position. But the newer phone models have incorporated a form of GPS triangulation that pulls much more precise information from a cluster of satellites constantly low-orbiting around our planet. The rapid cross-referencing of data can identify and place a phone to within 328 feet. Why 328, as opposed to 327 or 329, I have no idea.

Bill recited a street address on Serrano.

"Koreatown?"

"Close. Little Armenia."

"Thanks, Bill," I said.

"Don't thank me. Thank Big Foot." Big Foot, aka Melvin Skinner, was a Texas drug dealer whose "mule" was a deluxe motor home stuffed with thousands of pounds of marijuana. In 2006, the local cops used data from his throwaway cell phone to track him down en route to Alabama to make a delivery. He was arrested and charged for a laundry list of drug-dealing behaviors. His lawyers cried foul, claiming the DEA had violated his Fourth Amendment rights because they never issued a warrant, but those of us doing metropolitan police work cheered. The court ruled cell phone use to be a public, rather than a private act. That ruling was appealed, of course, and the case had been passed along to a higher court, but for now, no warrants were necessary.

"Thank you, Big Foot," I recited obediently.

I heard twin shrieks in the background.

"Gotta go," Bill said. "Lola has Maude in a headlock."

I traded the blazer for a dark blue windbreaker and retrieved my .38 from its nylon gun bag, locked in the safe in my closet. I had cleaned the Wilson only yesterday, and the stainless steel barrel and walnut handle gleamed. I hefted the weapon once or twice in my hand. It felt snug there, at home. Other cops preferred bigger guns, but most of them had bigger hands. I pulled out the Jackass Rig shoulder holster as well.

"I'm off," I said to Tank. "Wish me luck."

Tank blinked. That counted, I guess.

I activated the Guard-on deities yet again. They were armed for action, and so was I.

I switched to my beater Toyota, entered the address in my phone, and called upon MapQuest to get me there—so much easier than trying to decode the microscopic squiggles of the *Thomas Guide* while driving. Not that I'm complaining—Sherlock didn't even have that. Sunday afternoon traffic had started to build, and well over an hour later I was finally parked on Serrano Avenue, just around the corner from a massive church topped by multiple golden, onion-shaped domes that rivaled the Taj Mahal's.

Assuming Clara Fuentes's phone wasn't shopping in the Food 4 Less, there was only one building that made sense within my 328-foot radius of possibilities. The peeling three-story apartment house was a dingy rectangle, its faded tan the color of regret. A makeshift square of poured concrete out front housed a rusting pickup, canted to one side. Several swarthy old men, gray hair sprouting from beneath their undershirts, sat hunched on plastic lawn chairs dragged onto narrow balconies. They aimed rings of cigarette smoke at the pavement below. A baby was crying inconsolably, and a woman's voice shouted in frustration.

Across the street, graffiti disfigured the cement wall bordering the Food 4 Less, and a pile of blankets fenced in by overturned shopping carts indicated a homeless person had claimed one small piece of sidewalk real estate as his own. The whole block was derelict, the gleaming church around the corner a serious misplacement of priorities.

I holstered my gun under my windbreaker and got out of the car. I strolled up to the building's entrance, a metal gate meshed with chain-link, pushed it open, and walked to the front door of the apartment. The back of my neck prickled. I could feel the eyes of the old men following my every move, like silent prison guards.

The front door was not quite closed, a piece of luck. I stepped inside and studied a directory of names and apartment numbers hanging over a metal case of mailboxes. Half the handwritten names were too faded to read, and the other half were illegible. That meant a door-to-door. Three floors, six apartments per floor. I began at the beginning. The first two apartments were empty, or else no one was answering my knock. At the third door, I got a response, but the tiny, wrinkled woman, her walnut face bound in a flowered scarf tied tightly under her chin, spoke no English. I moved on.

47

Finally, upstairs on the second floor, in the second apartment, I got lucky again. A young Latino man not only opened the door but spoke English, and he used that English to invite me inside, once I told him why I was there.

"Sure," he said. "I know Clara. Best refried black beans in the city. She's Sofia's cousin, right? She visits here a lot."

"You know Sofia?"

"Not well enough." He grinned. "But that may have just changed." He pointed to a cage in the corner, half-covered with a striped beach towel. "Sorry about the towel. The bird wouldn't shut up."

He crossed the room and pulled off the towel. A gray parrot sporting a crown of yellow feathers and two orange spots for cheeks pinned us with a beady-eyed stare. "Cockatiel," the young man said.

SQUAWK!

He covered the cage quickly. "See what I mean? Harsh."

He indicated a lumpy sofa, and we sat. The apartment consisted of a 12-by-12-foot square that housed a twin bed; a desk and chair; a small sofa; a tiny kitchen area, including a wooden tray-table set up to eat on; one window; a bathroom the size of a postage stamp, and a cockatiel in a cage. No balcony.

"I'm bird-sitting," he explained. "Sofia came by earlier today in a big rush and asked me if I'd watch it for her. She loves that bird. No joke."

"When was that?"

"Let me think. Maybe two, three hours ago? She seemed pretty stressed."

"And Clara?"

"I haven't seen her for a few days. I'm Carlos, by the way."

"Ten," I answered.

"Ten?"

"Ten."

"Cool. So what, Clara's in some kind of trouble? Hard to believe."

I explained that an employer of hers was concerned and had hired me to look into her absence. "Can you show me Sofia's apartment?"

"Sure. Two doors down," Carlos said. I followed him into the hallway. The corridor was poorly lit, the linoleum underfoot sticky. A strong scent of stewing meat wafted from under one doorway, and I remembered I was starving.

"We're the only Latinos in the building," he said over his shoulder. "So, you know, we kind of got to know each other by default. Still, it's all good. My neighbors leave me alone, the rent's cheap, and I can catch the Red Line at Western and Hollywood to go downtown. I work two jobs, and at night I go to LACC. I'm studying to be a teacher. "

I found myself liking Carlos more and more.

"Here you go," he said. "Whoa. Shit, man. That's not good."

We stared at the wooden door frame. The jamb was splintered, as if the door had been jimmied open. I motioned Carlos behind me and slipped my right hand inside my windbreaker, curling my palm around the Wilson's wooden handle.

"Hello?" I said. "Sofia? Clara?" I nudged at the door with my foot. It swung open, revealing a one-room boxy studio identical to Carlos's. Either Sofia was the worst housekeeper in the world or someone had ransacked the place. A pullout futon lay in pieces, the mattress and pillows shredded, the wooden slats broken. A small coffee table was overturned, and torn clothing and broken dishes littered the floor. An entire sack of birdseed had been dumped onto a woven throw rug.

"Did Sofia leave you a key, by any chance?" I said.

"Um."

"Because if she did, technically, you're in charge of her place while she's gone."

Carlos was a bright boy. "In that case, I'm sure she did."

"Care to invite me in?"

"Por favor." He walked through the door.

I followed him in. I executed a quick visual search for signs of a violent altercation or hasty departure. No visible bodies. No bloodstains. No half-eaten plates of abandoned food. Most especially, no cell phone in sight.

"How many electrical outlets in your place?" I asked.

"Five," he said. "No, sorry, six. Three in the main room, two in the kitchen area, and one in the bathroom, stuck behind the toilet for some reason. I have to use an extension cord to charge my shaver and toothbrush."

I was in the bathroom in three steps. I got down on all fours. Sure enough, an iPhone was charging, resting on its back on the stained linoleum behind the toilet. I had forgotten to bring any latex gloves, but I had a handkerchief in my back pocket. I used it to recover the phone and charger.

I made a second assessment of the apartment, this time slowly and by foot. There was a small stack of unopened mail—mostly flyers, it looked like—on the kitchen counter, but I left it alone. Private mail, unlike phones, was not to be touched by private investigators, not under any circumstances. The same goes for garbage, unless it's been moved to the curb, and after the alleged break-in, the whole apartment qualified as trash. Nothing else jumped out at me, and I was fine with that. One, this was Sofia's place, not Clara's, and two, I had a feeling all the answers I needed were already wrapped inside my handkerchief.

I gave Carlos a business card. "Call me if either Sofia or Clara shows up, okay?"

"You think I should let the cops know, in case Sofia's missing, too?"

"Definitely report the break-in. As far as Sofia goes, it's up to you," I said. "But unless she's a minor or has Alzheimer's, you can't even file a missing person's report until she's been gone for twenty-four hours. Hopefully she'll be back by then."

Carlos stowed my card in his wallet. He fished a pen

from his other pocket and put out his hand. "Got another one?"

I did.

He scribbled his name and phone number on the back and returned it to me. "Let me know, man, if you need me for anything. That Clara's a nice lady. She reminds me of my *abuela*, my granny, you know?" He frowned at the upended room. "I don't have a good feeling about this," he said.

I didn't either, but I wasn't ready to say it out loud.

As I walked outside, I debated asking the Armenian death squad if they had seen or heard anything suspicious. I looked up at the balconies. The old men, with their impassive, smoke-wreathed stares, were as promising as a row of cement blocks. I took a step in their direction anyway, and as one, they seemed to melt back into their apartments. I was too hungry to pursue them further.

I drove straight to Langer's Delicatessen, at Seventh and Alvarado. I didn't care if the entire LAPD force was there to bear witness—after years of watching Bill inhale pastrami across the booth from me, I was finally going to have a number 19 all to myself.

Langer's was closed. I hit the steering wheel in frustration. By now, I was so hungry I couldn't think in a straight line, so I drove home on autopilot and had my mouth full of raw almonds before I had even set the keys down on the kitchen counter.

After two very unsatisfying bowls of cereal—I usually shopped on Sundays, and there weren't too many choices in my cupboards—I gargled with tap water and poured myself a Belgian Chimay. Time to do my part in supporting those busy little Trappist monk-brewers. The first sip was a perfect meditation, all on its own. By the third, I was finally myself.

I pulled out Clara's cell phone, still wrapped in my handkerchief, and used a corner of cotton to carefully swipe it on. This was a bare-bones iPhone: no e-mail activated and only the basic apps that came with the phone. I pulled up her most recent telephone activity. There were maybe 20 outgoing and incoming calls displayed on the screen, but only 3 sources. The majority of the calls were to or from either a 661 area code or a 213, identified as *Señora Bets* and *Sofia*, respectively. The third number was recent and unidentified. Bets and Sofia were also the only two stored contacts. I went back to the current calls.

True to her word, Bets McMurtry had called Clara over a dozen times since Friday. The most recent outgoing call, dated last Thursday, was to a long string of numbers, recipient unknown. I jotted down the date and time of the call in my notebook—the last indication that Clara Fuentes was still alive. I was tempted to call the number myself, but good sense prevailed. Instead, I texted the digits to Mike. With any luck, he'd be awake soon. PLEASE VERIFY THE SOURCE OF THIS NUMBER, ASAP, I added.

What else, what else? My eyes lit on the 661 area code. *Lancaster.* Right. I scrolled my own contact list for John D. Murphy. I pressed.

"Hello! Hello!"

I grinned with pleasure. John D always answered his phone as if half-convinced no one would actually be on the other end.

"John D," I said. "It's Ten."

"No kidding! It's been a coon's age. Thought you must have taken another vow of silence. How the hell are you?"

"I'm still standing," I said. "Sorry it's been so long. I was in India. My father died."

I felt rather than heard John D's heart quicken with sympathy. "You okay?"

My own heart softened at the old man's concern. "Yes, I'm okay. But what about you?"

"Well, you know, the legs aren't working too good, but good enough to chase after my granddaughter. Ashley's two-and-a-half years old already, and an absolute peach.

Talkin' up a storm. That child hangs the moon as far as her mother and I are concerned."

I had been somewhat instrumental in reuniting John D with his pregnant daughter-in-law, right after his estranged son, Norman, was murdered. I was glad the new little family was still intact.

"And you're healthy?"

"Still breathing, Ten, still breathing. I'm finally done with chemo, and it did its job shrinking the basketball in my gut down to a manageable size. Now we're at a geezer's standoff. Tumor's growing at about the same rate as I'm moving. I guess being older than God has its advantages. And the joints help." He chuckled. "Joints for my joints. I do still love my medicinal weed."

We shared a chuckle. John D wasn't just my first client as a private detective—he was still my favorite. We'd shared a single but memorable smoke, many moons ago.

"So what can I do you for?" John D asked. "Or is this call purely personal?"

"It's professional and highly confidential," I said.

"Understood."

I knew I could trust John D to keep our conversation to himself. I laid out the case as succinctly as I could. "Anything you can add to what I already know about your representative?" I asked. I liked to learn as much as I could about the people I was in business with. Google was fine, but there's nothing better than verifying facts with trusted friends.

"Not much." John D grunted. "McMurtry's a hard-line, anti-immigration, anti-drug, pro-life, Tea Party windbag. Can't stand her—can you tell? Thing is, she prances around in those tight skirts, acting all high and mighty, but she was in my son Norman's class in high school, and that girl was a hell-raiser, for sure. There wasn't a drug she didn't like, or a boy she didn't try to seduce. Then she found Jesus, like they do, got married, and made a fortune selling Christian beauty products, door-to-door at first and then at parties, like they did with that Tupperware stuff. My wife got invited to one of them wingdings once. I remember, because it was right before Charlie got blowed up in Iraq. After that she stopped going out."

I again felt, rather than heard, John D revisit an old sorrow inside.

"Anyhoo, my wife came home with a stick of free lipstick and reported that those women told the dirtiest jokes she'd ever heard, in between paintin' each other's faces 'til they looked like you-know-whats."

"Wow," I said.

"After she was saved, McMurtry turned into a mover and a shaker, I'll give her that. Her husband passed pretty early on, but that gal didn't miss a beat. She started a born-again school up here so her two kids could avoid learning about dinosaurs and monkeys, and the dang thing is still going strong. Don't worry. We're sending Ashley to one of them Montessori places."

I heard a door slam.

"Uh-oh, the light of my life's home from a birthday party, and she's going to need a scraper to get that icing offa her face." John D chuckled. "Better go. Nice talkin' to you, Ten. 'Bye now."

John D sounded as happy as I'd ever heard him. I fed Tank and cleaned his litter box with a light step, then rewarded myself with a second beer. I settled on the deck outside to savor it. But sometimes my spirit refuses to float above the clouds for long, and my inner hijacker soon intervened.

I haven't heard from Heather since breakfast. The nose-dive was swift—and swiftly made worse by my fishing the Post-it from my pocket. I frowned at the little hand-drawn daisy. Heather adored daisies and had taught me a favorite girlhood game early on in our courtship. Now I tried to decipher from the daintily sketched petals if we loved each other or loved each other not.

Tank brushed against my ankles. I reached down to stroke his back, and he arched slightly. No daisy petals necessary to read my feelings for him. Tank slipped from underneath my palm and ambled inside. I leaned back in my chair. The canyon sky was blue-black, and empty of stars. I finished my beer and followed my cat's lead.

As I was getting ready for bed my phone buzzed. It was a text from Heather: U STILL UP?

The obvious answer was yes, because yes, technically, I was up. But the question was, did I want to talk to her? That answer was no, but *no* hooked into an immediate and contradictory *you should,* and then it was on: *ignore the text and go to bed* was swiftly elbowed aside by *you read the text, so you owe her a reply.* They multiplied into so many dueling versions of *don't want to* and *you have to* that I had an entire courtyard of arguing monks in my head, just like the debating sessions of my Tibetan Buddhist youth. I knew what came next, and sure enough, I was soon visited by shame, the same shame that was so brilliantly instilled in me by my teachers years ago.

Shame was a big motivator at Dorje Yidam, its hot body crawl more feared than any of the stick-swats or ear-twists handed out. Whenever Yeshe, Lobsang, and I were caught misbehaving, we were informed that we had not only disappointed our teachers but had let down the entire Dharma, the lineage of teachings that stretched back to the Buddha. That's 2,600 years' worth of disappointment.

I shuddered, remembering the grave, pained look on the face of my tutor, Lama Sonam, or the angry look on my father's when I had broken yet another rule. It was a look nobody could ever fake, communicating something like, "Your behavior makes me question whether my whole life as a teacher has been a waste. Your behavior causes me to wonder if I've betrayed the Dharma and will be reborn as a horny toad."

I can testify that a shaming look is a very strong

deterrent to most people. I must have been about six the first time I experienced it at Dorje Yidam. My gut froze, as if a giant hand was gripping my entrails. A split-second later, fire bloomed in my calves and spread up through my thighs to meet the ice deep in my belly. The collision of these two—shame and fear—triggered an awful alchemy, sending toxicity throughout the body.

Right now, looking at Heather's text, my blood was streaming with it.

Breath is the only thing that will clear the taint of that particular poison. As I mutely stared at the text, I breathed deeply and slowly, in and out, until the toxin began to disperse. After about ten breaths, the disharmony was more or less resolved. But I still didn't know what to do.

Somewhere in the back of my mind I heard Lama Sonam's gentle voice: "Whenever possible, Lama Tenzing, do the thing you're most hoping to avoid."

I had promised myself today would be different. I found her name and pressed it. Her phone rang in my ear.

"Hi," she said.

"Hi back."

"You never called me back. Are you mad at me?"

A little fist of tension balled up between my shoulder blades. Part of me wanted to run my usual tactics and say, "I'm not mad at you. You're the one who's mad at me," but I was way too tired to sell that one with any confidence.

"I don't know what I am right now. It's been a hard day. I'm ready for bed."

"Ready because you're tired or because you'd prefer to avoid talking to me?"

Sometimes Heather can be maddeningly insightful. I felt my mental wheels spin in place.

How about telling the truth?

"A little bit of both, I guess." My shoulders relaxed. *Over to you, Heather.* I wondered if she was going to punish me for being honest.

To my amazement, she didn't. "Yeah, I'm pretty tired myself. I wound up working all afternoon. Check in tomorrow?"

"Yeah, let's do that." We both left off the love you's.

I activated the alarm and fell into bed. A solid *thunk* registered Tank's daredevil leap from dresser to mattress. He tucked up against me, and I felt honored, even as the tiny part of my brain still functioning smirked at my reaction. As I drifted off, I pondered the different ways cats and dogs— not to mention their deluded owners—handle affection. If you're a dog owner, you pay a little attention to your dog, and the dog thinks you're doing something miraculously wonderful. It licks, wags, pants, and dances in circles. Dog owners accept everything about this deal, despite the potential for well-earned ridicule as enablers of vulgar canine toadying.

If you're a cat owner, the reverse is true: your cat pays a little attention to you, and you think it's doing *you* a favor. Cat owners accept everything about *this* deal, despite the potential for well-deserved ridicule as easy marks, suckered in by cunning slackers who appear, at best, amused, when not subjecting their masters to long periods of feline disregard.

Either way, everybody's happy.

CHAPTER 6

I woke up rested and with a breakfast game plan—a gourmet version of what, when I first moved to Los Angeles from Dharamshala, seemed like the oddest food I'd ever tasted. The same teenagers I was introducing to Tibetan Buddhist chants introduced me to a P, B, and J. I was stunned at how good crushed peanuts and strawberry jam tasted, smeared on two slices of bread. Over the years, I continued to experiment with multiple variations on the original theme. These days, I started with handcrafted, organic, wholegrain bread from the local farmer's market and crunchy peanut butter, ground fresh while I watched at the natural foods store down the hill. To these basics, I would add slices of organic banana, when I had bananas around, and a drizzle of raw, wildflower honey.

I dressed quickly. My mouth watered just thinking about what lay ahead: the wild jungle sweetness of banana, combined with the earthy crunch of peanut butter, the low note of crusty bread, the hint of honey providing a tantalizing jazz riff in the far distance. I found a loaf of bread in the freezer, popped two slices in the toaster, and went to the cupboard for the peanut butter. It was gone. An almost full jar, if I remembered correctly. I checked all my cupboards, the refrigerator, and then all the cupboards again, in case I was merely suffering from a severe case of sudden-onset male blindness. Twenty minutes and two burned pieces of toast later, I was breakfastless and in a foul mood. Not even fresh-brewed coffee helped. I was seriously considering going back to bed with a pint of ice cream, when Mike called.

"Yo, boss-man," he said. "How's it hanging?"

"I can't find my peanut butter anywhere," I wailed into the phone. The wall of silence that greeted my words made me realize how ridiculous I sounded, and I started to laugh.

"Dude, for a minute I thought you were, like, six years old," Mike said. "Ask Heather. The women always know. So listen, I've been trying to trace that number you gave me, as in trying *all night*. And, well, the thing is, I'm stumped."

"I don't believe it." I had never heard the word *stumped* come out of Mike's mouth, not in the ten years I'd known him.

"Believe it. At first I thought it was one of those rerouting scams, you know, where they route the number through a buttload of countries, so you can't be sure where it first originated—well, I mean, most people can't, unless they're the FBI—but the thing is, I always can. Only this time, I couldn't. And it gets weirder."

"Go on," I said, checking under the sink. I needed that sandwich more than ever.

"Ten, I don't even recognize the network this cell phone number was using, or I should say, my algorithms don't. And that's not just strange. It's impossible!"

This day had started out bad and was rapidly getting worse.

"I'll keep trying," he said. "But first I gotta sleep for a couple hours. Later!" Mike hung up, his voice sounding almost ebullient at the challenge.

I called Heather.

"Hey," she said.

"Have you seen the peanut butter?"

"The *peanut butter?*" Now I felt ridiculous, as well as put upon. "Have you tried looking for it?" Heather's voice sounded taut and high-pitched, as if she were angry with me for asking. "Sorry, Ten, but I have to go."

I settled for toast and honey, but every bite rankled, as did the fact that I was back to square one and Clara's time clock was running out.

I walked into my designated meditation area and got as far as looking at my cushion before walking back out. I stared across the living room at my computer: I could Skype Yeshe and Lobsang, maybe bring them in on the meager facts at hand. My mind rebelled. I was a certified private investigator with more than a decade of police work behind me. I was the Sherlock Holmes of missing people. For once, I wanted to solve a case without resorting to the inner tools and secret weapons I'd inherited from the other side of the world.

The six-year-old in me still wanted to prove my father wrong.

For the next several hours, I used every non-meditation-based investigatory tool known to technology to try to track down Clara Fuentes. I entered my five-digit P.I. license number and executed various searches from simple to complex, using Merlin, TRACERS, and the LexisNexis offshoot People Search. By estimating Clara's age (mid-50s) and entering both Lancaster and Los Angeles as her cities of residence, all three sites turned up several dozen versions of Clara Fuentes, from a 16-year-old student in Covina, to a 75-year-old retired day care assistant in Fresno, as well as their neighbors, relatives, home addresses, and annual incomes. But not one of these Claras matched mine.

The California DMV was out: she didn't have a license, much less drive a car. And anyway, thanks to the tragic Rebecca Schaeffer case—a stalker hired a P.I. to acquire the actress's home address so he could shoot her—I wouldn't get much in the way of personal information via that department.

My Clara Fuentes had no record of arrests, no accidents, no bank accounts, no credit cards, no late payments—in fact, no payments at all. She was like a ghost, living beneath the social radar as effectively as if she were living under a bridge. I recalled an infamous case when I was still a rookie cop: one of our patrol units, answering a call about a bad smell wafting from a storage unit in the City of Industry, discovered inside a huddle of people, gaunt and filthy—illegal immigrants starved, beaten, and trapped like rats in a sewer. They were the victims of a "coyote" kidnapping, snatched and spirited across the border by a soulless Mexican smuggler—or coyote—and stashed out of sight while their captors used violence and threats to extort money from their families back home. These immigrants, too, had no identification. They, too, were ghosts.

Clara worked for a person with a public presence and money. Maybe there was a coyote behind this disappearance as well. But if so, why had there been no ransom note?

On the other hand, Bets McMurtry had a good reason for Clara to disappear. Illegal employees were a huge liability in politics, as Bets herself had pointed out.

But I remembered her clutching my wrist, her horizontal tears. I'd already experienced the aggressive, almost sexual charm, her "tell" as a con, and she was not conning her need for me to find Clara. I was almost 100 percent certain Bets McMurtry was not behind Clara's disappearance. I looked across the room at Tank, sprawled in a patch of sun.

"So who is responsible, Tank? Who is?"

I typed up a report of the first 24 hours, such as it was, and attached the document to an e-mail to Mac, subject: FOR YOUR EYES ONLY. My report took up maybe a page and a half.

My phone alarm pinged a reminder: time to return the Tesla and pick up my newly refurbished Mustang from the mechanic. I electronically transferred $1,500 from my savings to my checking account—thank you, Julius. Now the greatest challenge to my practice of non-attachment had adjusted valves, a jetted carburetor, an advanced distributor, and a balanced camshaft.

Tank was suddenly nowhere to be found and refused to come when I called him. I ate the last of the cereal dry from the box and dumped cat kibble in Tank's bowl—fair's fair.

I hurried outside and jumped in the Tesla for our final drive together. I dialed Heather as we zoomed down Topanga, and put her on speaker. Crossed wires aside, I was starting to really miss her.

"Good morning!" Heather was slightly breathless. I could hear a repetitive metallic squeak-squeak-squeak in the background. As a medical examiner, she spends her days doing forensic exams and autopsies. I tried not to visualize the cause of the squeaking.

"Good morning to you." I gave in to morbid curiosity. "What's that noise?"

"Oh, sorry," she said, "I'm pushing a gurney with a gangbanger on it. One of the wheels has a nasty habit of squealing, and I haven't had time to oil it."

"I presume this is a *deceased* gangbanger."

"Extremely deceased," she said. "Whoever killed him really wanted him to stay dead. I extracted fourteen slugs from his groin to his sternum, plus some knife wounds I'd rather not describe in detail to a fellow vegan. Let's just say it involves a few essential body parts. Weirdly, we've had a slew of these lately."

"Shooter probably emptied his magazine—seventeen rounds," I said, picturing the victim as target practice. "Only three bullets missed. Pretty good shot pattern."

"Well, Juan Doe here might disagree."

The nickname sparked an idea. "Have you come across any Juanita Does lately?"

"Not that I know of. You want me to ask around?"

"Thank you. Yes, I would."

Squeak-squeak-squeak.

Shoptalk was over. Which left personal talk. Heather didn't say another word. I took a deep breath, and executed an Acapulco high dive right into the middle of the silence. "When would you like to . . . to have our conversation?" I asked.

"Hold on a second." The squeaking stopped. "He's all

yours now," I heard Heather say to someone. "Okay, I'm back. How about tonight?" she asked. "I can come to you."

"Sure." I thought about the daisy Post-it note, and the dark forces took hold of me. "How about six o'clock?"

She paused. "Um, sorry, I'm working late today. I'll try to get there by eight, depending on traffic."

I wondered, snarkily, how many times this year bad traffic had been used as a cover for something else in Los Angeles. Had to be at least a million.

Make that a million and one.

"Okay," I said. "I'll keep my electronic eye out for you."

"And I'll bring my battery-operated buddy, just in case."

As the Tesla and I hit Pacific Coast Highway, fog was creeping across the road from the ocean, bringing a damp chill to the air. It matched the mood that had settled on me during the call with Heather. Yes, there'd been some humor in our banter, but like a lot of humor, it masked a deeper subject, which could be summarized in two questions Heather had posed to me at the Inn of the Seventh Ray on my birthday. I'd been thinking them myself but was too afraid to ask. Ever since, they'd hung over everything we did together, like dank ocean vapor: *Any idea where this relationship is going?* and *We hardly ever make love anymore, do we?*

So far, the only answers I'd been able to come up with were *No* and *I guess not*. Neither seemed remotely sufficient to either one of us.

The sex part was especially unpleasant to admit, but the truth was, except for our first few weeks together, Heather and I didn't work that well together in bed. Not that I'm an expert, but I've had a couple of relationships where the sex worked great, and I've had a couple where it didn't, and I've yet to figure out the magic formula. In fact, 90 percent of this whole sexual attraction thing still puzzles the hell out of me. With my ex-ex, Charlotte, aka She-who-hates-cats, the sex was rocket ship–ride fantastic, the rest of our interactions as toxic as botulism. With Heather, it was the other way around: we hummed like a top in the head and heart but got numb down toward the pelvis.

And Julie?

Sorry, I wasn't going there. Julie was old news.

Heather and I connected in so many ways. We liked the same music, the same kind of books, even got a kick out of each other's style of untutored but enthusiastic jump-and-flail dancing. We almost never fought. We loved to talk shop, not easy when you're dealing with corpses and drug dealers. It was only in bed that we couldn't seem to find the right rhythm. The first time we'd spent the night together was great. The first time we'd actually made love, I thought everything went pretty well, considering. But the next time, Heather had burst into tears and told me she was sorry, but she needed her vibrator to have an orgasm.

"Oh, okay," I'd said. "Fine by me." And it was. But ever since I'd returned from India, the vibrator issue had grown bigger and bigger between us. I could tell she was more and more bothered, and that made me want her less and less. I couldn't figure it out. I was starting to think the whole subject was a smokescreen for something else. But what?

I returned the Tesla to the dealership, full of praise but quick to fend off the salesman with the excuse that I was late for an appointment, thanks to that darned Los Angeles traffic. (One million and two.)

As I walked up the block to my auto mechanic's shop, the cutting edge of a headache pressed against my temples. Then I spotted my Shelby, displayed out front for all to admire. Call me shallow, but the sight of her gleaming yellow frame chased off my headache faster than three Advil and a week of meditation.

"She's a beauty, all right," my mechanic Scott said as he pocketed his check. Scott was a collector, as well as a fixer-upper. "You ever want to sell her . . ."

"Not going to happen, Scott."

He shrugged. He knew.

I decided to take my Mustang for a fast dash up the coast, to clean out both our pipes. The low roar of her V-8 engine sucked up my bad mood and blew it right out her dual exhaust pipes. I passed Malibu and was pointed toward Oxnard when my cell phone buzzed in my pocket. I pulled it out and squinted at the screen. Shit. It was Mac Gannon's landline. He'd probably read my report and wanted his money back.

I had to go all the way to Point Mugu State Park before I could pull off and call him back.

To my surprise, Melissa answered the phone.

"Hi Ten," she said, her voice subdued.

"Hi, Melissa. What's going on?"

"Nothing much," she said. "Daddy's gone away, and Mommy's in bed. She's having one of her little headaches, so I'm not s'posed to disturb her." I could hear Melissa parroting her mother's words, and I shuddered. How many times growing up had my own mother's "little headaches"—brought on by too much wine combined with other things—meant I was in for some lonely, scary hours? For the first time, I wondered what secrets Penelope Gannon might be harboring.

"How was school today?"

"Okay," she said. Definitely not the effervescent Melissa I was used to.

I waited.

"Um, uh, Ten? I have a detective question for you." She paused, and I pictured her hand creeping into her mouth for a quick gnaw. "You're still our detective, aren't you?"

The way she said "our detective" was charming, as if every family had a personal detective to go along with their gardener, plumber, and priest.

"Yes," I said. "I'm still your detective. What kind of detecting do you need?"

"Can you come over? It's not a telling thing; it's a showing thing."

"Can you show anyone else?"

"No," she said. "I need you."

I was back at Mac's compound in half an hour. I pressed the intercom, and a phone rang somewhere inside. Someone picked up.

Silence. Then a familiar, nine-year-old voice whispered, "Ten. Is that you?"

"Yes. It's me, Melissa, but what in the world are you . . .?"

The gate swung open.

Melissa was already in the driveway, bouncing from foot to foot. Her hair was a cascade of red, tumbling down her back, and she wore jeans and a T-shirt emblazoned with sequined butterflies.

"Melissa, do your parents know you've figured out how to open the front gate?"

She threw her arms around me. "I knew you'd come! I just knew it!" she said, and without another word raced up the hill toward a grove of swaying Monterey cypress. I followed, my feelings mixed. She veered right around the sentinel of trees and halted. As I reached her side, I spotted a tiny outbuilding surrounded by a miniature white picket fence. I gaped. I was guessing this was a child's playhouse, but it was also an architectural jewel, a light blue, Victorian-era structure of scalloped wood, complete with a wraparound porch, stained glass, and window boxes bursting with blooming geraniums—real ones.

Melissa tugged me over to the door.

"Shall I push the doorbell or use the brass knocker?" I asked, but Melissa had already run inside. I ducked in after her and was no less impressed, if that's the right word, by the interior. The curtains matched the upholstery, and the patterned walls had been sponge-painted. There was even a fireplace— and a baby grand piano, as in a grand piano for a baby-sized person. I calculated that the price tag for this playhouse was the equivalent of enough *dana*, or donated room and board, to sponsor 200 monks for a full year of study at Dorje Yidam.

I sat cross-legged on the hardwood floor, the only way I could fit, as Melissa dove behind the little sofa. "I found something today," her muffled voice announced. She reappeared, rolling a small steamer trunk behind her. "I hardly ever play here anymore, but I was feeling sad because of Mommy, and Maggie being gone to her other Mommy's, so I decided to have a pretend tea party. But I couldn't find the teapot anywhere, so I looked inside this."

She parked the trunk at my feet, her face solemn. "I didn't take it out, or anything."

"Take what out?"

Melissa's eyes filled. "I'm a little scared," she said.

"Do you want me to open this?"

"I don't know. I only turned nine a month ago. You decide."

"I tell you what," I said. "Why don't I take a look, and then we can decide what to do next."

I lifted the lid. Inside, a black nylon backpack was half-hidden beneath a pile of crocheted baby blankets. A small TSA lock, the kind you would use on a suitcase, secured the zipper.

"Is this yours, Melissa?"

Melissa shook her head. "It's Sofia's," she whispered. "She always brings it to work with her. I heard Mommy telling Daddy that Sofia's gone away. Mommy sounded mad. I really like Sofia. And . . . and I didn't touch it this time, I promise! I just found it! Mommy said to never, ever touch Sofia's backpack again, and so I didn't! Anyway, I only took it before because I needed it for my adventure, like Dora the Explorer!" Melissa's eyes filled with tears as she relived the unfairness of her life.

"I understand," I said. "You did the right thing by calling me. Excellent detective work." I picked up the backpack. "May I?"

She nodded, her mouth now fully occupied by four fingers.

It took me about 30 seconds to pick the lock, using the small blade on my pocketknife. Melissa stared, a little too fascinated, as I dug the blade into the opening on one side and alternately pressed and turned hard until the lock popped open. If travelers knew how easy picking was, they wouldn't bother locking.

A steel padlock, on the other hand, is a different story. That can take at least three minutes to break open.

I set the lock aside.

"Mommy says I shouldn't be a snoop," Melissa said. "She says snooping leads to trouble."

"How about you close your eyes and I'll tell you when to open them, okay?"

She squeezed her eyes shut.

I unzipped the backpack. Well, well, well. Mommy was right. The pack was crammed with quart-sized Ziploc bags, each loaded with smaller packets of prescription drugs of various types. I recognized many of the pills from my years on the force. There looked to be maybe 100 of each: Oxycontin, Ecstasy, Vicodin, Rohypnol, as well as Fentanyl patches and the skinny white elongated pills known as Xanax bars. I zipped the backpack closed.

"You can open your eyes now."

"What's in there?"

I considered what to say. She didn't seem like the kind of person one should lie to, even to protect her feelings. Finally I said, "Medicine."

"What kind of medicine?" She moved on to her thumbnail.

I decided it was time to deflect. "I notice you bite your nails, Melissa. Do you wish you could stop?"

She shoved her hands into her pockets. "Can't. I tried. Neither can Daddy."

"I can show you a secret way to do it. I learned it in the monastery. It helped me stop biting my nails when I was your age."

"You bited your nails?"

"Yes. It's a habit I got into at a time in my life when I felt kind of lonely. Want me to show you how I stopped?"

"Okay," she said. "But Mommy already painted bad-tasting stuff on my fingers and it didn't work."

"No, this is something you do with your mind," I said. "You . . ."

But now that I had taken charge of Melissa's secret, she was done with any more talking. She let out a squeal of delight and pounced on an old-fashioned, doll-sized perambulator tucked in the corner of the living room.

"My baby carriage! I have to go get Baby Baby and take her for a walk!"

She raced outside. The play door slammed behind her, just like a real one would.

I hefted the backpack in my hands, thinking. If Sofia was involved with a prescription drugs scam, then maybe Clara was as well, and that changed everything about my case. I had a lot of thinking to do. But first, I had to figure out what to do with the evidence.

Call Mac?

Call Bill?

Call the Malibu Police Department?

I wasn't ready to call the police yet. It might mean a world of trouble for me, but I finally had a lead. I needed time to determine how to parlay it into some answers. I made a snap decision. I would take temporary custody of the backpack. I certainly couldn't think of any good that would come from introducing a pharmacy's worth of pills to Mac Gannon's shaky sobriety, much less what such a discovery might do to the electoral hopes of one Bets McMurtry, should this somehow trace back to her.

Okay, it was tempting, but no.

Melissa charged back inside, clutching a baby doll with red hair and freckles. She deposited the doll in the baby carriage and wheeled it to face the door.

"Melissa?" I moved to her side and knelt so we were face to face. "I'm going to take this backpack and lock it in my car for now. I need some time to figure out what to do next. But you won't get in trouble, no matter what. And as soon as I can, I'll explain everything to your Dad."

She cocked her head. "Is this a shake kind of thing?"

"Definitely," I said.

We shook. I could see in the back of her eyes a look that said, *You better not let me down.* The trust of a child is like no other. Sometimes it's the only thing they have to call their own.

"No trouble. I promise," I said.

I carried the backpack to my car. The '65 Shelby Mustang doesn't have a trunk, so I tucked it just behind the driver's seat and covered it with my windbreaker. The Gannon house stood silent, the grounds empty of people, and I was spared the hassle of any further explanations. As I drove off, I saw Melissa wheeling her baby carriage around the circular driveway, her jaw working a mile a minute, which made me smile.

To President of the United States or leader of a criminal enterprise I added, *Melissa Gannon, Private Detective extraordinaire.*

Chapter 7

I made a beeline for Langer's. I didn't care if it was out of my way, I was not to be denied a moment longer. I parked in Langer's lot, off Langer's Square, and grabbed the backpack. I jogged around the corner, past a closed auto title loan office, Ana's Newsstand, and a couple of facilities for check-cashing fast. Inside Langer's, the blaring neon yellow, orange, and maroon stripes behind the food counter almost took away my appetite. Almost. I spotted my favorite—and currently harried—waitress, Jean, hustling to a crowded table by the front window, her arms lined with full plates. I took a small booth for hungry loners, smack in the middle of Jean's loading and unloading zone; the little brass circle imbedded in the wood let me know I was seated at table number 8.

"Ten-zing! You're back!" Jean's face was flushed with effort, but her blue eyes twinkled. "Did you miss me too much?" Her bobbed gray-blonde hair was shoved back from her forehead with a neon-green plastic band decorated with tiny kitten faces. Somehow, it suited her. Her other new accessory was an equally green compression bandage, wrapped around her right forearm.

"What's this?" I pointed.

"Oh, I know! Can you believe it? I have carpal tunnel syndrome. Too many years juggling plates of food." Jean's eyes darted around the room, as if checking for spies. Nineteen years with the Scientology organization, before finally breaking free, had trained Jean to be on the lookout for eavesdroppers and betrayers. Satisfied that all enemy eyes and ears were focused elsewhere, she leaned close to me.

"They gave me a prescription for Oxycodone," she said, her flat nasal Arizona accent seasoned with a dash of reverence. "All my normy friends and even some of my recovery buddies told me to fill it. Oh, Ten-zing, I was tempted. If you're in recovery and under a doctor's supervision, you get to treat pain medication as a freelapse—a high that doesn't count as a slip."

My skin prickled, as I thought of the stash on the seat next to me. It was all I could do not to snatch up the backpack and run.

"So did you fill your prescription?"

Jean shook her head so fiercely that her hair band slid over her forehead and she had to shove it back up. "Oh, no. Not me. No way, José. You might as well just shoot me up with heroin and put me back on the street in hot pants and stilettos. That's where one pill of oxy takes a girl like me. It's Advil or nothing for poor little Jean."

Her antenna must have registered someone watching. She straightened up with a jerk, all business.

"What are you eating today? Egg salad on whole wheat toast?"

I took a breath. "Number nineteen, please." I was aiming for casual.

Jean stared. "Ten-zing," she said, her own voice stern. "I have a very important question for you. I want you to think really hard before you answer."

I braced myself.

"Do you want a dill pickle with that?"

I laughed out loud, drawing a satisfied smile from Jean. "Why not?" I said.

She bustled away.

I stared blindly at the windows facing Seventh Street, thinking about what Jean had just said about oxy. Something about it triggered an idea, but it slithered away. I idly noticed a fancy set of wheels, a Mercedes four-door, gliding by outside, slow and elegant as a black swan. Car lovers like me notice things like that. The luxury sedan was incongruous in this neighborhood of mostly secondhand clunkers.

Jean slid a plate in front of me. I gazed at the contents in awe. I had done my research. Crusty twice-baked rye bread, warm hand-sliced pastrami, melted Swiss cheese, and fresh coleslaw. It was time. I compressed half a sandwich between my two hands, lifted the warm concoction to my mouth, sent a quick chant of gratitude to the cow that made this possible, and took a bite.

Oh. My. Goodness.

Jean hadn't moved. I saluted her with my sandwich and took a second, huge bite.

"If you come back on June fifteenth, you can have a number nineteen for free," Jean said. "Langer's is turning sixty-five this year. So am I, if this job doesn't kill me first."

I was entering a deep state of pastrami *samadhi.* "I just might have to come back."

A small frown creased Jean's forehead. "I know it's none of my business, my friend, but does Potato-latke-extra-applesauce-no-sour-cream-because-sorry-I'm-a-*vee*-gan approve?"

Jean never forgot an order.

"Heather? I haven't told her yet."

"Well, I predict she's not going to be happy about this. In my experience, *vee*-gans can be very judgmental. You ask me, that other one, the chef, sounded like a winner. I'll bet she ate everything. You should never have dumped her."

Like Bill and Martha, Jean was never going to let me hear the end of my blown romance with Martha's younger sister, Julia.

"I'm pretty sure she dumped me."

"Dumping is as dumping does," Jean announced, mysteriously. "Ten-zing, I'm not joking. Tell that to Heather soon."

"I will. Soon."

"Because, well, you know what they say, don't you, Ten-zing?"

"No, Jean. What do 'they' say?"

"Jean!" An older man gestured by the take-out area, his deep, unpleasant voice overriding the din like a Tibetan long horn. He ducked his double chin and barked something into a small mouthpiece clipped to his shirt, his eyes darting about like a Secret Service agent's. Deli orders were serious business. He signaled to Jean again, frowning. Jean leaned close. "That's one of the people I have to pray for daily," she said. She started to leave.

"Wait a second, Jean. You never finished your thought. What do 'they' say?"

She loomed over me, her blue eyes laser-beaming into my conscience.

"You're only as sick as your secrets." And off she went, my personal oracle, artfully disguised as a waitress at Langer's.

I stopped at Whole Foods, loaded up on groceries, and drove home, still floating on a cloud of smoked beef on rye. As I parked the glinting Shelby next to my trusty beater car, I experienced a brief flare of absolute contentment. Two cars outside, one cat inside—my little family was complete again. I'd been trained for over half my life that attachment to material things is a major source of suffering, but some things . . . well, they still gave me moments like this, of pure and simple joy. The trick lay in realizing these moments are fleeting, not in denying oneself the joy of experiencing them.

I decided to leave the backpack where it was for now. No one but me ever went into my garage. I did lock the side door, in deference to the pharmaceutical bonanza inside my car. I lugged four shopping bags of supplies into the kitchen and unloaded. Heather and I would have some decent food and wine to help us get through tonight, or I would, if the talk went badly and I ended the evening alone.

My nerves amped upward into high-anxiety range as I considered the conversation that lay ahead. I needed a run in the worst way—it had been more than three days, and even with a full stomach, my body was starting to emit sparks of tension.

I tried calling Mac first, but I was sent straight to voice mail and a new message: "This is Mac. I'm on location for a few days. I'll call you from the other side."

I wasn't unhappy.

"Ten Norbu. Call me when you can, please," I said. "I have some interesting news."

Tank deigned to come out from wherever he'd been hiding, and I deigned to feed him actual wet cat food—the dry kibble lay untouched in his bowl. As I dumped the pellets into the trash, I noticed a familiar glass container peeking out from under a wad of paper towels. The peanut butter jar, so recently full, was wiped clean, as empty of content as the Buddha's mind.

One mystery solved, only to be replaced by another one.

I changed, made sure that the Guard-on was awake and doing its macho thing—thousands of dollars' worth of pills now occupied my garage—and started off in a slow jog toward Topanga State Park, my phone clipped to the waistband of my running shorts, my feet decked out in my brand-new, super-expensive, biometric running shoes, manufactured somewhere in Denmark. A run would clear my head, so I could focus on what to do next with this baffling case.

Halfway up Musch Trail I was buckled over, having faced two immutable truths regarding Langer's number 19: One, hot pastrami, Swiss cheese, and coleslaw are an inspired combination. Two, hot pastrami, Swiss cheese, coleslaw, and high-speed sprints are a recipe for intestinal disaster.

My phone buzzed against my waist. I grabbed it, squinting through the forehead sweat dripping into my eyes. Mike was calling.

"You're up early," I huffed.

"Your perimeter just got breached."

"Ah. That explains it. Wasn't me, promise. I'm taking a run in the park, or trying to."

"Good. Listen up. This one's for real, boss. Some creep is sniffing around your house."

My heartbeat quickened. "Can you see who it is?"

"Sort of. The image is a little blurry. Skinny guy, I'm thinking maybe Hispanic, wearing a dark hoodie. Not skinny like ordinary skinny; skinny like a growing teenager, with big feet." Mike's voice rose up a notch. "Okay, okay, he's on the back deck now and looking in the back door, doing something to it. Now he's moved over to the kitchen window."

I started to jog down the path, the phone pressed to my ear.

"Now he's coming back down the steps and, uh, sprinting, I guess you could say, toward the perimeter. And . . . he's gone."

"Sprinting?"

"Well, more like hunched over and flailing his arms."

That description was too close to my own recent running endeavor for comfort.

"I wonder if it's Hector, the kid who comes around now and then to see if I want my cars washed."

"Can't help you there, my man."

"He usually pedals up on a bike, though."

"You can check it out when you get back to the house. Need any extra muscle?"

Mike's 6-foot 3-inch, 160-pound concept of himself as extra muscle made me realize how deluded we human beings can be. "Not yet."

I half-jogged, half-walked down the hill to my house, nursing my indigestion as I scrutinized the woods along both sides of the road for signs of things that shouldn't be there. I saw nothing.

I stepped onto the deck and studied the door jamb for signs of forced entry. The wood was untouched, but a small, poorly printed flyer had been half-slipped under the door. I pulled it out and read "Lawn work. Call Miguel Ortiz," followed by a phone number. I scanned my property one more time, but Miguel was long gone.

"Mike, you still there?"

"Yeah. Everything okay?"

"Seems to be. Looks like the guy just dropped off a flyer. Thanks for letting me know."

"No problem. I can set things up so the Guard-on will work on your cell phone. That way you can keep tabs anyplace you can get wireless."

"I don't know. It sounds a bit paranoid."

"Hey, it ain't paranoia if they really are—"

"Yeah, yeah, yeah," I interrupted. Mike gets most of his life wisdom from T-shirts. "Let me think about it, okay? Anything more on the mystery cell number?"

"Maybe. I'm not ready to commit yet."

"Join the club."

I carried the flyer inside. Tank was positioned just inside the door, a dour look in his eyes.

"Soon," I said. "Liver bits."

I moved to my computer and instigated a long, frustrating bout of fiddling with the patented Guard-on Image Retrieval System. I envy kids like Mike, who grew up with computers, remote controls, and other electronic wonders. While they were sitting around with their geek brethren playing video games and imprinting their DNA with computer skills, I was sitting around with the Tibetan Buddhist version of geek brethren, puzzling out what the Supreme Buddha was saying 2,600 years ago. Since nobody even bothered to write anything down for another 400 years, the Buddha's teachings were rich territory for puzzlement, also known as making shit up. We could have used a few YouTubes of the man, that's all I'm saying.

Finally. I actually managed to coax the recorded event of my interloper from the Guard-on's memory zone. I zeroed in on the image of Miguel Ortiz, or whoever he was. I ratcheted up to Level Orange immediately—Mike had neglected to tell me the kid had started out by looking in the window of my garage. As I watched, he rattled the side door, and I panicked briefly before remembering I had locked it. Talk about good timing.

Next, the image switched, and he was climbing up my wooden steps and poking around on the deck. He raised his fist and knocked once or twice. His body obscured the moment when he slid the flyer under the sill, but I could plainly see him move across to the kitchen window and shade his eyes, peering in. Then he was gone as quickly and silently as he'd arrived.

I hurried outside and found a pair of footprints in the soft soil below my deck. I placed my size 11 running shoe parallel to one of the prints. The outline was one or two shoe sizes smaller than mine. I followed the smudged imprints as they passed my favorite California oak and wove between the gnarled Manzanita trees lining the gravel driveway that connected me to Topanga Canyon Boulevard. Halfway along, I found a deep, clear print that revealed the distinctive waffle pattern of the brand. Adidas. So, now I was looking for a skinny kid in a hoodie who wore an Adidas running shoe, approximately size 9 or 10. As Mike would say, "Easy peasy." I had narrowed my search to a million or so suspects between here and San Diego.

On the other hand, maybe young Miguel really was looking to do lawn work. But I doubted it. I didn't have a lawn.

I moved onto parts two and three of my genius plan for identifying the intruder. I gave Tank a bowl of liver bits. Then I sat at my desk and punched in the number on the flyer. After three rings, the quavering voice of an elderly Hispanic male offered a shaky "*Hola.*"

"Miguel Ortiz, *por favor.*" This innocent request ignited a burst of excited Spanish that ended with a question. My understanding of Spanish is pretty rudimentary, especially when the words are delivered at the speed of a Gatling. I said, "*Que?*" and added a "*No comprende,*" for good measure, as he went into a second rapid-fire barrage, even louder and faster than the first.

I was losing this ground battle, so I resorted to underground subterfuge. As we spoke I punched the phone number into my reverse directory and identified the address connected to the voice. East L.A., the middle of gangland territory. Why was I not surprised?

A younger male voice came on the line. "Who is this?" he asked in heavily accented English.

I ignored his question. "Miguel Ortiz left a flyer on my door with this number on it. I'm looking for someone to care for my lawn. Can I talk to him?"

"He don' do that no more," the voice said. Then he hung up on me.

"Okay, then, if he don' do that no more, how come he put an ad for it on my door?" I said into the dead phone. I looked over at my cat. "Tank, I'm beginning to doubt the sincerity of Miguel's commitment to his business."

Tank lifted his head. "Excuse me, I got liver bits here," he answered in cat talk, one language in which I do happen to be fluent.

I checked the time and winced. Heather was about 20 minutes away from happy hour with the mysterious Dr. K., and I was about to possibly make things a whole lot worse between us. But my gut was whispering to me not to wait on this Miguel situation, and I had learned a while ago that ignoring such whispers never ended well.

I called Heather and got her machine.

"Heather, I am so, so sorry, but I can't do tonight. Something's come up, and it won't wait. I'll call you in the morning, okay?" I hesitated. "Love you. Sleep tight."

I retrieved the business card from my back jeans pocket and flipped it over for Carlos's information. Hopefully, he wasn't at work, in class, or taking Sofia's bird for a walk.

"Hi, Ten. Do you have news?" Carlos's voice was eager. I felt terrible that I hadn't considered that aspect of the call.

"No, sorry. Nothing so far. This is about a different situation, though the two may be connected." As I said this, I realized the truth of my words. I didn't know how or why yet, but the timing of my hiding Sofia's backpack and Miguel's visit was too coincidental to be random.

"How can I help?"

"I'm headed to East L.A. to gather information, and I may need a translator. My Spanish is rusty to nonexistent."

"When?"

"Now."

"Can you pick me up?"

"Sure."

Just like that, I was good to go. I went to my closet and unlocked my safe. Out came the Wilson again, as well as several $100 bills from my envelope of tax-free motivation.

The choice of car wasn't even a choice. I was heading into the Land of Clunkers.

Traffic wasn't bad—the evening hour had dislodged the normal logjam of late afternoon drivers. I picked Carlos up outside his apartment, and he read directions to me off my phone, until my Corolla was safely parked on the 500 block of Whittier Boulevard, across from the house where I hoped Miguel Ortiz still lived. The neighborhood was similar to many others I'd visited as a patrol officer, and scarily like the one where I'd met my first bullet, three years ago—an event that led to my leaving the LAPD.

A tumble of tiny, rundown houses, the faded colors of sherbet, made a jagged procession down either side of the boulevard. Some were boarded up, while others still attempted to appear homey with a coat of fresh paint here, a struggling but recognizable flower garden there. They wrestled for space with two fast-food franchises, a ramshackle bodega, and a corner bar. Every available surface, from walls to storefronts to telephone poles, served as a canvas for rival gangs to claim their turf with graffiti: even the trees were tagged. A few kids kicked a soccer ball around a small patch of dead grass, their shorts sagging to their ankles. Their older brothers occupied the buckled wooden porch of one of the abandoned homes, baseball caps pulled low, empty cans of beer piled next to them, like scat.

"Man," Carlos said. "Depressing."

I looked at the once-vibrant homesteads, now warped and peeling and listing to one side like invalids. I could sense rage behind the bold, overlapping slashes of graffiti warfare. Drugs had caused this. Drugs—and drug lords.

Like Chaco Morales.

His stocky form rose before my eyes: Chaco Morales, the big loose end in my life. He'd taken possession of my brain like no other criminal in the early days and weeks after the Julius Rosen case closed. I checked in periodically with Bill and the gang squad. No one had heard of or seen Chaco since his escape, but I didn't believe for a minute he was gone. His ruthlessness fed his ambition, and both were insatiable. Mexico was too small to satisfy such an appetite. No, Chaco Morales and I were not done with each other yet. I shivered. Even his name gave off the whiff of evil.

"You okay, man?"

"I'm fine," I said. "Let's get to work." I handed Carlos two crisp $100 bills.

"No, man. It's cool."

"Please," I said. "Otherwise, I'm leaving you in the car."

"Pay me after I've done something, then."

The soccer ball bounced onto the road in front of a low-slung Chevy Camaro. Horn blaring, the car swerved to avoid the two kids pounding after it.

"So, what exactly are we doing here?" Carlos asked.

I gave him a quick rundown on my "lawn-care" investigation. At the last minute, I decided not to mention

Sofia's backpack, but I forgot that Carlos was extremely intelligent.

"Sorry, *mi amigo*, but you said this might be connected to Clara and Sofia. I'm not seeing the connection."

Busted.

I filled in the blanks.

Carlos whistled. "You sure the kid wasn't confused? I've never seen Sofia with a black backpack. With any backpack, actually. And she's not on drugs. I'd know."

"Melissa had no reason to lie," I said. "Unless . . ." I pictured her older sister Maggie. But she'd been gone all month. "Either way, I still want to track down Miguel, if I can. Just to eliminate him as a suspect in my missing person's case, if nothing else."

"Okay. So what's the plan?"

"I haven't quite figured that out yet," I admitted.

Carlos smiled. "Fishing expedition, then?"

"Yes."

"Always did want to learn how to fish," he said. "Is there anything you can tell me about the two people you talked to on the phone?"

"Well, the first man I talked to, the one who didn't speak English, sounded elderly. He also sounded upset, but he was talking too fast for me to find out why. The second guy was younger and basically hung up on me."

"Hey, Ten, isn't that the house?"

Sure enough, the front door across from us had opened, and an elderly Hispanic man stepped outside. He was short and lean, dressed in clean khaki work clothes and brown cowboy boots. He smoothed his sparse hair and stuck a raffia cowboy hat on his head.

"*Mi Abuelo*, sorry, my grandfather has a straw hat just like that," Carlos said. "Makes me a little homesick for Mexico." Carlos was already getting into character. He pronounced Mexico Meh-hee-co. "Think maybe that's the old guy you talked to?"

"Let's hope," I said. The elderly man lit a thin, brown cigarillo, inhaled deeply and blew out a plume of smoke. He started walking briskly in our direction. We instinctively scooched lower in the Toyota's front seat, but he ignored us. He was spry for his age, which I estimated to be somewhere around 80, and he was marching in his cowboy boots like a man on a mission. He reached the end of the block and disappeared through the swinging doors of a cantina by the name of Los Gatos.

"Ah," said Carlos. "Happy hour."

"That's pretty local-looking," I said. "Do you think it's going to look weird if I go in there?"

Carlos looked me over. "I don't think it'll be a problem. You look non-Anglo enough to pass. What are you, anyway?"

"Tibetan father, American mother," I said.

He nodded. "Yeah, I can see that. Vaguely Asian."

That sounded about right. I'd inherited my father's thick black hair, which I had to keep mowed pretty short to prevent it from sticking straight up like the tip of a Magic Marker. I had my mother's nose, slightly thinner than the average Tibetan's. Her pale skin had mixed with my father's Tibetan ruddiness to give me a tannish tint, so I looked healthy even when I wasn't feeling it. My eyes, too, were a mix—not quite round like Valerie's and not quite slanted like my father's. Somehow her blue eyes and his brown ones had come together to make mine hazel, muddy brown, or green, depending on your-guess-is-as-good-as-mine.

"Ready?" I asked.

"Ready."

We crossed the street and sauntered up the block and into the bar. We were greeted by the *clack* of colliding balls from a pool table installed somewhere in the dim depths of the room. The sound provided percussion to a lively Mexican melody playing from a jukebox, the tune a kissing cousin of a polka.

A smattering of Hispanic men, all middle-aged or older, sprawled around a handful of round wooden tables. Their eyes were fixed on the two guys shooting pool. Señor Cowboy was sitting by himself at the bar. His eyes were glued on the bartender, who carefully poured a Dos Equis into a glass as if every drop was precious, which it is. I felt an instant connection: Dos Equis is one of my favorites.

We sat down at the bar as well, a few stools away from our man. The bartender finished pouring and stepped away. My mouth watered as I watched a Beer Moment happen, that first sacred swig that brings such meaning and purpose to the beer-lover's day. I was ready to encounter my own.

"Are you over twenty-one?" I asked Carlos.

"Twenty-three," he answered.

"Good. You order. I'll pay. Dos Equis for me."

The bartender moseyed over to us. He was clearly his own best customer; his massive belly strained the buttons on a shirt that had probably been white, and had actually fit, a few years back.

Carlos pointed down the bar to the old man's Dos Equis and said the Spanish equivalent of "We'll have what he's having." The bartender pulled two frosty bottles out of the cooler and set them on the bar, along with a couple of glasses. He carefully poured the amber beer into the glasses and stepped back, as he had with Señor Cowboy.

East L.A. isn't so bad, I thought.

I sipped, I savored, and I let out a sigh of satisfaction. You don't want to overwhelm the taste buds with too big a swallow at first. They prefer a nice, gentle stretch to a frontal assault.

The bartender, who doubled as waiter, had just returned after delivering fresh beers to the pool table gang, swapping full glasses for empty ones. He stepped close to Carlos and said something under his breath. Carlos's mouth thinned.

"What?" I said.

"Don't ask me why, but he's figured out you're a cop. He says he doesn't want any trouble."

I offered my best Buddhist smile.

The bartender said to Carlos, *"¿No habla español su amigo?"* Carlos shook his head and rattled off an answer. The bartender said something back, and they both chuckled. Carlos was turning out to be a natural at this.

"I told him you were cool. Asked him how we could make friends with the old man real quick," Carlos reported. "He says the guy loves ceviche but never has enough money to order it. He says they have great ceviche here. Should I order some?"

"Yeah," I said. "Get a double order, and we'll ask him over to share." I'd try to watch them eat it without regretting breakfast. Eating meat was one thing. Raw fish flesh? I don't think so.

The bartender disappeared into the kitchen and reappeared with a huge bowl of ceviche topped with slices of ripe avocado and wedges of fresh lime. He set it down in front of us. I slid $20 across the bar and waved him off making change. The bill disappeared into his pocket like magic. I glanced over at the old man. He was mesmerized by our bowl, a serious case of raw-fish lust if I've ever seen one. I made an exaggerated move of pushing the ceviche over to Carlos as I shook my head. Carlos turned to the old man, as if drawn by his longing, and gestured for him to come over and share. Moments later, we were seated three in a row—and ready for the next stage of interrogation.

Carlos seemed to enjoy the fishy concoction at least as much as Señor Cowboy did, but I didn't hold it against him. Meanwhile, I found that by defocusing my eyes slightly I could maintain a benign outer expression while watching them eat belly-white chunks of raw fish. Even a lifetime of rice and lentils was preferable.

I sipped my beer and waited as they ate and chatted. Finally, the old man wiped his mouth with a faded but clean-looking bandanna and let out a satisfied belch. Carlos and he were quickly immersed in a longer, fairly animated exchange, a blur of Spanish that lasted for several minutes.

The old man pushed away from the bar and headed for the men's room.

"I'm dying here," I said to Carlos. "Talk to me."

"Okay, well, I got him going by complaining about my two jobs, but he's outdoing me big-time: he's complaining about his job, his kids, his grandkids."

"Focus on the grandson Miguel, if you can."

The old man staggered back to his stool, and they finished up their conversation. Señor Cowboy was now into his third beer and clearly getting maudlin in any language. We slid off our stools and left our man staring down his weather-beaten reflection in the well-polished wood of the bar. One eyelid was drooping: he was closing in on bedtime, and fast.

Back in the Corolla, Carlos turned to fill me in. "Get this," he started, his eyes gleaming.

"Nah, ah, ah," I said. I passed over the bills. "A deal is a deal."

"You don't like to owe anyone, do you?" Carlos said, but he took the money. "Okay. So, his no-good daughter married a no-good man, and now their son, his no-good grandson Miguel, has dropped out of school and joined a gang. To make matters worse, his father, the son-in-law, has started running around with another woman, a *puta*, just as no-good as the rest of them. Miguel was the kid you were interested in, right?"

"Yeah. Did he say which gang Miguel joined?"

Carlos shook his head. "All he kept saying was it was a gang of gangs."

Gang of gangs. First I'd heard of it. Maybe Bill knew more.

Carlos laughed. "Maybe they're forming a union."

"Okay, I'll look into it. Chances are, the old guy was just talking beer-talk, but you never know. Thanks, Carlos. Really good work."

I drove Carlos home, both of us deep in thought. I was thinking about the bitter damage gangs inflict on families. Maybe he was, too.

I dropped him off on Serrano.

"Really, thanks," I repeated.

"Any time," he answered. His forehead creased. "Do you think I'll ever see Sofia again?"

"I don't know," I said. "I really don't."

He opened the car door. An ear-splitting Armenian mishmash of electric guitars and wailing horns blasted from one of the third-floor balcony apartments. Carlos straightened his shoulders and walked inside.

I had another potential clue, but I was out of ideas. As I headed up the 101 North, I called Bill. He sounded out of breath.

"Martha and I invested in an elliptical," he said. "Let me turn this thing off before I kill myself." After a moment, he said, "All yours."

"So, Bill," I said.

"Uh-oh," he answered.

I explained, in broad strokes, what had been going on. I left out the specifics of a certain backpack that was in my possession. No need to go crazy with the honesty thing.

"Let me get this straight, Ten. Your missing person, who may or may not exist, may or may not be related to Mac Gannon's maid, who may or may not be involved with a member of an alleged gang of gangs, a guy called Miguel Ortiz who may or may not have scoped out your home. Does that pretty much sum it up?"

"Pretty much."

"Okay, well, first of all—" Bill broke off. "You know what? I don't think I can handle this tonight. I'm going to finish my exercise routine, watch some mindless television with my beautiful wife, and call you in the morning. Think you can stay out of trouble until then?"

"Absolutely," I said.

"Gang of gangs," Bill muttered. "Shoot me now."

CHAPTER 8

Beep-beep-beep!

My eyes snapped open, the high-pitched warning tone piercing my sleep. It was 2:58 A.M., and somebody had just breached my perimeter. Again.

I slid my hand under the pillow next to me and found the .38 right where I'd tucked it, an impulsive midnight decision but apparently a good one. I thanked the various gods that Heather hadn't come over, we hadn't had our talk, and she hadn't spent the night. I swung out of bed. Sure enough, a shadowy figure was moving across the screen, captured in the eerie green glow of one of the infrared cameras. I couldn't tell if it was my lawn-caring friend from yesterday, but whoever he was, he was heading straight for my garage. He tried the side door. Slipped inside.

I am a creature of habit, and up until yesterday, it had never been my habit to lock the side door into my garage. I was tired last night and in a hurry to get to bed. Now my lack of mindfulness had boomeranged back to harm me.

My cell phone buzzed. Mike. He was probably sitting at his computer, seeing just what I was seeing.

"I'm on it, Mike. Can you call Bill for me?" He grunted and hung up.

I pocketed the phone, pulled on my running shoes, and slipped out of the bedroom. Moving quietly, I crept across the slick hardwood floor, making my silent way through the living room and into the kitchen. I needed to get a better sense of what I was up against. I crouched low and looked out the kitchen window. About 100 yards away, past the trees that line my property, a sliver of moonlight glinted off the big, square windshield of a Hummer. Did that mean I had more than one visitor?

Homeowner outrage hummed in my bloodstream. *This is private property. This is my safe space. You don't belong here.* I racked a round into the chamber of the .38.

I knew I should yell out—most intruders flee at the first indication of an inhabitant, armed or not. But I could feel the sizzle of adrenaline in my bloodstream urging me to deal with this the old-fashioned way. Besides, I was pretty sure I knew who was out there.

I cracked open the kitchen door and swept the barrel of the pistol across the grounds. Nothing. I dropped low and snuck around to the back of the garage, hugging the shadows. I peered into the small side window. It was Miguel all right, squatting beside my Shelby, a crowbar in one hand and a flashlight in the other.

He was about to jimmy a door I'd spent at least 20 hours restoring, on a car I'd just spent $1,500 tuning up.

Not my Mustang, Miguel. Not in this lifetime.

I took a deep breath and banged through the door, reaching over to hit the switch that illuminated the overhead light. I yelled at the top of my lungs and aimed the Wilson. Miguel jerked his head up. The flashlight clattered to the floor and rolled across the cement, coming to a stop at my feet as he groped in his pocket and pulled out a small pistol.

I pointed my gun at his chest. "Drop it!"

His arm jerked upward. Bad move. I lowered the sight and shot him in the meaty part of his left leg. He howled and fell hard, his head clunking against the Mustang's back bumper as he went down. He stopped moving, out cold.

I started toward him when two car doors slammed. Shit. I crouched down behind the Shelby and aimed into the inky darkness. Now I regretted switching on the light. It put me at a disadvantage. I could just make out a man—no, *two* men—sprinting through the trees and running straight for me. When they were about 20 yards out, I grabbed the flashlight and slung it to my right, aiming for the Toyota. It hit the sheet metal with a clang. They started firing in that direction but spotted me immediately when I stood up to return fire. Two muzzles swung my way.

There was no time for niceties. I aimed for center mass, just like the academy taught me. Two shots, two hits, square in two chests. The guy on the right toppled backward with a loud cry. The other one must have been wearing Kevlar because he just staggered for a moment, stopped in his tracks, but still very much alive. He got his footing back and fired, hitting the wall behind me with a series of muted *phut-phut-phut*s.

My police training sent up another instructional flare: *Take cover and hold fire until you can get a clean shot to the leg.* But I wasn't a cop anymore, was I? By my count, this guy had some kind of semiautomatic weapon. He'd fired a dozen times, leaving plenty of zip in what was probably a 30-round mag. I didn't like the odds.

I sighted the Wilson in for a head shot but missed low, hitting him directly in the Adam's apple. With no oxygen or equipment to make a sound, he sank to his knees and fell forward onto his face with a wet flop.

I let out a deep breath I didn't realize I was holding. With the smell of gunpowder lingering in the air, I realized I was witnessing karma happening right before my eyes. He'd gotten a reprieve when my first shot bounced off his bulletproof chest. But then he'd spurned that subtle gift from the universe and called in his destiny.

I heard a loud *thwock,* and my left foot jerked. Miguel! I took cover and checked the thick bottom of my running shoe—the ridiculously expensive running shoes I'd just treated myself to a couple of weeks ago. A .25 caliber bullet was now imbedded in its ruined sole.

Miguel was running out of strikes. Strike One: trying to jimmy the door of my Shelby. Strike Two: blowing away my new sneaker. The kid was clearly escalating.

I scooted backward so the Mustang's axle and wheels were between him and me. I heard the scuff of jeans against the concrete floor.

"Hey, Miguel!" The scuffing sound stopped. "*¿Habla inglés?*"

"*Un poco.*" A little. A little was better than nothing.

"I don't want to kill you," I said. "And you don't want to die. Give me the gun."

I waited. The silence grew. I curled my finger around the Wilson's trigger. Then I heard the scraping slide of gunmetal across cement. I leaned around the back of the Mustang and saw the flimsy little Browning on the concrete. I stretched down and got it.

"You carrying anything else?"

"No. Don' kill me, okay?"

I stuck the revolver in my pocket. Miguel was lying on his back, arms overhead, palms facing upward. Blood had pooled under his left thigh, but I was pleased to see I had just grazed him as I intended. I did a quick over-and-under frisk and came up empty, as he'd promised.

"Okay," I said. "You can put your arms down."

He lowered his arms.

"Now roll over. Put your hands behind your back."

I used a bungee cord to secure his wrists.

"Stay put," I said. I stepped outside to survey the damage to my other two assailants. It was extensive and permanent. The end for both of them had come quick. The first body had a hole in the chest, just right of center. The man lay flat on his back, so I couldn't tell if it was a through-and-through. The other sprawled facedown, his head at an odd angle. I half-rolled him over and saw that his throat was a ragged mess, before letting his body return to its original position. Two deadly MAC-10 semiautomatics—the earlier versions, complete with sound suppressors—lay next to their dead owners like attack dogs. Next to them, my Wilson looked like a younger, weaker breed. I was very lucky to be alive.

I stood up, feeling slightly light-headed, and focused

on my breathing to center myself. A river of feeling was flooding my body.

Relief. Sorrow. Remnants of rage. Shame.

Swimming up through it all was a deep and sure knowledge that this was a turning point in my life. I had never killed anyone—not in the line of duty as a police officer, not as a private investigator. Now everything was different. I had killed—not once, but twice.

I had taken two lives.

Nothing in my training as a monk or a cop had prepared me for the next sensation that welled up from my core—a hot wave of revulsion, as if my stomach was turning inside out. I tasted the bile on the back of my tongue and bent over to throw up.

The sudden roar of a big engine broke through my nausea. I stood up just in time to see the rear lights of the Hummer receding, wheels spitting gravel like grapeshot.

I ran back into the garage and saw the bungee cord on the floor, sliced in two. During my quick frisk of Miguel I must have somehow missed a hidden blade. I wanted to swear, but in my current overloaded brain state I had reverted to thinking in Tibetan, which has no real curse-words. My mind just kept repeating a Tibetan phrase that loosely translated as "I'm upset! I'm upset!"

The Hummer swerved onto Topanga Canyon Boulevard. I decided not to give chase—he'd be long gone by the time I got my car cranked up and hit those steep turns myself. I could feel the adrenaline, nausea, and other feelings fading in my body, replaced by a faint, grudging respect for the kid. Miguel had managed to get away on a badly wounded leg. He'd done it quickly and so quietly I hadn't even noticed. Even though he hadn't come to my house for honorable reasons, he'd certainly made a skillful escape. He was one tough kid. I found myself wishing him, if not well, then at least no more harm, in spite of his abuse of my hospitality.

Then that feeling subsided, replaced by a sharp twist of revulsion at my own actions.

What have I done?

I grabbed for my phone, to report the incident to the Malibu Sheriff's Station and give them the word on the Hummer. The cell phone vibrated in my hand. I glanced at the screen and saw it was Bill Bohannon, my ex-partner. In that moment, it seemed like light years since we'd been Detective IIs in LAPD's elite Robbery/Homicide division. Now Bill was a Detective III, and I was about to become one of his cases.

"Hey," I said.

Bill's voice was thick with sleep. "I thought I told you to stay out of trouble. Your buddy Mike said something triggered the security system. Everything okay?"

I looked at the two still bodies.

"Not exactly," I said. "I got two men down, one more wounded and at large."

Bill woke up fast. "Two men down. How down?"

"As down as they can get," I said.

Bill groaned.

"The kills were righteous," I said, but I wondered if that was true.

A siren wailed in the distance, drawing closer. Shit, Mike must have also called 911. My night was about to get even more complicated.

"Can you let them know about the Hummer? Black— no idea the license plate, but there's a young kid at the wheel with a leg wound. And Bill, I hate to ask, but—"

"I'm on my way," he barked. "Do not say one word to anyone until I get there."

The two lifeless bodies lay sprawled on the ground like a pair of unanswerable reproaches. I studied them and felt a second wave of shivers pass through my body.

Suddenly I remembered I wasn't the only member of my household that might be having some feelings.

Tank.

I hurried across the driveway and into the kitchen.

"Tank? Where are you, buddy?"

I heard a muffled squawk from the living room. I ran to the sofa and dropped to my knees, peering underneath it. Tank was huddled flat in his place of ultimate refuge, usually reserved for the rare thunderstorms we have in this part of the world.

"It's okay," I said. "I'm okay." I stretched out my hand to stroke his head.

He shrank against the far wall and made a small hissing sound. Maybe he was rattled by the smell of blood on me.

As I sat back on my haunches, unsure what to do next, my computer made that odd Skype sound, like a bubble popping. I looked at the screen.

It was a Skype video call from "lamalobsang." My heart rose, choking my throat with bittersweet relief. Yeshe and Lobsang—my lifeline between past and present, Dharamshala and Los Angeles, monk and detective. I had neglected them for months. I didn't deserve them, but here they were.

Over the years since I'd moved to Los Angeles, we'd communicated through snail mail and the occasional whispered telephone call between India and California, until last summer, when my father discovered our ongoing, forbidden contact. His "reasoned" response was to banish Yeshe and Lobsang to Lhasa, Tibet, where even snail mail was impossible. But this past December, at Apa's request, His Holiness had recalled them from Tibet to become head abbots of Dorje Yidam—my father's final act of healing before his death. Their journey back was, of course, harrowing but ultimately successful, and their safe arrival coincided with my time there for a few precious weeks, as I buried my father and they prepared for their new roles.

The change in leadership at Dorje Yidam brought with it many other changes, a lot of them technological. But I knew my friends' decision to get in touch with me this morning had nothing to do with modern technology and everything to do with ancient intuition.

I sat down at my desk and clicked on the Skype icon. Within moments, the gleaming, shaved heads and warm features of my two friends swam into view.

"Tenzing, dear brother! Greetings to you." Lobsang touched his forehead. Just to his right, Yeshe did the same.

"Lobsang. Yeshe. I am happy to hear from you," I said. As I said the words I felt my chest compress, as if two giant hands were squeezing it.

"Are you all right?" Yeshe's voice was breathless. "We had to reach you. I felt something . . . something dark."

I pictured the fresh corpses outside. I opened my mouth to answer, but the words stuck in my throat. These were my dearest friends in the world. But they were also Buddhist monks. They had dedicated their lives to the practice of ahimsa—to doing no harm to any and all sentient beings. How could I tell them that I had just killed two men?

Was it only two days ago, sitting at breakfast at Joe's, that I had made a new vow to be more mindful of the difference between privacy and secrecy, to make sure my natural reserve wasn't causing me to hide things from others that I ought to be revealing? Hadn't I just made a commitment to candor? Yet here I was at another crossroads, deciding whether or not to risk two more relationships by being totally honest. If I told the blunt truth to my brothers, would I lose the rock-solid respect we'd built up over a lifetime of shared secrets? And if I lied, would I lose even more?

I swallowed hard.

"I'm fine," I said. "Everything's great. But I can't talk right now. I'll call you as soon as I can."

I disconnected. For a minute I just sat, as the screaming siren grew closer and closer. I had spent most of my existence struggling with loneliness, but I had never felt more alone than at this moment.

Instincts kicked in, and I walked into the kitchen,

removing Miguel's .25 from my pocket and placing it on the counter. My hands were shaking, as if I suffered from palsy. I laid my Wilson alongside the other gun, as a patrol car skidded to a halt in my driveway. I looked out the window. My gut clenched. The door of the black-and-white displayed a six-sided star and the word "Sheriff." The Los Angeles County Sheriff's Department Malibu/Lost Hills Station had jurisdiction over this portion of Topanga Canyon, which meant I was screwed. If this fell under the jurisdiction of the L.A. Sheriff's Department, being ex-LAPD not only wouldn't help, it might hurt. The two agencies are notoriously competitive, with the Sheriff's Department constantly feeling like the underdog. Now the underdog had the upper hand.

The deputies remained in their cars, though the officer riding shotgun lowered his window slightly. I knew exactly what they were doing. Sheriff or police, we were all law enforcement, and the protocols for investigating a shooting incident were the same: observe; assess; be methodical; be cautious; protect the physical evidence; above all, treat the location as a crime scene until someone above your pay grade tells you otherwise. To which my frantic mind now added: if you were LASD and you could somehow stick it to the LAPD, so much the better.

I tried to remember to breathe, but my lungs weren't cooperating. The officers stayed put. I mentally went through the checklist with them: log relevant information; scan the perimeter for any suspicious people or vehicles; evaluate potential dangers, using your eyes, ears, and even your nose, to ensure there is no immediate threat; check victims for signs of life.

I was in for a long night. I revised my own list of priorities and started a pot of very strong coffee, using my very best beans. Whatever this visit from the authorities meant for my future, coffee was bound to help. With two dead bodies and an escaped gang-recruit in the mix, I wanted to make the best coffee they'd ever tasted.

I watched through the kitchen window as the deputies played their spotlight over the two sprawled bodies. They climbed out of the car, guns drawn. Time to make an appearance. I flashed my outside lights a couple of times to get their attention and inched onto the deck with my hands raised.

The driver was about 40, with a thickset body and the bushy overhang of mustache favored by law enforcement. His thick, black eyebrows canted sharply upwards, as if attempting to fly off his face, using his forehead as a launching pad. The other sheriff was younger, with high cheekbones and a shaved head. Like me, he looked vaguely Asian. Both wore the LASD uniform: tan shirts with epaulets, black-and-yellow arm patches, and a six-sided sheriff's badge pinned to the left front pocket. I had never laid eyes on either officer. This could get tricky.

The young one carefully walked over to the bodies to confirm they were dead. He nodded to his partner and rejoined him by the car, both still wielding their guns

"I'm the homeowner. I'm ex-LAPD," I called out. "Burglary/Homicide Division."

They approached, lowering their weapons slightly. "Deputy Sheriff Gatti," one of the cops said, "and this is Deputy Juan Herrera. Malibu/Lost Hills Station. You can lower your hands."

"Tenzing Norbu," I said. "Glad you're here, Deputies." Some lies are a matter of self-preservation.

Officer Gatti jerked his chin toward the two bodies. "You drop both those guys?"

"Yeah," I said. "I was under attack. Two semiautomatics and a .25, to be specific. I wounded the third man in the leg, but I took my eye off him, and he escaped in their vehicle. Black Hummer; couldn't read the plate in the dark."

Deputy Gatti jerked his chin toward the two bodies.

"Center mass?" he said, referring to the chest shot that brought my first assailant down.

"Yes. Plus a neck shot. One of the guys was wearing a vest."

He nodded, his expression neutral, but his eyes appeared to reassess me.

"How many rounds total?" Herrera asked.

"From me? Three," I said.

Herrera whistled. "Fuckin' A."

I assumed he meant this as a compliment, but two corpses didn't feel like such a great accomplishment. A big part of me wished I could rewind the previous 40 minutes and make a different choice.

"We have some questions for you," Gatti said, just as his radio crackled to life. He raised it to his ear; listened, nodding; and then grunted a few times. He ended the interchange and consulted with Herrera, both of them glancing at me, their expressions unreadable.

"Everything all right?" I attempted a weak smile.

"Guess we're waiting for the brass," Gatti said.

"Your brass," Herrera added.

Bill to the rescue. My shoulders lowered slightly.

"Did anyone catch the Hummer?"

Gatti and Herrera exchanged a glance. "We might have passed one on the way up here," Gatti said.

Typical Sheriff's Department tunnel vision, I thought. But who was I to judge. I was the one who let Miguel escape in the first place.

"Want to come in?" I motioned. "I've got coffee on."

They shrugged, as in "Why not?"

Inside, Gatti eyed the two guns on my counter but refrained from asking any more questions. I passed them both mugs of the fresh-brewed, French-roasted Sumatra. Herrera took a sip. His eyes widened. "Fuck, man, that's good." He gazed into his mug, his expression morose, as if he half-regretted having tasted such superior coffee.

Gatti got a call on his cell phone.

"Yessir," he said. "We're on it." They both stood up.

"Securing the scene?" I asked. They walked outside. "I've got spare barrier tape if you need any," I called to their backs. They ignored me.

More tires crunched outside. Moments later, Bill clumped into the kitchen. He headed straight for the coffeepot and poured himself a mug. He sat down in his usual chair.

"Okay, Cowboy," he said. "Want to tell me what the fuck happened here?"

For the first of many times that evening, I described the incident, starting with Miguel's visit the previous day. In good detective fashion, my ex-partner had me recount the sequence of events twice, to check for inconsistencies. When I was done, he had one question.

"What aren't you telling me?"

"What do you mean?" I widened my eyes, which was a rookie mistake.

"Ten, I've been interviewing suspects for almost twenty-five years and have known you for more than twelve of them. You're lying about something. And unless I know everything, I can't help you here."

So I had to give up the drug-filled backpack.

Bill stood up without another word and walked outside to confer with Gatti and Herrera. As the responding officers, they would pass anything we offered them along to the investigation team. Bill pointed to the garage, and my heart vacated my chest. Sure enough, Gatti and Herrera immediately walked over to the garage, unspooling barrier tape to include it within their crime scene. They opened the door and played their flashlights over the gleaming shanks of my Mustang, although, oddly, they didn't actually look inside it.

Bill ambled into the kitchen, replenished his coffee, and had a seat. I was dying to know what they had discussed, and he was going to draw this out as long as he could.

"Bill . . ."

"So here's what's going to happen," he said, finally

taking pity. "LASD has jurisdiction, so they'll be leading the investigation. But they're letting me tag along, and my plan is simple: to make sure your mouth doesn't get you into trouble. We'll leave out the little petty-theft of meds for now, okay? I think I've steered them in another direction. And for fuck's sake, don't tell them this whole thing started with Mac Gannon. He's not their favorite dude, you know."

"So what about the, um, backpack?" I asked.

"What backpack? Sounds to me like they were after the Mustang," Bill said. "How much is that car worth?"

"At least a hundred thousand," I said. "Maybe more."

"And your little escapee was trying to jimmy his way inside, right? Make sure you mention that early on. Question: You think you got all this on your security cameras?"

"Enough to show I'm not lying."

"Then we're good to go."

A County Coroner's van arrived, followed by a second Sheriff's Department car, no doubt carrying a crew of crime scene investigators armed with the usual kit of tools: high-intensity lights, bindle paper and tape for transporting evidence, protective clothing, cameras, a latent-print kit, biohazard bags, and the all-important tweezers.

It was a familiar enough scene; I had just never been the cause of it before. I twisted in my seat.

"Bill, they were going to kill me," I said.

Bill nodded. "Question is, why?"

Gatti and Herrera took me into their custody. It was time to remove me from the scene and transport me to the Lost Hills station for questioning. They placed me in the back seat of their black-and-white, but I wasn't cuffed. Bill followed us up and over the canyon and north on the deserted 101 to the sprawling, two-story brick station in Agoura. I was escorted to an interview room and dumped onto an uncomfortable metal chair, where I squirmed, on the wrong side of a slew of questions from two sheriffs from the Homicide Division. Bill sat to one side and listened. Toward the end, I slumped with exhaustion over the ugly Formica table, my elbows propping me up. My skin felt scalded.

After a couple of hours, which felt like a couple of days, they were done with me. Everything I'd said was supported by the evidence, most notably my Guard-on, which captured and affirmed the home invasion better than any description of mine could. I sent Julius an inner bow of gratitude.

The consensus? I was the victim of a possibly gang-related home-invasion burglary gone wrong, with my Shelby 350 as the target. It had just been on display at the mechanic's for all to see, and possibly the wrong people saw it. I reviewed and signed a statement. Herrera returned my gun, as Gatti stood to one side, arms folded, his eyebrows ready for blastoff.

The sky was glowing pink by the time Bill and I pulled back into my driveway. The bright yellow tape was still up, and it fluttered in the morning breeze, like the tattered remains of a garden party. The bodies were long gone.

Bill followed me into the kitchen. He stood wide-legged, pinning me with his eyes.

"Okay. Show-and-tell time, kiddo."

I didn't have to ask for further clarification.

I crossed to the garage, unlocked the Mustang, retrieved the backpack, and returned inside. I unzipped the pack and dumped the contents onto the table. Bill's eyes widened.

"You weren't kidding," he said. "That be a lot of contraband."

"What I still don't understand," I frowned, "is how they knew where I . . ."

My eyes narrowed. I snatched up the pack, fingering a slight bulge about the size of an electronic key fob in the nylon lining at the base of the pack.

I dropped the pack and ran to my bedroom, unlocked my safe, and grabbed my knife, a Microtech Halo. Back in the kitchen, one slim slice was all it took to reveal a small black plastic gadget, maybe two inches by four inches, with a flashing green LED indicator. I held the tracking device up for Bill to see.

"Well, hello there," Bill said. "Looks like you brought those three bozos right to your door."

For a few minutes, we chewed on this new piece of information in silence.

"This is pretty messed up," I said. "It doesn't make any sense. Two dead guys, a missing maid, a drug-filled backpack with a tracker, and I'm still no closer to finding Clara Fuentes."

Bill ran his hands through his gray-blond hair. "Hate to break it to you, but your missing persons case may be the least of your problems."

"What do you mean?"

"I mean, you may not be flying quite as far under the media radar from now on."

"I don't understand." And then, suddenly, I did. As of the 911 call at 2:58 A.M. this morning, I was dead meat, and somewhere out there, the vultures were gathering, ready to swoop.

"Can't you do anything to stop them?"

"Home invasion in upscale Topanga Canyon? Two dead, one more at large? There's no way to keep 'em from swarming. You are about to become extremely un-anonymous, my friend." Bill glanced at his watch. "I'm guessing you've got at best a couple hours left as a private citizen. Start practicing your smile."

He saluted me, his own expression wry, and pushed away from the table.

"Bill! A little help?" I said.

Bill sighed and sat back down. He held out his mug, and I filled it with the last of the coffee, which was stale and harsh but still the nectar of the gods compared to the swill they'd served at the Lost Hills station.

"Okay," Bill said. "I've had to deal with a lot more of this shit since I got promoted, and here's what I've learned, most of it the hard way. There are people whose entire job seems to consist of trawling for news bites, so you can bet the phones are already jangling over this. In the next hour or so, a bunch of news directors all across L.A. County are going to start marshaling their troops. They will do whatever it takes to snag your handsome, young, multi-ethnic face for their morning news broadcast."

"Is this supposed to make me feel better?"

Bill ignored me. "You're going to have maybe fifteen seconds on camera for people to decide if you're a good guy or a bad guy. Number one: Smile but not too much. Two men are dead, after all. You don't want to look like a bad mug shot, but you don't want to be reveling, either. Number two: Watch your mouth. Wiseass doesn't play well on the news. And you, my monkish friend, have been known to be a wiseass. Number three, and probably most important: Tell the truth. Look the camera in the eye and do your best to answer honestly, in a way that doesn't hang your butt out to dry later."

He stood up again.

"Aren't you staying?" My voice was more of a squeak.

Bill shook his head. "I would only complicate matters." He stuffed the drugs back into the backpack, grabbed the tracker, and stood. "I'm going to take custody of these for now. No argument. You're lucky as hell I intervened with this investigation so they didn't search your car."

I stood up as well, my voice stubborn. "I want to keep the tracker."

He stared at me.

"It's my only link between any of these events. I need it, Bill."

"Okay," he finally said. "But get that geek-freak of yours to hook your security system directly to the morgue, because that's where this business is going to land you

106

if you're not more careful. Ten, we're eventually going to have to bring the powers that be into this side of things. You know that, right?"

I did.

"And I can't promise you the Captain, or Chief Deputy Baca for that matter, won't send you a one-way ticket to Tibet. Hell, I might even drive you to the airport myself."

"Understood. But Bill, if I can't flush out whoever's running my attackers, I can't do my job."

He put the tracker on the table.

"Thanks."

"Yeah, well, we'll see about that. And good luck with the reporters." He shot me a rueful look and left.

I eyed the blinking tracker and felt my breath catch. There's a tiny Indonesian island, Komodo, which is famous for two things: convicts and giant lizards known as Komodo dragons. Heather's parents took her to Komodo once when she was a teenager, and she said the experience scarred her for life. In order to lure the scabby reptiles to within viewing distance, tourist guides would tether a small goat to a pole, serving up the perfect Komodo dragon snack. "I've never heard a sound quite so heart-wrenching," Heather said, "as that poor little goat's terrified bleating."

I wasn't quite at the bleating stage yet, but I could definitely relate to the feeling of being tethered bait. The fact that I'd just volunteered for goat duty didn't help much.

Tank had finally crawled out from under the sofa. He padded into the kitchen and nosed around his bowl.

"Hey, Tank. Apparently, we're about to be famous."

I gave him the rest of the liver bits—he'd earned that—as I downed two full glasses of water. I held my hands out in front of me, turning them front to back. They had stopped shaking, but I felt as if they were drenched in invisible blood. I undressed and moved into the shower and stood under the stinging hot water, scrubbing my hands and body until my skin was raw and red. As I toweled off, a wave of tiredness broke over my body, so dense I almost buckled under its weight. I staggered into the bedroom and collapsed, face down. After a moment, I rolled onto my back and closed my eyes, but every time I started to drift off, two figures approached me through the darkness. Adrenaline firing off multiple synapses, I raised my weapon, and my body was shocked awake. I opted for simply lying still, as my skin sparked and flickered.

Tell the truth. So Bill, too, had joined the chorus of sooth-sayers, urging me to change my ways. I knew why, too. Dozens of interrogations with even the most skilled pathological liars underscored the foolishness of doing anything else. "It's like this," Bill told me once, over celebratory beers after a particularly boneheaded slip-up by a murder suspect. "Guy tells the truth, he doesn't have to remember what he said. Boom. No worries. Guy lies, he's gotta keep telling more to cover up the ones he's already told. He gets so busy trying to keep track of what's what, pretty soon he can't remember his own goddamned name. It's just a matter of time 'til he fucks up."

I wondered how much time I had left.

My doorbell let out a hearty *bing-bong!*

Shit. I glanced at my phone. Barely 8 A.M. I'd been resting for less than an hour. Now somebody was at my rarely used front door, ringing my rarely used doorbell, which meant it was somebody I didn't know, who didn't know me.

I pulled on a clean pair of jeans and a black T-shirt, and used the bedroom door to block my body as I craned my head around. I wanted a clear sightline on my visitor before I stepped into view.

For a moment, my heart stopped. Pema. I shook my head. I was losing it. Lack of sleep and post-traumatic shooting syndrome had loosened a few bolts in my brain.

But the resemblance to my first love was uncanny. Pema, age 13, glowing with fresh beauty. The Tibetan village girl who carried groceries up the hill to my monastery the summer of my 12th year. The girl who gave me my first kiss.

Now, it was like looking at an age-progression image. Like Pema, this woman had angular cheekbones, glossy black hair, honey-colored skin, and dark brown eyes fringed with thick lashes. She was in her 20s and wearing a navy dress of some kind of clingy material that enthusiastically wrapped around her body a few times before meeting itself in front again. As I watched, the woman tossed her hair back with both hands, and her dress tightened across a perfect pair of breasts.

I crossed the living room and opened the door. She flashed a shiny smile. Up close, I could see I was mistaken. Her lineage was Central or South American, not Tibetan. But my body couldn't care less.

She held out a slim hand. "Mr. Norbu? My name is Cielo," she said. "Cielo Lodera, Channel 5 News."

Is she the one?

"Cielo?"

"It means *heaven*," she said and laughed. "My mother loves to say she asked for an angel, but God sent her a hell-raiser instead." She leaned past me and quickly scanned my living room. "Tell me I'm dreaming. Am I actually the first reporter here?"

"You are," I said. "And with any luck, the last."

"Don't count on it," she said. "Listen, can I come in? I might be able to help you with that." She stepped inside before I could formulate an answer.

Her eyes darted from my office area to my sofa to my kitchen, as if she didn't believe there wasn't another reporter hunkered down in some corner. Then she seemed to relax.

"Your place is very neat," she said, nodding with approval.

"Thank you," I said. "I used to live in a Buddhist monastery. Tidiness was encouraged."

Her eyes widened. "A monastery? Where?"

"India. Dharamshala, to be exact."

"Where the Dalai Lama lives?" She practically thrummed with excitement. "I knew this was going to be good."

"Uh, what is?" I sounded like an idiot. Cielo's uncanny resemblance to Pema, coupled with her own sultry phero-mones, were interfering with my brain-to-mouth connec-tion. I tried to rein in the attraction. I had just shot two men in my backyard. What was wrong with me?

Her eyes gleamed. "Look, the word is the killings may be gang-related. Add to that, you're an ex-cop. So I ask myself, what are a couple of cholos doing in the backyard of some ex-cop living way out in the sticks of Topanga Canyon?" Her eyes narrowed, as she started to weave the story elements together. "No, not just any ex-cop. A peace-loving, nonvi-olent, Buddhist monk ex-cop trying to get away from the madness of it all. This is huge." She grabbed my hand. The electricity was palpable, at least to me. She didn't seem to notice. "You're a licensed private investigator now, right?"

"How did you . . . ?"

"I can help you play this any way you want to, Detec-tive Norbu. You want to be an innocent pacifist forced to stand his ground? Great, my viewers love a reluctant hero. Or maybe you want publicity for your private detective agency. No problem, I'm happy to throw you a major plug. Hell, I'll learn to meditate if you want. But only if you work with me. Me and nobody else. I want an exclusive, under-stand? I'm good at this. Really good. Maybe the best. Let me in, Detective. I know how to take care of you."

I'm halfway there already, I almost said. I withdrew my hand, so I could think. For whatever reason, my close brush with death was making her particular brand of life force tantalizing.

She pulled some kind of release form out of a soft leather messenger bag. "Do we have a deal?"

A memory fluttered—something Julius Rosen once told me. "Some of the best deals you'll ever make are the ones you don't make at all." I took this wisdom with a grain of salt at the time, seeing as how he dispensed it directly after getting us both almost killed over one of his non-deals. But for now, it was the only wisdom I had going for me.

I let the form hover in space until the right words came. "I can promise you this: I'll never deliberately mislead you. But I can't make any deals that limit what I can or can't say."

"Are you sure?" Cielo smiled, and her eyes seemed to darken. "There are definite benefits to giving me an exclusive."

Was I reading her correctly? Bill hadn't mentioned this aspect of media work. I felt my pulse accelerate. Whatever else was going on with me, I was still in shock, and even I knew not to assume anything.

"Sorry," I said. "I can't."

A flash of amusement and, possibly, regret, registered on Cielo's face. Or maybe I was imagining that, too. She snapped her smile back into place. She tucked the form back in her leather case, her professional-reporter persona once again in charge.

"Okay, no exclusive, but at least let me be your first."

Everything that came out of this woman's mouth was trouble. Her mother had a point.

"Deal?" she smiled.

"Deal."

"Good enough for me," she said. "My crew's right out-side." She opened the door and shouted something. A couple of semi-dozing cameramen leapt to attention.

Forty-five minutes later, the interview was over. I had no idea how well I'd done, but thanks to Bill I didn't smile too much, I wasn't a complete wiseass, and I mostly told the truth. Cielo kissed my cheek and told me I was the best she'd ever had, but I'm sure she told that to all her interviewees.

As she followed her crew out, she paused in the doorway. The sun framed her curves, and I was catapulted back to an equally breath-stopping glimpse of Pema silhouetted against sunlight, almost two decades ago outside the monastery kitchen. Yes, I had a girlfriend, but chemistry is still chemistry.

Cielo flipped her lustrous mane one last time. "You won't be sorry we did this," she said, and left.

Somehow, I doubted that.

I looked outside. Two news trucks were now parked in the driveway, with two more pulling in. The carrion-hunters were gathering.

I paced back and forth between my kitchen and living room until Tank emitted a low cat-growl from his bed. He doesn't like it when I'm anxious. It disturbs his naps.

"Okay, okay," I said.

I took a deep breath, sending oxygen down into the middle of my anxiety, and headed outside to face my inquisitors.

Chapter 9

"I've got some bad news." Bill's voice was grim on the phone.

"Mmff." I rubbed my face and eyelids. It was just past noon. I'd done a face-first pillow-plant after the last news truck left, slept for two hours without moving, and now I felt worse than ever.

"That Ortiz kid?" he went on. "The one you winged in the thigh? He's dead. He took a gang-style hit sometime before dawn this morning—big time. If you're lucky, it may even knock you off the news. Which, by the way, you are all over. Have you been watching?"

"No. I don't have a television, remember?"

"Luddite. Channels 2, 4, 7, and 9. Nine led with the story. CNN had a little something, too."

"How'd I do?"

"Okay," he said. "You obviously had a superior coach. Next thing, you'll be on all the talk shows, spouting opinions as Mr. Crime Expert."

"If that happens, you have my permission to plug me. At close range."

Bill's familiar bark of laughter was reassuring. "Martha's loving every minute of this," he said. "She's predicting you're going to get a lot of marriage proposals."

"She would." Martha Bohannon may have been a retired court reporter of German descent and the overworked mother of twin preschoolers, but her main job in life was to get me married. Probably so I could become an overworked father. As later-in-life parents, Bill and Martha had exhibited stunned, slightly awestruck expressions pretty much since the day the girls were born. "It's like being on LSD," Martha had confessed to me once after too much wine. "Only you never come down." If that was the case, she and Bill were having a pretty good trip. That was the upside. The downside was that Martha suffered from constant sleep-deprivation, and Bill went from "first cop through the door," in live-fire situations, to "cop stapled to a desk chair," while other officers raced toward the action, hands reaching for their 9-mm Glocks. The only live fire Bill experienced these days crackled behind his fireplace grate. And who could blame him? One look at his expression when he had those two girls on his lap was enough to tell you what he'd come to this planet for.

I bolted upright, Bill's earlier words sinking in.

"Wait. What? Miguel Ortiz is *dead*?"

"Like I said, big-time. Tijuana-style, no less. What they call a two-zip hit."

"Two-zip?"

"Pure nastiness. They leave the head in one zip code and drop the body off in another. The Tijuana boys sometimes use two-zips as a way to let their rivals know they're moving in on new territory. But here? This is new. Kid was also missing a few vital organs, so God only knows what message his killers were trying to send."

The image of a slashed-up Miguel triggered a violent upheaval in my gut area. I spontaneously sent out an all-purpose prayer of protection: *May I learn anything I need to learn about two-zip executions by received wisdom rather than through personal experience.*

Then I felt terrible about the semi-flippant route my mind had taken. I was using glibness to detour from fear, plain and simple. Miguel's murderers were ruthless butchers.

"What do you think happened, Bill?"

"Best guess? He got punished for screwing up twice in a row. A lot of these gangs have no tolerance for error with new recruits. Bastards."

This made sense. Miguel hadn't looked or acted like an entrenched banger to me—just a scared kid dressed up as one, trying to find some way out of the 'hood. A second image flicked through my mind: Miguel's grandfather buckled over in mourning. His future grief prompted a surge of my own, here and now. I breathed into the sadness, reaching for the compassion that often hides behind it, but instead I tasted the slightly cloying flavor of pity. *Such a waste,* I thought, picturing all the life events ahead of Miguel that he would miss. *Such a pitiful waste of a lifetime.*

I stopped myself. The calm voice of Lama Tashi, our resident healer at the monastery, came to me from long ago. "Lama Tenzing, we are all equal beings in the universe," he'd told me more than once. "If you hold others in the thought that they are victims, you rob them of their power. If you hold others as fully responsible for their own destiny, you ennoble them by treating them as equals."

I honor you, Miguel Ortiz.

"Anyway," Bill's voice broke in, "I thought you should know. I'll call again as soon as we figure out who's responsible. The gang squad here is saying Miguel was training to be a mule for a small-time guy by the name of Chuy Uno—sorry, that would be Chuy Dos. Chuy Uno is doing time in Tijuana. Which means he's probably still running things, come to think of it."

"Chewy, like gum?"

"C-H-U-Y," he spelled. "Pronounced Chewy, short for Jesus, pronounced Hay-Soos. Do try to keep up. The thing is, my guys tell me this isn't either Chuy's typical calling card—Uno and Dos tend to be one-pop-in-the-back-of-the-skull kind of guys—so who knows?"

"Who, indeed."

"Whoops, gotta go. Boss is calling. If you require more gory details, ask your girlfriend. Miguel came in on her shift."

Heather. I never called Heather. Oh, man. This day had started out bad and was getting worse by the minute.

"And Ten?" Bill's voice was laced with amusement. "I hope you remember all the little people who were here for you when you were just a humble private eye."

"I'm sorry. Remind me again—who is this I'm talking to?"

Bill hung up laughing. I was glad I could still make someone I loved laugh.

I called Heather immediately, before I lost my nerve.

"Ten! Thank God! Didn't you get my texts? Are you okay?"

"I'm fine," I said. I checked my phone. Sure enough, there were several increasingly frantic texts from Heather, starting about two hours ago. "This is the first chance I've had to call," I told her. "I'm sorry. It's just been crazy around here."

"But you're really okay? Promise?"

"Yes. Promise."

"And Tank?'

"Tank's fine, too."

"Good."

The quality of communication seemed to change, as a sense of frostiness chilled the air between us.

"Heather? Are you okay?"

"I'm fine," she said, but her tone indicated the opposite.

"What is it?"

"It's nothing. It's stupid, okay? I don't feel like talking about it."

I sensed real distress underneath the dismissal. I was tempted to ignore the signal, but I'd been doing far too much ignoring lately.

"Why are you mad at me this time?" I asked. Then I flinched; I should have left out the *this time* bit. In interpersonal combat, even the slightest passive-aggressive move can lead to instant escalation.

"Oh, let's see. Besides the fact that you shot two men, almost got yourself killed, and didn't think to call me— much less let me know you were going to be all over the news with this? I had to learn about it alongside my co-workers. Everyone's been watching here at work. Asking me about it. I was mortified."

"I said I was sorry. I *am* sorry, Heather. I just didn't have a chance to."

She interrupted her voice low. "You were totally flirting with her."

"Excuse me?"

"That reporter. You were all over her."

Leave it to Heather to sniff out a buried mine of potentially explosive material. I feigned innocence, as my inner negotiator scrambled for a toehold.

"Which reporter?"

"The hair-tosser with the big rack, as if you didn't know," she hissed. Her voice rose. "You were practically drooling!"

"I was not!"

"Oh, please."

"I wasn't!"

"Liar, liar, pants on fire!"

Now we had both regressed to squabbling kids. I put my mental brakes on and took a couple of deep breaths. "What's your proof, counselor?" I said, trying for a little adult levity.

It worked. Heather's voice lightened. "Ha! Exhibit One: the reporter in question kept cocking her head to one side. Women do that when they're flirting. Exhibit Two: the interviewee had a little half-smile on his face while talking. As I happen to know from experience, said interviewee does that when he's flirting."

Or trying not to smile too much, I wanted to protest but didn't. "Pretty slim evidence."

"Shall I go on?"

"No need. You've made your case."

I felt a little iron blob form in my belly, the one that can very quickly become a big iron blob. Heather was right, of course, but I didn't want to discuss it. As far as I was concerned, my moment with Cielo, such as it was, had passed. I was sure if I tried to explain myself further, I'd be heading into a rat-maze that had no nutrition at the end of it.

"Heather, nothing happened. She interviewed me, and she left. Case closed." Time to change the subject. "So listen, Bill tells me you're doing the autopsy on Miguel Ortiz, the young gangbanger who tried to rob me."

"Already did it. First thing this morning. Poor kid. Just like the others, only worse."

"Can you tell me anything more about the cause of death?"

Heather sighed. "Ten, it's an active homicide investigation that may or may not link back to the incident at your house last night. You know I can't discuss the cause of death, or anything else about the autopsy."

Neither of us spoke for a minute or so.

"Baby?" she said.

"Yes."

"I'm really glad you're okay. I meant to say that first, you know."

For some reason, I suddenly felt like crying. Must be the tiredness.

"I'm working late again," she said. "But I'll call you. Be safe, okay?"

"Sure thing," I said, my voice a little thick.

My office landline had been ringing constantly throughout our conversation. I checked the voice mail. I had 13 messages, a record for me. Work was picking up.

Or not. Three hang-ups, seven reporters wanting quotes, a matchmaking agency offering to represent me to a select crop of bachelorettes, and a car collector in The Valley salivating for the Shelby. Absent was anyone calling to hire me. I'd heard that fame and money went hand in hand, but so far I was getting only one handful—the absolute wrong one for my specialized line of work. Also missing: any word from Mac. The silence was a little deafening on that front. Only the final voice mail was remotely interesting: "Cielo Lodera here. Just wondering how you liked the interview."

I'll bet, I thought. But I saved the message.

I made a second round of hospital, jail, and morgue calls, just in case, but there was still no sign of Clara, alive or dead.

I jumped in the shower, finishing with a bracing ice-water chaser. I toweled off and put on a cotton kimono, cinching it tight, like a shield. Time to address myself more rigorously to the task at hand: finding out exactly what kind of mess I'd landed myself in, and then finding out who was on the other end of this particular knotted string of karma, so I could maybe, maybe locate Clara Fuentes for my client. I had never before failed so miserably on a misper case, for so many hours in a row.

I began by applying myself to the actual mess in my living room. Having film crews on the premises is effectively like inviting a series of earthquakes into your home. It's no doubt a by-product of my monastic training, but I can't think if I'm surrounded by chaos. Anyway, the act of cleaning is itself one of my best investigative tools. Just the simple back-and-forth motion of pushing a mop across a wooden floor often generates *aha* moments for me. So I mopped, and I mopped. And I mopped some more, until I threw down the mop in frustration. The handle hit the floor with a bang.

Tank yowled and leapt from the windowsill.

"Sorry, buddy," I said. "I feel like I'm running in increasingly smaller circles here."

Tank responded by licking his right paw and drawing it over his face like a washcloth.

"I already showered."

He strolled to the kitchen door and brushed his body up against it.

"Good idea," I said. Call me crazy, but I knew exactly what he was saying, although the psychic communication between me and my cat was one secret I would take with me into the bardo realm and beyond.

I changed into my riding gear, packed a water bottle and a few snacks into a small, insulated nylon case that doubled as a bike pack, and grabbed my helmet out of the closet. Soon I was slipping and sliding along the gravel drive on my 21-speed, all-terrain cruiser. An exhilarating half-hour of downhill racing later, I braked to a halt in the parking lot at Zuma Beach. I locked my bike to a pole and took off along the packed sand, beginning with a measured jog.

I reviewed the past 16 hours of insanity. *Something . . .* An idea was niggling at me, but for the life of me, I couldn't figure out what it was.

The beach was deserted. After a quarter-mile, I hid my bike case and shoes behind a bleached and peeling log about 15 yards from the water and burned another quarter-mile at a faster clip. I then emptied every ounce of energy I had into a final sprint to the end of the cove. I wheeled left and pelted into the ocean up to my thighs. The shock of cold bit into my leg muscles. I turned and sprinted back onto the sand, angling upward until I again reached the fallen log. Retrieving my belongings, I started back at a steady trot.

Something Heather had said . . .

As I rounded the last curve of beach, I drew up short. Two men were standing near my bike in the parking lot. They were several hundred yards away, so I couldn't make out much detail, except for the fact that they were physically big. Really big. One man handed a pair of binoculars to the other, who aimed them directly at me. Not good.

I wanted to waggle my fingers, or maybe make a different statement with just one of them, but that didn't seem like a smart way to go. Instead, I quickened the pace to full speed, my heels spitting divots of damp sand.

As I closed in on the pair, they responded by lumbering across the lot to a familiar-looking black van, a Ford. They climbed inside and accelerated toward the exit. I managed to read the license number: industrial plates. I couldn't quite decipher the logo on the side; the van was too far away. There were three initials, but the design was quite small, with an even smaller phrase printed underneath. I mentally recited the license plate as I fished a pen out of my bike case. I jotted the sequence of numbers and letters on the back of my hand.

My ribs were heaving. I thumbed Bill on my speed dial.

"What? I'm on my way into a meeting. We can't keep meeting like this, Ten."

". . . run a plate . . . me?" I gasped.

"Slow down," he said. "As a guy I know likes to say: breathe."

I steadied my breath and tried again. "I really need you to run a plate for me. A van. Commercial, I think."

"Ah," he said. "Sorry, but no. I'm too busy massaging crime statistics." Bill spent most of his time now attending meetings, pressing the flesh, and managing data. His newer, safer job came with a daily dose of mind-numbing, energy-draining bureaucracy. "Use that fancy service you subscribe to."

"I'm on my bike. And there's no time. Please?"

"The magic word," he said. "Fine. I'll get to it after the powwow."

I guess he must have heard my loud silence, because he said, "Okay, okay. Jesus. What's the number?"

I read it off the back of my hand.

"Let me switch to my other line to make a call. Gimme thirty seconds."

I counted through five impatient breath cycles.

Finally, Bill was back. "It's commercial, part of a permanent fleet."

"Who's it registered to?"

Chapter 10

I pedaled home in record time, my normally sluggish uphill pace fueled by the information from Bill. I had a name, and in a moment I would have an address. I'd put in a second call from the Zuma lot, this one to Mike. My personal data-jockey was on the hunt as I powered up Topanga Canyon Boulevard.

For the second time today, I blasted my skin with cold water. Before my cropped hair was even dry, Mike called back.

"Okay, boss. Here's what I got. GTG Services, Incorporated, is like one of those freshwater polyps—you know, a hydra: one head, a shitload of tentacles. Not just here, either. These suckers—pun intended—reach statewide and into a few other states as well."

"But the headquarters are downtown, right?"

"Right. I can see the building from my living-room window." Mike and his live-in girlfriend occupied a spacious loft downtown, filled with DJ and electronic equipment and little else. "You know that tall, skinny rectangle on Wilshire?"

"With all the black glass?"

"That's the one. The Aon. Sixty-two floors, but the lobby counts as two. Somewhere on the sixty-first, or penthouse floor, is GTG, the hydra's nerve center, you might say."

"So they own the van?"

"Vans, plural. Over a hundred statewide, maybe twenty-five of them here in L.A."

"What business are they in?"

"You're not listening. *Businesses,* plural. As in, what

123

service business aren't they in? It's all GTG, but they switch up the slogan depending on the service rendered. Here's the shortlist: 'GTG Services: We Bring Healthy to You.' That one's medical supplies. 'GTG Services: We Bring Safe to You'—barbed wire, chain link fences, et cetera. That little offshoot took off post-nine-eleven and lately has expanded to all the states that border Mexico. Wonder why. Let's see, what else? 'GTG Services: We Bring Clean to You.' Some kind of very high-end maid service. And then . . ."

"Stop," I said, crossing to my computer desk, phone to my ear. "That's the one. Can you follow that tentacle?"

I heard mad tapping on the other end of the line. Mike started humming off-key, under his breath, which was a very good sign. "Interesting," he said. "Their office is based in the cracked-out broken heart of East L.A."

"Gangland?"

"Exactamundo."

"Got an address?"

"Does one hand clapping in a forest make noise?" Sometimes I think Mike's mind is solely populated by Zen meta-masters spouting confused koans.

Mike gave me an address in Boyle Heights, not that far from Los Gatos Cantina of ceviche fame.

"So, boss," he said, "got any idea who's behind this thing?"

I admitted I didn't.

"Okay, well, let me know when you do. I've accessed their business slogans and addresses galore, but the actual identities of G, T, and G are in data lockdown. You know how I much I fucking hate firewalls. Ciao." The last thing I heard before he hung up was the peel of a pop-top, probably belonging to Mike's sixth Red Bull of the day.

I stared at the two addresses in front of me. Unless I could do a fast clone of myself, I was faced with a hard choice: Do I post watch at the head of the hydra? Or do I start my surveillance by tracking down the tentacle that recently crawled into view? I flipped and flopped until a brilliant third possibility came to me: I could eat something and then decide.

I was inhaling my latest invention, "Greek" pizza—warm pita layered with black olive spread, creamy hummus, and tart tzatziki, topped with a heap of chopped and olive oil–drizzled tomatoes, feta, cucumbers, and avocado—when my business line rang. I glanced at the caller ID, instantly suspicious. I had just deleted seven more useless, annoying requests from the message center. I smiled. This caller was from my past, and someone I was happy to reconnect with.

"Ten, my man! I just heard your story on the radio. Almost crashed my car. You're more gangsta than Diddy!"

"Hi, Clancy."

"Too bad I quit being a pap—I'd be all over your Tibetan ass right now."

We shared a laugh. I pictured his wide smile and coffee-colored skin, topped with a crown of black dreadlocks.

"How's the private eye business?" I asked. "You official yet?" Clancy had helped enormously with the Marv Rudolph case last year, multitasking as both paparazzo and amateur investigator. In return, I'd finagled a way for him to get that elusive freelance photographer's prize known as the "money shot"—an exclusive, preferably forbidden snapshot of a major celebrity doing something unusual. Gossip sites hand over tens of thousands of dollars for a money shot, and paparazzi live to take one. Clancy had used the windfall from his photograph of megastar Keith Connor embracing a mystery woman—Heather, long story—to pay off his student loans, get ahead on his mortgage, and quit a job he'd come to loathe. The last I'd heard Clancy was in the process of getting a P.I. license for himself. It turns out the skill sets necessary for both paparazzi and private eyes are startlingly similar.

"Nah. Still interning," Clancy said. "I'm on'y fifteen

hundred hours into my three thousand. You got off easy, bein' a cop and all."

"Yeah, well, now you know why so many ex-cops are private investigators. If police hours didn't count and we had to clock three thousand working under someone else, we'd never make it."

"Right. Well, I'm gettin' there, little by little. Some dude in Glendora's my supervisor. I musta sent out fifty résumés; he's the only P.I. called me in. All he did—looked me over, walked outside to my ride and looked *it* over, then handed me a list of hardware I needed: digital camera, laptop, like that. All of it I already had, except puttin' the tint on my windows. He had me doin' surveillance on some dude with a bogus liability claim the next day."

"Wow. Good for you."

"Pay's for shit, but it's steady. Or was. Things are slow right now in the slip-and-fall world, don't ask me why. How about you? Did you really off those two guys?"

"I'm afraid so," I said.

"What was that like?"

"I don't recommend it." My voice was clipped.

"I feel you," Clancy said, after a short silence. "Well, I just wanted to say 'hey.' See how you were. Let's keep in touch, a' right?"

"You got it," I said.

I hung up. A minute later, the lightbulb went on, and I was speed-dialing Clancy back. I didn't need to look any farther; the solution to my surveillance dilemma had actually just found me: Clancy Williams, recovering paparazzo and P.I.-in-training.

"Yo."

"Me again," I said. "I might have a job for you, Clancy. Surveillance."

"For real? When?"

"Now, actually." I checked the time. "Can you meet me downtown in an hour? I could really use your help."

"I'm there."

I gave him the Boyle Heights address. "Park two blocks south, on East Cummings Street."

"I'm there," he said again. "Look for a sweet gangsta ride with tinted windows . . . Oh, wait: Boyle Heights. Never mind. I'll look for you."

Using my computer, I printed out a business label, attached it to a manila envelope, stuffed it with three empty sheets of paper, and sealed it. Then I crossed to the bedroom and grabbed several $100 bills from the envelope of cash locked in my closet safe, along with my gun, binoculars, Dodgers cap, and new camera—a Canon EOS 1-D Mark IV, identical to Clancy's. Before I left, I made two more calls. The first was to Mac's cell. I finally had something to report. I got his voice mail again. Maybe he'd caught the news and was avoiding me. I didn't leave a message. The second was to Heather. She picked up immediately.

"Hey," I said.

"Hay is for horses," she answered, her voice teasing.

"I can't talk," I said. "But I forgot to say something before. I don't think you should come over here right now."

"Okaaay . . ." Her tone had cooled noticeably.

"No, not that," I said. "I just . . . I don't think it's safe yet, that's all."

"Is this even open for discussion?"

"Heather . . ."

"Oh, great: now you're Heather-ing me."

That tone had crept into Heather's voice, a sour, dull tone I interpreted as "I'm unhappy and it's your fault. You're not meeting my expectations." It usually led to information I didn't want, like a wet newspaper landing with a thud on my doorstep.

Heather's sigh matched my own.

"I just . . . I wish you wouldn't do that," she said. "Call me to tell me you can't talk."

The irritation crept from my shoulders to my jaws.

I tamped it down. "I'm sorry," I said. "I thought it was important."

She plowed ahead. "Maybe if I knew we were solid it wouldn't bother me so much."

Her logic seemed shaky. I smiled, remembering a conversation I'd had with Julie once, when I was upset at her for doing something without including me. "Ten," she'd explained, "handing out claim checks on your well-being to other people is just . . . is never a good idea. If you think it's my job to make you feel okay, you're not only avoiding responsibility but you're giving all your emotional authority to me. Eventually, you'll resent me for that, guaranteed." Wise woman, that Julie, but somehow I didn't think Heather would appreciate my ex-girlfriend's insight.

I said, "I disagree, but now's not the time." Heather made a sound like the low speed on a dental drill. "There you go again."

"What?"

"And now that . . . that other infuriating thing: pretending not to know what I'm talking about."

I started to emit a small peep of defense but didn't have the heart to push it into the air. Any conversation that leaned toward the personal was becoming impossibly complex between us. And if Julie was right, we shared equal responsibility.

Heather's voice was small. "Maybe it's good I can't come over," she said. "Maybe we should take a little time off, you know, apart from each other. Get to know ourselves again, maybe explore other options . . ." She trailed off, but I knew what she was doing. The daisy Post-it was proof she had already started down that road, and now she wanted my permission. The nerve she touched was shockingly raw.

In my early training as a monk, the principle of *ma chags pa*, nonattachment, was drilled into me constantly until it was part of every breath I took. In spite of all that training, I'd experienced the polar opposite of nonattachment with girlfriends. Especially Heather. I clung to her at times like a parasite. I'd never been with such a physically exquisite woman, and I still wondered at her beauty. But nobody mentioned that the experience came with a price tag. My gut clutched whenever another man gave her a second look or talked to her, innocently or not, and such incidents happened all the time.

As I started a downward slide into a sinkhole of past jealousies and futile arguments, Lama Sonam's calm face came to my rescue. "Clinging doesn't lead to suffering, Lama Tenzing," he told me. "Clinging *is* suffering." I used a deep breath to help propel me up to firm ground.

"Let's not decide anything right now, Heather. We're not at our best."

"Okay," Heather said. "Okay. You're right. Sorry."

As I hung up, it occurred to me that I might actually be the more emotionally mature partner in this relationship. Now, *there* was a terrifying thought.

I took another long breath, inhaling deep into my belly. En route, I passed a cluster of emotions. Sadness, for sure, and a queasy sensation of fear. But underneath the fear I tuned in to a slight bubble of elation. What if I was a free man again—not now, but soon? A certain female reporter's face floated up, unannounced and uninvited . . .

I activated my Guard-on before leaving. I had to smile: *You'll be a free man, all right. A free man who lives inside an electronic fence.*

Within the hour my Toyota was parked behind Clancy's Impala. Clancy climbed out and stretched, unfolding like a ruler. He had shorter hair and more muscles than the last time we'd met. He looked great. I made a mental note to start lifting weights again. I joined him on the sidewalk, and we did an awkward man-hug consisting of shoulder clapping and hip avoiding, before stepping back and grinning at each other.

"Good to see you, man," Clancy said.

"And you."

We got right down to business. I had just done a quick drive-by of the address and was able to tell him about his target.

"It's a one-story storefront," I said. "Some kind of housekeeping service. Their logo is on the window, with the slogan 'We Bring Clean to You.' But I'm primarily interested in the lot behind the building. It's full of maybe a dozen of their vans, and I'm hoping there's one van in particular with this plate." I gave him the license number and described the two heavyset men I'd seen at the beach. "You bring your telephoto?"

Clancy nodded.

"Good. I want you to try to locate that van, without being too obvious. If it's not there, call me. If it's there, call me and start watching it. If you see two huge cholos approaching that or any other van, call me. If they or anyone else visits the van, if the van so much as changes parking places, you call me. If it hits the road, you follow it, and you call me. I want to know everything, okay?"

"Dude, you lookin' at the king of surveillance. I plan on rackin' me up some serious extra hours. I even brought an empty super-size cup, 'case I need to take a piss."

"Okay, *that* I didn't need to know."

We shared another laugh. My smile faded.

"Clancy, be really, really careful, all right? These are not good guys."

Clancy nodded. "I figured." His eyes narrowed. "How 'bout you? You doin' okay?"

"I'm fine. Why?"

"I dunno. You seem a little skeeved out to me. Like, not as mellow as I remembered."

I opened my mouth. Closed it again. I shrugged. "Long week," I said.

I left Clancy getting all his gear in order before he set up shop down the block from the GTG lot.

In 20 minutes, I was circling the slender, stealthy black skyscraper known as the Aon. My first order of business was to determine how to get in and how to get out. According to their website, the underground in-house parking facility was open to visitors. But it wasn't that big, and I suspected it was already full. I quickly discovered the entrance to a second underground lot, for valet parking and residents with monthly passes, located just around the corner. I drove down the ramp to the valet area. An attendant ambled to my window.

"Help you?"

"I'm a messenger. Can I get to the Aon easily from here?"

He nodded. "Tunnel's that way," he said, motioning with his chin.

"I'll only be here a few minutes," I added.

He gave me and my beat-up car a chilly once-over, but his eyes widened at the sight of a folded $20 in my hand.

"I'm really backed up. Time is money," I added.

He pocketed the $20. "Over there," he said, pointing to a space right next to the cashier's window and very close to the exit ramp back to the street.

I grabbed the labeled and sealed manila envelope from the back seat, jammed the Dodgers cap low over my face, and ran through the underground pedestrian walkway connecting the lot with the skyscraper. Three decades ago a fatal fire had broken out in the Aon building, and firefighters had used this tunnel to evacuate panicking occupants. Thanks to that tragedy, every office building, old or new, is now required to have an installed and functioning sprinkler system. I wondered what other history these reinforced walls contained.

I found the elevator leading up to the main lobby and pressed the button. Checking my phone, I saw that Clancy had left me a message while I was traversing the underground tunnel.

"Yeah, so I found the van. Got my eyes on it. Nothin' much else goin' on here, but the situation's sweet. I'm goin' off the grid now, so I can focus. Later."

I took the elevator up two floors, got off, and found myself facing a wall, a desk, and a uniformed concierge planted there to direct, as well as inspect visitors. My Dodgers cap low over my brow, I exited the elevator quickly, clutching the manila envelope to my chest. Time to instigate the time-honored activity known to private investigators as "pretexting" and to normal people as lying. My pretext? I was a harried messenger with a late delivery.

I approached the concierge, a young, handsome African-American man standing behind a long desk. A false wall, decorated with a huge rainbow-hued modern painting, separated us from the actual lobby and office elevators. I was breathing fast to emphasize the urgency of my delivery.

"Excuse me," I panted. "I have an urgent express delivery for GTG Services." I flashed the envelope at him, GTG's pre-printed address on the label and the word RUSH added by me in block letters, front and back.

He picked up the phone, pushing a sign-up sheet and a ballpoint pen toward me. I signed my name with a flourish, making sure the writing was illegible.

He must have been on hold. He studied my signature, his brow furrowed. "Name," he said.

"Name?" I swallowed.

"Name of the messenger service. It's not on here."

I was starting to sweat for real, when a seemingly familiar figure rounded the corner. Although the man wasn't immediately recognizable, his thousand-dollar suit was. My eyes moved up the pinstripes to their owner with his stony face and slicked-back hair, as I shuffled through my memory files. *Mark Goodhue.* Goodhue, Bets McMurtry's go-to man. One of the G's in GTG, unless the universe was playing a ridiculous joke.

"Just let them know it's here," I said and made a swift retreat to the elevator, pushing the down button. I knelt, as if to tie a shoelace. The concierge said something to Goodhue. Sure enough, he took my bogus envelope. He opened it and removed the three blank sheets of paper.

Bing!

I stepped inside the elevator. As the doors closed, I saw Goodhue shrug and hand the envelope back.

As I ran back through the tunnel, I wracked my brain to remember Goodhue's car. I pictured Gannon's driveway and retrieved the image of a sleek black Mercedes S-Class sedan.

As my mind attempted to unlock the reason behind Goodhue's presence, a separate lever fell into place: I was almost positive this same Mercedes had cruised by Langer's while I was eating inside.

I was in my car and on the street in record time and waited a half-block away from the exit, hoping I'd remembered right.

I had. The black Benz nosed out of the exit and turned north up Wilshire. I waited until the sedan had a block-and-a-half on me and then pulled into Wilshire myself, keeping the car in sight. If I had guessed right, Goodhue was at the wheel. In a few blocks, the driver maneuvered from Hope to Flower to Third and then merged onto the 110 South. I followed, maintaining several car lengths between us. When the car merged again, onto the 105, I realized where we were headed. LAX was about 13 miles west. I frowned, adjusting my thinking. Los Angeles Airport could be incredibly tricky for a one-man tail.

But I was wrong. Maybe three miles later, the Mercedes took the Crenshaw exit and disappeared off the ramp. I followed, trying to guess: left or right, left or right. I settled for left and, sure enough, saw the sedan just ahead. I followed, keeping my distance, as the traffic was now sparse. Several blocks ahead, the Mercedes took an odd jump. I slowed way down, pulling my car left to avoid a deep cleft in the middle of the street. Welcome to the wrong side of the tracks, where potholes stayed potholes for years.

I continued following the Mercedes, turning right onto 120th Street, and was startled to see a fenced-in airport, complete with diner, airstrip, and several private planes parked along the edges of the terminal, smack in the middle of the Crenshaw district in Hawthorne. Who knew?

I pulled over and watched as the Mercedes drove inside. I continued along 120th Street, looking for a sight line. Finally I found a spot where I could see past the building to the solitary landing strip. The black sedan was parked near a private jet, a Gulfstream. I lifted my binoculars. *Yes.* Goodhue swam into view, climbing out of his car. He waved one hand, looking upward. I swung the glass sideways, and my lenses filled with the stiff helmet-hair of Bets McMurtry, ducking out of the plane. Giant red-framed sunglasses covered half her face—odd, considering the afternoon sky was overcast—and she was wearing a checkered black-and-white coat. She looked like a distressed, big-eyed fly. She picked her way down the steep stairway from the plane, gripping the rail and moving gingerly, as if she were in some pain. Goodhue hurried to her side and eased her into the passenger side of his car.

I again kept my distance, as Goodhue backtracked to the 105. This time, he transitioned to the 405. I was a little more relaxed. With Bets in the car, no doubt talking a blue streak, Goodhue was much less likely to spot a tail. I followed for ten miles or so at a pretty good clip before Goodhue left the freeway and zigzagged from Cotner to Santa Monica Boulevard to a smaller side street in the Flats area generously—and sometimes snidely—referred to as "Beverly Hills adjacent."

I hung back as he parked in front of a small but tasteful one-story Spanish bungalow in the middle of the block. He escorted Bets through the front door. This must be her mother's house, the one she suffered in as a girl and later inherited. Didn't look that awful to me, but what do I know about deprivation in Beverly Hills?

I was just about to claim a good viewing area and settle in when Goodhue marched out again. Soon, we were back on the 405 South. Goodhue was a busy boy today. Now where was he headed?

Within 15 minutes, we had entered the uninviting heart of Culver City's industrial badlands. The shadows were lengthening. By now I was wishing that I, too, had brought a super-sized cup to take care of my urinary needs. I dropped back even farther, leaving several blocks between us as we weaved through a maze of cement warehouses and one-story brick buildings. Finally, the sedan nosed up to an industrial chain-link fence of thick galvanized steel, woven through with dark green slats for privacy and enclosing who knows what. My detective antennae started to quiver as I noted the barbed-wire reinforcements jutting inward from the slatted boundary. "We Bring Secure to You," indeed. This circumference had the feel of a state prison. I again wondered what lay inside. Nothing good.

An electric barrier gate, wide enough for a tank to pass through, slid open. The Mercedes eased into the lot. The gate closed firmly behind it.

I parked a block-and-a-half away. Even with binoculars, I couldn't see much through the green slatted vinyl, though I just made out two large warehouses, situated side by side, with what looked like a modular trailer sandwiched in between. I used my iPhone to take a GPS snapshot of the location; otherwise I'd never find my way back here. Switching back to my binoculars, I carefully scanned the front and side perimeters of the chain-link barricade. Unless I wanted to shimmy up the spiked trunk of a huge, three-limbed saguaro cactus planted at the front corner of the boundary, it appeared as if there was no other way in. I took a second series of photographs with my Canon.

After waiting several minutes, I slipped out of my car and sidled past the cactus to the back of the enclosure, to double-check if there was any other mode of entry, as well as take care of my urgent need to pee. I noted a large dumpster and a Toyota Tercel hatchback from another decade, its dented hood and passenger door sporting different shades of blue.

After marking a ficus tree like a territorial dog, I was able to think again. I stepped from behind the twisted gray-green trunk and froze as a red pickup truck pulled into the narrow dirt-lined alley paralleling the rear of the enclosure. The truck parked behind the Toyota. A thin man in a security guard's all-purpose navy blue uniform, complete with epaulets, emblems, and gun, climbed out of the pickup. He tugged on his holster and crossed the alley to the fence. Like magic, a batch of chain link opened inward, and I realized there was indeed a small, padlocked gate back here, camouflaged by overlapping fence slats.

As I watched, a second uniformed and armed guard, as thick as this guy was thin, let him in. My binoculars offered up a brief glimpse of a third warehouse within the enclosure, as well as a small metal shack, the perfect size for a guardhouse. The small gate closed. After five minutes, it reopened, and the heavy guy exited, yawning. He climbed into the rundown Tercel, and soon man and car huffed away.

I checked my watch. It was 8 P.M. Shift change. I waited, and sure enough, the thin guard stepped out of the guardhouse and took a long, careful meander around the grounds before returning to his tiny quarters. Still no sign of Goodhue.

I returned to my car and settled in for what I assumed would be a long night of sitting and watching, punctuated by a few location changes and drive-bys, to avoid suspicion. My stomach grumbled. I ate a stale protein bar I found tucked in the back of the glove compartment.

I leaned against the headrest and waited.

Two hours passed, and I had just allowed myself a quick catnap, the kind you take with one ear cocked and one eye open, when the faint *beep-beep-beep* of a reversing truck alerted me to a change. I scrambled upright. A large semi was backing out of the lot, a sidelifter loaded with two movable containers and equipped with a pair of hydraulic-powered cranes. Its cab and trailer executed a complex reverse three-point turn, straightened out, and drove right past me. I ducked below the driver's line of sight, but I could clearly make out the writing as the truck rolled by— "GTG Services: We Bring Clean to You," printed on both containers and the passenger door of the semi.

The truck might as well have been printed with giant question marks. I decided to follow.

I'd started this adventure with a full tank of gas. Two-and-a-half hours later, the semi pulled into a second warehouse facility, equally well-enclosed, equally well-protected, only this one was all the way in fucking San Diego, just off the last possible exit before Tijuana. The Corolla was driving on fumes, and I was hungry enough to eat its fraying upholstery.

For the second time tonight, I peed on a tree that didn't belong to me. For the second time, I rolled silently around the perimeter of an enclosed storage warehouse set in an industrial park, with another huge, three-limbed cactus standing guard at one corner. But this time, when I rounded the empty block to the front entrance, a black Hummer was waiting for me, head lowered, revving its engine like a giant bull.

The fear-fueled flight response was immediate. As I wrenched the wheel, executing a crazy, screeching U-turn, both rear passenger windows exploded. My car had just taken a through-and-through meant for my skull. Hunching as low as possible, I jammed hard on the accelerator, very grateful for the darkness. I wove back and forth on the deserted road, the little Toyota's engine revved up to a high-pitched shriek, as several more shots whanged off my back fender. I was bleating with fear, definitely the goat of goats, as the Hummer closed the gap. I almost wept with relief when I caught sight of a well-lit 24-hour gas station up ahead. Sure enough, the Hummer stopped giving chase. It sat for a minute on the road, then turned around and drove off, like a slavering dog that has made its point.

I ran inside the 24-hour Stop and Shop and spent 20 nervous minutes surveying shelves of junk food with one eye on the window. The Hummer didn't reappear, and finally I filled my car's tank with gas and left, armed with beef jerky, vinegar-flavored potato chips, and a can of root beer. I would have bought actual beer, but I was too paranoid to put anything into my system that might soften the razor-edge of attentiveness honed by the Hummer. I might need it again tonight.

As I started the drive, I opened the beef jerky and popped one strip into my mouth. It tasted exactly the way it looked—like highly seasoned, desiccated animal flesh. As I slowly chewed, though, I tasted something else behind the processed hide. I tasted the fear and helplessness of a trapped animal that has given up its life, flavors that were now lodged in my own body, after the recent spate of attacks. I spat the half-chewed mouthful into my hand and threw it out the window.

Maybe my brief romance with meat was officially over. Maybe no one else need ever know.

The rest of the drive home was uneventful. I pulled into my driveway just after 3 A.M. I did a brief walkaround of my car, stumbling with exhaustion as I checked out the damage. The back seat was littered with kernels of shattered glass, the left fender had a big tear in it, and the entire right flank was pocked with bullet holes. I laid my hand on the damaged sheet metal and shuddered. This car had been my partner longer even than Bill. It had kept me safe, and tonight it had probably saved my life. But these wounds felt irreparable, psychically if not in reality. Time to buy a new old car.

I trudged into the house. Tank ran to me yowling. I knelt down, but he stalked away a few feet and glared. Like Heather, he was furious now that he knew I was safe.

I checked my office messages and had three, plus a hang-up.

The first was from Cielo, but she didn't leave a message. The second was from Melissa, her voice shy. "Ten? Hi, Ten. It's me, Melissa. Where are you? I miss you. Are you ever coming for a visit with your cat?" Next, from Carlos: "Hey, just wondering if . . . you know . . . It's just that Sofia's still gone, and I was hoping you might have found something out." And finally, Mrs. O'Malley: "Mac is wondering if you have anything further to report on that matter you discussed. He heard from your mutual friend, and she's very concerned at the lack of progress."

Four calls and at least three needed something from me, something I couldn't give at the moment.

I fed Tank quickly and silently, before readying myself for bed. I tumbled under the covers and shifted from stomach to back, my body itching. I'd washed my face and brushed my teeth, but dejection coated my skin, and disappointment lodged at the back of my throat. I'd made some kind of connection between the Hummer and Goodhue, but what did it mean? Could I rule anything out, really? Exhaustion acted like an accelerant on this flicker of self-doubt. Instead of breaths, I started counting the long parade of hours I'd spent so far, trying to learn something of value with this case that would lead me to Clara Fuentes and coming away empty-handed. She was still out there somewhere, waiting for someone to rescue her, and I was the wrong man for the job. Like my poor car, I was badly damaged goods.

Go to sleep, Tenzing. All will be well. Go to sleep.

CHAPTER 11

Tank kneaded me awake, his claws mostly retracted. That proof of forgiveness, combined with sleep and the warm spill of sunshine pouring in my bedroom window, eased my mood considerably.

Before I could change my mind, I put in a call to Clunkers for Cops, an LAPD non-profit organization that provides financial assistance to widows and orphans of fallen officers. The cheerful gal at the other end promised to have a tow truck there within the hour.

I made a pot of coffee and moved to the deck to assess. As I sipped from my mug, I could still feel the lingering traces of disappointment from the night before. I doubt if anybody likes running away with their tail between their legs. I certainly didn't.

My cell phone buzzed, and I saw it was Clancy.

"Clancy! How's it going?"

"Going okay," he said. "Still no movement on your van, but several others took off first thing this morning. They were gone a few hours. Now they're back."

"Are you cool staying there for now?"

"No worries. The wife and kid are at her mother's this week. I still got some food, and I got my iPod all set up. I'm learning Spanish, did I tell you?"

"Smart."

"*Gracias, amigo.*"

I did a few stretching exercises on the deck as I went over what I'd learned. Not only was Mark Goodhue involved with my client Bets, but he was up to his eyeballs in everything else pertaining to my world at the moment.

The question was, why? Was McMurtry ignorant, or behind all of this? If not, who was? I had a hard time picturing Goodhue as the chief honcho here. He was well groomed, but there was that hint of weakness in his eyes, the soft corners of his mouth, and the prissy crease of his suit trousers. I didn't think he had the stones to be behind an operation this vast.

I sent Mike a text, letting him know Goodhue was probably one of the G's in GTG. Mike was no doubt fast asleep, but later today he'd be all over this fact. I needed to call Bill next, to fill him in on my second armed attack in as many days, though hopefully this one was far enough from his jurisdiction to remain off the LAPD grid for now. I certainly didn't need any more reporters ringing my doorbell, any more gorgeous, sloe-eyed, curvaceous . . .

As if on cue, my cell phone buzzed. When I saw it was Heather, my face flooded with heat, caught fantasizing. Her words quickly eradicated my embarrassment.

"Ten, a Juanita Doe just came in. Definite homicide. Autopsy's pending. They're still trying to ID her."

"Where's the body?'

"One-one-oh-four," she said, referring to the building at the county coroner's office where autopsies take place.

"I'm on my way," I said.

I raced around the house, my heart pained, but also eager to know if this was Clara. As I ran to the Shelby, a tow truck pulled up, ready to haul my mortally wounded Toyota to its next incarnation. They attached the chain and raised the carcass until it was balanced on its rear tires, then drove away, towing the battered vehicle behind them.

I offered thanks to my Corolla for its service: *May you serve well into the future, even if only as parts.* Something prickled at the nape of my neck, gone before I could catch it, as my monkey mind next wondered: *If a Toyota leads a good life, does it come back as a Lexus?*

I made a brief but essential stop en route downtown

and arrived at the county coroner's bearing a peace offer-ing. Heather met me in the parking lot. Even in scrubs, she glowed. I handed over a nonfat vanilla soy latte, and we shared the bittersweet smile linked to better times. The first time I'd exchanged any actual words with Heather was in this very lot, and the second time, I'd tried to woo her with this very drink.

She glanced around before giving me a quick kiss on the lips.

"Thanks for the heads-up," I said.

"Well, don't thank me too much. Bhatnager just informed us that only those directly involved in the inves-tigation can see the body until we get an ID."

Bhatnager was the Chief Medical Examiner, and Heath-er's boss. My face fell.

"But I can tell you this. It's a Hispanic female, medium height and weight, twenty-eight to thirty-five years old."

Not Clara then. I was conflicted—half relieved, half disappointed. Conflicted was my normal state so far in this Tibetan year of contradictions.

"Anything else you can tell me? Was she cut up?"

"No." She lowered her voice. "Shot in the back of the head. Although her tongue was missing."

So this was an old-school hit and probably about snitching. Which led to my next question.

"Was she wearing a uniform of any sort? Like a maid might wear?"

Heather shook her head. "No. Jeans. Why?"

"Just curious," I said. This was proving to be a complete dead end.

"There was one odd thing, though. I found some weird grain in her pocket."

"Grain?"

"Yeah, you know, like millet and stuff."

My heart picked up speed.

"Could it be birdseed?"

Heather's face lit up. "Ten, you're a genius! That's exactly what it is. Birdseed!"

"I know who she is," I said. "And I know who can identify her."

I gave Heather Carlos's number and told her to break the news gently—that his heart was involved. We stood outside for a few more minutes, as she finished her coffee. She crumpled the cup. The gap of silence slowly expanded into a yawning crevasse between us.

"Ten—" she started, at the same moment I said, "Want to meet for a drink later?"

"I can't," she said. "I have plans."

I'll bet.

"Doing what?"

"Nothing," she said, her skin flushing. "Just, I'd rather not say right now, okay?" Heather's phone pinged. She glanced down. "Bhatnager. I'll call you later tonight. I promise." Another quick peck, this one on the cheek, and she was gone.

The sun beat down on me, its touch harsh.

Don't do it.

I reached for my phone.

Don't.

I found the number I'd entered yesterday morning and pressed it. Maybe she wouldn't answer.

She picked up before the second ring. "I wondered how long it would take before you called." Cielo's voice was playful and light.

"How did you know I would call? Am I that predictable?"

"Yes," she said. "So I'm done with work for the day. Want to play?"

I drove with my brain turned firmly off. Twenty minutes later, Cielo admitted me to her Santa Monica apartment, a location disturbingly close to Heather's condominium. She was wrapped up tight in a white terry-cloth robe, drying her hair with a towel. She smelled like night-blooming jasmine.

Her toenails were painted an edible tangerine. In her bare feet, she was a few inches shorter than me. That made me happy.

Cielo stepped closer and slipped her arms around my waist. I lowered my face to her hair and inhaled. I'm a sucker for anything jasmine. She lifted her mouth and met mine for a deep kiss. I finally pulled away, so she wouldn't feel my heart trying to pound its way out of my chest. She moved her hands to my shoulders and studied my face. Reaching up, she softly brushed a palm over my head.

"Oh," she said. "I've been dying to do that. I love the feel of your hair."

"Really?"

"Mmm. Like a soft brush."

I've hated my hair ever since I was young, struggling to tame its brazen vertical thrust. Once I moved into the monastery, the issue changed, but the strained relationship remained. I never could decide which was worse—hating my hair or having no hair to hate.

Cielo continued to run her hand across my fuzzy scalp, in soft, delicious strokes.

An unfamiliar sensation spread through my limbs; I was on the border of feeling faint, but in a good way. I think they call it swooning.

I pulled her close again. Heaven indeed. She was everything I never got to have when I first had feelings for a girl. She was my do-over, my Pema, right here and right now. I closed my eyes, loving the way her soft contours fit into my body's angles so snugly. *Pema.*

Cielo chuckled. "I'm feeling a lot of activity down here in your jeans, Detective," she said. "I have an idea." She pulled on the belt of her robe and gave a little shoulder wriggle. The garment slid to the floor. I had a fleeting thought that this wasn't the first time she'd executed that move—it was a little too smooth—when her breasts jutted against my chest.

My throat clutched. I cleared it. "I should probably tell you—"

She covered my mouth with her hand. "Let me guess. You're in another relationship that's not going so great, and you're pretty confused about it."

My startled blink was answer enough.

"Consider me warned. Now shut up, Detective. You're ruining the moment."

I definitely did not want to do that. Which is how—an intense and extended session of sexual acrobatics, and a long bath later—I ended up back outside her apartment, walking toward my Shelby, wondering what the hell I'd just done.

Right before I'd left, I had made a second clunky attempt to tell her about my relationship quandaries. By then, she was several bong hits into a post-sex marijuana high, reclining in the tub where we both had been soaking moments before.

She waved my words off. "Tell it to your life coach."

"But—"

She cut me off. "But nothing. Look, you're a few years older than I am. Maybe you're at that settling-down stage. I'm not. I'm twenty-six, I've got a good career going, and I want to experience everything I can. Today, that was you."

"And if I want to see you again?"

"One day at a time. Now go away, Ten." She smiled. "Detect something else, okay?"

I got in my car and drove, my mind conjuring that last image of her in the tub, her swells and curves peeking through a blanket of soap bubbles.

Halfway up Topanga, the damp, itchy blanket of guilt descended. I didn't know whether I was guided to Cielo by divine inspiration or by an unconscious intent to mess up my life. Either way, one thing was clear: I had once again proven that between Heather and me, I was the less mature and more self-destructive romantic partner.

By the time I reached my turnoff, a full-scale Tibetan debate was playing out in my head, complete with dueling lamas punctuating their points of view with lunging feet and clapping hands. The topic was honesty. "You must discuss your erotic activities with Heather immediately!" CLAP! "No! The Buddha says, practice moderation in all things!" CLAP!

Unfortunately, in this case, moderation was just another excuse for keeping a secret. The interchange had an unsettling effect on my stomach, and little waves of nausea formed and dissolved as I parked the Shelby in the garage.

I started for the house and then stopped abruptly.

Well isn't that just perfect.

I was face to face with the relentless laws of karma. This being a just and fair universe, my property had once again been burgled. This time, the burglar or burglars had entered by busting the kitchen window on the far side of the deck. So much for my security system.

I groaned, remembering my hasty departure that morning. Even a $6,000 security system isn't much use if you neglect to activate it.

I walked inside the kitchen, broken glass crunching underfoot. The LED tracker, which I'd left on the kitchen table, was now smashed on the floor, as if in anger. My living room and bedroom were tossed as thoroughly as Sofia's had been. At least the burglars had been unable to break into my safe.

But the Guard-on system was gone. Both monitors, the electronic brains, all of it. Gone. Where the bedroom monitor used to be, I found a crudely scrawled note:

"¡¡¡Chinga tu!!!"

I was pretty sure what the words meant without calling Carlos to translate.

I heard a low cat-growl from behind my hamper, one of Tank's emergency hiding places. I ran to him.

"You want to come out? It's safe now."

He blinked, staying put.

"I know," I said. "I don't blame you."

I filled Tank's food and water bowls. He'd surface when he was ready. I stepped onto the deck to check for the infrared cameras. They were gone, too. A swell of rage broadsided me, washing away all other thoughts—of guilt, of pleasure, of truth, of lies.

My phone buzzed. Mike.

"Hey," I said.

"So, something's wrong with your Guard-on," he said. "I can't seem to . . ."

"It's gone," I said. "Fuckers stole it. I'll call you later." I hung up on his sputters of disbelief.

I changed into a pair of black jeans, a black T-shirt, and my black windbreaker, and went out into the evening like a good ninja. I had a plan, and it involved being back at the Culver City warehouse by 8 P.M., when the shift changed for the guardhouse occupants. This time I was doubly armed, with the comforting weight of my Wilson Supergrade in the right-hand pocket of my jacket and an equally comforting wad of $100 bills—removed from the envelope stored inside my safe—in the left-hand pocket of my jeans.

In ancient China, the ruling parties behind the building of the Great Wall made a strategic error that proved to be their downfall. The wall itself was almost impossible to penetrate physically. The guards, however, were not so impenetrable. Human corruptibility proved to be the weak link in the blockade, and invading forces soon learned to use a bag of gold for their opening salvo. Once palms were greased, the guards would cheerfully open the gate to let invading forces through, and emperors would fall.

I parked three blocks away from the warehouse with ten minutes to spare, and hugged the shadows as I made a stealth approach into the alley, then crouched behind the dumpster. I waited patiently, and sure enough, about five minutes before eight, a red pickup truck pulled into the alley. I took a big, slow breath and crept to the back of the truck, stooping low. The driver opened the door and climbed out. In two steps, I had the barrel of the Wilson pressed against his temple. "Freeze and you won't get hurt."

"Jesus," he hissed. He started to turn his head but changed his mind. He was rail thin, with a hawk face and a gray buzz cut. "What do you want?" he asked.

"I want inside the lot," I replied.

"I can't do that," he said.

"*Chinga tu*," I whispered.

"Huh?"

"Nothing. What's your name?"

"Oh. Larry." I noticed his holstered gun was a Glock.

"You ex-LAPD?"

"Nah. Ex-military. Private, army reserve." From National Guard to security guard. Well, he wasn't the first one to take that career route.

I removed the Glock from his belt holster and pocketed it. Lowering my Wilson, I pulled the roll of hundreds out of my jeans pocket. "Look, Larry," I said. "All I want to do is sneak a quick look inside. Ten minutes, tops." I peeled off five $100 bills and fanned them one-handed, like playing cards. "Five brand-new Ben Franklins, yours for doing nothing. A non-action."

"Hell, no," he said. "I could lose my job."

I counted out five more hundreds. "A thousand dollars," I said. "Final offer."

He considered the bait for all of about two seconds before he bit. "What the hell, I could use the cash. My wife likes to go to the Indian casino."

I held up my hand. "No explanation needed."

"Gimme a minute or two, until Vern leaves."

"No problem," I said. "I can wait for Vern."

I gave him one of the hundreds, for incentive, and waved the other nine at him one more time before stepping behind the dumpster. Larry unlocked the small side gate and disappeared inside. A few minutes later Vern ambled out to the alley, securing the padlock behind him. He hitched his pants and climbed into his hatchback. Engine coughing, the car disappeared around the corner.

Larry unlocked the gate a few minutes later and gestured me inside with a single, sharp arm jerk. We stood by the guardhouse.

"Save me some time," I said. "What's inside those warehouses?"

His face twitched, as if his nerve endings were frayed. "I get paid to guard, not to stick my nose where it don't belong," he said.

"Do you have keys?"

"I got keys." He scratched the side of his nose with a bony forefinger.

Oh, right.

"Are they worth five hundred dollars?"

I handed him a second bill but flashed four more, which I conspicuously transferred to the on-hold stash.

He passed over a key ring. "Ten minutes."

"Ten minutes," I said and ran to the modular trailer, the one I'd seen Mark Goodhue enter. I found that key easily. Once inside, my flashlight illuminated what looked like a standard industrial front office, with metal desks and chairs, and a poster board covered with some sort of complex scheduling grid attached to one wall. There was a tall, locked storage unit in the corner, also metal, but the room itself was empty of computers, filing cabinets, or anything remotely removable. These were careful men. I ran outside and fumbled with the keys until I found one that unlocked the first warehouse. I stepped into a dark cavern and again played my flashlight across the space. A dozen or so identical compact trailers, the size and shape of Airstreams, barely filled one end of the warehouse. The trailers were locked, and even up close I couldn't see inside. A little metal plaque on the outside of each door announced "Model EOT3.1 GTG Medical Supplies, Inc. Goleta, California."

I pointed my phone and snapped some pictures.

My beam picked up a row of large, barrel-shaped containers, complete with spigots, like beer kegs, lined against a second wall. "GTG Organic Products: We Bring Clean to You!" I read. Maybe the maids came with their own home-grown cleaning products. Nice vertical manufacturing ploy, but nothing illegal about it.

I locked up and hustled to the second warehouse. I didn't have much sand left in the hourglass. I let myself inside. Before I'd even switched on my flashlight, my nose told me at least part of what was in the building, and sure enough my light revealed hundreds of neatly-tended marijuana plants in transportable, hydroponic containers. This was more like it. I estimated the street value at a couple of million dollars. I walked to the far end of the warehouse— and whistled. Stacked rows of portable, industrial shelving housed hundreds of extra-large Ziploc bags bulging with multicolored pills, a megaversion of Sofia's backpack stash.

I was out of time, but I assumed the third building held much of the same. I had seen enough. I stopped by the shack and gave Larry his money.

"I'll leave the keys and your gun just outside the gate," I said.

He pocketed the bills, his smile revealing jagged, stained teeth. "See you around?"

"Probably not, but you never know."

"You keep bringin' them hundreds, you can drop by any night you want," he said.

Somewhere, a Chinese emperor shuddered.

Chapter 12

I was famished. On the way home I stopped at a 24-hour deli, and nothing would do but hot pastrami. So much for my brief relapse into vegetarianism. I was at war. I needed my meat. The restaurant was surprisingly busy. I found a stool at the counter, joining half a dozen other exhausted diners hunched over their plates, like crows on a telephone wire. While I waited for my sandwich, I browsed the Internet to see if I could find any information on the Airstream wannabes. I tried a few different variations on the words *portable* and *trailer,* but nothing useful came up. I added *cleaners* and *security.* Lots of images, none of them relevant. What were those trailers for?

I sat back and thought: bags of prescription painkillers, marijuana plants, a company offshoot providing medical supplies, and a place in Goleta that manufactured portable trailers. I entered a different set of parameters, including the serial number of the first van, and pressed SEARCH.

My eyes widened. I was looking at a mobile operating room, eerily similar to the ones in the warehouse. I moved on to the manufacturer's website and continued to explore. When I saw how much each unit cost, my blood slowed. They were close to $250,000 each, and various add-ons could drive the cost up to $400,000.

If I was right, and that's what the warehouse was housing, those guys not only had truck-loads of painkillers, as well as pot but also a portable means of creating the demand for them. Holy cow.

How the maids fit in, I had no idea.

Speaking of holy cows, a greasy sandwich landed in

front of me. My neighboring counter-dweller, a toothless vagrant nursing a lukewarm cup of coffee, aimed a pair of rheumy eyes at my plate. His hands were cracked and grimy, and trembled as he cupped the thick china mug. His expression was one of pure longing. My appetite took a rare back seat to my compassion, and I slid the plate his way.

"Enjoy," I said, my appetite subdued by his need. I got up to pay the bill.

As I was cashing out, my phone buzzed, and a text from Mike popped up: EITHER YOU'RE IN W. HOLLYWOOD IN THE MIDDLE OF THE NIGHT OR SOMEBODY STOLE YOUR PHONE TOO. GIVE ME A CALL.

Mike keeps my iPhone GPS on his computer—he doesn't trust me to know who or where I am at any given point in time. I glimpsed a dog-tired man in the mirror behind the cashier, and it was two beats before I realized the man was me. Maybe Mike had a point.

I called him on the way home, putting him on speaker.

"Guess what?" Mike sounded jazzed. "Your Guard-on unit just showed up.for sale on Craigslist."

"That was quick. What makes you think it's mine?"

"Timing. Plus, from the pictures I can just make out a few digits on the serial number, and they match your receipt. Plus, you almost never see one of these for sale used. At six grand, people feel pretty committed to loving them, even if they hate them."

"How much are they asking for it?"

"Two grand."

I felt vaguely insulted at the steep discount, which made no sense, considering it was a gift to begin with. "Okay, can you send me the details?"

"Texting as we speak. Hey, Boss, you need any backup on this?"

"No, thanks. I've got it covered."

I was an occasional bad-boy motorist, guilty of texting and driving. This time, though, I pulled over to extract the information from Mike's text. I checked the time. Probably way too late to call. On the other hand, they did just post the item. I punched in the number.

A high-pitched male voice said, *"Si."*

"Is this"—I checked the information—"Manolo?"

"Yeah."

I slipped into Conscious Lying mode. "Hey, my name's . . . Bill." I mentally apologized to my ex-partner. It was late, and I had only a few brain cells still working.

"Yeah, what you want?" He spoke with a pronounced Hispanic accent.

"I got your number off Craigslist. I'm looking for a Guard-on."

"Yeah, okay. We got a nice one, looks pretty much brand new."

It ought to, I thought.

"Where did you get it?" I asked. "Those are hard to find."

He had his story all ready. "My uncle give it to me," he said. "He don' need it no more." He was about as convincing at Conscious Lying as I was.

"I'd like to buy it," I said, "but the problem is, I only have seventeen hundred." No Craigslist seller would take me seriously if I didn't try to bargain him down a little.

"No, man," he said, falling into the universal singsong cadence of deal-making. "That's too low. Tell you what, though—how 'bout you coming off a hundred, I coming off a hundred?"

"Nineteen then?"

"Yeah, okay, deal. Cash, though. Gotta be in cash."

"Cash is fine. How soon can I pick it up?" I was banking on him being in a hurry to unload the stolen property.

He held a hasty conference in Spanish with someone in the background. He came back on and said, "Where you calling from?"

"Santa Monica." That seemed far enough from Topanga Canyon to keep any suspicions at bay.

Another rapid-fire exchange in Spanish.

"You know Tuna Canyon Park, just before Malibu?"

"Sure do."

"Okay. The park there? It's no open this time of night, but we parking across from the entrance and waiting for you. Okay?"

"That's where you want to do this?"

"No, man. We meeting you there, then you follow us, okay?"

"Got it."

"We driving a Ford van. Black."

Now that was interesting.

"What you driving?"

Oops. I hadn't thought this through. The Corolla had gone to the graveyard, and my Shelby was, well, if these guys had anything to do with the other crew that broke in, my Shelby was a dead giveaway, no pun intended.

"I'll call you right back," I said.

My mind sorted through options. I tried calling Bill first, but his phone went straight to voice mail. Either he was on a case, or, more likely, sick of my 2:00 A.M. calls. Mike, however, was just getting going. But Mike motored around on an electric pedal bike. I'd never braved the eROCKIT solo, and I wouldn't fit behind him, even riding sidesaddle. Mike's girlfriend, on the other hand . . .

I called Mike back. He and Tricia both worked the vampire shift, so I had no fears he'd gone to bed.

"Mike, is that offer of backup still good?"

"Absolutely! What do you need?"

"You, and, uh, Tricia's MINI?" I heard the murmur of voices, one low and pleading, the other high and a little resistant. Low had the last word.

"It's on. How about artillery?"

That gave me pause. Before he went upscale by purchasing a downtown loft, Mike lived, as he put it, "in Manson country." He still had an ancient shotgun he'd acquired at the time, for premise-protection. I had to balance the danger to my own well-being if Mike wielded a shotgun against the impression Mike carrying a shotgun might make. Come to think of it, they both landed on the wrong side of the protection scale.

Still karma was karma. I couldn't count on my current streak of bullet-dodging luck to hold forever. And he sounded so excited.

"Fine, bring artillery."

I called Manolo back. "I'll be in a Brown MINI Cooper." Mike's girlfriend, Tricia, drove a MINI, a car the color and size of a Hershey's Chocolate Kiss. All the better if they thought I was a wimp.

"Okay, we meeting you there in maybe half an hour."

"Better make that an hour," I said.

I turned into my drive just in time to see the chocolate-colored MINI up ahead, chugging through the gravel to my house like a piece of fudge on wheels. Mike's long torso was slightly bent as he drove; even so, his curly halo of hair nearly brushed against the inside roof of the compact car. He rolled down the window and offered a sharp salute. His eyes gleamed. Even his goatee stood at attention. The fact that he was packing heat had clearly gone straight to his head.

"Five minutes," I said. "Try not to shoot anything."

I ran to my closet safe and counted out a thick fistful of hundreds. My Julius Rosen–funded cash stash was shrinking by the hour. Tank stalked the bedroom perimeter, tail high. I explained the situation to him as best I could. That, plus a nightcap of tuna water, seemed to satisfy him.

I ducked into the passenger seat of the MINI still in ninja-wear, still armed. "Let's go."

Mike urged the little go-cart down Topanga as I provided background information, talking over the rattle and vroom of the engine.

"So I want you to stay in the car and cover me while I

deal with these guys," I concluded. I glanced at the shotgun in the backseat. "Never mind, don't even cover me—just keep the gun within reach, in case things get rough."

Mike nodded happily.

"Cool," he said. "Very cool."

The black Ford van sat opposite the Tuna Canyon Park entrance. Wrong license plate number but right everything else, up to the tinted windows and small logo and slogan printed on the side door. The back of my neck prickled, and I patted the Wilson in my windbreaker pocket, double-checking.

"Pull up directly in front of them," I said, and Mike did so. He, too, was quivering in anticipation.

"Deep breath," I said, and we both took a moment to breathe in and out.

I reached across the seat and flashed the MINI's brights a couple of times. The headlights illuminated two males slouched in the front seat of the van. The driver answered with a flick of his lights, executed an awkward U-turn and headed back in the direction of Santa Monica. We followed. After a half-mile or so the van turned onto a narrow rutted dirt road that wound toward the ocean. The van slowed to a crawl. We maintained a slight distance. The road petered out completely at a stretch of dunes. The driver reverse-turned the van to face us.

"Okay, here," I told Mike. He stopped the car, leaving about 20 feet between vehicles. The male on the passenger side of the van climbed out, clutching a cardboard box. He was just a kid, maybe 18. Narrow face and skinny arms, combined with a shaved head and tattoos. A scrawny scarecrow, trying to be something he was not.

He moved to the middle of the dirt road, took a wide-legged stance, and gave us a flat-eyed stare.

"*Shaun of the Dead,* man," Mike said.

"What? Who?"

"You know: Mexican stand-off, only with real Mexicans

instead of zombies." I would have to parse Mike's twisted cultural references later. I climbed out of the MINI and started walking, my right hand in my pocket, my breath shallow.

The kid was nervous, too. His eyes darted from side to side, and his thin arms, holding tight to the box, were trembling. The Guard-on unit, including the little cameras, hardly weighed 20 pounds, so I knew the quivering wasn't caused by muscle strain. I scanned his body. He wasn't armed, as far as I could see. Mind you, the waist of his baggy jeans started almost at his knees, but there was no telltale bulge in either pocket.

"Manolo?"

"Pedro," he said. "Manolo's back there." He jerked his chin at the van. "You Bill?"

I nodded.

He set the box down. "Here it is. You bring the cash?"

"Right here." I waved a wad of bills at him. This was becoming a regular habit of mine. "I need to take a look, okay?"

Pedro nodded and took a step back, crossing his arms.

I moved to the box and knelt, prodding at the contents, although I already knew it was mine. As I bent closer, as if to count the outdoor cameras, my eye caught a telltale arm-swiping movement. I rolled to the left just as Pedro whipped a foot-long piece of pipe from the back of his pants and chopped. I was quick, but not quick enough. A white-hot blast of nerve-pain shot through my right shoulder. I kept rolling, thinking *Stupid! So stupid!* Now my right arm was numb and not taking orders from my brain, which kept begging the hand to grab my gun. I clambered to my feet awkwardly as I attempted to fish the Wilson out of my right-hand pocket with my left hand. Pedro raised his arm a second time. A second glancing blow ricocheted off my upper back as I twisted away.

I was finally able to grab my .38, transfer it to both hands, and point. Pedro froze, mid-lunge, and yelled something at Manolo. No time, or need, to guess what he said. I tucked and rolled as a gun flash-fired from the direction of the van, and a bullet streaked by my left ear. *WHUP!* The sand puffed and settled.

An ear-splitting bellow erupted from the MINI Cooper. I had completely forgotten about my own trusty backup man, but not for long. The air exploded with the sonic blast of a 12-gauge. Now I was wounded in one wing and partially deaf. I tried to shake the ringing from my ears as I checked the vicinity for damage.

An enormous hole gaped in the side of the van. Mike's shot was at least six feet wide of Manolo, another thin-limbed teenager in over his head. He stared at the mortally wounded van, his mouth hanging open. Maybe Mike's marksmanship wasn't great, but give him an *attaboy* for Shock and Awe.

I trained my Wilson.

"Drop it," I shouted. "Drop your gun. And put your hands up where I can see them!"

Between my .38 and Mike's cannon, Manolo knew his odds had changed. He placed the handgun at his feet and straightened up, arms raised. I glanced down at it. What the hell was a kid his age doing with an FN Herstal Five-seveN semiautomatic pistol? Pedro made a slight move, and I flicked my barrel at him. He got the message and dropped the pipe onto the sand. I motioned for him to kneel down. He complied. I sensed he was new to the gangster life; a spreading stain of urine darkened the front of his jeans, adding an unpleasant tang to the night air.

"Cover this guy, Mike!"

"Okay!" Mike's gangly body advanced, shotgun pointed. I worried that he might blow the kid away accidentally. Then I realized I was rooting for a kid who'd attacked me with a pipe not too many seconds ago. I sometimes have difficulty figuring out what's compassion and what's being a complete idiot.

"Easy with that thing," I said.

"Yeah, okay." Mike turned to me. "What should I—"

Pedro scrambled to his feet and broke into a sprint. By the time Mike got the shotgun raised, his target was already up and over the dunes.

"Mike!" I shouted.

Mike looked over his shoulder at me.

"Let him go," I told him. "One's all we need." Who knows what he'd hit this time. For sure, it wasn't going to be Pedro.

Mike lowered his shotgun, his expression half relieved, half disappointed.

I moved to the young man by the van, still standing with his hands in the air. His dark eyes were in constant motion, making them hard to read, and his arms, like Pedro's, were covered with ink. But not his neck. That was a good thing. Neck tattoos as good as shouted to the world, "I do not ever intend to have a real job." Maybe this kid was keeping his options open. Maybe I could persuade him to step away from the dark side.

"Are you Manolo?"

He nodded, his gaze shifting back and forth, up and down, anywhere but at me.

"I'm giving you a choice here, Manolo. If you answer me honestly, I'll let you go. You screw around with me . . . Well, you won't like it."

His voice was skeptical. "You're gonna let me go, huh? You think I'm *loco? Estupido?*"

"I mean it. Mike, tell him I wouldn't lie about something like that."

"He wouldn't lie," Mike said.

A confused look came and went from the kid's old-young face.

"So what do you say, Manolo?"

Manolo's eyes narrowed, as he aimed his words somewhere to the left of me. "You *la Tira*, you setting me up? You some kind of cop?"

Some kind of cop—that's me. "I'm a private investigator," I said. "And no. I'm not setting you up."

Manolo glanced at the Wilson in my hand. "What that piece cost you? Ten thousand?"

"Who's your boss, Manolo? Who do you work for?"

His Adam's apple bobbed a couple of times while his brain tried to calculate what would lead to more harm—telling the truth or lying. I knew the feeling.

"I can' tell you that, man," he finally muttered.

I decided to help him out. "Do you work for Chuy?"

His eyes widened, which gave me the answer I needed. "Uno or Dos?"

He swallowed. "Dos," he said his voice low. "He work for Uno."

"So Chuy Uno's the boss?"

"Uno's not the *jefe*, the boss, either. Everything's changed. New jefe now."

Was Manolo referring to the leader of the rumored gang of gangs?

"Who is it?" I motioned with my gun. "Who's the new boss, Manolo?"

He swallowed hard again. "Carnaté," he whispered.

"Say that again?"

"Carnaté." His eyes flicked across the sand, as if he thought the dunes had ears. I made a mental note to call my contact in the gang unit to see if a "Carnaté" was on their radar. I'd never heard of the guy.

"Carnaté, as in *meat*?"

His look was one of pity, mixed with genuine terror. "You don' know shit, do you?"

I changed tactics. "So you worked for Chuy Uno, and then, what, he joined another gang?"

A flash of anger straightened his spine. "It's bullshit, man. I was doin' six months in juvie, and when I get out, it don' mean shit. All that new money going straight to Chuy's head. And less and less coming down here to us now."

162

"All what new money?"

"Carnaté pay Chuy a lot of money to bring his *clica* over. I heard sixty thousand, all in hundreds, clean and pure as the Virgin Mary." Manolo crossed himself.

"Ah, so Chuy's *clica,* his gang, joined forces with this Carnaté."

"That's what I just said. And fucking Chuy, he went out and got himself a brand-new chopper. Rides that thing like he a king or something. Meantime, what do I get? A stinkin' Ford van a few nights a week and a job driving *puta*s around like a pussy."

"You can put your hands down," I said.

He dropped them to his side. He still wouldn't meet my gaze. "You gonna let me go now?"

"Not quite yet. Is Chuy Uno still in jail in Tijuana?"

Manolo nodded.

"Where can I find Chuy Dos?"

Manolo's shifty eyes fired off a rapid set of blinks.

I let him blink.

Finally he said, "At work."

"Where and when?"

He named a street very familiar to me and an address that Clancy was no doubt surveying at this very moment. Well, well, well.

"He there most days, eight to three. Can I go now?"

"Soon. Talk to me about the Guard-on unit."

"Man!" He jerked his chin toward the dunes. "Pedro and me, after we busting in, we couldn't find the dope. Instead, we grab the machine. Taking all the cameras out of the trees, like that."

"I noticed," I said. "So Chuy told you to steal my Guard-on unit?"

He shook his head. "Naw, man, Chuy just want his dope back, 'cause he know Carnaté gonna squeeze his nuts for losing track of product. Jacking the machine, that was my idea." Manolo brightened, as if expecting praise.

Mike walked up.

"Are you almost done here? Tricia needs her car."

At three in the morning? I wanted to say, but didn't. Vampires have their own mysterious nocturnal activities.

"Almost." I turned back to my captive. "You're not going back to Chuy with what happened here tonight, are you, Manolo?"

"You shittin' me? He kill me for sure, he find out I got caught jacking, you know, stealing on the side. I can' let him kill me." His voice rose. "No way, man. You let me go, I'm gone. You and Chuy never see me again. You don' know that man, what he like to do." He made another sign of the cross.

I gentled my voice. This kid was clearly terrified of something. "What does Chuy like to do?"

A gentle salt breeze was blowing in from just over the dunes, but he shuddered, as if hit by an arctic blast.

"I'm done talking," he said.

The image of a young banger's butchered body, squeak-squeaking on Heather's gurney, flicked through my mind. I prayed I was wrong about this. But if I wasn't wrong, the kid had every right to be scared.

I turned my attention back to Manolo, whose skin was slick with sweat.

"I'm taking your pistol," I said. I counted out eight $100 bills. "Here. That should cover it. I suggest you and your buddy Pedro use this money to get as far away from here—and Carnaté—as possible.

Manolo shoved the bills in his pocket, which hung down around his calves. He looked away, scuffing at the sand. Without his gun and bravado, he was just another lost, scared adolescent, wearing pants five sizes too big.

He licked his lips. "He gonna know you did this."

"Chuy Dos?"

"Naw. Carnaté. Carnaté knows everything."

Beyond the dunes, an ocean lullaby was ebbing and

flowing, ebbing and flowing. "I hear Canada's nice this time of year," I said.

He finally met my eyes, dead serious. "Maybe I see you there, amigo."

He ran across the dunes and into the darkness. I waited until he was out of sight.

Mike was snapping shots of the blasted side panel with his iPhone, for posterity.

"Mike, when you get home, can you call the Lost Hills Station and make an anonymous report on this van?" Let them deal with it.

"Sure thing, boss."

I called Bill, and this time he picked up. Turned out, he hadn't been asleep after all. He was called out on an officer-involved, drive-by shooting in Echo Park.

"I'm sorry, you're saying what now?" Bill said, his voice low.

"I need to follow up on something," I said. "It has to do with this gang of gangs. You up for a little joyride?"

Bill groaned, but I knew I had him. Anyway, he was already up.

I had Mike drop off my boxed Guard-on system and me at the 24-hour Jack in the Box farther up the PCH. I shoveled down a breakfast sandwich and a small greasy loaf of shredded potato generously called hash browns, and downed a scalding cup of bitter coffee. Bill pulled into the parking lot 40 minutes later, and I climbed into his car.

I turned the Herstal over to him. Maybe a trace would shed some light on this new gang.

"I'd forgotten this about you, Tenzing. How much you love to ruin a guy's beauty sleep," Bill said. He bagged the Herstal and locked it in his glove box. "Okay, Cowboy. Where to?"

I brought up the GPS tag on my phone and filled him in, as we merged onto the 10 and sped along the mostly deserted freeway and surface streets until we got to the

Culver City industrial lot. I directed him to park up the block. The front of the lot was dead still, although the silence was underpinned by a constant, low-frequency hum. I couldn't locate the source, but it was close by. I checked the office module, but there was no light on inside. In fact, the whole place was suspiciously bathed in inky darkness.

"Now what?" Bill asked, one eyebrow cocked.

I led him to the back alley. The guard's hut, too, was dark. I looked up and down the alley. No pickup truck. No Tercel hatchback. I crossed to the spot in the fence where the guard's entrance was masked by overlapping slats. I kicked at the hidden gate in frustration.

It swung open.

We called out a few times before entering the lot, on high alert, but the site appeared vacant. I led Bill to the first warehouse. It was locked up tight, but I was able to hitch Bill onto my shoulders so he could play my flashlight through one of the high windows. A youthful memory flared, only back then it had been me standing on Lobsang's shoulders, stealing an ancient text from the monastery library. I shook the recollection off. Bill's weight dug into my shoulders as he peered inside.

"There's nothing in there, Ten. Just a big room."

"Are you sure?"

"It's empty, pal."

All three warehouses were stripped clean: not a pill, pot plant, or mobile unit in sight. Back in the car, I sat in stony silence, my body stiff with disappointment. Bill finally cleared his throat.

"I'm going to assume you weren't tripping on some special Tibetan juju medicine, Ten, and that those warehouses actually had something in them."

"Someone must have gotten spooked by my earlier visit. I'm telling you, they were full of drugs and marijuana plants and . . . and portable operating units."

"Emphasis on *portable*," he said.

"Agh!" I hit the dashboard, realizing. "Everything—the shelving, the hydroponic systems—all of it was on rollers!"

"Modern gangs," Bill said, philosophically. "They think of everything." He yawned. "I don't know about you, partner, but I'm ready to call it a night."

Chapter 13

The concrete floor presses against my cheek, cold and unyielding. I am stretched out, prone. I have been here before. I lift my head to look around. A man steps out of the corner shadows. It can't be. But it is. My father lifts his right hand with the palm facing me. With his left hand, he points to the ground. The first gesture is meant to dispel fear, the other to call the earth as witness.

"You can't be here," I say. "You're dead."

"You only think I am," my father answers, and his eyes turn the color of blood.

I run outside, into a barren stretch of desert sand. Sere. Lifeless. Carcasses litter the perimeter; maybe human, maybe animal, they've been left to rot by their attacker—me. I look at the horizon, which comes alive with whirling sand. The cloud of dust envelops me. The air swirls, dark and full of grit.

I start to walk, when a second man—more a boy, really— appears before me in the billowing sand storm. His hands are cupped in front of his chest. A beating heart rests in the shell formed by his palms.

Miguel. Dead Miguel.

And then I know. I am back. Back in my recurring lucid dream.

"Show me," I say.

Then I am standing at the base of a tall stone watchtower. As I look up, the tower sprouts limbs, like a human. Or a cactus.

I step inside. It is pitch black. I feel my way up the steep stairs, past the first level, past the second. My legs are heavy. Climbing is like lifting concrete, but I force my way up the rough-hewn steps to the third level.

I can go no farther.

"Help me," I say. "I am lost."

A low voice speaks into my ear. It is androgynous, neither male nor female. For the first time, I wonder if it is my own voice I am hearing.

"Go back," it says, and the impenetrable dark fills with the ringing of bells.

I was jolted awake. My cell phone was clanging—I had recently changed the ringtone to Bell Tower—and for a moment I was confused, straddling two realities.

I cleared my throat and answered. "Hello?"

"Tenzing? It's Bets, Bets McMurtry." Her voice was low but frantic and laced with fear. "Clara called me! I just got the message. She must have called last night after I went to bed! She's still alive, but you have to find her! She's in trouble!"

"Hang on," I said. *Did I oversleep?* I checked the time, my heart thud-thudding in the disjointed rhythm of panic, but it wasn't even 6:30 A.M. yet. I'd been out for only a few hours. I was okay.

I sat up in bed, shoulder-hunched the phone under one ear, and grabbed a pen and my notebook.

"Okay. What did she say? Tell me exactly."

"She said, she said, *'Ayúdame,'*" Bets wailed. "She said it twice. *'Ayúdame! Ayúdame!'*"

Help me. Something tightened across my chest, like a leather strap.

"That's all she said. Then she hung up. Ten, she sounded so scared!"

"Can you give me the number of the phone she called you from?"

"I think so," Bets said. I waited, but without much hope. "Oh, no. It says 'number unknown.'"

"Bets, I'd like to come get your phone."

"But that's impossible . . . I mean, I don't think I can . . ."

I heard a doorbell ring in the background. "Shit! I have to go. Please, Ten. Find her before it's too late."

"Bets! I need that phone!"

I heard raised voices, and a man came on the phone.

"Detective Norbu? Mark Goodhue. I'm sorry, but we're dealing with an emergency over here. We will get back to you shortly."

Just like that, they were gone. Apologies to the Buddha, but I wanted to throttle both of them.

I jumped out of bed. My eyes itched with exhaustion, but there was no time to lose.

I coffee'd up and was on my way to East L.A. and Clancy's lookout point well before 7 A.M. The key to everything rested inside those cleaning vans, and I was not going to be caught flat-footed a second time. Clara had been missing for almost a week. The odds had been solidly against her survival. But as of earlier this morning, she was alive enough to beg for help. I intended to provide it.

I found the parked Impala and tapped on Clancy's window. He lowered it, stifling a yawn. With his stubbled cheeks and raccoon eyes he, too, resembled—as Bets had so graphically put it—warmed-over roadkill. Three days of round-the-clock surveillance will do that to a man. I was right on his heels in that department. I'd even spooked Tank this morning.

"Yo," Clancy said. "Just in time."

"What's their schedule?"

"Well, in about twenty, if all goes as usual, most of these puppies will pull out, empty. Not the one I been keeping my eyes on, mind you, but most of the rest. Your favorite hasn't moved once. It's like they know why we're here and who we're watching. Weird. Anyway, eight o'clock, out they go. Empty. Two hours later, back they come. Empty. Around three o'clock, same thing. Out, empty; in, empty. Whatever they're transporting ain't from here."

Clancy yawned again.

"Thanks," I said. "Now, go home. Get some solid in-your-bed sleep. Once you wake up, if you're up to it, go to the Aon downtown and watch for this car." I gave him the make, model, and license-plate number of Mark Goodhue's Mercedes and showed him a snap I took of Mark. "If you catch this man on the move, follow him. Are you keeping track of your time?"

"Oh, I'm keeping track," Clancy said. "This rate, I'll be done with my hours and ready to set up on my own before next week!" He ran his hands through his hair, which was a good deal less halo-like. In truth, it more closely resembled a pelt from an unidentifiable animal. "Anything else?"

"You might want to take a shower." I smiled. "You know, before your wife and daughter get back. You look like crap."

"Now who's callin' the kettle black?" He drove off, laughing.

Sure enough, at 8 A.M. sharp, several Hispanic men, all dressed in navy coveralls, a small white logo sewn on their front pockets, appeared like magic from the one-story office building and climbed into their assigned black Ford vans. Not my two bruisers, though, and sure enough, the van I'd spotted at the beach stayed put. I followed the exodus at a discreet distance, as they all drove maybe ten blocks east before pulling into another lot. Whoever was running this operation clearly understood the benefits of mobility in all things—moving targets are much harder to hit.

I pulled over and parked two blocks before their stopping place; my Shelby's noticeable frame and color had me at a distinct disadvantage. Through my windshield, I could see this second lot belonged to a rundown church, its paint peeling and the cross on its roof tilted to one side, as if it, too, had experienced a rough night. I lifted my binoculars. The church's sign was too faded and chipped to read, and it occurred to me I was looking at an abandoned house of God. Any praying going on inside wasn't officially sanctioned.

A side door opened, and a young man with a thick billow of shiny black hair slicked straight back from his brow wheeled out a garment rack. He was about my size and shape, and also wearing the navy coverall uniform. His arms were covered in tats; he could be from the same litter of puppies as Manolo and Pedro. He leaned back on his heels, halting the rack's progress, and the long row of black backpacks dangling from the top pole swung from side to side like bodies.

I snapped some photos, but I already knew the backpacks matched Sofia's. Switching back to my binoculars, I zoomed in and, sure enough, spotted the telltale bulges of tracking devices sewn into the nylon at the base of the packs. Just then, a city bus trundled by and pulled over at a bus stop just past the church. The automatic doors opened and discharged a small army of chattering women in matching navy maids' uniforms. They bustled into the lot. A second Metro bus followed suit, along with several junky cars and pickups, as more and more maids joined the growing throng.

My cell phone buzzed. Heather's text was brief: AT WORK. CALL ME?

SOON, I texted back, as a slight, bowlegged man a few years shy of 40 strutted out of the building with the cocky confidence and build of a bantam rooster. I was betting on this being Chuy Dos, the alpha fowl. He clapped his hands, and the women clustered around him. He was dressed Mexican *caballero*-style, with tight jeans, pointed boots with steel toes, a dazzling white shirt, and a straw hat. He removed the hat and held it over his heart. He began to speak. Some of the maids bowed their heads. I wondered if perhaps they were praying, until one of the women raised her hand and said a few words. Chuy Dos jammed the hat back on his head and talked heatedly, pounding his fist in his hand. Two more women chimed in, and he interrupted again, this time more calmly.

I wished I could read lips. I couldn't tell if Chuy had dissension in the ranks or was just conducting business as usual. He clapped his hands a final time. The maids formed a line, and he distributed the backpacks, sliding them off the pole individually. His young assistant stood nearby, writing on a clipboard, as each woman collected her prize and climbed into her assigned van.

All aboard. The vans squeezed through the exit one by one, like cows through a chute. I decided to follow the last one out, and eased onto the street behind it. I trailed along without incident as the others peeled off. After several turns, we found our way onto the 10, heading west.

Once we were safely on the freeway, and I had put a few cars between us, I called Heather.

"Yes," she said, her tone a little businesslike. Maybe one of her superiors was nearby.

"It's me. Can you talk?"

"Sure. What's up?"

"I have an organ-transplant question."

"How romantic," she said, but I knew Heather. She loved shoptalk, and there was an undercurrent of curiosity in her tease. "Mind you, anything I say about transplants will have to be theoretical," she added. "I take organs out; I've never installed one."

"No problem, I'm looking for basic information. Do you know how much organ transplants cost these days?"

"Which organ? And which hospital? More importantly, with or without insurance?"

"Actually, I was thinking black-market value, but now that you mention it, why would anyone in their right mind go that route, instead of doing it legitimately? Heather, can you hang on a moment?"

The van merged onto Pacific Coast Highway, and I wondered if I was going to wind up back at Mac Gannon's. That would be interesting. I slowed down, once again allowing several cars to move between us.

"Okay," I said. "Where were we?"

"You were wondering who might want to buy black-market organs," she said. "My hunch would be rich people who need them. I'm guessing really wealthy people don't appreciate all the rules that govern transplant medicine. Any medicine, for that matter."

"What kind of rules?"

"You have no idea the hoops you have to jump through. And everybody has to jump. No exceptions. Hospitals like ours are very sensitive to bad publicity. We could lose all our funding if some mogul or other bought his way to the top of the list for a new liver, say, or lung or heart. Organ donation may be the last remaining situation, at least here in Los Angeles, where fame and fortune don't buy faster results. You know the One Percent—they do not like to wait, period. My guess is they'd happily pay black-market prices if they could get that kidney or lung right now. Why?"

"Just curious. So what's a good transplant go for these days?"

Heather paused.

"Round figures," I said.

"I'm not sure, Ten. I'd have to double-check."

"Well, how about if you wanted to purchase an organ?"

"Hello? Not my bailiwick. I mean, I assume a donor-cycle organ is pretty valuable."

"Donor-cycle?"

"Sorry. Morgue lingo. It's what we call motorcycles. Almost all the best organs come from eighteen-to-twenty-five-year-old motorcycle crash victims. They're the healthiest ones around, providing the kid hasn't been hitting the alcohol and cigarettes too hard yet."

Same with young gang members, I thought. "So, who performs the transplants? With these black market organs, I mean?"

"Jesus, Ten! How on earth would I know that? All I do know is we've got one of the best legit guys right here at USC, on our hospital staff. Dr. Kestrel. Perfect name, by the way: he looks exactly like a bird of prey. I must have told you about him."

"Dr. Kestrel? Don't think so." My neck tensed.

"He's a legend, travels all over the world lecturing to other surgeons. The joke around here is that Dr. K. could transplant your soul without leaving a scar. All the nurses are in love with him. They think he's a god; he's that good with his hands."

Had I found Heather's Dr. K.? Did she, too, love him, or did she not?

I swallowed back something bitter-tasting. Now was not the time.

"Sorry I can't be more help," she said.

I remembered the question that had been nudging at me all week.

"Heather, you remember when you told me about that first banger, the one with all the knife wounds?"

"Of course," she said.

"What did you mean when you said he was like the others, only worse? What others?"

"There's been an upsurge in gang hits. At least we think that's what they are. Young Hispanic males with neck tattoos and terrible knife wounds . . ."

"Heather, were they missing any organs?"

"Yes. Yes, they were." Her voice faltered. "Oh, my God, Ten. What are you saying?"

The van moved into the left lane, as its turn signal blinked.

"I can't explain. I'm so sorry, but I have to go. I'm on surveillance. But Heather?"

I took a deep breath. It was time.

"Can I come see you later? You know, to talk?"

"Yes," she said, her voice quieter.

"I'll call you as soon as I'm free."

Her last words were "Be careful."

I moved left as the van turned north up Sunset and accelerated, barely making the traffic light. As I passed the Self-Realization Center on my right, I mentally sent a greeting to the miscellaneous bodhisattvas within. The van snaked up Sunset, through the village of Pacific Palisades, veering right onto Bienveneda.

If memory served, that whole area was a nightmarish maze of tiny cul-de-sacs, but there was no other major thoroughfare to connect to on the other end. In other words, no way out. I continued up Sunset and pulled into the Temescal Gateway Park entrance to wait. Sure enough, the van reappeared on Sunset about ten minutes later. I followed again, at a cautious distance, as it turned south on Amalfi Drive. This time, I kept following. If I had to make a quick getaway, I knew I could head north and eventually hook onto Temescal Canyon and disappear.

Amalfi Drive parallels the Riviera Country Club, and I could practically smell the heady scent of self-satisfaction coming off all those perfectly tended golf course greens. The van passed several sprawling mansions before pulling into the circular drive of a heap of dark brown wood topped with green slate. The thick stand of eucalyptus and sycamore trees had been around long enough to cut off any direct Southern California sunshine.

I kept driving and stopped a few equally musty mansions further up. Why would anyone living in sunny Southern California choose to live in these places? Out came the binoculars. As I watched, a uniformed maid walked up to the front door, backpack in hand. The door opened, and she disappeared inside. The van pulled away, and I stayed back, allowing a spectacular dark green Bentley, the color of "rich," to come between us. The Bentley turned left on Sunset, but the van and I continued north on Amalfi Drive, heading into the hillier part of the Palisades. The van made yet another stop, pulling into yet another circular driveway of yet another mansion, this one a three-story brick manor of ivied turrets and gables, fit for more than a few skeletons and ghosts.

A slight young woman climbed out of the van. Dark brown skin, a single black braid coiled around her head like a garden hose. Her uniform hung loose on her frame. She rang the doorbell, backpack in hand, and I timed it so I could catch sight of the person who opened the door as I slowly rolled by. I prayed the van driver was too preoccupied with his multiple maids and backpacks to notice me skulking around. I was definitely pushing my undercover limit by now.

The occupant of the home was elderly, perhaps 75, spider-thin and elegantly dressed in crisp navy trousers, a striped blouse, and a matching navy sweater with polished gold buttons. She took the backpack from the cleaning lady and patted her on the arm as they walked inside. I pulled around the corner and parked on a side street, Casale Road. Channeling Tank, I licked my palms and attempted to bring a little order to my hair. I grabbed a wrinkled sport coat stashed on the fiberglass shelf in the back of my Shelby for just such emergencies. I slipped it on, took two deep breaths, and walked back to Amalfi Drive. Using a tree trunk to shield myself, I checked the driveway. The van was gone.

I jogged the 20 yards or so to the front entrance. The doorbell echoed inside, as if in a hollow chamber. The door opened, and I was face-to-face with the refined, elegant, but freakishly unlined features of the elderly woman. The air inside was stale, as if she hadn't opened a window in decades. She squinted at me. Large tortoise-shell glasses magnified a startled pair of turquoise eyes, and her hair was a fine puff of pure white. "Yes?" she said, peering closer. Her smile was glued to her face like a postage stamp. "Do I know you?"

"No, ma'am," I said.

"Was I expecting you?"

"Probably not," I said, stifling a smile at this odd question.

"Oh. Well, then." Confusion flooded her eyes, although her smooth forehead, startled eyebrows, and frozen smile didn't change. I wondered if this was what Heather meant by having some "work" done. The total absence of wrinkles was disconcerting. Could she even blink?

"Do I know you?" she asked again, and I realized she might not be operating with the full complement of mental skills. A small movement caught my attention, and I turned. The maid hovered in the kitchen doorway, watching me with dark eyes. I flashed my P.I. license, snapping my wallet shut too quickly to make out details. The maid melted away, as She-of-the-frozen-smile patted her heart with one hand.

"Oh, dear," she said.

I waded right in, pretexting like the fallen ex-monk I am. In my most authoritative cop-voice, I said, "I'm sorry, ma'am, but I'm going to have to search the contents of the backpack you just received. I have reason to believe it may contain illegal contraband."

She made a small, whimpering sound, shooting a panicked look at the backpack, set on a glass-topped table nearby.

"I'm Detective Tenzing Norbu. What's your name, ma'am?"

"Hilda Shwartz Billingham MacRae Sweeney," she recited obediently, as if answering a roll call.

"I'm sorry we have to meet like this, Miz, uh, Miz Sweeney, but I'm just doing my job." I could almost hear Bill guffawing at the clichéd cop-speak. I held out my hand.

She reluctantly passed me the backpack. I noticed this one had no TSA lock.

I unzipped it and neatly stacked the contents onto the table: one wrapped cellophane package of marijuana; two baggies containing about 20 Xanax bars each; 30 or so

Oxycontin pills in a clear plastic vial; a third baggy of pale green pills I couldn't identify on sight but looked suspiciously like Ecstasy. Also, two dishwashing sponges, a pair of rubber gloves, and a spray bottle of blue liquid, all of which I ignored. I calculated the value of the prescription drugs in my head. Not exactly Sofia's bonanza, but I had a feeling that her bloated stash, probably skimmed and stored over time, may have been one of the things that got Sofia killed. According to Manolo, Chuy Dos had little appreciation for jacking.

Assuming all this was for tiny Hilda Sweeney, though, she was a fairly serious doper. Now I had my answer as to how anyone could tolerate living in a BelAir mausoleum. Xanax, anyone?

Suddenly a more authoritative version of Hilda Sweeney pushed through the over-sedated brain cells. "Young man, can't you find anything better to do?"

"I beg your pardon?"

"Can't you go arrest some real criminals, instead of taking away the one source of relief I have?" A single tear escaped, and she brushed it away. "I have acute arthritis, not to mention chronic fibromyalgia. I am in some degree of pain every waking moment of my life, ranging from extreme to excruciating. That contraband, as you put it, is the only thing that makes my world remotely tolerable."

I didn't tell her this, but whatever evidence I found as a private investigator through pretexting would be inadmissible in any court of law. "I'm not going to take away anything from you," I said. I would pass this information along to Bill, but that would be the extent of my intrusion.

"You're not?" She stared, her features as motionless as a lizard's.

"No. I just needed to see what was in the backpack. You can keep it."

"Oh," she said, sounding genuinely relieved. "Well, then."

"But I do have some questions. What is your maid's name?"

"Maria."

"Maria what?"

She waved the question off. "Garcia? Gonzales? You'll have to ask her. I pay the agency directly. In cash."

I stored that particular piece of information for later. I indicated the drugs. "And does the agency provide these every week as well? For cash?"

"I'd prefer not to say." She lowered her voice. "Confidentiality agreement."

"I understand," I said.

"But I'm not addicted," she went on. "If you're careless, these pills can get a real grip on you. I watch how many I take. I have extraordinary self-discipline."

"I believe that."

"I wouldn't have married and buried four husbands if I didn't have will power." Her perfectly pointed nose quivered, as if daring me to challenge her.

"And this method of purchasing painkillers, it's legal?"

Her eyes blinked twice, allaying my earlier concern. But rather than answer, she changed the subject. "I'm sorry, Detective. Where are my manners? Would you care for a little something to drink or eat?" Her hands fluttered. The way she was eyeing her stash, I suspected she had some other snack in mind for herself.

"No, thank you, I'm fine." I excused myself and stepped into the kitchen as Hilda et cetera, et cetera, et cetera Sweeney grabbed the vial of Oxy and disappeared up the curved wooden staircase.

I found Maria hunched over a clunky old-fashioned cell phone, a discarded sponge and spray bottle on the counter next to her. She shoved the phone in her uniform's front pocket as I walked to her side.

"*Hola,* Maria. *¿Habla inglés?*" I asked. She gave her head a shake, her body language somewhere between a scowl and a cringe. I pointed to her pocket.

"*¿Teléfono?* Who were you just calling? Chuy Dos?" She

shook her head again, a little too quickly, and a red flush crept up her neck. Some people should never try to lie.

Well, maybe she was lying about speaking English as well.

I tried again. "Maria. Do you speak English?" I enunciated each word slowly. "Tell . . . the . . . truth . . . and . . . you . . . won't . . . get . . . into . . . trouble. Trouble. Do you understand? *Comprende*?"

She glanced at the kitchen door. "No trouble, please, *señor*," she whispered. "No leave country. Chuy Dos, he promise."

My mind started to race.

"Chuy Dos has promised to keep you here, in America?"

"*Si*. We working for Chuy Dos. He making us legal."

"Working as a maid, cleaning houses?"

"*Si*. Cleaning. And also," she nodded toward the doorway, "bringing the *drogas*."

Why was she telling me this? My inner alarm went off. I grasped her arms, my grip firm.

"Were you talking to Chuy Dos, Maria? Just now, on the phone?"

Her eyes filled, and I felt terrible, but I had to know.

"What did you say to him? Tell me, Maria," I ordered, raising my voice slightly. I stepped away and pounded my right hand into my left fist, as I had seen Chuy Dos do earlier. It worked.

"He tell us to look for white man! I tell him white man coming here," she cried. "In this house!"

I took off, charging up the hill to my car, even as a small part of my brain had to chuckle. I'd been called a lot of names since moving to Los Angeles but never "white man."

I fired up the Shelby. Which way, which way? North or south? I decided to retrace my path toward Sunset and pulled off at Chatauqua to watch and wait. Within moments, Chuy Dos's two favorite burly enforcers screamed by, the driver's meaty paws gripping the steering wheel. I counted three breaths and peeled down Chatauqua until I was safely on the coast highway and headed for Topanga Canyon Boulevard once again. My mind frantically rearranged the tiles on this complex mosaic of a case.

I had encountered a period of several fallow months between leaving the force and fulfilling the numerous legal and professional requirements necessary to become a licensed private investigator. I'd used the unexpected free time to read up on a few things, including starting your own business. I needed help if I was going to start my own; "How to be an Entrepreneur" was nowhere to be found in Dorje Yidam's Buddha-centric curriculum. To my surprise, I'd found that I really enjoyed studying entrepreneurial success stories. And now I couldn't help but admire the business model coming into focus before me, even as it horrified me: procure an army of illegals willing to *do* anything to achieve legal status and have them deliver drugs to upscale clients willing to *pay* anything for a high-quality product and absolute confidentiality. Quality and privacy. With a start, I realized my own little business promised clients the same two services.

Legal and moral issues aside, this distribution system was highly viable, the potential margin of profit enormous. And the cash-based economy meant other drug money could be laundered through the maids-for-hire business. "We Bring Clean to You," indeed. Add to these the possible organ-transplant connection, not to mention who knows what other medical procedures, and you were potentially generating a lifelong need for prescription pain medication that you then would provide. All they needed to do was add babysitting and funeral homes (We Bring Serene to You?), and they'd have a perfect cradle-to-grave operation. As it was, the vertical became horizontal, the horizontal vertical, as business upon business stacked on and supported one another. Sitting high atop this very lucrative pyramid were guys like Carnaté. No wonder so many cartel leaders were popping up on the Forbes list of billionaires. With illegal models like these, they were easily taking home multiple millions every month.

I shook my head at the intricacy. If drug lords—at least the ones who survived over time, like "El Chapo" Guzman, the late Pablo Escobar, and my personal nemesis, Chaco Morales—ever put the same energy and time they invested in creating and executing crimes into building a legitimate empire, they would probably be equally successful, without blood on their hands and a bounty on their heads. But who could truly understand the labyrinth of the criminal mind? The Buddha, maybe, but he was long gone, and as far as I know, he didn't leave a teaching on this subject.

Probably 98 percent of criminals are driven by poverty, addiction, and the misguided notion that they remain invisible while breaking the law. The L.A. jails are full of them, cycling in and out of locked pods, sure that things will be different, the next time.

Then there are the remaining 2 percent, masterminds like Chaco. A rare and dangerous breed, he was truly evil—a modern Moriarty. His addiction was to power, his morality that of a highly intelligent, stone-cold killer.

For me, Chaco was more than just a really bad, bad guy: he was the one who got away. I let him slip, even though I had him wounded on the pavement. It rankled me deeply, like a taunting itch I couldn't quite reach.

I clung to the idea of him, in a most un-Buddhist fashion.

During Chaco's fairly brief reign, at least during my interactions with him, he had built an impressive empire, one that rivaled Guzman's and even Escobar's. Chaco was obviously capable of what entrepreneurs call outside-the-box thinking. Now, apparently, there was a new dog on the block: Carnaté. This new model in front of me—using maids as dope distributors to the wealthy; carving up gangbangers to provide other rich clientele with desperately needed organs; manipulating people's innate greed, on the one hand, and desperation on the other to loosen their moral fiber—had the fingerprints of another Chaco all over it.

Heightened alertness tap-tapped the edges of my mind, coupled with a feather-tickle deep in my belly. I balanced on the borderland between excitement and fear.

According to Bill's sources, including the DEA, Chaco had completely disappeared off everybody's radar, here and in Mexico. Then word came down from the Mexican Army, as well as Los Zetas, the Mexican crime syndicate: Chaco was dead.

I didn't believe it. Chaco and I were hooked at a level I might not understand, but I trusted my instincts on this one. I would know if Chaco Morales had died, as surely as I sensed he was still alive.

CHAPTER 14

I called Heather as I turned into my driveway.

"How about Langer's, say four o'clock? Can you get away that early?"

"Perfect," Heather said.

Once home, I followed the advice I'd given Clancy and took a very long, very hot shower, scrubbing the past two days from my body with multiple rounds of soap and shampoo. I toweled off briskly and scraped what few whisker bristles there were from my non-white Tibetan cheeks. I was still bone-tired, with the charcoal smudges under my eyes to prove it, but at least my skin and hair were clean.

I met my dark-ringed eyes in the mirror. "Are you really ready to tell Heather the truth?" I said out loud. "The whole truth?" Just the words alone made my stomach tighten and the inside of my mouth go dry. As I turned from my reflection, Tank wandered in and gave my ankle a light bump with his nose. He always senses when my emotions start gyrating.

I reached for him, lifting him into my arms as I moved to the edge of my bed to sit.

"Heather and I used to take showers together," I told Tank. "I can't even remember the last time we did that."

Tank turned his emerald green eyes toward me.

"I know. It was so good, and now it isn't." I gathered up the loose fur on Tank's neck, gave it a little tug, and then released it. "I've been trying, Tank. Really trying this time."

This was crazy. In the past week alone I'd been burgled, shot at, stalked, and struck with a pipe. Yet the thought of telling Heather the truth—of upsetting her, maybe even making her cry—was far more terrifying then any one of these assaults. My chest literally clenched with fear at the thought of what lay ahead.

My eyes felt scratchy, and I rubbed them with my palms.

Why was I so scared? Why was I so bad at reading relationship clues? I was a trained detective. Why couldn't I act like one, instead of a . . . a . . . ?

Tank meowed.

"Right, a complete idiot who knows nothing about women."

I rubbed at my eyes again. And suddenly I understood what was going on. I had seen Lola and Maude make exactly this gesture when they were trying hard *not* to cry. Ooph. Maybe it wasn't Heather's tears I feared. Maybe it was my own.

The simple act of owning the truth seemed to be directly connected to a deep well of feeling inside. I took a deep breath and dove further.

My guilt, my avoiding Heather wasn't about eating meat or feeling judged or even sleeping with Cielo. These were evidence of a deeper, much more serious reality. The truth was, I didn't love Heather anymore. I hadn't for some time. And Heather deserved to know. I really didn't want to fail at this relationship, but I was holding onto a chimera, an idea of closeness, as opposed to actual intimacy. One of the biggest clues? I had been in several life-threatening situations, had actually killed two men, over the past few days, yet I hadn't thought to call her, had barely even missed her.

Worse, I had been keeping things from her for months—things I did, things I felt—because I didn't want to upset her. But the more I hid this growing pile of issues from her, the more compelled I was to find fault with her. My mind marveled at this mechanism, all the more amazing because I hadn't been aware of it until now.

And she's been doing the same with me.

I breathed in the painful truth of this and exhaled.

Heather and I were victims of the same patterns, pre-programmed to create the same cycles of suffering in our relationship. Somehow both of us got love and pain entangled at an early age and felt bound to keep repeating the same equation over and over and over again. But it was a lousy form of arithmetic: Love + Pain = Life.

I was way too familiar with this formula. In fact, only one woman had ever offered me an alternative, and I had run Julia off before we could test whether hers might lead to a happier result. The tears finally flowed, for Heather's wounds as well as my own, and the release made room for a sense of calm I hadn't felt in some time.

I put on a clean pair of jeans and a sky-blue dress shirt Martha had given me last year. She'd told me Bill didn't like the color, but I knew better. Bill hadn't worn a shirt this size in decades. Martha was sick of seeing the same three T-shirts every time I came over for dinner. I tucked my shirttails in and added a belt. It was a little warm for the cashmere blazer, but I set it on the bed to take anyway. I felt as if I was getting ready for a first date, rather than a probable breakup, but I wanted to look my best, even if I was heading for the termination of our romance. All rites of passage deserve respect.

I still had two hours—and the unexpected gift of calm. Who knows how long it would last? I moved to the deck and sat in the afternoon haze, mentally sorting through all the recent twists and turns of this case. For a detective, this, too, is working. I had a real mess on my hands. Time to try and make some order out of it and, if I was lucky, work out what to do next. Tank jumped onto my lap, and I let him stay, digging my hands into his soft blue-gray fur. His heartbeat was strong and steady, and his purr sounded like a tiny buzz saw.

Here's what I knew:

CLARA FUENTES. Status: missing, but still alive as of this morning. Last seen in the apartment of her relative, Sofia. Clara's last call on the day she went missing was from her iPhone to an untraceable cell number. (I should call Mike to check on his progress tracking down that number.) Clara had made another call to her boss this morning, a cry for help. This time, the number was blocked, possibly also untraceable.

SOFIA, LAST NAME UNKNOWN. Worked for GTG Services, Inc., as a maid and, apparently, a high-end drug courier. May have been chipping the product. Fled her apartment, which was ransacked. Shot in the back of the head, execution-style. Tongue removed, indicating she had probably talked out of turn, possibly about her employer's illegal activities. I was guessing that the someone she talked to was her cousin, Clara Fuentes. But how had Sofia's killers found out?

MARK GOODHUE. Bets McMurtry's go-to man and an executive at GTG Services, Inc. Perhaps the head of the hydra, but I had my doubts.

TENZING NORBU. Hired to find Clara Fuentes. In the course of his investigation, stumbled (coincidence?) onto the seemingly broad-based and highly illegal shenanigans of GTG, for which he currently has next to no proof. Still no closer to finding his missing person and has no indication other than intuition that the two incidents are connected.

BETS MCMURTRY . . .

My iPhone erupted with pealing bells, inside the house. I stood up, dumping Tank onto the deck, and walked to the kitchen to grab my phone.

Mac Gannon had finally surfaced.

"Hello?"

"Where th' fuck've ya been? And what th' fuck're ya doing, ya stupid fuckin' chink?" he slurred. It occurred to me that *on location* might be Mac's pretexting code for *on a binge.*

"Bets lef' me a message; sh'wuz bawlin' like a baby," he went on. ". . . th' fuck m'I payin' you for?"

"Mac, where are you?"

"None've yer goddam biznizz. Goddamn chinks, takin' over ev'ything."

I didn't have the strength to remind him of my Tibetan heritage. Mac was too far gone to hear me, in any case.

Now he was saying, "Wha're you . . . ? Stupid bitch! Gimme tha'—"

"Is this Mr. Norbu?" I heard. I recognized the Irish lilt, though Constance O'Malley's voice was pitched an octave higher than the first time I'd spoken with her.

"Is Mac okay?" I asked.

"He will be. I do apologize."

Why? I wanted to say. *He's the one being a jerk.* But in my limited experience, guys like Mac Gannon somehow always managed to find women like Constance O'Malley to take care of them—women who are pragmatic, efficient, yet strongly attracted to craziness, as if by controlling another's wild side, they can avoid ever acknowledging their own. Just another example of the human heart's confused relationship math.

"Not to worry," I now said. "Maybe you can have him call me another time. When he's feeling, um, better?"

The relief in her voice was palpable. "Yes, yes, I'll do that. Thank you."

I checked the time again. I should leave in an hour. The temptation to rehearse my lines was strong, but I knew that in order to be fully present with Heather, I would need to listen with mindful attention and answer with my most open self. Besides, whenever I rehearsed difficult conversations, I somehow always gave the imaginary person on the other side lines of dialogue highly favorable to my own point of view.

I went over my mental checklist regarding the case and remembered my follow-up question for Mike about these mysteriously untraceable cell phone numbers. But Mike was no doubt dead asleep. I wouldn't get anything from him for another three hours. I sent him a quick text message instead.

My restlessness was growing. I decided to leave now and take the alternate Topanga Canyon Boulevard route, over the hill to the 101. There was a Woodland Hills car wash right off the freeway where I liked to get my Shelby bathed and waxed. After several days of surveillance, cars, too, can take on the look of homeless vagrants.

The car wash was almost empty, and I watched my baby go through the shampoo, rinse, and hand-dry cycles with a weirdly personal pleasure. Car washes were a secret vice of mine—I couldn't believe it the first time I took my Corolla to one and personally witnessed the mechanical swaying and sudsing and rinsing and waxing, followed by the drying and detailing by human hands. In India, a car wash consisted of one impoverished car-care wallah with a wad of damp rags, which left both you and your sheet metal feeling slightly smeared with guilt.

I'd just tipped the gnome-like man who tended to the windshield when Clancy called.

"Good. You're alive," I said.

"Dude, where you at?"

"Just about to get on the 101 and head downtown."

"Perfect. Because I been watching the Aon, like you asked, and the Mercedes left there about half an hour ago. I followed it, and now we're at some church."

"The abandoned one Chuy uses?"

"What? No, a real one, man, in Echo Park. Catholic. Our Lady of . . ." He paused, as if to read something. "Our Lady of Loretto, whoever she is. And get this. Some kind of big hoo-ha happening here. Bunch of limos starting to pull up. Lotta fancy threads and bling, you feel me? And your man Goodhue, he just got out of the car, and he's in a tux. I'm thinking you'd better get your ass over here."

"What about you? Can you stay?"

"I can stay, a'right. But I still look like shit, not to mention bein' the wrong color for this crowd. Couple of dudes hanging by the front door of the church, they're bodyguards for sure. No way can I get near the action. Why, you busy?"

I thought of Heather and our talk. The Year of the Male Water Dragon, of contradictions and mixed blessings, strikes again.

"I'm in Woodland Hills. I'll be there in half an hour," I said. "Take lots of pictures."

But the contradictory forces had intervened with Heather as well. I was about to call her, when she called me.

"Hey," I said. "I was just about to—"

"Tenzing," she interrupted, "I'm so, so sorry, but there's been a huge pile-up on the 105, several fatalities, and it's all hands on deck here until further notice. Can you forgive me?"

"Absolutely," I said. "Good luck."

I entered the church address in my phone, double-checked the actual location on Google Maps, and kept one eye on the speedometer and another on the freeway for Highway Patrol cars. Estimated driving time, 30 minutes. I was there in 14.

As I turned onto the exit ramp, I had to brake behind the long line of luxury cars snaking toward Union Avenue. To my right a tall, modern spire housing a bell and topped by a wrought-iron cross pierced the sky—a marker, I presumed, for our destination.

The line of cars inched toward Union, past a squat brick building on the left, its face gashed with the spray-painted monograms of gangbangers, and opposite it, a rundown liquor mart sporting a competing wall fresco, with flames, tusked beasts, and its own set of rival tags. Mere yards away, I turned right onto a neat block of homes and apartment buildings trumpeting their values via well-tended rose gardens, fresh coats of paint, and a small, outdoor shrine to the Virgin Mary.

As I continued around the block to get a sense of the geography, I counted three churches, including Our Lady of Loretto, on one short street alone. At the end of it, a barbed wire fence, an abandoned warehouse, and a second graffiti-riddled liquor store announced the end of the safety zone. Churches, three: liquor stores, two. For now, this neighborhood was holding its own.

I drove slowly past Our Lady a second time. The church and adjoining school shared a parking lot, which was already packed with cars, including, I was sure, Goodhue's Mercedes. More limousines, as incongruous in this simple neighborhood as giant peacocks, unloaded families dressed in their best finery. Women and girls fluttered about like tropical birds in brightly colored gowns, their shoulders covered with shawls of lace and embroidered silk. The men and boys wore too-tight tuxedos and brand new suits, with satin bow ties in pastel blue, pink, and lavender.

One little girl, urged by her mother, deposited a bouquet of daisies at the base of a life-sized statue of the Virgin Mary on the church's front lawn. Above the front entrance of the church, another Mary, her hands clasped at her chest in prayer, as if she were about to execute a perfect prostration, balanced on what looked suspiciously like a Viking helmet, horns included. But that couldn't be right, could it?

More guests arrived. Was this a wedding? A religious holiday of some sort? People seemed too perky for a funeral. I was really rusty on my Catholic rites, so any guess would be just that.

With a start, I recognized the two massive men posted at the entrance, stuffed into matching suits the iridescent gray of a shark's skin. They were my stalkers from the beach. I now had my first definitive link between Goodhue and Chuy Dos.

I continued up the block to Council Street and parked at the far end. I shrugged into my black cashmere blazer. I found a yellow silk tie rolled up in the right pocket, where I'd stuck it before my meeting with Mac, and knotted it neatly around my neck. I left my gun in the glove box. This was church, after all.

I made my way on foot to the far end of Mission, where Clancy was stationed with his telephoto lens, digital camera, and laptop.

"Woodland Hills, my ass," he said, glancing at his watch. "You juice your ride or what?"

"I have my ways," I said.

Clancy looked me over and nodded appreciatively. "S'what I'm talkin' about. You'll pass for sure in there. Why you so fine all of a sudden?"

"Always prepared, that's me."

Clancy's eyes widened as he glanced past me. "Whoa. What's up with that?" He picked up his camera and started firing off pictures like shots from a Tommy gun. I turned just as two white Hummer limousines, each triple the length of an ordinary Hummer, glided up to the church. End to end, they took up a third of the block. The first driver, in a black suit, dark glasses, and chauffeur's cap, slid open the passenger door with a flourish. Out spilled a clutch of girls, graduated in age from about 5 to 15, dressed identically in short pink dresses slathered with lace and finished off with something frothy. They reconfigured on the sidewalk, smallest to tallest like nesting dolls, as their male counterparts, in matching pale blue tuxedos and ruffled shirts, tumbled out of the second limo. For a moment, chaos reigned. Then a young woman with an iPad emerged from the girls' limo and briskly paired up the couples.

I counted 14 girls and 15 boys, which left 1 gangly young man, his tuxedo pants short by two or three inches, standing alone. But not for long. A pale pink ballet flat poked from the passenger door of the first Hummer, followed by a second foot. The driver leaned in, his hand outstretched.

After a brief struggle, the owner of the feet emerged in an awkward mass of white shiny material shaped into dozens of roses. The material snapped into a billowing skirt, like an automatic umbrella shooting open.

The girl's face was broad, her body blocky and a little stout, not particularly helped by her gown's tightly laced top and massive skirt. But she had a glorious tumble of black curls, and clutched a small bouquet of pink and cream baby roses. Her dark shining eyes and shy smile made clear to me that this was the most beautiful she had ever felt, and a bittersweet pang unexpectedly invaded my heart area. She lurched over to her waiting prince, who was clumsily shifting from foot to foot. Her dress must have weighed 50 pounds. He reached across the expanse to take her elbow. They were both unable to meet each other's eyes.

"You got a clue what we looking at here?" Clancy asked, his camera clicking away. "I'd say wedding, but that girl's mos' definitely jailbait."

"No idea. But I know someone who might," I said, as I pressed Carlos's number. He answered after one ring.

"Ten," he said. "I'm glad you called."

I felt a pang of guilt. "Carlos, I'm so, so sorry about Sofia," I said. "I meant to talk to you right away, but this case has been nonstop. I know you cared about her. Did you—?"

"Yeah. I identified her." Carlos cleared his throat. "I don't ever want to do that for a friend again. Ever. Have they figured out who killed her?"

"Not yet. But I might be getting close. That's why I called. I have a question for you."

"Anything."

I described the scene in front of me.

"*Quinceañera*," he answered instantly. "When a girl from our culture turns fifteen, it's huge. Kind of like sweet sixteen, plus a debutante's coming-out party, plus I don't know, maybe a coronation, all rolled into one. I'm guessing you're outside their family church, probably the one she's grown up in, for a *misa de acción de gracias*—you know, a Catholic mass to give thanks for her, welcome her to womanhood, celebrate her purity, that kind of thing."

As I watched, the two lines of children processed from the sidewalk to the church entrance, youngest first. "What's with all the other kids?"

"*Damas* and *chambelanés*," Carlos said. "They're friends, cousins, kids of their parents' friends—each one symbolizes a year of her life—though usually you only have fourteen total, not fourteen of each! They're like her entourage, you know? It's strange, though. Usually a *quinceañera* is on Saturday, so the entire congregation can attend."

"Maybe they want to keep it private. That would explain the bodyguards." As I watched, the birthday girl took a step and stumbled. Her beet-red escort barely kept them both from disappearing into the folds of white satin. My heart went out to them. Fifteen—I wouldn't go back to that time of my life if you promised me an ocean of bliss.

"Well, whoever is hosting this *quinceañera* has dough, for sure," Carlos added. "I've also never heard of stretch Hummers for the kids. That's going to be some follow-up fiesta."

"What do you mean?"

"Oh, the church service is just the beginning. You're in for a long night, Ten. Hope you're up for it. You think her dress is big? Wait until you see her cake."

"Where do they usually hold these fiestas?"

"Depends. My second cousin in Mexico had hers outside, at her *madrina's*—sorry, godmother's—orchard. Sometimes people just rent a big hall near their church. But this one? This one sounds like it could wind up anywhere. The richer the parents, the bigger their need to show off. Or maybe the godparents are paying. That can happen, too."

The burly bodyguards surveyed the street, finally empty of scurrying last-minute guests, and stepped inside the church. The tall wooden doors closed behind them. I thanked Carlos and hung up. I stared at the doors, my mind racing.

"Clancy, any idea who the girl's parents are?"

Clancy shook his head. "Hard to tell. But I did snap just about everyone who came in. Only one dude wearing a corsage, and his old lady, too. Here, take a look."

Clancy pulled up his pictures and scrolled through them one by one. "Here's Goodhue," Clancy muttered. Mark Goodhue had arrived solo, looking like a stiff penguin in his tuxedo. The sequence of shots showed him quickly entering the church, head down, not talking to anyone. I kept skimming the long parade of dressy couples. Some went straight inside; others clustered by the entrance to chat.

"Stop!" I said, pointing. "There's Chuy Dos!"

Chuy Dos was almost unrecognizable in his immaculate tuxedo, without his cowboy hat, but his bowlegged, puffed-chest stance gave him away. He held the arm of a slight woman in a long turquoise gown, crowned with an elaborate crest of matching feathers. Chuy Dos was half-waving at someone ahead of them and smiling, but there was something off about his smile.

"Clancy, can you zoom in on his face?"

Clancy filled the screen with the narrow features of Chuy Dos. Now it was clear as day. His mouth was as much grimacing as smiling, his eyes wide and frozen. He resembled a mongoose facing a cobra.

"Who is he looking at?" I wondered out loud.

"Lemme see if I can figure it out," Clancy said. He clicked back and forth between photographs, before giving a short nod.

"I think maybe it's this dude. Arrived right before them. Look how the bodyguards . . . how everyone's eyes are on him and his old lady. And like I said, they're the only ones wearing flowers. Wow, she is one hot mama!" He tipped the screen toward me.

I stared. The woman was stunning, although she hardly looked old enough to have a teenage child. Her skin was like amber honey, and thick black hair cascaded in soft waves over her toned shoulders. A pair of delicate eyebrows perched over dark, fathomless eyes, and her lips were lush and mysterious, curved ever so slightly upward, as if inviting you into a secret world of promise. Her sparkling, emerald-green dress clung to her curves and then flared out, spilling onto the sidewalk in sequined waves. A small spray of roses, cream and pink like those in the girl's bouquet, was pinned to one shoulder.

She resembled a sea goddess. A married sea goddess—a huge diamond solitaire and thick gold wedding band took up most of her ring finger. If she was the mother of that stocky, self-conscious girl, I understood why I had felt a commiserative twinge; glittering tiara or not, the child would never outshine her mother in anyone's eyes, most especially her father's. I, too, had grown up under the shadow of two larger-than-life parents. Makes it hard to thrive.

I shifted my attention to the woman's companion, presumably her husband and the father of the girl. His left arm was locked around her shoulders, and his ring finger, like hers, sported a thick band, this one studded with diamonds. He was wearing dark glasses, and his chin was tucked, so it was difficult to make out his features. His hair was a fuzzy nest of curls, a lighter shade of brown than his fashionable, three-day-old beard. His shoulders were wide, his torso trim. He looked about 35, maybe a touch older than his wife. As I studied his image, though, my gut sounded a warning, like sonar detecting hidden danger beneath the surface of things.

I wish I could see his eyes.

He had a single scarlet rose, the color of fresh blood, pinned to the lapel of his tuxedo. His right arm hung at his side, thick fingers slightly curled. In fact, his whole body seemed coiled. I scrolled through the next few photographs and noticed, as Clancy had pointed out, the tension, if not terror, emanating from everyone around this quietly threatening man. His mere presence activated an internal Code Red, the highest state of readiness, reserved for terrorists.

Terrorists—and cartel kings.

I was looking at Carnaté.

"I'm going inside," I said to Clancy.

"For real?"

"Don't worry. My mother was Catholic," I said. And I crossed myself, to prove it.

I slipped inside the church. It was at least ten degrees cooler than outside and as dim and dusky as I'd hoped. As my eyes adjusted, I counted some 60 wooden pews, 30 on each side of the carpeted middle aisle. Each pew seated about eight or ten people, and almost all were full, which meant there were close to five hundred people in the church. At first, the bodyguards were nowhere to be seen. Then I spotted them sitting about halfway up on the far left, their broad shoulders and thick necks unmistakable.

The back pew still had a couple of empty seats on the aisle. I moved to it and paused. My body reached back decades to retrieve the muscle memory of genuflecting while making the sign of the cross on my chest. The 11-year-old me had been briefly entranced by the mysterious rituals in Saint Joseph, the Catholic church in Paris my mother had dragged me to during one of her "confused" spiritual phases, this one brought on by a short-lived attempt at sobriety. After a few months, her belief had lapsed—right before she did—but the ingrained shame and longing for forgiveness remained alive inside her to the end. She died of a massive drug-and-alcohol overdose a year and a half later. When I found her, collapsed on our living-room floor, I also found a tiny gold cross I had never seen before hanging from a delicate chain around her mottled neck.

I looked around the church. The architecture was simple but elegant. Several small shrines lined the walls, complete with clusters of votive candles and fresh flowers—offerings laid at the feet of statues of Mary, with or without her infant child. Mary as a bride. Mary as a mother. Mary as a wife. Mary grieving the loss of her son. The natural light was muted, filtered through tall windows of brilliant stained glass. Looming over everything was a large wooden crucifix above the altar.

Standing at the front, the girl in white faced the crowd, her shoulders hunched with self-consciousness. Her retinue spilled out on either side of her. Mark Goodhue, Chuy Dos, and Chuy's wife sat in the front left pew, and the Sea Goddess was seated on the right. Up by the altar, an elderly priest gazed up at the lectern, where the man I suspected to be Carnaté was reading a lesson in accented but understandable English. He kept his eyes firmly pinned on the text in front of him; so once again, I couldn't get a clear look at his eyes.

He seemed to be sneering. Then I realized that a thin scar, probably from a knife wound, had pulled the left corner of his mouth into a permanent sneer. Or maybe he'd always had the sneer inside, and the scar had merely allowed his mouth to catch up.

To my surprise, the service was in English, perhaps as a favor to Goodhue.

"'Then the Lord extended my hand and touched my mouth,'" the man at the lectern read, "'saying, See, I place my words in your mouth.'"

He turned up the volume, and people shifted in their seats. "'This day I set you over nations and over kingdoms! To root up and to tear down! To destroy and to demolish! To build and to plant!'"

The ringing voice faded into silence, but there was no peace in the collective stillness. More like a palpable sense of suppressed dread.

"The word of the Lord," he concluded, his misshapen mouth in a half smile.

"Thanks be to God," came the reply from the assembled. The man slipped on his sunglasses and rejoined his goddess, draping his arm around her shoulders possessively.

It was the *quinceañera*'s turn next, but she fared less

well. Her voice was trembling and barely audible. I caught a few words, like "daughter" and "Mary, Mother of Jesus," before she blurted out "Amen!" loud and clear.

The priest smiled at that and proclaimed, "Gloria Teresa Garcia, may God, who has begun this good work in you, bring it to completion."

Good. I now had a first, middle, and last name with which to work. The priest sprinkled Gloria Teresa with water. She maneuvered to the right of the altar and placed her bouquet of roses at the foot of a statue of the Virgin Mary, draped in blue. The priest then motioned to the left front pew. Chuy Dos joined Gloria Teresa at the altar and handed her a black leather Bible. Goodhue stiffly followed suit, passing over a delicate set of prayer beads with a silver cross dangling from one end. *Rosary beads,* I corrected myself.

I looked around. The closed eyes, the carved deities, the flowers and beads, the memorized words of devotion and thanksgiving, the chanting in unison, the hymns of praise—was any of it so different from the Buddhist rites and rituals that defined so much of my early life? Each tribe comes with its own spiritual instructions and safety measures, but all are aimed at assuaging terror around the inevitability of death. The only real difference I could see was that other tribes felt justified in killing their enemies in the name of their beliefs, while mine was more likely to immolate itself.

The deep blast of a pipe organ startled me out of my reverie, as the congregation joined in on a haunting hymn about a soul magnifying its lord. People were reaching for their coats as they sang; the service must be winding down. I had escaped notice for now. Time to return to my car and post Clancy at the other end of Union Avenue, in order not to lose the troops en route to the party. As for me, if I managed to lose two white stretch Hummers in Echo Park, I would personally shred my P. I. license, with Tank as my witness.

CHAPTER 15

Clancy left first, and I fell in several cars behind the girls' Hummer. Within minutes, we were back on the 101 South, but not before the first limo's sunroof opened, and the birthday girl popped her tiara-clad head out to blow kisses at a couple of astonished homeless men stationed at the freeway entrance. I liked her more and more.

I had no idea where we were going, only that our destination was somewhere west of downtown, off the 10 freeway. Forty minutes later I had my answer, as both Hummers, followed by a steady stream of Beamers, Benzes, and rented town cars, exited on Fourth Street in Santa Monica and snaked their way seaward, until they crossed Ocean Avenue and passed underneath the iconic arched sign of the Santa Monica Pier.

The cars were headed for the pier parking lot, half of which was taken up by a giant, blue-striped tent. Beyond the tent I could see the smaller neon sign announcing the local carnival of delights called Pacific Park. Beyond that lay the ocean, swabbed with a broad brushstroke of gold by the setting sun. A pale crescent moon was barely visible above the skyline.

I called Clancy.

"Yo," he said. "I haven't been to the Santa Monica Pier since high school, when I rode the old coaster, high on weed."

"No rides for you today. Sorry. I need you to keep your eye on the lot, in case Goodhue or Chuy Dos takes off. Especially Goodhue," I said. "He's still our main target."

"What about you?"

"Be a shame to waste my party clothes," I said.

"Sounds reckless," Clancy warned.

"I'm running out of time," I said.

Uniformed parking valets were checking the cars against their lists, so I detoured up the hill then drove back down Appian Way and into the public "Hot Dog Stick" lot, named after the tiny shack next to it that is famous for its corn dogs.

I made my way back to the entrance to the pier, as more and more cars inched along the boardwalk leading toward the parking lot. The empty Ferris wheel, roller coaster, and numerous other rides awaited the onslaught of guests, as did a courtyard of fast-food franchises. Whoever was paying for this had booked the entire pier and had no doubt bought off all the concessions as well. Paid them handsomely, I thought, given the benign expressions on the vendors' faces. A small fleet of catering trucks told me that high-end food was also on the menu; stacked crates of champagne, tequila, and Mexican beer promised a high-octane party. I estimated the price tag for Gloria Teresa's fiesta at well over $100,000. Pretty nice party.

A familiar clip-clopping sounded behind me. I turned, half-expecting another pair of reins to be handed to me. Instead, I was greeted by the startling sight of Gloria Teresa sitting sidesaddle on a gigantic white horse at the far end of the wooden byway, her skirt spilling down one flank like a blanket of roses. Her escort was holding the bridle and looked about as happy doing so as I would be.

iPad Lady directed them off to one side, as the two Hummers let out the rest of the entourage at the pier entrance, reversed course, and drove away. The pedestrian walkways flanking the wide wooden thoroughfare were rapidly filling up with guests entering on foot. Gloria Teresa's royal court hustled past the guests and into the tent.

Meanwhile, several harried uniformed guards were checking people against their guest lists. It seemed as good a time as any to join the crowd. I affixed myself to a large, multigenerational family shuffling up to the entrance. As soon as we reached the checkpoint, I bent down to "retrieve" a quarter I had palmed from my pocket and then tapped one of the young daughters on the shoulder.

"Excuse me, did you just drop this?" I asked, smiling and holding out the quarter.

She shook her head, smiling as well.

"Are you friends with Gloria Teresa?" I continued.

"Yes," she said, as our guard tried to count heads. "She's in the class ahead of me at school."

And we were inside.

Just in time, it seemed.

"Señoras y Señores, ladies and gentlemen!" The female leader of a mariachi band tapped on her microphone and beckoned everyone to the front of the tent. Like her nine male bandmates, she was dressed in a ruffled white shirt with a soft red tie, black tuxedo pants striped with silver studs and belted in red, and a black-and-silver bolero jacket with a jaunty matching sombrero. Behind her, I counted several horns and electric guitars, as well as a hefty drum set. "Please join Gloria Teresa's family in welcoming their *princessa* to her ball!" the leader called out.

Horse and rider, led by Gloria Teresa's attendant, made their way up the wide wooden thoroughfare and into the tent, their entrance marred only by the steed's decision to lift his tail midway for a quick dump, thus confirming my opinion of his kind.

I stuck close to my adopted family, who moved inside with the rest of the crowd and positioned themselves at one end of the tent. We held our collective breath as Gloria Teresa slid off the horse and into the arms of her escort. He staggered slightly but successfully deposited her onto the ground, to huge applause. I ducked behind the crowd, trying to keep a low profile.

More guests pushed inside and pooled around a large

dance floor, in front of the dais where the band had set up. A gigantic, three-tiered cake, decorated with frothy flowers and glittering candies, took up most of a table next to the dais. Set beside it, under a glass dome, was a slightly disturbing porcelain doll with frozen eyes, black sausage curls, and a diamond tiara, dressed in a white gown identical to Gloria Teresa's and looking eerily like her.

I scanned the room. Goodhue, Chuy Dos, and the couple I assumed were the girl's parents were downing shots of tequila at a bar in one corner. The bandleader again tapped on her mike.

"Señoras y señores, a special treat by Gloria Teresa, and her *chambelanes!*" The drummer rolled out a fanfare of sorts, and all the escorts moved to the middle of the dance floor, arranged themselves in a circle, and dropped to one knee, their heads bowed. Gloria Teresa waited until the guitars started up, then made her way to their center of the circle, measuring her steps to match the three-four time. The choreographed number that followed was part waltz, part theater, with random curtsies and bows thrown in for good measure, as Gloria Teresa spun from boy to boy. After a few minutes, the other girls joined in, but Gloria Teresa was the star of this show. She was a surprisingly graceful dancer, and her eyes sparkled. She finished with a final deep curtsey, to thunderous applause. Her companions left and the woman in green approached her daughter with a pair of white satin high heels.

"Let's all welcome Gloria Teresa's beautiful mama!"

The crowd burst into warm applause. Clancy and I had guessed right.

Next to the tall, elegant sea goddess, Gloria Teresa quickly regressed into an awkward child. As she struggled with her voluminous skirt, a slight frown creased her mother's brow.

I willed her to succeed. *You can do it, Gloria Teresa. I know you can.*

Finally, she managed to kick off her ballet flats and slip into the heels.

"And now, the moment we've all been waiting for!" the band leader announced. "Señorita Gloria Teresa and her papa will perform their father-daughter waltz."

The man with the blood-red rose in his lapel strode across the dance floor smiling and took his daughter in his arms. I tried to push a little closer, but no one was budging. I craned my head to get a better look, but I could only catch glimpses of father and daughter as they spun around the dance floor in tight, careful circles.

My heart opened, warming at the sight of this twirling pair, and a second girl, a nine-year-old redhead, hurtled her way into my consciousness, propelled by trust and roller blades. I remembered, too, the light that blazed in Bill's face whenever his twins, Lola and Maude, ran into the room.

Maybe if I had a daughter, I'd be okay as a father.

The couple circled closer, and I registered two very different smiles, one sweet, one slashed by a brutal scar. My heart chilled unexpectedly.

I know this man, I thought.

He maneuvered his daughter to a spot near where I stood and for a split second, looked directly at me. I took an awkward step backward—and felt the hard muzzle of a gun pressing between my shoulder blades.

"Do not make a sound, señor," I heard, as strong hands gripped my arms. There were two of them. They steered me outside, the gun barrel incentive enough not to cause a fuss. The sky was now dark and peppered with stars. Some of the party guests had already made their way onto the roller coaster, and ecstatic shrieks erupted overhead. A sharp *pop,* like the report of a revolver, made my heart stop, until I heard three more and placed the sound. A partygoer was exploding balloons with darts at one of the game booths.

I craned my neck around and saw that I was in the meaty grip of Chuy Dos's two enforcers. There was no sign of Clancy as they dragged me down a set of steep wooden steps to the beach, then pulled me underneath the pier. The dank air smelled of dead fish and urine. The ocean was maybe five yards away, and inky waves slapped at the peeling wooden pylons.

"I come in peace," I told them. Thug One's response was to shove me against a wooden pillar, while Thug Two patted me down. He pulled out my phone and slung it sideways into the shallow seawater.

"Really? My iPhone?"

Next, he removed my shoes and socks, and tossed them into the oily scum. Now I was out about $700.

"Tell Carnaté I expect reimbursement," I told them. They exchanged a startled glance. So I had guessed right—not that being right helped me any. Thug One bound my wrists behind my back with nylon rope, then moved a couple of steps away and took off his suit jacket. His avid smile was just enough warning. I braced myself.

They proceeded to take turns landing blows, as peals of delight rained down on us from the gyrating rides overhead. After what felt like hours of assault but was probably only minutes, to my relief a phone buzzed. Thug One answered it, listened, then muttered something in Spanish to Thug Two. By now, my lip had swollen to twice its normal size, and my left ear felt like it was made of sea sponge.

The thugs grabbed me by the shoulders. Powerless, I felt like a terrified toddler locked in a nightmare between a pair of giant kidnappers—only this nightmare was real. As they dragged me out from under the pier, my bare heels dug parallel trenches in the sand. I hung like dead weight between the two men. I wasn't going to make things easy for them, not after they'd roughed me up and tossed my shoes and phone.

They strong-armed me across the damp, packed sand to a beach cabaña close to the shore. The rest of the beach was deserted. They shoved me inside the cabaña, and suddenly I was face to face with Carnaté, reclining like a Roman emperor on a striped canvas chaise lounge that took up half the room. He had discarded his tux and tie and exchanged his starched white shirt for a short-sleeved Hawaiian one, black with hot-pink flamingos. He still wore dark glasses, though night had long since fallen. Two battery-operated lanterns cast sharp shadows across his face. An open bottle of chilled Pacifico beer was sweating beads of condensation on a white plastic side table. I couldn't blame it. Next to the bottle lay an ominous companion: a Glock 17, its barrel snugly fitted with a silencer.

Carnaté waved an arm toward the only other piece of furniture, a low, blue canvas beach chair, its seat slung like a hammock between wooden arms.

"Sit," he ordered.

I lowered myself awkwardly onto the chair, my knees almost touching my chin. I winced; my bruises were beginning to sing to me. I peered up at Carnaté, again feeling like a small child trapped in a world of big people. I was unarmed, trussed up, and aching from top to bottom. But I still had all my teeth—and I could still do battle with my mind.

I chuckled.

"You find this situation funny?" he snapped.

"It's the look," I said. I cocked my head. "I can't decide if you're reaching for Caligula or surfer-dude."

He said nothing, but a ripple of irritation passed across his face. Score one for me.

He pointed to the beer. *"Cerveza?"*

I shook my head. "None for me thanks, but please help yourself. With a wife like that, you need to keep up your strength."

Another ripple of anger. I changed tactics. I wanted to keep him off balance but not push him to the point where he reached for that gun.

"So, I take it you like meat?"

This time, Carnaté merely seemed startled. "Meat?" he said.

"Yeah. Your name's Carnaté, right?"

He burst out laughing, and just as I realized I had made a huge mistake, he pulled off his dark glasses.

My world imploded.

The lighter hair, the scar, even the slimmer body—they were all decoys, and they had done their job well. But the flat, cold eyes? Those I would know anywhere. *You can't be here. You're dead.* In my dream, I had been addressing my father. But sometimes even lucid dreams get confused. Chaco Morales, *El Gato* of the nine lives, had made expert use of chemicals and a plastic surgeon's knife to buy himself at least one more.

"Carnaté," I repeated, realizing. "Incarnated."

"Yes," he said. "Or in my case, reincarnated." He spread his arms. "I came back, amigo."

I took a deep breath, thoughts darting around my skull like frantic moths looking for a way out.

"You didn't think I'd miss my own daughter's *quince anño*, did you?" he said. "What kind of father would that make me?"

I stayed quiet, as I tried to work myself free of the bind I was in, mentally as well as physically.

"I saw you at the back of the church," Chaco went on. "Goodhue said you wouldn't show up, that you were following another lead entirely, but I knew better."

"The police know I'm here," I lied.

"No, they don't," he said. He picked up the Glock and fondled it, like a favorite toy. My throat closed. Then he put the gun back down again. "Let's talk, shall we?"

I finally hit on a ploy—pathetic, but better than nothing.

"In that case, I think I will have that beer," I said. "But you're going to have to free my hands, unless you want to feed me my bottle like a baby."

Chaco rolled to his feet easily and stepped outside. I

heard voices. So the two gorillas were still there, keeping watch. Too bad. I struggled to sit up but couldn't maneuver out of the chair. Thug Two followed Chaco back inside. He was holding an opened switchblade.

He crossed to my chair and tipped me forward in a rough embrace, as he reached around behind me to slice through the nylon rope binding my wrists. My nostrils filled with his rancid body odor, a mixture of stale garlic and stupidity. As the blood rushed into my numb hands, multiple pricks of pain caused my fingers to flex. Thug Two grunted and pushed me back into the chair, then nodded to Chaco and returned to his post outside.

Chaco handed me a beer from a cooler next to his chaise lounge. I struggled forward to take the bottle, my hands still tingling.

I nodded toward the Glock. "Hasn't anybody told you that silencers are against the law?"

His turn to chuckle. "When they kill me, I don't think it will be for owning a silencer."

"When?"

"Do you know the life expectancy of a man in my line of business?" he said. "The surgeon did well to make me look so young, but I recently passed the age of forty-five. In narco-years, that makes me at least a hundred and fifty."

He took a deep pull of beer. I did the same, taking a moment to enjoy the yeasty burst of what might turn out to be my last one ever.

"Interesting you can recognize that truth," I said. In spite of myself, I've always been fascinated by the inner workings of a genius, evil or not. And whatever else Chaco was, he was brilliant in his chosen field.

"The bargain is implicit," he explained. "We live the life of myths and legends—in my country, ballads are written, films are made about men like me—but our time on this earth is short and always, always terminates in prison or the grave. As for me, when it comes to that, I will make

211

sure to die a spectacular death, out in the open, rather than behind bars, like an animal."

"Death by cop, in a hail of bullets," I said.

He eyed me. "Something like that." His smile was more like a grimace, sinister and cruel, or maybe that was the scar talking. "For one such as me, there is no other way to live but this—close to the flame that eventually must destroy me. In that sense, you and I are alike. Otherwise, you would not be sitting here across from me, inviting death."

A swell of cheers reached our cabaña, as the band returned to the dais and began a new set. This mariachi song was more old-school. Chaco tapped one hand on his thigh, keeping time.

"I'd offer to do a hat dance with you," I said, "but I lack rhythm."

Chaco laughed again. "See, this is why I like you. Everyone else is always so afraid to joke with me." He finished off his beer and pulled a new one from the cooler. "Another for you?"

I shook my head. He saluted me with the bottle before drinking deeply. I felt like I had entered a fourth dimension of reality. I was sitting in a cabaña on a beach in Santa Monica, California, sharing beer and conversation with one of the FBI's most wanted men—a cartel kingpin, a titan in the global drug market, whose annual earnings probably figured in the billions, counted out in laundered dollars and paid in buckets of blood. In Mexico alone, Chaco and his equals had claimed more than 50,000 lives just in the past five or six years, not to mention the damage caused to their customers here in the United States. Yet nothing seemed to slow them down. I faced a monster not only surviving the global recession but thriving during it, by being both ruthless and nimble.

A man everyone assumed was dead.

Well, if I was going to die at the end of this conversation, at least I would die better informed. One thing I knew for sure—men like Chaco did not succeed in a vacuum. The Buddha says the root of all suffering is our innate desire to avoid pain and cling to happiness. As long as that desire exists, ambitious people will make money fulfilling it.

As if reading my mind, Chaco said, "This country you live in is insatiable. More, more, more, always more. Do you know how much I spent on Gloria Teresa's fiesta? Almost two hundred thousand dollars!" He shrugged. "Do you think it is accidental that the world's biggest provider of drugs and the world's hungriest consumers just happen to share borders? Porfirio Diaz, my country's president in the last century, had it right: '*Pobre Mexico*—'" He caught himself and switched to English. "'Poor Mexico, so far from God and so close to the United States.'"

"And yet your wife and daughter live here."

He shrugged again. "The Mexico I grew up in no longer exists." He changed the subject. "Have you ever been shot, Señor Ten?"

I pointed to the scar on my temple. "Once, but it was just a graze."

"Four times for me. Death and I have danced cheek to cheek four times." He nodded to himself, as if remembering the gun battles fondly.

"What am I doing here?" I asked.

Chaco set down his beer quietly and fixed me with his flat, unblinking eyes. "Last year, because of you, a good deal of my product was confiscated. My brother Pepé was arrested, along with my wife's brother. They remain behind bars. Some might see that as a disaster. I saw it as a blessing. They were becoming too close to each other. Pepé was on that *panga* moored in the cove without asking my permission, and my wife's brother was not supposed to be anywhere near that aspect of my business."

He smiled. "You thought you caused me harm. You did not. Thanks to you, the two biggest threats to my authority were removed, without my having to lift a finger against my own blood. And by exposing the weakness in my smuggling method, you inspired me to make much-needed changes. To reinvent myself, if you will. To be born again. Not only that, you forced me to move away from a saturated market, to diversify. I have tripled my income since we last met."

He lifted his bottle again, as if toasting me, and drained it.

"You're welcome," I said.

He grabbed beer number three. "For me," he continued, his voice expansive, "there are no mistakes. Every personal interaction offers either an opportunity for pleasure or a lesson to be learned. But with you, I seem to experience both outcomes at once."

"What have you done with Clara Fuentes?" I said.

Chaco narrowed his eyes, as if calculating the worth of my words. "I understand you very well, Señor Ten. You are a man who does not give up. Your actions over the past week? They have added—what to call it?—a certain spice to my life. And yet, I find myself having to once again dismantle what I have so recently built. Because of you." His voice hardened. "Immigrants who have found a way to blend into this country will be returned to their previous hell because of you. People in constant pain will go back on the streets to quench their need for relief because of you. So I ask you, who is bad and who is good?" He gave a little shrug. "Still, you impress me. Even as I know I must kill you, I have come to admire you. This is not a frequent occurrence in my world. In fact, I cannot remember feeling such esteem for another man since my mentor, years ago."

"Who was your mentor?"

He smiled. "You see? You do not ask why I admire you. Instead you ask about my mentor. Always choosing knowledge over praise. A man with such a loose hold on his ego is very powerful—and very dangerous." He leaned forward. "Tell me, Señor Ten, what do you think of me, now that we've had a chance to talk?"

"I think you're surprisingly intelligent," I said. *For a greedy, murdering brute.*

"You expected me to be an illiterate peasant." It was a statement, not a question, but I decided to answer anyway.

"Yes," I said.

"I am a peasant, that much is true. But I spent four years in a Mexican prison when I was very young, and I was befriended by a brilliant man, a Ph.D. in philosophy, who was a victim of a roundup of corrupt bureaucrats by corrupt politicians. He taught me English and made me read at least one book a week. I owe everything to Tio José."

Good old Uncle Joe. Touching. "Is he still alive?"

Chaco shook his head. His face darkened, and my blood chilled at the look in his eyes. He grabbed his beer and chugged it. He reached for another, his fourth.

I took note.

"What happened to José?" I said.

"He died," Chaco said. "It was necessary. After four years he could not control himself. He was desperate with loneliness. He begged to touch me. He tried to touch me."

"Ah. So you killed him. That must have been hard on you."

In this way, at least, Chaco proved no different from the rest of humanity, today or back in the time of the Buddha. He took a long pull of beer to numb the pain of an unhealed wound. "I did not want to be touched. He knew that. He had weaknesses. In prison, as in life, one must control one's weaknesses."

I probed deeper. "He should have shown you more respect. A man of your brilliance."

Chaco nodded. He was now on beer five, in addition to several shots of tequila he'd downed earlier at the party. His eyes still looked deadly, but they were coated with the sheen of too much alcohol.

I might just have a chance.

I tested the looseness of his tongue.

"Tell me," I said. "How did you evolve from a peasant to the man you are today?" I waved toward the party. "A man who can afford all this?"

"It is not so difficult to reinvent yourself. You, of all people, should understand this. How? Simple." He held up a fist and unfolded three fingers, one at a time. "Bribes. Bribes. And bribes." He laughed softly, glancing at the gun. "Also violence, but only as a last resort. Alas, narcos do not have recourse to the courts to enforce their laws, as others do."

"But how did you get your start?"

He shrugged. "Family business," he said. "Some people inherit a farm. I inherited a smuggling route. Turned out, I was very good at smuggling."

"What about now? Goodhue? And Chuy Dos, for that matter? They don't strike me as your equals in any way."

"You really don't know, do you?" Chaco said. "You really don't know how far the greed reaches."

For some reason, this comment bothered me more than any of his others. I opened my mouth to dig further, when the band's rousing rendition of a nationalistic march wafted across the sand, amplified by the drunken singing of the fiesta revelers. Chaco put one hand over his heart and slid directly into the land of the maudlin.

"You want to understand me? To understand how I ripened from peasant to warrior? Listen to my country's song. 'War! War without a truce!' We are called to shake the earth at its core!" He made a fist. "I feel the suffering of my people, Señor Ten. Here!" He thumped his chest. "In my heart, in my blood! Do you have any idea what it feels like to live for centuries with the heel of the enemy's boot on your neck?" His face looked like that of a gargoyle, his twisted lip menacing in the half-light of the cabaña.

"Yes," I said. "Although in my case, the boot is Chinese."

"S'not the same," he said. "S'not the same at all."

Good. He was starting to slur his words, and his inner

victim was surfacing. Deep down, most people think their suffering is worse than everyone else's. I don't buy the premise. Three hundred years of suffering is no better or worse than three years or three seconds. Suffering is suffering.

Chaco's eyelids had lowered to half-mast. His reaction time, not to mention his aim, would be sorely tested in a fight. I calculated the distance between my right hand and the Glock. Chaco's head dropped toward his chest.

I started to shift my weight forward.

He moved like a striking snake and pointed the muzzle straight at my sternum, his finger curled around the trigger. So this was it, then. I had completely underestimated my enemy—again.

I closed my eyes and silently repeated *Om mani padme hum.*

I'm sorry, my friends, I thought, *sorry for my failure to save others, to save myself.*

"Get out," I heard.

I opened my eyes. The gun was still trained on me, Chaco's hand as steady as a rock. Why was he sparing me my life?

"Get out," he said again. "And stay the fuck out of my business. I love my wife, Señor Ten. She was Miss Tijuana. Did you know that? So beautiful, my Gloria Teresa. I went under the knife for her. Risked my life to return here for her. Named our only child for her. And I promised her no blood would be shed on a day that celebrates our daughter's purity."

He sighed. "I have kept my promise. But if I ever lay eyes on you again, I will not only kill you, I will slaughter you like a pig, and mail your dripping parts to your loved ones, free of charge."

Any semblance of intelligence—of humanity, for that matter—had left his face. He glittered with malice, and for that instant, I believed in the Satan of his Catholic faith. Carnaté, evil incarnate.

"And just so we're clear, you were never here." His eyes were slits. I half-expected a forked tongue to flicker from between his lips. "And neither was I."

I stood upright, expecting at any moment to feel the gut-punch of a close-range bullet and then to feel nothing at all. I walked to the opening in the cabaña and ducked outside. The two bodyguards were gone. Maybe they were finally getting to dance.

I started to run, alone in the dark except for a sliver of moon, a devil, and a big, black ocean.

Chapter 16

I woke up with a headache burrowing behind my forehead and settling in for the day. I barely remembered getting into bed last night. I had jogged up the beach and back to my car, avoiding the blue-and-white tent, still filled with revelers. Clancy's car was gone. Only the fish would know if he'd called me. I was weak with hunger and headed to a nearby strip mall, where I found a Thai hole-in-the-wall. It was full of hipsters dressed like gangsters, if gangsters cared about being hip. I was starving and needed something fast—and soft enough for my swollen mouth to negotiate. When I stepped inside, the small but fierce female proprietress scurried up to me. My upper lip made smiling a challenge, but I gave it my best shot.

"What's fast and good?"

"No service," she said.

"But the sign says you're open until midnight."

She pointed to my bare feet. "No shoe, no service."

Oh.

I stepped outside the door, then leaned back in. "What's fast and good?"

That earned a half-smile. "Soup. *Tom yam nam khon.* Cook just made fresh. Or we have—"

"I'll have that," I said, my wounded mouth watering in anticipation of the mix of spicy lemongrass and sweet coconut milk. "To go."

I'd downed the entire container of soup then and there, on the sidewalk, before driving straight home. As I approached my house, I reached for my iPhone to disengage the Guard-on. Then I remembered I didn't have a phone anymore. Then I remembered I didn't have a connected Guard-on, either. I was shedding electronics faster than Tank shed hair in the summertime.

Tank himself had been ready to disown me, but I couldn't deal with him. I fed him the last of the liver bits and crashed without even flossing.

Now I found his warm body with my foot and stroked his back with my bare sole. His low purr let me know I was once again forgiven. We humans could learn a lot from our cats about letting go of resentment.

I lifted my head, which felt like a bowling ball. From the rectangle of sunlight reflected on my wall, I deduced it was mid-morning already. I explored the laceration inside my upper lip with my tongue. It was mostly healed, though the lip itself was still puffy.

I swung out of bed, wincing. I had a long day ahead of me. But first on my list, after two Advil, was trying to make contact with Yeshe and Lobsang. My near-death moment last night had knocked some clarity into me—woken me up to my stubbornness, like the loud gong the elder monks used to strike at Dorje Yidam every dawn, to rouse us from our sleep.

It was 12 hours later there. With any luck, I would catch them before they went to bed. I moved to my computer, opened the Skype app, and put in a call. As I waited for a response, my heart unfurled like the petals of a lotus, and I wondered what perverse instinct had made me think I should deny myself their support.

Yeshe's image swam into focus. He was smiling so hard that his eyes were squinting. "Tenzing!" he shouted. Deep down, Yeshe didn't believe I could hear him on the computer unless he pitched his voice loud enough to reach across the miles.

"You don't have to shout, Yeshe. I can hear you, my friend," I said, smiling.

"Yes. I remember that now," he said. "Can you wait for a moment?" He disappeared from view, and I found myself staring at the familiar simple furnishings of their shared abbot's office, the same space that my father had once occupied while fulfilling his monastic responsibilities. A sharp twinge in my heart, like a muscle cramping, let me know I still harbored hurt from my father's death.

Yeshe reappeared. Next to him, Lobsang's bald head floated, as bright and round as the moon.

"*Tashi delek*," I said, touching my hands to my forehead in greeting.

"Good health to you as well, venerable brother," Lobsang replied. His eyes narrowed with concern. "Your lip is swollen." His expression grew stern. "Where are you?"

I tipped my screen. "Here, in my living room in Topanga Canyon," I said.

"No, Ten. I mean inside." Lobsang's voice rang with authority, and I realized he was not only growing up, he was growing into his position as abbot. "Where *are* you inside? Where has your *spirit* gone?"

"Are you in danger?" Yeshe added. "Ever since we last communicated, I've been feeling dark emanations, a concentration of shadow-energy surrounding you."

I wasn't ready to go there yet—to the two corpses sprawled outside my garage. Instead, I told them about the previous night: the quinceañera celebration, the cabaña incident, my close encounter with two thugs, a gangster, and a Glock.

Lobsang and Yeshe already knew about Chaco from the previous time he and I had tangled.

"I do not like that you have attracted this man back into your life," Lobsang said. "You are inviting great risk. Why?"

"Funny, Chaco said almost the same thing," I said, keeping my voice light. "Don't worry. I've got Tank here to keep me nice and safe."

Yeshe smiled, but Lobsang's expression remained serious. He was not fooled, not one bit.

"I am concerned, Tenzing," Lobsang said. "I feel you may be dancing very near the edge of a steep cliff."

I didn't reply. He was right, but that didn't mean I would step back.

"How can we help?" Yeshe asked.

"Connecting with you is already helping," I admitted. I sidled a little closer to honesty. "Lately, I've been noticing this growing tendency, you know, to keep things to myself. To isolate, go it alone."

Lobsang finally allowed himself a small smile. "*Lately?* Forgive me for disagreeing, dear Tenzing, but you have preferred to go it alone for as long as I've known you, and I've known you for most of your life."

I heard the echo of Lama Sonam's voice, gently chiding me when I was a boy: "Trust the *sangha*, Tenzing. Let the sangha support you. You do not have to battle the world all by yourself."

Yesterday I had witnessed Gloria Teresa's *sangha*, her built-in spiritual community, surrounding her. They celebrated her transition from girl to woman, rejoiced in her growth, and publicly honored her love for her God. At Dorje Yidam, our *sangha* was also a community of like-minded practitioners, in our case dedicated to the spiritual teachings and liberating techniques of the Buddha. As with any such group, we were encouraged to feel at one with the *sangha*, to invite its support rather than rebel against its rules, as I had been in the habit of doing back then.

And now?

Then, I'd rebelled. Now, I'd rejected my spiritual family entirely. Given my current lack of any spiritual practice whatsoever, what *sangha* in their right mind would want me? And my sincere but misguided attempt to make Heather and me a *sangha* of two had backfired. No relationship can bear that weight, not if the foundation is shaky.

"You're right," I said. For a brief moment, it felt good to admit the truth, but almost immediately my inner defender stepped in with a lame excuse. "But it's not easy staying connected to the *sangha*, living over here, doing what I do."

Excuses, lame or otherwise, usually evoked the same reaction from Yeshe and Lobsang: absolute, utter disinterest. Their unwillingness to engage in my habitual defensiveness was one of the reasons I loved them and needed them in my life.

"Staying connected to the *sangha* is hard anywhere," Lobsang said.

Yeshe's big smile broke through. "Yes! Have you forgotten what it's like living in a monastery?"

We all laughed at the truth of that. As novices, we made a daily sport of pointing out the inconsistencies and hypocrisies of the old monks who taught us. We defined ourselves as much by our opposition to the *sangha* as by our identification with it. Our favorite target was old Lama Jamyang, a lifelong celibate and sweetly harmless elder, who had the bad-luck assignment of informing us about matters pertaining to sex. As far as his qualifications for teaching such a course went, what can I say? Lama Jamyang was brilliant at making butter sculptures. Period. He knew less than we did about sex, and we didn't know much. All secular courses at Dorje Yidam were taught in English, a language that the old monk spoke haltingly. No matter, because his fundamental lesson wasn't complicated. His attitude toward any and all interactions with the opposite sex boiled down to one key concept: "Don't stick thing in girl." He didn't elaborate—he just repeated the phrase over and over, accenting different words: "Don't *stick* thing in girl!" followed by "Don't stick thing in *girl*!"

As a self-appointed rebel, I, of course, had to press. "Which particular thing?" The shocked hush that followed was worth the sure punishment my father would mete out later on.

"Any thing!" Lama Jamyang bellowed, before banishing me from class.

Sadly, this severe approach to a natural instinct is not the sole province of Tibetan Buddhists. The world is rife with extreme, shame-based attitudes toward the opposite sex. Even Bets McMurtry's born-again gang had a name for *Don't stick thing in girl:* abstinence education. I doubt it works any better here and now than it did with me over there back then.

"Tenzing?"

I herded my wandering mind back to the present. I looked at the screen, at the openhearted concern radiating from my friends' faces. Their unquestioning love tapped against the wall of resistance, and a small crack opened up.

"I need your help," I said. "With the case I'm working on now. I'm a little lost."

Without hesitation, they nodded in unison. "We are at your service," Yeshe said. "Always."

I rubbed my eyes. "I'm like a mongrel chasing his tail, utterly convinced he's closing in on his target. I'm running in circles, and I'm running out of time."

Lobsang said, "There's also the small issue of bad men kidnapping you, of a gangster wanting you dead. Such things would affect any person's serenity."

I nodded.

"Can you tell us more about your adversary?" Yeshe's eyes were steady. He, too, was maturing. There was a time not that long ago when he didn't want to hear anything bad said about any other sentient being.

I told them what I could about my complicated foe, including what my research had uncovered: the hundreds of brutal deaths; the billions of corrupt dollars; the sense I had that there was no destroying this creature, that its tentacles were too numerous, too easily replaceable by others. They listened in silence, eyes closed, breathing in and out. They were Buddhist monks committed to *ahimsa*, to nonharming, but they were also Tibetans, victims of an enemy regime responsible for mass cruelty, if not genocide.

"But I have no visible proof," I continued. "All the evidence keeps disappearing. He's been one step ahead of me this whole time, and I don't know what to do." I reached toward the screen, as if to touch them. "Do you have any intuitions based on what I've told you so far?"

Yeshe opened his eyes. His head bobbed. "Something came to me as you were talking. When did this start, Tenzing? Can you remember when you first tugged on these particular strings of karma? Where were you when it happened? Can you go back?"

I blinked, as the voice in my dream came back to me, clear and low. *Go back.*

"Back to the beginning?"

I reached back, sorting through the past week.

Impressions formed: *Mac Gannon's estate . . . Bets McMurtry, Mac, and me drinking iced tea . . . Bets scratching her arms . . . Mark Goodhue's pursed lips and stiff back . . . Melissa leading me to the forbidden nylon backpack, the tracker planted inside it like a ticking bomb . . . A maid delivering drugs to a woman with ongoing pain in her hip and probably her heart.*

All that felt like eons ago. Had it only been a matter of days?

I shared the incidents with Yeshe and Lobsang. I told them about Bets and her missing housekeeper, and how the misper case had catapulted me into this underground world, linked to the first like a bardo state and filled with danger.

Lobsang, ever the practical one, said, "So, who is paying you?"

I started to say "Mac Gannon," but then I realized I didn't know the answer. He might be paying me, but then again, he might merely be funneling money from elsewhere, including from Bets. And the payment was specifically for finding a missing person, Clara Fuentes. Who was paying me to do whatever I was doing now, chasing down Chaco and Chuy Dos and the rest of them?

Lobsang saw the look on my face and said, "Nobody?"

"Bets, I think. Or Mac Gannon. I don't even know anymore." I sighed.

"Don't waste time judging yourself," Lobsang warned. "It is an indulgence. Whatever is, is. You know that."

"Listen to you, venerable Lobsang," I teased. "You're starting to sound like a real abbot."

He ducked his head and smiled.

Yeshe was following his own train of thought. "The real question is not who is paying you but what is driving you. I trust you have a higher motive. But Tenzing, if your motivation stems from lower intentions, from forces of your unconscious mind, you must bring them to the light right away. Remember what the Buddha says: we must always explore the root cause of our actions; to cling to our ignorance is to return to the mud. And in your case, to invite danger."

I took a deep breath. Then another. I was sorely out of the habit of tuning in to myself. I closed my eyes and floated a couple of questions through my mind: *What is so important about this case? Why am I putting myself in danger?*

Chaco's flat eyes looked back at me. I opened mine and said, "One thing I feel is a drive toward completion. I don't like loose ends. I can't walk away from a situation unless I know order has been restored."

They both leaned toward me. The slight bow meant, *You are on the right track. Please continue.*

"It's a feeling, deep in my belly," I said, sensing further into the physical clues offered by my midsection.

Yeshe's answer was prompt. "Then you are experiencing fear, hunger, or thrill. Those are the key sensations all of us feel in our bellies. Can you tell which one it is?"

I drew another slow breath down into my abdomen, trying to explore the river of sense impressions flowing through me. Talk about muddy. The only clarity available was the fact that I was really out of practice.

Finally I said, "Half fear and, uh, half thrill . . . maybe?"

Lobsang shook his head. "There are no halves in the belly. It's all one thing."

Aah. I felt a shift, a bigger area opening up, and then a vast spaciousness. The sensation was disorienting, dizzying even. I realized how tightly I'd been separating my feelings, trapping fear inside one tributary, anger in another, excitement off to the left, shame to the right, and surrounding any hint of sadness with the strongest sea wall of all. For one brief moment, I felt all the barricades drop. I was liberated. Free. The expansion was dizzying: suddenly I could experience everything I felt, all at once. A deep wave of unity and calm washed through me.

Lobsang gave me all of three seconds to ride the sweet rush before marching, in his methodical way, directly into the heart of the matter. He'd always had a knack for gently nudging me into wisdom and then kicking my butt.

"Of all your feelings," he pressed, "what is the one you have kept most hidden from yourself?"

Out of nowhere an overwhelming upsurge of sadness, like a rogue wave, loomed. I started to back-paddle furiously. Then I caught myself. *No, allow.* I was swept into a vast gulf of grief, awash with the ancient debris of my parents' divorce and my mother's suicide. I shuddered. Opened my eyes wide and looked into Yeshe's, then Lobsang's.

"Oh," I said. "Sadness. My father and mother, their relationship. Her . . ." My voice trailed off, as a lump of hardened grief caught in my throat. They nodded. They knew my story.

"Do you know what your parents' struggle and your mother's suicide have in common?" Lobsang's voice was kind.

My mind was blank. I shook my head.

"Both were beyond your control. You were powerless to help your parents get along with each other. You were powerless to make your mother happy."

All that time, all that energy I'd expended, trying to

cajole my mother out of her drinking and depression, trying to keep my parents from fighting.

"Tenzing, do not judge," Yeshe broke in. I nodded, grateful for the intervention.

"There is another thing," Lobsang said. "Your parents' relationship and your mother's suicide were both loose ends. Loose ends you could never tie up. No wonder you have chosen this line of work."

I felt a prickle of irritation. "That's not what's driving me," I said. "That's not the only reason I'm a detective." I bristled, a sure sign he was close to another truth.

They both laughed. Yeshe said, "I agree! Certainly not the only one! Fear, thrill, compassion, old family patterns—you probably have a dozen motives that drive you, just like the rest of us. Don't think you're so special all of a sudden. But whatever the motives, you must learn to recognize them and, who knows, maybe even make them your friends. Inquire into all your motives, Tenzing. Don't wall them off from each other or yourself."

Irritation shifted into grudging acceptance, which in turn moved into relief at hearing the truth.

Lobsang stifled a yawn, and I realized with a start how long we had been talking.

"I've kept you from your sleep," I said.

Yeshe smiled. "Knowing you are better, I will sleep better."

"But yes, we should go now," Lobsang said. "Tomorrow, we welcome a new crop of novices. And do you know what I am certain of?"

"What?"

"They will be in every way just as maddening as we were at their age."

"You have my sympathy," I said. "All I have to deal with are gangsters and drug lords."

"There are days when I would gladly switch roles," Lobsang said.

I placed my hand over my heart. "You've helped me. Thank you."

"*Yin dang yin*," Yeshe answered. "You are most welcome. But Tenzing, thanks are not necessary among dharma brothers."

"Be well, Lama Tenzing," Lobsang added, reaching toward the computer. "And remember: whenever darkness draws you in, choose the *sangha*. Choose the light." A blip and they were gone.

I sat back. I felt a little spaced out after our conversation, light-headed and light-bodied as if my physical form was inflated with helium. Deep conversations with Yeshe and Lobsang tended to have that effect on me. I was relieved when Tank wandered in and started to slalom back and forth between my shins. I reached down to stroke his back, using his warm body to ground me. My office telephone was blinking. Looked like once again, I had several messages. I stood, stretched, made myself a pot of coffee and Tank a bowl of wet food. I ate the last banana.

Finally I listened to my messages from the night before:

Heather, unable to reach me on my cell. Exhausted from dealing with multiple vehicular deaths. Turning in. Maybe we could talk tomorrow. (Which was today.)

Clancy, wondering why the hell I wasn't answering my cell.

Bill, ditto.

Mike, ditto.

Cielo Lodera, asking, "How's my hero of the hour doing?"

And finally, a sheepish-sounding Mac Gannon, just checking in.

I started at the end, which was also the beginning. I called Mac.

I got his voice mail. "You know who it is. Speak after the beep."

"Mac, Ten here. I need to talk to you, as soon as possible."

I had no sooner ended the call than Mac returned it.

"Ten? What's up? Any news?"

"No," I said. "But we need to have a conversation. When can we meet?"

A moment of silence, followed by, "Why not now? I just finished sucking at eighteen holes of golf, and I'm almost home. Come by whenever. The girls are out riding all day, or some fucking thing, so it'll just be me."

He sounded sober, if a little irritable. I told him that would be fine.

My next call was to Mike. It took three calls to wake him and tell him he was a complete genius and I was wrong again. Mike being Mike, a few months ago he'd insisted, against my protests, that I purchase a back-up iPhone and give it to him for safekeeping, as well as a memory stick onto which I'd downloaded my list of contacts.

"Told ja," was all Mike now said.

I showered, changed, brushed my teeth, collected my gun, and fueled both tanks, feline and automotive. An hour and a half later, after a detour downtown to pick up the new phone from a sleepy Mike, I was knocking at Mac's office door.

"Come in!" he yelled.

He was sitting in the rattan chair by the coffee table. Two glasses and an untouched pitcher of water completed the picture. Mac's right knee was jittering up and down like a jackhammer. In fact, he looked a little twitchy all over. Mrs. O'Malley hovered nearby—I guess Mac's concept of "It'll just be me" didn't include her. Mac gestured me toward the other chair.

"Want a bite to eat?" He focused on my face. "Th' fuck happened to your lip? I wouldn't have pegged you as a brawler."

"Nothing. And no thank you."

"A drink, then? You look like you could use one."

"Not for me."

"Suit yourself." He reached behind him in a single fluid motion, finding, without having to look, a bottle of expensive-looking single-malt Scotch positioned just so in the middle of the bookshelf. He twisted the cap open and poured himself a generous tumbler of amber liquid. His look was defiant, as if daring either of us to comment.

"Cheers," he said.

I noted that Mrs. O'Malley's pretty mouth had suddenly thinned into a narrow, disapproving line. I also noticed that Mrs. O'Malley's hair, like Mac's, was damp, as if they had both just stepped out of the same shower. I quickly stuffed these observations in the giant box called "None of My Business."

Mrs. O'Malley withdrew, but not before confiscating the Scotch bottle. Mac scowled but didn't stop her. He admired his drink like a lover, before taking a swig. He savored, then swallowed, and it was as if a large, soft hand had smoothed down all the prickly places on his skin.

"So, what brings you here, Ten?" His voice was instantly expansive.

I opened my mouth. Closed it again. Where to start? "I've been . . . following several lines of inquiry having to do with Clara Fuentes's disappearance," I said. "And all of them lead back to here."

"Here?"

"Well, to that first meeting here, with Assemblywoman McMurtry and Mark Goodhue."

A thought occurred to me. "Do you even know?"

"Know what?"

"About the drugs? About Sofia's murder?"

He reached behind for the bottle, although there was plenty of Scotch left in his glass. Realized his booze had been impounded. "Goddamn busybody," he muttered. "They're all the same. Like fucking fourth-grade schoolteachers." He took another long swallow from his glass and met my eyes. "You want to tell me what the hell you're talking about?"

I knew from intimate personal experience that I had maybe 20 minutes of lucidity to work with before the alcohol hijacked Mac's personality. Then all bets were off.

I skipped past the hidden backpack of drugs, mentioning only that Sofia may have been connected to a small-time dealer. I wasn't going to throw Melissa under the bus, especially not if Mac was drinking again. Instead, I concentrated on my growing suspicions concerning Mark Goodhue and his company, GTG.

"What kind of suspicions?" Mac asked.

"There seems to be a connection between Goodhue, a local dealer called Chuy Dos, and a drug lord. A bad one. Mexican-cartel bad," I said. "Bets McMurtry may be involved, as well."

He looked skeptical. "Bets and a drug lord? You're reaching there, buddy. You ever listened to her on the subject of drugs?"

"Tell me about Goodhue," I said.

He leaned back in his chair, thinking. "Bets and I go back to high school, as you know. We lost touch for years, sure, but I still consider her a friend. But Goodhue? I really don't know the guy. I met him for the first time that day you were over here." He scowled. "Mexican cartel. Jesus fucking Christ. That's all I need." He drained his glass. Mac's face was starting to flush; his liquid medicine would soon move from calming to fraying his temper. If I weren't careful, in a matter of minutes he'd again be accusing me—and my Chinese relatives—of ruining his life and taking over the world.

I glanced out the window, where the afternoon sun was painting dapples of light on the trees, and compared that dance of nature with the reddening glower on Mac Gannon's face. So much good fortune, so little contentment. I wondered what big feelings he was avoiding, what secrets he was keeping. They must be substantial. Fate had conspired to make him a major movie star, with a few hundred million dollars in the bank, a beautiful wife and family, and a fabulous estate in Malibu, and yet at the slightest hint of trouble, he ran to his favorite victim role for comfort, like a child to his security blanket. It was sad, really.

I adopted the soothing voice I'd used so many times on my mother. "I'm just trying to put pieces together, Mac. And it's worth your paying attention to what's been happening. You don't want blowback if there's something illegal going on with those two. Not to mention what it might do to Bets McMurtry's political aspirations."

He shrugged irritably, as in *I don't want to hear this.* "Look, I adore Bets," he said. "I think she's the best thing to come along since Sarah Palin. She's crazy as a loon, and I should know, but she's fifty times smarter than any of those other bimbos. Bets gets people fired up, *plus* she's got a brain. And as far as I know, she's as straight an arrow as they come." He leaned closer. "Let me tell you something. It's people like Bets who're gonna save this country."

Here we go, I thought.

"She'll take strong measures. She's not afraid to do the things that need to be done."

A chill wriggled up my spine, into my neck. "Like what?"

"Like, keeping those goddamned wetbacks from crossing our borders. Like taking illegal drugs off our streets once and for all. Like shoving fucking Obamacare where the sun don't shine. Count me in as a big supporter."

And then I got it. Immigration. Drugs. Medicine. What did they all have in common? Who would stand to lose the most if these issues were solved through legalization and implementation?

GTG Services, Incorporated.

Mac stood up, turned to face the bookcase, and reached behind a row of leather-bound books on the top shelf, retrieving a fifth of Scotch. He refilled his glass, muttering something that sounded like "bad pony."

"I'm sorry, I didn't quite hear you," I said.

He focused on me, as if surprised I was still there. The alcohol was doing a number on his brain cells. "I said, 'I hope I haven't wasted my money on a bad pony.'"

"Who, Bets? You've donated to her campaign?"

He waved off my question. "Not Bets. With these god-damned spending limits, I couldn't give her much even if I wanted to. No, I'm talking about the PAC, New Americans for Freedom."

He covered his mouth. "Oops. Nobody's supposed to know I put my money in that. Ten fucking million, to be exact." He shrugged again. "Not that they give a fuck anymore. That's chump change. These days, you gotta have at leas' one billionaire behind you to get your people elected, somebody who can write those checks for a hunnerd mil without flinching, y'know? And New Americans for Freedom's fuckin' landed one."

"Really? Who's that?"

"They're not saying." Mac's eyes grew sly. "And why d'you care s'much, anyway? All I know's wha' Bets told me the other day: 'Fuckers've brought a whale in.'" He swung his head back and forth, like a wounded bull looking for someone to charge.

I pushed to my feet. My time was up. But something was still niggling at me.

"One last question, Mac. How did Bets know to hire me?"

"Wha'?"

"When Clara went missing. How did our meeting come about? Did you recommend me?"

"Lemme think . . ." Mac leaned back and closed his eyes for a moment. Then he shook his head, meeting my eyes. "Can't remember. The firs' call came from Bets, for sure. Then Goodhue got involved, once he found out I'd set up a meeting with you 'n Bets. Tried to call it off, but Bets wasn't having it." Mac shook his head. "Guy's a fuckin' prig. Don' know why she doesn' get rid of him."

Goodhue again. Goodhue, Chuy, and behind it all, the head of the hydra, Carnaté aka Chaco Morales. The grand puppeteer, manipulating the strings, making everyone else, including me, dance. Another man who hated unfinished business. I was his loose end, just as he was mine. But he was the one who had me tied up in knots.

I left Mac sinking into a bog of self-pity, belting back Scotch straight from the bottle. I was safely out of there and had pulled out my phone to call Clancy, when Mrs. O'Malley ambushed me next to my opened car door. I inwardly rolled my eyes. The last thing I needed was a long heart-to-heart with Mac Gannon's secret mistress.

"A moment, Mr. Norbu?" She gestured toward the office. "I heard raised voices. Is everything all right?"

"Absolutely fine."

Anxiety spiked her voice. "So he didn't . . . ? No politics? No conspiracy theories?"

I shook my head. "None at all." She was probably worried that I had TMZ on my speed dial.

"I'm glad," she said. A tear formed at the corner of one eye. She brushed it away. *Not my business. Not my business. Not. My . . .* I rested my hand lightly on her shoulder. "Are you okay?"

More tears. "It's just that Mac . . ." She crossed her arms, clutching at her shoulders. "I'm afraid he's destroying himself," she said. "I'm afraid the whole thing is about to collapse."

"The whole thing?"

"His career, his reputation, all his hard work. His entire world. Everything's teetering on the brink."

"Because . . . ?"

"People used to love him. Now everybody hates him. Or worse, they think he's a foolish idiot. I'm so afraid for Mac."

She was avoiding the obvious. *What would Lobsang say?* "What about you? What are your fears for yourself?

235

What are you hiding from?" I tried to keep any judgment out of my voice. "What aren't you admitting? The hardest thing?"

"The hardest?" Her eyes were pools of pain.

"Yes."

"I . . . I don't . . ."

I said, as gently as I could, "How long have you been . . . with Mac?"

Her whole body slumped, though whether with relief or shame, I couldn't tell. "In love with him? Since I was a teenager in Dublin and saw his first movie," she said. "Half my life. Pathetic, right? As far as the other goes, we only got . . . intimate a year or so ago."

I stayed silent, trying not to glance at my watch. The woman was in a lot of pain.

"I moved to Los Angeles after I left university, and got a job as a nanny for an actor who knows Mac; his daughter and Melissa go to the same school. Mac spotted me at a birthday party. He needed an assistant and offered me a job. I thought it was a sign that we were meant to be." She made a bitter little mouth movement. "I know! I know! It's all such a fucking cliché."

"What about Mac. Does he love you?"

Her smile was resigned, though surprisingly without bitterness. "I'm pretty sure that's not in Mac's repertoire. Not with adult women anyway. We have opinions, you know? He adores Melissa, but that'll start changing as soon as she hits puberty, just like it did with Maggie."

"Well, at least your eyes are open, Mrs. O'Malley."

Her eyes flashed. "That's another thing. My last name's O'Malley, but I'm not anybody's missus. Mac just started calling me Mrs. O'Malley because he thought it was funny. He did the same thing to poor Penelope—she was always Penny before. I guess he likes branding his women, you know, after he charms them and before he starts blaming them for everything. No wonder she pops so many pain pills."

As I watched, something inside her shifted. She only straightened her spine, but as a result she seemed to actually grow several inches taller. "You know what?" she said. "I think I may be done." She took a deep breath and looked around, as if seeing her surroundings more clearly. "Fuck him. Just . . . fuck him." She met my eyes. "Thank you, Mr. Norbu. This little talk has helped."

Don't thank me, thank Lobsang. "I'm glad" is all I said.

She took a step toward the office and then appeared to think better of it. "Nope. Not going there. I'll mail in my notice." She smiled at me. "I think I'll address it to 'Penny.'"

She strode back toward the house, a tall and graceful warrior, at least for this moment in time.

I stood in the harsh sunlight. Without Melissa's bright, darting presence, the compound, though surrounded by lush greenery, felt strangely lifeless.

I hoped she was doing okay.

My new iPhone strummed in my pocket like a guitar, an unfamiliar but welcome ringtone. Mike must have decided I needed a change.

I checked the screen. Heather.

"Hey," I said. "Sorry about yesterday. Things got out of hand."

"Mike told me. Me, too, by the way. What a crazy night. Not to worry. We'll get there." Her voice was light, with none of the undertone of blame I'd come to dread. I smiled. *We'll get there* was a favorite catchphrase of ours, from our early days of heady courtship.

"You sound great," I said.

"Maybe not great, but I am better," she answered, somewhat mysteriously. "Anyway, never mind about that. Listen, I was trying to find out more about the organ-transplant stuff, so I put in a call to Dr. K. just now."

"Doctor K.?" My voice climbed the scales toward high squeak.

"Kestrel. Gustolf Kestrel. Transplant guy, remember? He

wasn't around, but I wound up chatting with one of the nurses in his department. They were all buzzing about Dr. K.'s new patient. Ten, you'll never guess who checked into hematology this morning for blood tests."

"Um," I said, still recovering from the blatant Dr. K. reference.

"I'll give you a hint. As far as I'm concerned, this patient doesn't need a new liver, she needs a new brain, preferably cloned from Hillary Clinton's."

As her words registered, my heart started pounding so hard in my ears I could barely hear the name I had already guessed.

"Bets McMurtry," Heather said. She lowered her voice. "She's right here in County-USC, can you believe it?"

CHAPTER 17

I drove straight to Boyle Heights, which was becoming a bad habit I couldn't seem to break. I soon found myself in a vigorous, losing debate with the elderly receptionist the powers that be had chosen to guard the lobby of County-USC. I soon determined why. Myrtle Fishbein may have looked like someone's granny, but in fact she was a manifestation of the wrathful protector deity, the six-armed *Mahakala*, minus the crown of skulls. She had pulled up Bets's information and was reading something off her computer.

"I'm sorry, sir, but the patient in question has left strict instructions. In fact, I'm very surprised you were apprised of the patient in question's presence." She pulled her attention from the screen, removed her reading glasses, and set them carefully in the pinkish-gray hair on the top of her head. Her fiery eyes bulged, as if to wither me with their stare. "What did you say your name was?"

I hadn't said, nor was I about to. I didn't want anyone later connecting the dots between my presence here and Heather's offhand comment.

"Can you at least let her know she has a visitor?" I said.

She crossed all six arms. "No," she said.

I played the only card I had left. "Then let me speak to your supervisor."

She sniffed, but protocol was protocol, even for wrathful Tibetan protectors. She set a "Back in five minutes" sign on her desk and marched off, tiny but mighty, her joints stiff with indignation. As soon as she'd turned the corner, I hustled past the desk and down the corridor to find the hematology ward myself. Maybe I'd get busted, but I've discovered through years of experience that there are times it's easier to beg forgiveness than get permission.

After a quick sidestep into the hospital gift shop for camouflage aids, I placed myself in front of a doctor frowning over a patient's chart near the elevator. He looked busy, which meant he'd take the easiest route from me bothering him to me being gone.

"Hematology?" I asked, shifting my vase of flowers and box of chocolates to hide the fact that I didn't have a visitor's badge.

"Sixth floor," he answered, without looking up from the chart.

I made a beeline up the elevator and out the door to the sixth-floor duty station. A couple of nurses had their heads together, chatting, their voices low. I quick-scanned the inpatient message board and soon spotted a "Ms. Jane Smith" in room 617. Nothing, if not original, these people. There was a Sally Williams in the room next to hers.

One of the nurses said, "May I help you?"

I shifted the flowers. "Just checking in on Sally," I said. "Sally Williams. Room 618, right?" She glanced at the board, and nodded, smiling at me. "That way," she said, pointing at a hallway to her left.

An armed security guard, his hair gone to gray, his belly putting pressure on his shirt buttons, was slouched in a folding metal chair outside a door halfway down the hall. His nose was buried in a *Guns & Ammo* magazine.

Bingo.

As I drew closer he reluctantly tore his gaze from the centerfold, which featured the latest in sexy munitions. He narrowed his eyes with as much gravitas as a minimum wage rent-a-cop can muster. As gatekeepers go, he was a piker compared to the receptionist downstairs.

The patient's door was open. White curtains bunched across a metal frame, blocking any view into the room.

"Hello," I said. "I'm here to see the assemblywoman."

A crease deepened between his eyebrows. "First I heard a this. She expecting you?"

I waved the box of Godiva chocolates before him. I've found that sometimes no answer is the best answer. Let him fill in the blanks, work out what I meant by the gesture.

His imagination appeared to be stalled, or at best struggling. I guess I had to spell it out.

"Errand of mercy," I said. "Chocoholic."

As he wrestled with this piece of intel, a raucous voice rang like a bell from inside. "Who's talking? Who the hell's out there?"

I interpreted that as an invitation. I parted the curtains and stuck my head inside. Bets was propped up in bed with a glossy magazine on her lap, the subject matter, in this case, high fashion; the ammo, clothes and cosmetics. She was dangling her left hand like royalty before a tiny Vietnamese woman, who was sitting on a folding metal chair and applying bright orange polish to Bets's long nails.

Bets snatched her hand back and pushed herself upright. "Tell me you found her. Tell me you found Clara."

I shook my head.

"Well, shit," she said. She flopped back onto her pillow. "Shit on a fucking stick. Now what?"

I shot a meaningful look at the manicurist.

"She's okay," Bets said. "Doesn't speak a lick of English. None of them do."

I winced, but the manicurist didn't appear to react. I set the flowers on a side table and moved to the foot of the bed. Up close, I could make out dark circles, like smudged coal dust, under Bets's eyes, and the unsuccessful attempt to erase them with makeup. And her eyes? Her eyes looked more catlike than ever, with their slightly yellowish tinge. And yet, she exuded charisma.

From my years of observation, both as a cop and as a student of humanity, there seem to be four basic facial

241

types—bird, horse, pig, and fox. Bets was mostly fox. She'd gotten herself a world-class haircut and a brand new color of hair since the last time I saw her: the streaky-blonde cap, short and shiny, was as vivacious as she was. Although her politics repelled me, her animal energy was strangely forceful. A memory from my teenage years flashed through my mind, a fleeting image of the sexy mother of one of the novice monks. I reached for his name. Lama Chodak? No, Choden, that was it. His mother lived in Lower Dharamshala, the lonely wife of a carpet merchant who was away a lot on business. My father had ordered me to accompany the young monk to his mother's house one afternoon, shortly after he took his initial vows, probably to make sure he didn't break any. Lama Choden wasn't the one my father should have worried about.

Choden's mother greeted us at the door wrapped in a gauzy Indian sari that outlined her curves in all sorts of interesting ways, especially to an 18-year-old. While her son chattered away over cups of tea, she studied my mouth, my shoulders, my hands as I lifted my cup, as if simultaneously appraising and devouring every motion I made. I found the encounter highly confusing, and for weeks afterward that look in her eyes invaded every meditation. Bets McMurtry had the same Sexy Mother energy, and I was sure it had won her more than a few votes.

I handed her the chocolates.

She glanced at the box. "Sweet," she said. "But not why you're here. So why *are* you? Take a load off, why don't you?"

The manicurist immediately moved from her chair and retreated to the other side of the room, her eyes lowered.

Bets didn't make the connection, but I smiled my thanks to the woman, making a mental note never to assume people don't understand a language they don't speak.

"I've hit a wall," I said, sitting. "I need some answers from you."

Bets nodded. "Go for it."

I did, a full-frontal assault. Time was awasting. "Bets, why and how are you involved with Chaco Morales? What's the connection?"

"I'm sorry," she said. "Chaco who?"

"Morales. The drug lord. Mexican cartel." As if she didn't know.

Her face purpled with rage. "What the fuck are you talking about? Who sent you here? Are you wired? Goddamn Democratic pricks. I should have known. Goodhue told me you weren't to be trusted. You get the fuck out of here! *Now!*" She swept her arm, knocking over the manicurist's rolling tray of implements. Little glass bottles of maroon and blue and peach polish clattered onto the floor. One of them exploded, and red liquid dotted the floor and wall like blood spatter. With a small cry, the Vietnamese woman dropped to her knees and started trying to mop the stains with some cotton balls.

I jumped to my feet as the security guard burst in, hand at his gun.

"Everything okay?" he said.

"How dare you," Bets spat at me. "You're fired, do you hear me?" She turned to the guard. "Get him out of here!" she ordered.

"I'm leaving, I'm leaving," I said as I tried to squeeze past the guard, his bulk blocking the doorway. He grabbed me by the shoulders.

"Hey! I said I'm leaving!"

I was face-to-face with a large expanse of overfed solar plexus and sorely tempted to drive my fist straight into it. For once, I practiced restraint, instead executing a police academy-style twist-and-drop to slip free of his grip. I brisk-walked past the stares of the nurses at the duty station. The guard didn't follow. Bets must have come to her senses and called him off. I got out before one of us made things much, much worse.

Driving home, still trying to breathe through the anger, I received a text from Mac Gannon. YOU'RE OFF THE CASE, it said. KEEP THE CHANGE.

In a way, I felt relieved. If I really was just working for myself now, I didn't have to be so cagey with everyone. I hadn't signed any nondisclosure agreements, right?

I called Bill at work.

"I think I may have stumbled onto a connection between the politician Bets McMurtry and Chaco Morales," I said.

"Jesus Christ, Ten, what's next?" he said. "Did you figure out where Hoffa's buried, too?"

"Bill, I'm serious. I met with Chaco last night. He's changed his appearance, but it's him. He's still alive."

"Oh really? Then why are you?" He sighed. "Do you have any proof?"

"I don't," I said.

"I suspected as much. FYI, I sent a few of our drug and gang guys down to San Diego to meet a few of their drug and gang guys, to check out that warehouse. And guess what they found?"

I didn't have to guess. I knew. "Nothing."

"*Nada*. Zip-all, my friend. Oh, except for two thousand gallons of organic cleaning solution. All of which have now been tested and therefore contaminated, which means a hefty reimbursement is forthcoming from my department's already over-stretched budget. Which makes me look like a newly promoted D-Three asshole."

"Sorry," I said.

"Yeah, well, what are you gonna do?" Bill sighed again. I pictured him rubbing the bridge of his nose. "The hell of it is, I believe you, Ten. But listen: from now on, I need absolute, irrefutable proof before I lift another finger. And I'm not talking about a few baggies of untraceable prescription pills and medical marijuana from a missing woman's backpack."

"I understand."

"And Ten, you know how you get these vibes about things?"

"Yes."

"Well, I'm getting a real strong vibe that you should leave this noodle alone."

One of Bill's earliest pieces of advice to his overzealous rookie partner came while we were eating rice noodles at Sanam Luang Cafe, a Thai place in North Hollywood. Our case at the time, a hit-and-run vehicular homicide, wasn't going anywhere. Bill was ready to call it quits for the day and head home to relieve his exhausted wife of babysitting duty. I was lobbying hard to keep knocking on doors.

Bill had pushed his empty plate to one side, while I tried, unsuccessfully, to fork up my three remaining rice noodles. I'd already swished a final mushroom through the last of the spicy black soy sauce and popped it in my mouth.

Bill pointed the tip of his fork at my plate.

"Some cases? They're slippery." He nudged at one noodle. "Frustrating, you know, like pushing a noodle around, trying to pick it up. No matter how many different ways you try, you can't get ahold of it." He illustrated, and I watched, fascinated, as the noodle kept slithering away. "See?"

"So, what's the secret?" I remember asking him. "What do you do?"

He shook his head. "There aren't any secrets. You just keep pushing the noodle around the plate until something happens. Sometimes you break a case with actual detective work. You uncover a clue—some new piece of forensics, say—or you catch a weasel in a lie. Sometimes, it's more like dumb luck."

"Luck, huh?" They didn't talk too much about "dumb luck" at the Police Academy.

He'd shrugged. "Maybe luck's the wrong word. More like a reward for not giving up. You know, like that old saying, *Even a blind squirrel finds an acorn now and then.*"

"So that's your advice? Just keep pushing the noodle around until you get hold of it?"

"Or don't. Sometimes cases just never break."

I had trouble with that last part. My face must have given me away.

"You know those crime statistics they pass around every month back at the shop?" Bill smiled. "The last one I saw? Guess what? Even the FBI, with all their resources, only closed sixty-five percent of their homicides."

"So what's your point?"

"My point is, sometimes you just gotta walk away. Say to yourself, *That's one mysterious noodle there, and I'm just gonna leave it that way.*"

I remember setting my own fork aside and using my finger and thumb to pincer up the noodle and place it in my mouth.

"And sometimes," I said, chewing, "you make your own luck."

Clancy was the next guy to bail on me, for an entirely different reason.

"Bets McMurtry? Man, you didn't tell me she was part of this deal. My other boss is nutso about her and not in a good way. He catches wind I'm involved, he'll take away all my intern hours. He already did that to this other dude. They got into a shouting match over McMurtry's speech dissing Obamacare. Next thing you know, he shows the guy the door, takes away his hours, and now the poor bastard's back to square one. I want to help, Ten, and I can't stand that bitch, you know I can't. But we're talking about me risking losing two thousand hours . . ."

"I understand."

"I wish you woulda told me earlier, man."

"I'm sorry."

Finally, I called Heather and recounted my run-in with Bets at County-USC, just in case it came up.

"What the hell were you thinking?" she said. "Do you

know how much trouble I could be in?" Then she said, "Wait, are you telling me you were working for her? For Bets frigging McMurtry? And you didn't let me know?" I could practically hear her teeth gnashing.

"I'm sorry," I said.

"I'm never ever talking to you about work stuff again."

"I understand."

I didn't bother calling Mike (asleep), or Cielo (trouble). I trudged into my house exhausted and embarrassed, my shoulders bowed under the weight of all my missteps and apologies. Tank met me at the door.

"Looks like it's just you and me, Tank," I said. I spooned a can of food into his bowl. Then I sent myself to bed without supper.

Chapter 18

But the next day found me hunkered down in the Shelby with my binoculars, my camera, and a large cup, listening on the radio to a KNX 1070 news report on none other than Tea Party darling Bets McMurtry. According to the newscaster, the assemblywoman had checked into the hospital overnight for some routine tests but was absolutely fine and back on the fund-raising trail for her causes. I could confirm that information, because at that very moment I was looking through my binoculars at the candidate herself. She and Goodhue had stepped out of the J.W. Marriot downtown, where KNX told me Bets had just delivered a rousing speech to a herd of hedge-fund managers.

I'm sure they loved her.

Bets, her larger-than-life, red-rimmed sunglasses shielding her face, climbed into the front passenger seat of Mark Goodhue's Mercedes, which I had followed from the Aon two hours earlier. I'd been parked downtown since 7 A.M. What can I say? I had woken up with lots of free time on my hands and a gigantic flea bite to scratch.

Goodhue was the only route left to the flea.

I didn't have Bill. I didn't have Clancy. I didn't even have Heather, not really. But I did have my intuition, my determination, misguided though it might be, and $93,000 dollars left in the fund willed to me by Julius Rosen, who represented the real beginning of the Chaco Morales tale. I hoped it was enough.

The Mercedes swerved out of the hotel parking lot. I could see the two occupants having what looked like a heated conversation in the front seat. Good. As long as they were fighting, they wouldn't pay any attention to me and my yellow Mustang, trailing a few cars behind them. As soon as we merged onto the 105, I knew. Bets was about to become airborne again. This time, I was determined to follow her all the way to her destination.

I ignored the heart palpitations, letting me know I hadn't addressed my recently acquired fear of flying in toy planes or any other small aircraft.

I skirted around the cavernous pothole, now marked by traffic cones. It was even deeper, if that was possible. Two blocks on, the Hawthorne airport looked as innocuous and unobtrusive as the last time I paid it a visit. The diner was quiet, the parking lot virtually empty. I circled the block and reclaimed my previous surveillance post, keeping watch as Goodhue continued past the entrance. Now what? He drove along the fenced perimeter, continuing past three large helicopters lined up in a row, and pulled into the private parking area of a small building next to the control tower. Goodhue helped Bets out of the car, and both disappeared through the door.

I started my car and circled the large block surrounding the airport. I lucked out. There was a commuter parking area directly across from the tower. I claimed a good space, facing the airport. I zoomed in on the building across the road from me and found the name of the business, etched in glass on the front door.

Oh, no. No, no, no.

The sign on the door said:

PREMIER CHARTERS
Helicopter Charter Solutions
Since 1989

I sat for a few minutes, hoping I was mistaken. Watched as McMurtry and Goodhue stepped out the backdoor of the building and slowly crossed the tarmac toward the metallic flying impossibility awaiting them. Goodhue and anoth-er man—the pilot, I assumed—helped Bets into the crea-ture's stomach.

You don't have to do this, Tenzing.

The last time I was this close to a helicopter, there was a crazed man inside, aiming a gun at my head. Which felt safer than the last and only time I was inside one. We had just landed, if you could call it that. I was in pursuit of the same crazed man when the giant iron insect dangled precariously off one side of a precipice, holding on by one thin strut. I bailed out immediately. Since then, my healthy discomfort about flying in anything dependent on rotary blades had deepened into what I considered a completely rational terror.

I aimed my binoculars at the chopper. The body was cream-colored, the dark blue undercarriage striped in white, turquoise, yellow, and red. With its twin engines and dual rotors—large blades overhead, small ones at the tail—the machinery seemed sturdy enough, but my innards weren't fooled.

"Fear," I announced out loud. *No doubt about it this time, Lama Yeshe. My belly is one big ball of fear.*

The front and back rotors whirred to life, quickly accel-erating into a blur of blades. The helicopter rose, hovered for a few moments like a hummingbird, and then angled up, up, and away. I pulled on my windbreaker and packed my weapon of choice—the final wad of bills from my Julius Rosen Memorial Petty Cash Stash. Chaco's three-step route to the top echoed in my brain: bribes, bribes, and bribes. Like a martial arts master, I would now turn Chaco's best offensive move against him.

I crossed the road after checking both sides for oncom-ing traffic, though getting hit by a car might be preferable to what lay ahead. I entered the office of Premier Charters. The décor was 'coptor-centric, with several framed aer-ial photographs of Los Angeles on the walls and a small tin helicopter dangling from the ceiling like a toy bug. I counted two small offices to the left and a fridge and coffee maker to the right. A hidden speaker blared an old Doors song, "Riders on the Storm," which I recognized because Valerie, my mother, played it incessantly when I was a child.

Maybe I'd get lucky. Maybe Premier Charters owned only one of the choppers outside. I approached the counter, where a young, bouncy blonde, her hair streaked with purple, peered at a computer screen as her jaws worked a wad of gum.

"Good afternoon? Can I help you? I'm Amber?" she chirped, in that adolescent singsong that lifts every statement into a question. She reached under the counter to lower the volume of Jim Morrison's wail.

"Yes," I said. "How do I go about finding out where that helicopter is going?"

Instead of eyeing me with suspicion, hers widened with excitement. "Omigod, I knew it, I knew that was her. Are you the paparazzi?" She removed her gum and looked around for somewhere to stash it, settling on folding it inside a glossy tourist brochure.

Rather than answer, I smiled mysteriously. She was free to interpret in any way she wished. What I did say was, "Did you know that paparazzi pay real cash for good tips?"

She looked around, although we were the only two people there. "I think I may have heard that? Like, with TMZ?"

Chaco's tutelage aside, I've traveled in and out of India most of my life, so bribery has been a necessary evil. In any case, it didn't take a black belt in Green Fu to melt this girl's heart. I slid two Benjamins across the counter. She picked them up, her expression reverent.

"This is my first time," she said, fingering the $100 bills. "We've never had paparazzi here before."

I waited. I didn't want to sully the purity of the moment for her.

"Right," she said, suddenly officious. "So, do you just want the coordinates, or would you prefer to charter your own helicopter?"

My vocal chords tightened. "You have more than one?"

"Oh, yes, we have three helicopters? They're all AW109's? Two for passengers, one for rescues?"

She pecked on the computer and squinted at the screen. "Sam's available right now?"

This was good news for my case and disastrous news for my equilibrium. I inhaled deeply and let my breath out slowly. "How much to follow that other helicopter?"

More pecking, more squinting. "That will be, well, about five hours total? Round trip? Two down, the same coming back, plus you pay for wait-time if he sits there longer than fifteen minutes?" She tapped a few keys and said, "Okay, um, seven thousand. Do you want me to book it for you?"

I shuddered at the thought, and the cost, but I did.

I gave her my credit card, which had recently been bumped up to a $30,000 limit, as if the powers that be had learned about my new nest egg, even though my savings account was with a different bank. I wouldn't put it past them.

She ran the card, which didn't burst into flames at the unusually high charge. Then she turned away and had a quick conversation on her office phone, her cheeks pink from all the excitement. Within moments, a helicopter pilot with hair the color of a raw carrot emerged from one of the small side offices and strode directly outside to one of the remaining parked choppers. He disappeared inside.

Amber passed over a form to fill out. "For the passenger manifesto?" She opened one hand. "Passport, please?"

"I'm sorry?"

"I need your passport," she said. "For coming back?"

"Coming back?" I was starting to sound like her.

"Across the border? You're going to Mexico?"

Well, shit on a stick, as Bets would say.

I peeled off eight more $100 bills. "I, um, I forgot my passport? But I think I can get a copy of it sent here?"

She nodded. She understood me perfectly.

I filled out the information.

An hour later, I was strapping myself into a luxurious leather passenger seat the same rich cream color as the helicopter. As Bill likes to say, all systems were go, once I had managed to rouse Mike from bed so he could e-mail Amber a PDF of my passport. Luckily I'd sent a color scan of it to him, photo included, for safekeeping when I traveled to India to be with my father. At Mike's urging. Now I owed him two favors.

I was seated directly behind Pilot Sam. He turned from the blinking electronic console. "Buckled up? Ready?"

I nodded. Another lie. My stomach was telling me the opposite. Many things in nature have wings on them, from pesky mosquitoes to majestic eagles. But as far as I know, nature has yet to evolve a creature, hummingbird aside, with a spinning object on its head that propels it straight upward, turning the whole flying deal into something completely unnatural. To my primitive mind, anything that rises straight up is equally capable of returning to earth in a vertical plummet. I've been told that helicopters don't drop like a bowling ball if the engine quits, but then, I've been told a lot of things that turned out to be dead wrong.

Sam motioned for me to put on the aviation headset lying on the empty seat next to me. Ever since I'd lined his pockets with an extra $500, he was Mr. Share-the-Helicopter-Love. My plump earphones crackled to life as Sam exchanged takeoff chatter with the tiny control tower. He goosed the engine, and we lifted off, smoothly enough. Despite that fact, my stomach flipped over, registering the unlikely defiance of gravity. We banked left, and I attempted slow, steady breaths, trying to reunite with the bottom third of my stomach, the part that was pretending I was still on the ground.

"Off we go," Sam said.

I opted for silence.

We pulled out of the L.A. haze and headed a few miles offshore. Then Sam banked left again and took us southward, hugging the coastline. I popped two pieces of spearmint gum in my mouth, a parting gift from Amber, and focused on chewing and counting breaths. My single goal was to keep the choppy waves of anxiety from turning into an embarrassing mini-tsunami. Just in case, I had mapped out the location of the white barf bag tucked into a compartment under my seat.

After 35 grim minutes we alighted on a runway just north of the main Tijuana International Airport Terminal. Sam did a little of this and that, before turning to me.

"Wait here," he said.

I waited. He was in and out of an official-looking customs building in about five minutes.

"That was fast," I said.

"General Aviation Building. These guys know us well. They approve of our job: ferrying rich tourists to Mexico to spend *mucho dinero*. By the way, anybody asks, you're going fishing in Baja for the day. Like they do." He chuckled to himself, an inside joke.

"Okay, then," I said. "I'm going fishing." It wasn't untrue.

After I'd done another hour of white-knuckle battle with my dread, I saw Sam murmur into his mouthpiece. He leaned right, as if to check on something outside. He turned to me and pointed to his headset. I put mine on and heard, "There's Jack, our other pilot, coming back. He wants to know where I'm going."

Just then, our twin flew past us, some distance away and a half-mile or so closer to land. Sam answered my concerns before I could express them. "Don't worry. I got this covered."

He switched to a different frequency to have a private conversation. Then he was back. "Jack says good luck."

"Good luck?"

"With the fishing."

The flight stabilized slightly, along with my stomach, as we moved farther inward, chopping our way south down the western peninsula of Baja California. The signs of civilization, from housing to smog to green irrigated fields, fell away, replaced by a dry landscape dotted with gnarled creosote and the occasional cactus, arms up as if imploring the cloudless sky for rain. We passed a tiny village. Then, nothing. No wonder Sam chuckled about our fishing expedition. We had crossed into a waterless land.

Soon, I'd have some answers.

I was curious. "How far south of the border are we now?"

Sam glanced at the GPS coordinates and punched a button. "A couple hundred kilometers, maybe?"

The helicopter slowed its course, and Sam's voice was loud in my ears. "Getting close. We should be there in about ten more minutes."

"Okay," I said. "I want you to hang back a little, if you can. I'm not sure what we'll find. And I'd rather not be seen."

"Will do," Sam said.

I assessed the rumpled terrain below. No roads. No houses. No obvious signs of civilization. No easy way in or out, except by chopper.

An idea niggled.

"Sam, do you happen to know if your company has recently contracted with any major new corporate clients? Like GTG Services, for example?"

He shrugged. "Not my area of expertise. But Jack's a part owner. He mentioned there might be something big in the works. He's hoping that means they can get another couple of birds, maybe the new AW169 ten-seater, plus a second aeromedical chopper. I have no idea who the deal's with, though. I just fly these things. If I was any good at business I'd be running my own charter company, and my kids would be in private schools, you know?"

"You have kids?"

"Two. Boy and a girl. He's six, she's eight. Both already much smarter and better-looking than their dad, thank God." Sam's wide smile transformed his face, and I was exposed to another example of what unconditional fatherly pride looks like.

He pointed to two o'clock on the horizon: "Look. Over there."

In the distance, a white building shimmered; it was the size and shape of a medium-sized warehouse. Two pristine concrete helipads, marked with bright yellow circles, sat a short way beyond the building. The helipads were brand new, the cement barely dry.

Sam hovered the chopper in midair, keeping his distance. The spinning rotors caused the sandy terrain to riffle out in gritty waves right below us.

I fished for my binoculars and scanned the surroundings.

The building looked as if it had been dropped from the sky, right in the middle of a vast cactus- and mesquite-riddled wasteland. Two narrow, rutted dirt roads angled out from the building into acres and acres of flat desert.

I focused on a tall, three-pronged saguaro by one corner of the building. I sharpened the image, a memory tugging. Was I imagining things, or was this cactus the twin of the tall, three-pronged saguaro in Culver City? Another memory twanged: a third visual of a third cactus next to a third warehouse, in San Diego.

This cactus wasn't a twin, it was an identical triplet. I zoomed in for a closer inspection, and the bright sunlight emphasized some oddities. Each "limb" of the giant saguaro had a horizontal seam midway through it, as if it had been manually attached. The "skin" of the cactus was waxy and roughly ridged to look real, but free of any actual spines. The limbs themselves were too perfectly asymmetrical to be natural. This saguaro and two more like it were both masterfully camouflaged and clearly man-made. But what purpose were they man-made for?

I recalled the mysterious electronic hum I'd heard but been unable to identify at the Culver City warehouse. And then the answer strummed loud and clear, an unmistakable chord of truth. The cactus was not a cactus at all, but a cell tower disguised as a succulent. Three cell towers, in three separate locations. Chaco Morales had built, and now controlled, a personal, covert telecommunications network. Which also answered a second mystery: why Mike hadn't been able to link Sofia's, Clara's, and Mark Goodhue's cell phones to any known service providers. Our hydra had a secondary set of tentacles—invisible, wireless ones. Who knows how far they reached.

"Oh, my God," I said.

"What?" I'd forgotten that Sam could hear me.

"Nothing," I said. "Just, I think I figured something out."

I swung my lenses back to the main structure. The row of narrow windows winked at me in the afternoon sun, as if to say, "The joke's on you!"

How does one even begin to challenge such a man? I shook off the feeling of hopelessness threatening to engulf me. *You got this far, didn't you? Take advantage.* I continued my risk assessment. A lone Hummer and a smattering of four- wheel-drive jeeps dotted a narrow parking area along one side of the structure. No security cameras. No barbed wire. No armed guards, at least none visible. This didn't have the feel of anybody's command center. So why was this building constructed here? Not to mention, how? And what were Mark Goodhue and Bets McMurtry doing inside?

"Can you move just a little closer, Sam? I'd love to know what that thing's made of. I can't imagine anybody trucking heavy materials across this terrain."

"Oh, I can tell you that," Sam said. "You're looking at

one of those instant buildings from China. They ship the modules over in containers and then basically just bolt them together. All you need is a foundation, and you can have yourself a warehouse in under a week."

"No kidding. I'm surprised I haven't seen one of these before."

"You can't build them in California."

"Why not?"

"Earthquake codes."

"They don't have earthquakes down here?"

"Oh, yeah, plenty of earthquakes," Sam said. "Just no codes."

I snapped a series of pictures with my digital camera.

I took a closer look at the scrubby surroundings. Other than the insta-building, there wasn't much to see, certainly no paved roads suitable for ordinary vehicles. I didn't see any airstrips for landing small aircraft, either. Helicopters were the only practical way to bring people in and out—*practical* being a relative term.

"What do you want me to do?" Sam asked.

An idea shoved its way to the front of the line. I could have Sam drop me off at the nearest village. I thought I'd spotted one about 15 miles north of here. Perhaps I could find the local law and get them to talk about Chaco, with the help of my greenback persuaders.

Good sense pushed back. This was a very bad idea. I'd never heard of anyone speaking fondly about doing time in a Mexican prison. If Chaco had the clout necessary to build something out here in the middle of nowhere, as well as outfit it with his own personal cellular network, he was likely to own the local law enforcement authorities. He was a drug lord, with an army of illegitimate and legitimate soldiers. I was an ex-monk with a .38 and a 17-pound Persian cat.

"Let's go home," I said.

Sam nodded and executed a 180-degree turn so that we were facing north. We flew in silence for some time.

"So what are you, exactly?" Sam's voice broke in.

Good question.

"I'm . . . I'm just a man," I said, "trying to do some good."

Sam twisted around to look at me. After a moment, he returned his gaze to his console.

"Cool," he said.

We flew steadily for an hour or so. I was actually growing accustomed to the experience of acres of ground rushing beneath my feet. With a pang, I realized how much Heather would enjoy this slight inner shift. During one long night of pillow talk early on, trading professional war stories, Heather had described to me in some detail insights she'd gleaned from her Psych rotation, specifically, the wonderful results of "exposure" therapy in treating people with phobias. I had been skeptical at the time, but now I was a believer. After several hours of intense chopper-exposure, I was actually able to lean my head against the plush leather headrest and fall into a light doze.

"Crap." Sam's voice broke into my nap, followed, oddly, by the word "Brown."

"Wha . . . ?" I pushed upright.

He motioned to the right of the curved window. A second helicopter, army green, was keeping pace, maintaining a soccer field's distance between us.

"What's the problem?"

"Feds, I'm pretty sure. That's a Bell 407. Probably just took off from Brown. It's close."

"Brown?"

"U.S. Customs checkpoint, at Brown Field Municipal Airport. Shit. Look at that. He's definitely tracking us."

"Why? You aren't doing anything illegal," I said.

He glanced at me with something less than warmth. "I know," his voice rang in my earphones, "but how do I know you aren't?"

He switched channels and proceeded to hold a tense

conversation with someone on the other end. He didn't speak again until he had set the helicopter gently down on one of three small helipads just southeast of the Brown Field control tower. He cut the engines, and we watched as the ATF chopper settled on a helipad adjacent to ours.

"Showtime," Sam said. He moved behind me, swung open the door, and stepped outside. By the time I had my own feet on the tarmac, a man and woman were striding toward us, wearing black ATF windbreakers and grim expressions. The woman was sturdy, with strong shoulders and a crop of curly brown hair. She was a few inches taller than me and a few years older. The male agent was well over six feet and lean, sixtyish, with a gray comb-over that wasn't faring well in the whipping wind.

Behind them, a uniformed pilot descended the steps and started spot-checking his machine.

The male agent flashed his badge, and I caught a glimpse of a Glock G22 holstered to his waist. "Agent Willard, Bureau of Alcohol, Tobacco, Firearms and Explosives. This is Agent Gustafson." Neither offered their hand.

Sam handed Agent Willard his card. "I'm the charter pilot," he said. He motioned toward me with his chin. "He's the customer."

Willard waved Sam inside. "Go do your thing," he said. "I'll talk with you in a minute."

Sam hurried off, avoiding eye contact with me.

Agent Willard turned toward me. "Now then, who the hell are you?"

I explained who I was and pulled out my P.I. license as supporting evidence. Willard grabbed it and squinted at the print, before returning the license.

"Ex-LAPD," I added.

"How long were you with the force, Detective Norbu?" Willard asked.

"Eight years. Two on patrol, six as a detective, Robbery/ Homicide."

"What were you doing in Baja?"

"Um," I said. "Fishing?"

"Good enough for me," Willard said, shooting a look at Agent Gustafson. "I'm outta here. I need to take a piss." He turned and strode away. The pilot, inspection completed, followed. Gustafson stayed put.

"So you were with the force for eight years?"

"Yes, I was. And before that, I was a Tibetan Buddhist monk, teaching meditation."

"Sure you were."

"I was, actually."

She looked at me a little more closely. "Okay," she said. "Got it. You're one of the good guys. Do you mind telling me what in the holy hell you were doing in a helicopter circling that site in Baja California, Mexico? And do me a favor? Don't say fishing."

Personal intentions and new rules aside, I've found it to be generally unwise to lie to or stonewall a Federal agent, especially if she already knows that's what you're doing. On the other hand, I wasn't about to give this woman the whole story. I'd be kicked to the curb so far and so fast I might never find my way back. This was my mystery to solve, my killer whale to land.

Yeshe's voice pleaded with me. *You are weakened by your attachment to winning. Let this one go, Tenzing.*

I couldn't.

I resorted to the time-honored practice of not exactly telling the truth while not exactly lying.

"I was fishing but for information, not for, you know, fish. I'm putting some pieces together in an investigation. That building in Baja is one of the pieces."

"You mind being a little more specific?" Gustafson's gaze was steady. Huh. One of her eyes was blue, the other brown. Contact lenses or nature?

I reeled in my wandering attention and tried a different tack. "Mind if I ask a question or two of my own first?"

She waited.

I pointed to the ATF insignia on her windbreaker. "Does your interest in the building concern alcohol, tobacco, or firearms? I'm guessing firearms." I couldn't picture the ATF sweating over, much less Chaco Morales smuggling, tequila and smokes.

"You guessed right," she said, after a pause. She'd chosen to be forthcoming, so I did the same.

"Well, if it matters, my investigation has nothing to do with them, at least not directly."

She continued to observe me closely, her mismatched eyes alert to any sign I might be lying. She apparently decided I wasn't. She nodded.

"Sorry I can't be more helpful," I added. "But I'm in a bit of a hurry. I need to get back to L.A. Any chance we can wrap this up?"

Gustafson's mouth tightened. "So you're not going to tell me what your investigation *is* about?"

"I'd rather not," I said, keeping my voice mild.

"And I'd rather not run you in on an obstruction charge, but I will if I have to."

When people with authority dangle a threat, I am usually struck with the overwhelming urge to tug on it and see if they're serious. As a child, my reactive behavior resulted in more missed meals and mandatory kitchen duty at the monastery than I care to mention. But as a grown man, sometimes calling a bluff worked. I hoped this was one of those times.

I turned my back to Gustafson and crossed my wrists behind my back, ready for the handcuffs. I waited two long inhales and exhales.

I heard Gustafson sigh. "Turn around, Norbu."

I faced her, relaxing my arms. Gustafson's own were crossed, protecting her chest. She slowly lowered them, a conscious gesture of reconciliation. Her eyes were ever so slightly amused. "Let's be on the same side here, Detective."

That was fine with me. I didn't have any personal argument with the ATF. I just didn't want them trampling over my investigation, not when I was getting close to some answers. From my LAPD days, I had firsthand knowledge of their deservedly bad reputation for obstruction, miscommunication, and generally making boneheaded decisions they later denied. Operation Fast and Furious was a perfect example, when they allowed weapons to be passed into the hands of suspected drug smugglers under the misguided assumption that the weapons could then be traced to cartel leaders. The ATF officials in Mexico hadn't even known the score from their American counterparts. Speaking before Congress, one of the ATF's own deputy attachés later called the entire gun-walking fiasco a "perfect storm of idiocy." Bill and I had shared a laugh over that one. And for every exposed Federal blunder like Fast and Furious, 20 more dumb decisions remained safely barricaded behind unbreakable claims of national security.

Although Gustafson didn't strike me as dumb. Quite the opposite.

My fellow cops referred to the FBI as either "the Feebs," in honor of their dubious investigatory skills, or "the Shoes," for the clunky wingtips they wore. I glanced down at Gustafson's feet. She was pushing the edge of the ATF fashion envelope with a sleek pair of black running shoes. A rebel, like me. I liked that.

Agent Gustafson waited. I made a decision. Who knows? Maybe she could help me find Clara. "I've been following up on a misper case. My investigation has to do with drugs, money, and some new information I haven't quite figured out. Not yet."

"Okay." She nodded. "So you're saying, no connection to firearms? No bullets? No unusual weapons of any kind?"

"Nope." Maybe hers had to do with the rest of the Fast and Furious cache. Thousands of the weapons the ATF had allowed to walk were still at large and in circulation out there, the last I'd heard.

"Who's paying your fees?" Gustafson asked next.

"I can't tell you that," I said. Then I got cute. "All I can say is he's never been in trouble with the law. He's one of the good guys." My little inside joke backfired.

She jumped all over my words. "Wait a minute. Are you your own client here? Some sort of . . . vigilante? Isn't that against your religion?"

Now I had proof. Gustafson was that rare and dangerous land mammal, the Smartus Agentus Federalus. She was also just a semantic hair away from the truth. I only quibbled over her word choice. *Vigilante* brought to mind crazed outlaws, enraged mobs looting, and killing innocent victims. I preferred to think of myself as a concerned citizen, willing to go the extra mile for the good of the community. In this case, I might have gone a little farther than the extra mile, but all for a noble cause.

"Well?" Gustafson crossed her arms again.

I tried smiling. "You make vigilante sound like a bad thing."

She stared back with bicolored eyes, neither color amused. "Detective Norbu, the sooner you talk to me, the sooner you can go."

I changed course. She clearly shared my own tenacious need for answers. Plus, she had the bigger badge. "Fine. As I mentioned, I was hired to find a missing person. A woman, an illegal alien as it turned out, named Clara Fuentes. I worked the case for several days, until my client called me off. In the course of my investigation I opened up a second, massive can of unexpected worms, having to do with Mexican gangs. I've got an active curiosity and a need to close my cases, paid or not, so I'm following up on things. I don't know where any of this will lead, beyond Baja. Honestly."

Gustafson appraised me, puzzled.

"Do I know you?" she said. "I feel like I've seen you before."

That's all I needed. Once she realized I was the ex-cop

on prime time who plugged two gang members in my back-yard, all bets were off.

I shrugged. "I don't know why you would." I changed the subject. "I'm curious, Agent Gustafson. When did that building go up, anyway? I haven't checked the coordinates on Google Earth yet, but I'm betting it's so recent, nothing will show up but empty desert."

Gustafson said nothing.

"So, what?" I continued. "You just happened to be watching a bare patch of sand when boom, this building appears?"

Gustafson still stayed silent. I recalled Sam's commentary regarding the construction technique for putting up an insta-building.

"Let me guess. A big hole in the ground suddenly showed up on some random satellite feed. Were you the one who picked up on that? Nice work!"

Her eyes glinted, as if she appreciated running into another not-dumb member of the warrior tribe. "Close," she said.

I waited. She seemed to make a decision.

"How much do you know about deeply buried facilities? Modern ones?"

"You mean, like tunnels?"

"Tunnels, caves, bunkers, hidden storage vaults."

I thought it over. "Not much," I admitted. "The Tora Bora caves. Those facilities in Iraq, where the WMD's weren't, I guess. Why? Should I know more?"

Gustafson chewed her lower lip, frowning. "Let's just say I'm a little obsessed with the subject. To my mind, deeply buried facilities pose a great threat to our national security, maybe the greatest, and nothing's more critical than finding and eliminating them before they are used to eliminate us."

"All right," I said. "And you think you've found one?"

"Don't know yet. Can't be sure. But that site sure looks like a potential cut and cover."

"Sorry. 'Cut and cover'?"

"There are really only two viable techniques for constructing deeply buried facilities," she explained. "Tunneling, and cut and cover. Cut and cover's exactly what it sounds like—dig a deep hole, reinforce it, fill it with whatever nastiness you want to keep secret, cover it up."

I pictured the Baja site. "Like with a building?"

"Sometimes. More often soil, but yes. Sometimes. We call that dissimulation. Making the construction of an underground facility appear as if you're actually building something else."

"So how do you know which one this place is?"

"I don't. It's just, a hunch, you know? Unfortunately, there's no silver bullet when it comes to detecting these fuckers. I mean, sure, we have our ways. Satellite imagery, heat-detecting intel, radio intercepts. The Defense Department's even working on a quantum gravity sensor they can send into space to serve as a trip-wire, an early warning sign that will justify using our other intelligence assets."

"Uh-huh." *Have you ever met my friend Mike Koenigs?* I wanted to say. My brain was starting to melt.

"But unless you can get actual boots on the ground and eyes on what's there, or intel from a mole, it's almost impossible to prove anything."

I said nothing, because I had nothing to add. Not yet.

"So, to answer your question, yes. I was the first one to spot an uptick in activity," she admitted. "The digging of a big hole, the pouring of concrete, the building plopped on top. Satellites don't lie. I was also the one to ask the question, why? Why that? Why there? No one else seemed to care, but I checked it out, found some anomalies, and I've been keeping an eye on that area from a distance ever since. My partner thinks I'm paranoid, and my superiors could care less, but something's off. I just know it."

I nodded. I knew the feeling. "Anomalies? What kind of anomalies?"

She shook her head. "Sorry, that's as far as I can go. My

boss finds out I've been briefing some lunatic P.I. obsessed with his own mission, and my ass is grass."

"I can appreciate that," I said. "You're probably better off avoiding a paranoid Tibetan vigilante. On the other hand"—I mentally thanked Mike and his T-shirt philosophizing—"you know what they say about paranoia . . ."

At long last, Gustafson cracked a tiny smile. I handed her my card. She pocketed it without looking.

"You drink coffee?"

My look said it all.

Her strong legs scissored across the blacktop to her helicopter. She climbed inside and soon returned with a thermos and two ATF mugs.

"It's been a long day," she said and opened the thermos. The smell weakened my knees.

"You're not only smart, you're a genius," I said. "I think you just became my favorite *federale*."

Another smile. She filled our mugs with steaming coffee. I took a sip, and my body broke into a chant of gratitude as I savored the rich, bitter-yet-mellow liquid. The tiny, dry ache lodged between my eyebrows disappeared. Up until that moment, I hadn't registered Gustafson as real, much less female. Her role was strictly two-dimensional. Simply put, she was Authority and I was not. One sip of this elixir, though, and she bloomed into a fully evolved entity of the female variety. Anybody who could make coffee this good was worth getting to know a little better.

I registered the bright crinkle of laugh lines, a rarity in her line of work, and the way her lips moved as she savored her coffee. I noted her unusual eyes, themselves a pair of anomalies. She was very fit, though not the lean, wiry kind of fit. Her kind was sturdy and curvaceous, and it suited me just fine.

Is she the one?

"This coffee is outrageous," I said. "Are you sure it's legal, Agent Gustafson?"

She brightened. "I always soak the ground beans in a little hot water first—hot, but not quite boiling. After forty seconds or so I pour the rest over the grounds. You wouldn't believe how much difference that first little steep makes. It brings out all the natural oils."

"Wouldn't want to stifle those," I said.

Her gaze stilled. "Detective Norbu, are you flirting with me?"

I drew an indignant breath before realizing she was right. I was flirting with her.

"Do you have a problem with that?" I smiled.

She took my mug and emptied the coffee onto the tarmac.

I took that as a yes.

Just then, Sam poked his head out of the customs building and gestured me over.

"Shall I call you?" I said to Gustafson, eliciting an expression bordering on panic. I quickly added, "If I find out anything more about that site in Baja. That's all I meant."

She flushed and awkwardly fished out an ATF business card, scribbling a number on the back. As she passed me the card, her odd, bicolored eyes met mine. "Don't go there again, Detective Norbu."

As I walked away, I wondered which *there* she meant. And if she really meant it.

CHAPTER 19

By the time I finally got home, I was too hungry, exhausted, and overwhelmed by the day's events to pursue that thought, or any others. I'd spent the short flight back to L.A. persuading Sam I wasn't a terrorist in the making. I think he believed me. The huge tip helped.

The sun had long since dropped below the rim of the earth, leaving a sky wrapped in darkness. One lone star blinked overhead, or maybe it was one of Agent Gustafson's wandering satellites.

I peeled off my clothes, pulling on my cotton kimono and cinching the sash. I fed Tank, changed his box, and spent a mindless hour using a fine-toothed cat-comb on his thick fur while he yowled in low but steady protest. He was already mad at me, so it seemed economical.

I checked my messages, both phones. I had two more from Heather on my iPhone and a third from Cielo Lodero, who had called my office line. My stomach began to ache, but I chose to blame hunger. As I made myself a grilled avocado, heirloom tomato, and cheddar cheese sandwich, I recalled a piece of wisdom I once heard, though I couldn't say from where: *You know your life is getting too complicated when you're contemplating cheating on your mistress.*

My cell phone strummed. I didn't recognize the number, but I had a feeling I knew who the caller was.

"Yes," I said.

"Detective Norbu?" Her voice was lower, huskier than I'd remembered.

"Tenzing. Call me Ten, please."

"Ten." She tried it on. "Okay, Ten, but only if you call me Gus."

"Gus?" I said.

"Gus. Take it or leave it." Her chuckle sounded hollow.

I heard the clink of ice cubes, a long swallow. She was drinking, and it wasn't beer.

"I mean, don't get me wrong," she said, as if continuing a conversation in her head. "I actually like you, Ten. So, but . . . " She cleared her throat. "I . . . I . . . Ah, shit."

I was growing increasingly baffled by the direction this conversation was taking.

"Agent Gustafson, Gus, I mean, you don't . . ."

"I'm gay," she blurted. "I'm a lesbian. A friggin' . . . I'm a dyke, okay?"

No, not okay. More like, acutely embarrassing. Take any crowd of admiring men, and Heather could always instantly identify which ones wanted to bed her and which were merely drawn to her beauty for aesthetic reasons. She called this skill her gaydar.

My gaydar was obviously in need of serious adjustment.

Now I was the one to clear my throat. "Well," I finally said, "don't take this wrong, but if I was a . . . a woman, you'd be my type." Wow. Did that even make sense?

She laughed, although I could hear a current of pain underlying her mirth.

"God, this is mortifying," she said.

"For you and me both."

"I just . . . You have no idea what a nightmare this is. A gay ATF agent. I mean, hard enough just being a woman there, never mind the rest of it. The never getting asked; the never telling."

"But they repealed that policy, right?" I said. "And anyway, I thought 'Don't ask, don't tell' was just for the military."

"It's part of the whole macho, flag-waving bullshit." She paused. "And the thing is, once you're in the habit of keeping certain behaviors secret, it's not so easy to change. That part's on me."

I understood, all too well.

"Unwritten rules," she went on. "Meanwhile, my love life is nonexistent. Who wants to be with someone whose sense of normal includes living a lie? But I'm convinced, rightly or wrongly, that the minute I come out, I can wave any promotions good-bye."

Another rattle of ice on glass. I didn't have to guess at her favorite nighttime companion, or why her tongue was suddenly loosened.

"Listen to me," she said. "Jesus. I hear you're a monk, and next thing, I'm confessing right and left."

I laughed. "I don't mind," I said.

"Well, true confessions aside, I'm also calling to say thanks."

"For what?"

"For noticing that I'm smart, and for finding me attractive—I know, weird, right? But it's been a while—and also, for backing off when I asked. I can't remember the last time any of those things happened to me, especially with a man from law enforcement."

I felt a surge of compassion for Agent Gus Gustafson. What a lonely world she inhabited, pretending to be someone she wasn't and feel things she didn't.

My irony alarm sounded a second time inside—my own little tripwire, to be pursued more fully later.

"Thank you for your honesty," I said. "I respect that. And I'm really sorry if I made you uncomfortable."

"Ah, shit," Gus said, but I could tell she was smiling. "You really are one of the good guys, aren't you? It's almost enough to make me consider switching teams." Another clink and swallow. The edges of her voice were starting to go slurry on her. "So, I'm thinking we should join forces on this Baja thing, Mr. Buddhist Cop-who-likes-dykes. Nobody else around here seems to give a flying fuck, y'know?"

"I do," I said.

"Ask me anything you want. I'll give you an answer, unless, you know, it compromises my dead-in-the-water investigation."

"Fair enough," I said. "So, what were those anomalies you picked up?"

Silence. Maybe I'd gone too far.

"Okay," Gus said, "but this is in absolute, total confidence. We're talking Fourth Amendment issues. Congress tends to go nuts over this kind of stuff."

"Got it."

"A couple of things don't add up. Mainly, a UAV picked up some heat."

"I'm sorry, UAV?"

"Unmanned Aerial Vehicle. A drone. Homeland's been known to loan out the occasional UAV to the DEA, Customs and Border Protection, local police—but you probably know that already. And even us, once in a blue moon. Certain drones are equipped with heat sensors—infrared radiation imaging, like that—and the Feds have been deploying them more and more along the U.S.-Mexico border, all the way from Southern California to Texas. Mostly to identify grow houses, though they're also interested in tracking unauthorized crossings, illegal drug and weapon smuggling, that sort of thing."

"The Baja site's a bit far south to qualify as a border, isn't it?"

"Yeah, well, this whole area of border surveillance is pretty fuzzy legally. That's sure to change. But you'd be surprised how many of these little mechanical peeping Toms are out there right now."

"How did Homeland Security get on board?"

"They didn't. This was a one-shot deal. Let's just say I called in a favor and leave it at that."

I pictured Chaco's portable pot-growing facilities, his pharmacies on wheels, and his mobile medical Airstreams in Culver City, all of them able to disappear overnight. This large, stationary building didn't fit his M.O. "So, are you thinking someone is growing marijuana in there?"

"No. For one thing, that requires major sources of electrical power. We'd have spotted those on our own. They did detect this odd extra heat somewhere in the general vicinity. But since, according to them, the heat wasn't caused by growers, my bosses blew me off. Especially since the authorities down there not only weren't concerned but told us to back off from the investigation. ATF isn't exactly popular in Mexico, not since that last royal fuck-up."

"Any idea what caused the hot spot?"

"Nope," she said. "Willard insists it could be as simple as old hot springs running somewhere underground. He says, best case scenario, digging the hole for the slab probably jiggered something under the surface."

That sounded highly unlikely. "What's the worst case?"

Another long silence. "The worst-case scenario is why I drink instead of sleep at night," she admitted. "But what I also keep wondering is, who dug that hole? Poured that foundation? Who put that building up there? It's located in no-man's land, on the boundary between Sinaloa and Tijuana cartel territory, but I've been hearing the odd rumor that Los Zetas might somehow be involved as well. If I didn't know better, I'd say they were all in cahoots. You know, conspiring. But who's behind the conspiracy?"

I inhaled deeply. If I spoke his name to Gustafson, I might be signing my own death sentence.

Oh, well. As the Buddha says, death is inevitable.

"Have you considered Chaco Morales?"

"El Gato? He's dead. Los Zetas, remember? They claimed responsibility. They even sent out a picture, I think."

"What if I told you his death was faked? That the cat has started yet another life? Because Chaco's not dead, Gus. He's . . . reincarnated."

Her laughter was skeptical.

"I'm serious. He's alive. I just saw him."

"But, how . . . ?"

"He had surgery to change his appearance. He goes by the name Carnaté now."

"Holy fuck. Carnaté is Chaco Morales?"

"And I'm sure he's the guy behind that place. But as you said, not for growing pot." I hesitated. I was tiptoeing into territory I could scarcely believe was true myself. "The thing is, Gus, I'm starting to think it's some kind of medical facility, though I wouldn't put it past Chaco to also be hiding something there. Something the rest of the cartels might want a piece of."

"A *medical* facility?"

"Yeah. But, it's weird, right? I mean, why would he . . . ?" Our minds did the same math.

"Oh shit, Ten. Are you thinking what I'm thinking?"

"I think I am."

"What's the one kind of building that is absolutely off limits to any kind of military attack, ever? Geneva Convention–prohibited."

We said it together: "A hospital."

We were both stunned into a temporary hush.

"So let me ask you again," I said, breaking the silence. "What's the worst-case scenario?"

"WMDs," she said, her voice reluctant. "Even saying that out loud makes me think I should have my head examined. Do you know how hard they are to purchase, much less hide? Why haven't we seen anything, heard anything from the Mexican authorities? Shit, from anybody? Where's the chatter?"

You really don't know, do you? You really don't know how far the greed reaches.

So I told Gus about *my* worst-case scenario: a gang of gangs. An über-cartel, with its own telecommunications system and sophisticated weaponry, bribing its way deep into the political and financial systems of both countries; a hydra reaching its feelers easily between borders, with Carnaté as its head.

After a long silence, Gustafson let out a long sigh, as if she'd been holding her breath.

"Sorry you called?" I said.

"Yeah. But also relieved. At least I'm not crazy. Or if I am, at least there are two of us."

We were winding down. A final question plucked.

"What's the other discrepancy?" I said.

"Sorry?"

"You said two things didn't add up."

"Oh. Right. Well, this may not mean anything, but it looks to me like the foundation they dug and reinforced might have been bigger than the building they constructed, by maybe a dozen meters, extending west."

"Interesting." I carefully filed that information alongside the rest of our conversation.

"I've got some major digging of my own to do, Ten. I'll be in touch. You take care, okay?"

"You, too. Be well."

"And Ten?"

"Yeah?"

"Just so you know, if I was straight, you'd totally be my type, too."

I disconnected with a smile on my face but a cannonball of dread forming in my belly.

I had to get a full night's sleep. I'd been averaging less than three hours a day. I switched my cell phone to mute, drank a full glass of water, opened the window, and climbed beneath the covers. Tank leapt to the bottom of my bed and settled on top of my feet. I let him stay there, enjoying the feeling of dense weight, of warmth.

I nudged at him with my toes, breaking the mood. He rolled off and settled in the crook of my knees with a contented purr.

"Good night, Tank," I said. "Sleep tight."

An image of my ex-girlfriend Julie, gently caressing my face as we lay side by side, arrived unannounced. I let the impression float away, like a bubble. *May you be safe. May you be happy.* Then my mind must have changed channels, because the last thing I remembered as I coasted into sleep was a big, white building with something lava-hot bubbling underneath, liquefying its foundations.

CHAPTER 20

The distant, insistent ring of my office phone broke through my fog-filled brain.

"Mmmph," I groaned. I sat up and checked the time: 4:39 A.M. I had been dead to the outside world for almost seven hours.

Whoever was calling my landline this early should know better. I lay back down.

No one calls at this hour unless it's urgent.

I swung my feet to the floor. Maybe it was a false alarm. Or maybe pushing the noodle around had finally changed my luck.

I felt my way through the dark living room to my desk and grabbed the phone. My eyes widened at the glowing ID of the caller. "Clancy?"

"Ten, what the hell?" Clancy's hushed voice was clenched with tension. "You turn off your phone, or what? I've been calling you all night!"

"Sorry." I tapped caller ID, and sure enough, Clancy had called the office number twice already. I must have slept through everything until now. "So what's up?"

"Some weirdness," he said. "Weirdness you might be interested in. Having to do with Chuy Dos and Goodhue."

"Back up, back up. What are you talking about? I thought you wanted out."

"I did. Then I changed my mind. Short version? I been watching the Chuy Dos operation on my off hours. Something stinks about this whole McMurtry deal, Ten, and I hate being that dude, the one who bails. I figure, what I do on my own time is my own business. Screw the hours, you know? This is about finishing what I started."

"I get it. So where are you?"

"I'm not sure. Somewhere east of Inglewood. Culver City, maybe? I was watching that GTG van lot—more like dozing than watching—when something woke me up. A loud voice—urgent, you know, like "don't fuck this up, it's important." It was Goodhue, hollering orders at Chuy Dos outside the office building. Goodhue must have driven in while I was catching some zzz's. Anyway, he jumped back in his Benz and booked it out of there. Didn't get my act together fast enough to tail him, so I decided the next best thing was to stay put. I couldn't reach you, a'right? But it paid off."

He paused to take a breath. I remembered to do the same.

"Twenty minutes later, here come two of Chuy's men, the clipboard dude and another one I didn't recognize, and they jump in a van and take off. So I follow, and next thing they pull up next to some sort of mobile home, parked in an empty lot. Crib looks like an Airstream but not, you know? I'm here now, keeping an eye."

"Does it have the GTG logo on the side panel? Did you get the license plate?"

"Yeah, got the license. And yeah, the logo's on the panel.You can't miss it. There's nothing else in the lot. Now the van's just sitting outside, engine idling. I'm parked a block away, waiting to see what happens next. I'm telling you, Ten, there's some weird-ass business going down."

I was back in my bedroom zipping up my jeans, phone wedged between my left shoulder and ear. "Tell me exactly where you are," I said. I pulled on my running shoes.

"Lemme check."

I grabbed my iPhone from the side table to enter the address.

"Okay, says I'm on Mesmer Avenue . . . damn!"

"What?"

"This dude in, in fuckin' scrubs, just ran out of the trailer and handed over some kind of fuckin' . . . Jesus, some kind of cooler, I think! The van's taking off. What do I do?"

"Follow them!" I said. "I'll meet you there!"

"But—?"

"I know where they're going!"

I wasted two minutes circling the room with choppy, directionless steps. My brain was on fire.

Okay. Okay. Slow down.

The action felt counterintuitive, but I took two slow breaths and stretched my arms as high as they could reach before bending forward until I touched the floor with my fingertips, then lowered myself even further and pressed my opened palms against the hard wood, the first of two sun salutations. The elongated breathing and body movement created just enough mental space for me to focus.

Passport. Gun. Cash.

I unlocked my closet safe and retrieved all three.

Tank.

I moved to the kitchen and scraped a full can of cat food into Tank's bowl.

Bill.

I called Bill from my car, winding my way up and over the hill to the 101. With no traffic, I could be downtown in 20 minutes. I'd done that once already this week.

Bill's "hello" was more of a verbalized groan of despair than a greeting.

"Bill, I need you to track down an Airstream, white with the logo GTG on the panel. It's parked in an empty lot on, uh"—I read my phone—"somewhere on Mesmer Avenue in Culver City. I don't have the exact address. Pretty sure the vehicle is one of Chaco's mobile medical units I was telling you about. With any luck it's still there. We're talking possible homicide, but send an ambulance just in case, okay?" I took a deep breath. "I think the victim may be Clara Fuentes."

"Got it." Bill knew me well enough to translate the tone in my voice as *life or death situation*. "What about you? Where are you headed?"

"Hawthorne airstrip," I said. "And don't ask."

Then I checked on Clancy.

"We're already on the 405, heading north," he said. "These fuckers mean business. I didn't know a Ford tank could move this fast."

I floored the Shelby, praying the highway patrol officers were all in bed where they belonged. I was four blocks away from the airstrip in Hawthorne when my phone chimed, at the exact moment I spotted Clancy's Impala in the middle of the street, hazard lights flashing. I slammed on the brakes. Just in front of the Impala, the black van rested on its left side, like a tired puppy taking a nap. Orange construction cones were scattered across the street like giant pieces of candy corn, leaving the jagged gap in the asphalt exposed. The skid marks told a frantic story. A speeding van swerving too late to avoid a giant pothole; a hungry pothole swallowing up a rear tire, causing the van to tip over. For once, I was glad the city hadn't done its job.

The accident must have just occurred. Clancy was climbing out of his car, phone to his ear, but otherwise the street was deserted. He saw me and waved, ending his call and cutting off my chiming ringtone.

The front passenger door in the van pushed open, and Chuy Dos's young clipboard attendant, dressed in his navy GTG coveralls, clambered out, grabbing the door handle for balance. He dropped to the ground and landed in a clumsy heap. His forehead sported a large, rapidly swelling purple bruise, and his eyes were dazed.

"How's the driver?" I called out to Clancy, who had reached the van. He cupped his eyes and peered through the windshield.

"He's okay," Clancy replied, giving me a thumbs-up. "Conscious. Breathing. No blood. Just trapped, it looks like."

Good. I had a few minutes. Time to make my own luck. Time to pick up the noodle with my bare hands.

I ran to the other guy, who was still on the road where he'd landed, though he'd pushed himself into a seated position. His arms hugged his raised knees. His body was starting to shake, and he was muttering to himself. I got close and checked his vital signs. His pulse was thready, his skin damp and clammy.

"*Higado,*" he said. "*Higado. Higado.*" Whatever that was, he needed it badly.

"Call 911," I yelled to Clancy. "This one's going into shock! And bring a blanket if you have one!"

I unzipped his coveralls and awkwardly peeled them off him. Clancy ran to his car and returned with a rumpled flannel sleeping bag—a P.I.'s best buddy for long surveillance gigs.

I wrapped the soft sleeping bag around the victim's trembling shoulders.

"Now what?" Clancy said.

"Now, you stay put until help comes."

"What about you?"

I stepped into the coveralls and zipped them over my clothes, windbreaker, and shoulder-holstered gun. They fit fine.

"I'm going fishing," I said.

I jogged over to the van, where the front passenger door hung ajar like a wayward wing. I hiked up and over the opening and leaned inside to take a look. The wide eyes of the driver, still belted behind the steering wheel, blinked up at me from below. I hoped he was confused enough by the accident that his addled brain would see my uniform and take me for another courier, sent by Chuy Dos.

"*Higado?*" I said, my voice urgent.

He pointed next to him. A white plastic box with a black lid and handle, slightly bigger than a picnic cooler, was wedged at an angle between the seat and the dashboard. Every cell in my body ratcheted up to a state of high alert. ORGAN TRANSPLANT: HANDLE WITH EXTREME CARE was stamped in red on the side of the container.

Even though I had guessed what was going on, I hadn't completely believed it until I read those words. So it was true. Chaco was stripping gangbangers for parts.

I shimmied farther until I was bent in half at the waist and somehow grasped the black handle with my right hand. I tugged. The container wasn't heavy, maybe five pounds, but the angle made retrieval impossible. I needed help, but I didn't know how to ask for it.

And then I did.

"Ayúdame!" I gasped to the driver. *"Ayúdame!"* He freed one arm from the seat belt and pushed as I pulled. Two more tries, and I had it.

I speed-walked to my car, the cooler cradled to my chest as I sent its contents good thoughts. I had no idea what protocol to follow when transporting live organs, but I figured a little loving-kindness couldn't hurt.

In five minutes, I was at the airfield. I parked on the far side of the lot. Goodhue's Mercedes was there. Then I heard a loud *phut-phut-phut*, and a cream-and-striped helicopter, lights flashing, lifted skyward and took off. Hopefully, Goodhue was on it. That would make my job a lot easier.

I paused to pat my chest and underarm, making sure my gun was snugly tucked away in the shoulder holster. My passport and extra money were also safe and sound. What was I forgetting?

Gus.

I set the cooler down gently, unzipped my coveralls, fished out my phone, and pressed her number. Her voice mail picked up right away. She must have turned her phone off. I decided to text her instead: BAHA IS ON. TEN.

Cryptic as hell, but I didn't have time to explain. She was smart. She'd figure out what to do.

I hustled inside Premier Charters, holding tight to the

cooler, a few folded $100 bills damp in one hand. But I didn't need them.

"Hurry! They're waiting for you." The young man at the desk waved me straight out the back exit.

A second helicopter was poised on the tarmac, rotors turning slowly. This one was white, with a bright yellow nose and the initials EMS stenciled on its side in red. EMS: Emergency Medical Services. I was looking at the third steed in Premier Charter's stable, and maybe the most essential one for GTG Services, Incorporated's new line of business.

I took a deep breath, crossed the tarmac, and ducked inside. So far, I was getting by with the ruse. Amazing what the right uniform will do for a man. I was also helped by the fact that I didn't have to pass through any security—the Wilson Combat Supergrade strapped against my chest would have ended this journey before it began, and I'd be begging for forgiveness from inside jail.

I moved farther into the cabin and nodded to the pilot, seated up front. It was Sam, another piece of luck. I widened my eyes and made the slightest of shakes with my head. He responded with a curt duck of the chin before returning to his instruments.

The spotless passenger area was about the same size as the other helicopter's, but the far wall was taken up with a cot the length and width of a stretcher, cushioned with blue foam and belted with several wide red nylon straps. The headrest was slightly elevated, but the bed itself was empty. The surroundings mimicked an ICU. Several medical monitors hung overhead, and the locked metal storage lockers underneath were no doubt stocked with medical supplies. A pair of opaque curtains blocked any view from the large, curved side window.

Two high-backed leather seats faced each other on the near side of the cabin, each with their own set of plump aviation headsets tucked into a side pocket. One seat was occupied. I took the other and found myself facing a short, bushy-browed man in jeans and a tan linen sport coat, with a hooked nose, prematurely snow-white hair, and piercing black eyes. His hands were clasped in his lap, his fingers strong yet tapered, like a musician's. He wasn't so much handsome as compelling. And yes, he resembled a bird of prey.

I set the container gently on the floor in front of me and strapped in.

"You're late," he said.

"Sorry. The van got into a little accident on the way here."

He jerked backward, as if punched by my words. "Jesus! How's the liver?"

Hidago. Liver in Spanish.

"Don't know," I said.

He reached for the container, but I clamped my legs around it.

"Sorry," I said, thinking fast. "Orders. Not until we land."

His round black eyes narrowed. "They didn't tell me anybody else was coming."

"They didn't tell me, either." I shrugged, indifferent.

We had a brief stare-down. I mentally crossed my fingers and executed a wild leap, suicidal, if I guessed wrong.

"My boss likes to keep things separate, Dr. Kestrel," I said, and that did the trick.

He moved up front to Sam and tapped him on the shoulder. Sam lifted one cushioned earpiece to hear. "Let's go," Kestrel said, before returning to his seat and buckling in. He was clearly used to giving orders and used to people obeying them.

I studied him surreptitiously, as the helicopter machinery hummed to life. He gave off his own hum, one of sheer power, the total confidence that comes from being the best in your field. Genius carries a charisma all its own. I shook off the image of what his musician fingers might choose to do in their off hours. With Heather, say.

We lifted off. I took in several deep lungfuls of oxygen and tried to keep my mind on the job and my stomach in the same general vicinity as my head.

Kestrel watched me curiously. "You get airsick?"

"Only small aircraft," I said.

"You get used to it," he said. "I've got drugs, if you want anything."

I'll bet he does.

"No, thanks."

Kestrel reached for a water bottle, set in a cup holder on his armrest. He twisted it open and fished a small Ziploc out of the front pocket of his sport coat. The contents were like a micro-version of Chaco's bulging bags of pills. I spotted Oxycodone, Ecstasy, a couple of Xanax bars. He had a tiny trove of mind-altering treasure.

Dr. Kestrel sorted through the contents, his sharp nose overseeing the search like a predator's beak. Finally, he pounced on two capsules, half blue, half white. He resealed the bag and returned it to his pocket. Then he tossed the pills back, followed by a chaser of water—a practiced, two-step motion. He noticed my stare. "We call these 'Physicians' Assistants'— they'll keep you going for at least eight hours."

"And they are . . . ?"

"Diet pills. Phentermine, to be exact. Lousy for weight loss but miraculous when you're trying to function on little-to-no sleep."

"They don't interfere with your surgery skills?"

"I guess not," he said. "I've been taking them for years." His smile was smug. "Once I'm done with this procedure, it'll be back to business. So no sleep tonight, either." He patted his pocket. "Never mind, two more of these'll keep me going until tomorrow night, when I'll switch to Ambien. Welcome to the romantic life of a surgeon." He didn't seem too cut up about it. Maybe the speed had already started to dance in his bloodstream.

I thought through my next step. Kestrel obviously bought my new role as courier and didn't seem to notice that I wasn't tattooed or Hispanic: once again, my "vaguely Asian" looks were helping me pass as something foreign, but not too foreign. I cleared my mind of any distracting jealous tugs and revisited what Heather had told me about Dr. K.: how the man was considered a god in his field. Fine, I would treat him like one.

"I find your talent humbling," I said.

He beetled his brows, but his eyes glinted with interest.

"I mean, you hold people's lives in your hands on a daily basis."

He chuckled. "Along with their kidneys, lungs, and livers."

"I can't even imagine," I said. "Clearly, you're the best, since my boss chose you. If you don't mind my asking, how much do you get paid for . . . ?" I nudged the cooler with my foot. "You know . . ."

He preened. "Performing a highly complicated emergency transplant procedure in a foreign country under impossibly challenging circumstances?"

I liked his attitude. I wouldn't necessarily want a surgeon on uppers swapping out my liver, but as a talker, he was a detective's dream.

He settled into his chair. "Maybe seventy grand per, but that's gross pay. We net a helluva lot less. Not for this one, mind you. This one pays more."

"So how long does an operation like this take?"

He motioned to the container. "This one? Six-to-eight hours. Maybe a little less. I'm fast. All depends on the state of that liver in there. You have to treat organs like newborns. If you put a banged-up liver into somebody, you're asking for complications."

Good to know. I made a vow to treat my liver like a brand new baby from now on. "How can you tell? If it's damaged, I mean."

He shook his head. "Can't. Not until you remove it from the isosmotic solution. And even then, it's not obvious."

I nodded, as if I knew what he meant. The next couple of questions were delicate, but important.

"So this procedure, it's . . . risky, right?"

Dr. K's knee started jiggling. Excitement? Anxiety? I couldn't tell.

"I've never done a partial before," he admitted. "Live donor to patient."

Partial? Live donor? I hoped he didn't register the shock these words triggered.

He ticked off more concerns. "Donor's almost fifty. Patient's a heavy drinker until recently. Not to mention the hepatitis B business. So, yeah, you could say it's risky."

I recalled John D's tales of Bets McMurtry's wild early years. "A sordid past, coming back to haunt her, eh?" I hoped he wouldn't notice I'd switched to a gender-specific pronoun. It was a little interrogation trick that often worked wonders when digging for more information. Sure enough, he walked straight into my trap.

"Ha! I was part of the evaluation panel that turned her down in the first place. Her MELD score was off the charts." He caught my raised eyebrows. "Model for End-stage Liver Disease. The higher the score, the faster you move up the list. But the rest of her numbers were in the cellar. Red flags all over the place. Hospitals tend to steer clear of transplants with elevated probabilities of rejection. They're all about avoiding potential liability claims."

"Right."

"And even if the graft took, she'd probably require interferon treatment for the hep B afterward. Otherwise, we could be looking at the same story within a few years. So, like I said, the panel turned her down." He smiled slightly. "And yet here we are. Ironic."

"Very."

Kestrel stretched his arms in front of him. He was

compact, but his biceps were very strong and defined. Maybe he self-prescribed steroids, too. "We'll see. The liver will take, or it won't. She'll stay off the sauce, or she won't. Either way, I'm the best chance she has. Either way, I'll get paid."

He glanced at his watch.

"Hope we're close. Livers last twelve hours max outside of their donor."

I pictured Bets, with her cat eyes and acerbic mouth, lying somewhere inside that big white building in the desert, awaiting a second chance at health. She must be so scared. I glanced at the plastic container. What was I doing in the middle of all this?

But I kept going. I had to. I couldn't bail even if I wanted to. I was 20,000 feet above sea level without a parachute. "So, they put up that medical facility fast, huh? Any idea who might have picked up the tab?"

He shook his head. "No idea. The place isn't finished, but I guess they put a hurry-up on an OR and a single ICU unit when your boss's numbers started crashing."

My integrity machinery let out a small squeak. She wasn't my boss, not anymore. And I might be about to cause her irreparable harm.

May I be serving the higher good. May my intentions and action, be noble and true.

"Whoever built it, though, guy's a fucking genius," Kestrel continued. "You wait and see. All those baby boomers desperate to jump the line for new hearts and lungs? We're talking a multi-billion-dollar business. Standing room only."

I glanced up front. Sam had moved one side of his headset just enough to free one ear.

Kestrel let out a small throat-sound of disgust. "As usual, we doctors will just get served the crumbs."

"Pretty good-sized crumbs," I said. As soon as the words left my mouth, I wanted to haul them back in. Why risk insulting him now? Plus, I knew better. Never offer logic to a person locked in a personal drama of victimhood. Might as well tell a wounded soldier whose thigh has been shattered by a bullet, "Cheer up, at least you still have one good leg."

Kestrel angled away from me. He closed his eyes, resting his cheek on the back cushion. The message was clear: our conversation was done.

The chopper flew steadily south.

Kestrel appeared asleep, despite the diet pills. He let out a soft snore.

I picked up the headset tucked beside my seat and slipped it on. I adjusted the mouthpiece.

"Sam?"

The headset crackled.

"This shit's fucked up," I heard. "I was eavesdropping a little bit. Caught the gist."

"I know," I said, my voice low. "Listen, I don't have much time. After we land, are you supposed to stay put or return to your headquarters?"

"Stay put," he said. "Not Jack; he was drop-off only. But they told me I might be needed for a medical transfer."

"Good," I said. "I'm glad."

Kestrel shifted positions, his eyes fluttering. I quickly removed the headset and moved across to the curved window.

Behind the curtains, the sky was light. The sun must have risen. I dared a quick look below, parting the sheer material. Recognizably inhospitable terrain streamed beneath us. I craned my head to look frontward, and soon a small speck of white appeared, swiftly growing larger and larger up ahead. The chopper began to lose altitude, just as the other Premier Helicopter floated by at a distance, already heading back to California.

I hurried to my seat and buckled up, using deep, slow breaths to keep the descent-flutters from erupting into full-blown nausea. My phobia was slightly better but by no means cured. The story of most of the challenges in my life.

Kestrel checked his iPhone and frowned. "Do you have service?" he asked.

I powered up.

"No," I said. I hadn't banked on that. An added wrinkle.

We settled on the ground with a light bump.

Sam hurried to the side door and pulled it open. Scalding air flooded the cabin. A man in green scrubs waded through the heat toward us.

Kestrel was hurriedly unbuckling his seat belt. He pushed to his feet. He held out his hand.

I passed the container over to Dr. Kestrel. He, in turn, handed it to the other man, who turned and took off. Kestrel followed him.

"I'll be back," I said to Sam.

And I followed Kestrel.

CHAPTER 21

The heat was unbearable. Every inhale was a mouthful of seared oxygen. The nylon coveralls didn't help. My left armpit, harboring the .38, was literally streaming sweat by the time we reached the entrance to the building. The man in scrubs pushed inside, and we followed. He was Hispanic and harried-looking, his thick black mustache hooking around both sides of his mouth like twin scimitars. He set the cooler down.

"You're late," he barked, echoing Kestrel. A second man appeared, a stone-faced soldier boy. He was dressed in short-sleeved black fatigues; his uniform included handcuffs and a Heckler & Koch self-loading pistol. No safety vest—probably too hot for one. Finally, an older woman hurried up, in nurse's white.

Mustachio Man frowned in my direction. "*¿Quién es este?* Who's this?"

Kestrel waved toward the inside of the building. "He's one of theirs."

He said it, not me. I tried to look as crisply official as possible, given the rivulets of sweat freely flowing down my body.

"Dr. Gomez is assisting me," Kestrel said to me.

I nodded to Gomez. "Good to meet you."

The expression on his face stated otherwise. "Our nurse, Señora Delgado," he said. Delgado, at least, had a kind face.

Niceties over, Gomez waved us in, past the security guard. I checked out his uniform. Mexican Municipal Police. Probably moonlighting as a hospital guard. If I got paid less than $600 a month, I'd moonlight, too.

The air was as icy inside as it was scorching out. I shivered, surveying the interior with interest. Impressively clean and painted a pale hospital gray-green, the structure was basically one large box. The left side was divided into ten rooms, with ten closed doors. An assortment of unfinished office cubicles in various states of construction lined the other side. A freestanding, diesel-fueled generator hummed away from the far corner of the building, the kind normal hospitals used as backup, in case of a power outage. Maybe these guys had two.

At present, we seemed to be the only people in the building. It had the hastily vacated appearance of a schoolyard during an air raid.

Kestrel said, "Have you concluded the pre-op?"

"Yes," Dr. Gomez nodded. "Just administered the hundred milligrams of Demerol."

I jumped in. "I need a word with Assemblywoman McMurtry before she goes under. Where is she?"

Gomez checked with Kestrel. He shrugged his okay. "But make it quick," he said. He nodded to the nurse. "Take him." She reacted to his order with an adoring gaze. I guess his particular brand of sex appeal crossed borders.

Nurse Delgado led me across the empty floor. One of the side doors was ajar, and I saw open cardboard boxes and an empty hospital bed, the mattress still wrapped in plastic.

"Is Goodhue with the patient?" I asked. My hand crept toward my shoulder holster, hidden inside my coveralls.

"No. Señor Goodhue take a jeep into town. Doctor Gomez tell him to come back when la Señora is in the recovery room."

We reached the last door. She knocked lightly, before opening it. "Señora, your friend would like to speak to you."

She withdrew. This room was not only finished but it was a replica of any state-of-the-art pre-op room in any top medical facility. I crossed to the hospital bed, where a very different version of Bets McMurtry lay. No make-up. No sunglasses. No fire. I would have walked right past her on the street without recognizing her. Her skin was parchment and had the telltale yellowish tinge of a liver on strike. Her tawny eyeballs told the same tale. She looked ten years older than the day before.

The Demerol had worked its magic, and she eyed me with benign amusement, stoned to the gills. "Detective," she said. "I think I'm mad at you, but I'm not remembering why." She rested her head back on the pillow. "What are you doing here?"

"I'm here to help you," I said.

"Sweet of you. Why?"

"Bets, you're in business with a really bad man."

She groaned. "Ah, shit—not that again. Now I'm remembering why I stopped liking you, Norbu."

"Listen," I said. "You have big dreams. If you're lucky, an even bigger future. Do you really want to tie that to a drug lord and a killer?"

She rested her eyes on mine. Her pupils were like pancakes. She was too under the influence to think straight, and her next words proved it. "Here's what I know. Everybody's hiding a nasty secret or two. My last drug run I was so desperate I gave a stranger a blow job for fifty bucks. Brought me to my knees"—her smile was beatific—"in more ways than one. The next day, I got down on those same knees and accepted Jesus as my Lord and Savior. Best day of my life, right after the worst one." She tried to focus on me, with little success. "I got news for you. I'm going to die without this procedure, and I need someone who's willing to break a few rules to save my life."

"Break a few rules? Is that your definition of what he's up to?"

She sank into her pillow. Her eyelids were at half-mast, and I knew my time was almost up.

"Don't you worry about me and Mr. Morales. They got

crooks in the White House that eat guys like Chaco for breakfast." She lifted a forefinger, pointing vaguely. "That's where I'm going, Ten," she intoned, like a stoned seer of the future. "Sacramento first, then D.C. You're looking at the second governor of California who will make it to the White House. Morales is nothing. Just another blow job, so I can live long enough do the real work God's got planned for me."

I heard a brisk knock. Dr. Gomez stepped inside. "Almost time," he said to Bets. She barely nodded. He caught my eye and beckoned toward the door.

"You're wanted," he said. His mouth twitched strangely.

I stepped out the door and into the point-blank range of a pair of guns at the end of a pair of extended arms. One pistol, the Heckler, belonged to the security guard; the other, an older but equally deadly Beretta 92, to Mark Goodhue.

Gomez withdrew, closing the door softly behind me.

A cop can always tell whether a person aiming a gun is an amateur or a professional. The "tell" is the steadiness of the shooter's hand. The security guard's grip was stable as a rock, and the quiet gleam in his gaze informed me he had experience pulling the trigger and it was an experience he'd enjoyed.

In contrast, Goodhue's two-plus pounds of pistol fluttered and waved like a flag in a fickle wind.

Police Academy training teaches a variety of complex physical maneuvers that should work when faced with a close-range, armed perp. Should is one thing. Reality is another. I'd learned the hard way that the wisest way to disarm a dangerous shooter was with my mouth. In this situation, though, I was hampered by the fact that the expert shot and I were fluent in different languages. Where was Carlos when I needed him?

The language barrier was the least of my worries. Goodhue concerned me more. He'd probably never pointed anything heavier than a Montblanc pen before now. Berettas aren't light, and some 92s don't have manual safeties.

The gun waggled in the general direction of my head.

Criminals aren't used to the truth. It confuses them. "You're scaring the shit out of me, Goodhue," I said.

"What?"

"Could you point your Beretta somewhere else, before you shoot me in the face?"

Goodhue had an MBA and a designer suit, but he was still a criminal. He blinked, as if suddenly realizing how much his gun hand was wobbling.

He said something in Spanish to the guard, who stepped back two feet and raised his second hand to steady his first. The new angle gave him a better direct shot. Goodhue lowered his own arm with a visible sigh of relief. He reached a hand to massage his shoulder muscle before replacing gun-wielding with a more familiar weapon of choice: honcho arrogance.

"Representative McMurtry and I are deeply disappointed that you are meddling in our affairs again," he sniffed. "Against explicit orders."

I wasn't all that happy at the moment, either. The only thing that gave me cheer was that nobody had frisked me. I could feel the comforting touch of my pal and partner, the Wilson Supergrade, tucked alongside my rib cage.

"Who told?" I said.

He jerked his head toward the guard. "He called me in town. Said there was some Chinese-looking guy here. I knew right away."

He turned to the guard and fired off another sentence in Spanish. I may not speak the language, but I know blood-lust when I see it. The guard practically licked his lips, as his hand tightened on his weapon. So Goodhue was giving him my killing orders.

For the third time this week, I was in the company of

a stone-cold shooter, with a target on my chest. The guard jerked his chin toward the door. I stayed put.

Goodhue said to me, "Don't worry. He's just taking you to the helicopter."

Right.

Goodhue turned, as if to walk away.

"Mr. Goodhue?"

He stopped. Faced me, his eyebrows raised.

"Why? Why Chaco Morales?"

If he talked, I knew I really was dead. But at least I'd die knowing a little more about the nature of greed. Goodhue's look danced between smugness and pity. "You haven't been around politics much, have you?"

I shook my head.

"You ought to hang around Washington for a while. Or even Sacramento. You deal with those guys for a few years, and you're grateful to do business with a guy like Chaco. At least he doesn't waste your time pretending he's not a crook."

"That's your justification?"

"You can't possibly be that naive, Detective Norbu. Hell, no. My justification is the same as everyone else's. I want to be rich, and I want to be powerful. I was just an entrepreneurial peon with an MBA, trying to get a small medical supplies business off the ground, when I stumbled onto Chuy Dos's cleaning-service model. We met, and we hit it off. The more he told me, the more I liked what I was hearing. He and his partner were sitting on a gold mine with this concierge cleaning–slash–drug delivery scheme they'd hatched, and I told them so. They had a database of a couple thousand wealthy people around L.A. who didn't mind bending the law to get their special treats. It was a niche opportunity of a lifetime. I pitched the idea of using the same model to locate and satisfy transplant candidates. Put together a business plan, combined forces, formed a new company under their umbrella one, and *voilà*, here we are. We've got over four hundred people on the waiting list. Once we're up and running, we're talking half a billion a year. Net."

Just saying the numbers made him shine with glee.

"And the organ suppliers?"

"That's Chuy's end of the business. I don't ask. But gangbangers are vermin, Tenzing. You show me someone who says otherwise, and I'll show you a liar. Mr. Morales is a generous man. The family of every dead banger gets five thousand in cash. It's a triple win."

"How does Bets feel about that?"

"Bets doesn't know the details. She doesn't want to. She's got long-term political plans, and so does our PAC, New Americans for Freedom. With a rising star as our political mouthpiece, one who literally owes her life to us, we can keep all our business models nice and lucrative. I'm sorry, did I say triple? I should have said, home run!"

"All very impressive," I said.

You're a stain on this little patch of the universe. I'd like to . . .

Settle down, I thought. *You need this stain to keep talking.*

"So, what about the other thing, the heat under the building? What's that about?"

He frowned. "I'm sorry?"

"What are you guys storing down there?"

"I have no idea what you're talking about," he said.

This, I wasn't expecting. Now what? I decided to rattle his cage. "The foundation showed up hot on a satellite heat scan. A drone confirmed it."

Goodhue reddened. "What are you . . . ?" His voice climbed the scale. "What satellite? What drone?"

I held up my hands, but kept pushing. "Sorry, I assumed you knew. Homeland Security picked up unusual heat readings somewhere around here."

"Homeland Security? Jesus Christ!" Goodhue swayed from foot to foot, his right fist clenching and unclenching.

The guard chose this moment to pull out a cigarette and light it, one-handed, while still keeping his pistol trained on my heart.

Goodhue snapped at him. "You can't smoke in here! It's a goddamn hospital!" Apparently the tension was getting to him. Good.

The guard removed the cigarette from his mouth. He didn't put it out, though.

"You want to see heat?" he said. "I show you." So his English was serviceable.

I was vibrating with eagerness to get something into motion. In addition to the tension of being held at gunpoint, my muscles were shivering with the chill. The temperature had lowered to the point of human refrigeration.

The guard led us back through the building, opened the front door, and waved me out with the gun barrel. Emerging into the dry Baja heat was like diving into a pizza oven. The shock of scalding air caused me to exhale forcefully. Behind me, Goodhue yelped.

The guard waved his cigarette around. "Heat," he said, and laughed harshly.

Everybody's a comedian, as Bill loves to say.

But we were finally outside, and I sensed a small shift in my survival odds.

"Sorry, but I'm melting here. I gotta unzip this," I told Goodhue. I calmly unzipped my coveralls.

The guard lifted the cigarette to his lips for a long-awaited drag.

Now!

I dropped and rolled, hitting the ground sideways and coming up on my knees with my Wilson in my right hand. The split-second the guard's brain took to abandon the pleasures of addiction for his duties as a killer was all I needed. I dodged left. He fired and missed. I got my own shot off as I crashed into Goodhue with my left shoulder, taking us both down. My ears were screaming from the shots, but I didn't hear any human screams added to the mix.

I pressed my Wilson hard in Goodhue's heaving chest, pinning him with my knees as my other hand pocketed his Beretta, after making sure the safety was, indeed, engaged. I checked on the guard. He was on his back, head turned toward me, eyes wide with surprise and leaking life. I'd hit him lower than I'd intended, square in the navel. He was illustrating what they say about gut shots: *You're already dead, but your head don't know it.*

I waited for the nausea, the self-disgust to kick in. Nothing.

I felt . . . nothing.

I watched with as much reverence as I could muster, given my numb state, and the fact that I was pressing a steel barrel into another man's chest. The light slowly left the guard's eyes. *Om mani padme hum.* I said the words, but I didn't feel them, either.

I swung back to Goodhue, who appeared appropriately shaken. His expensive suit was blooming stains of sweat, and his skin had taken on a greenish tint.

"Let's go," I said.

"What? What?" He pulled his eyes away from the corpse and focused on me. Fury flared across his face, and his lips drew back as he swiped his slick brow with the back of a fist. Then he remembered I was the one with the gun. He visibly retracted his fangs, like a viper. I'd never seen a person so angry and yet so contained—an explosive combination.

"We need to check the foundation," I said.

"I'm not doing a goddamn thing until you get that gun off me."

I considered his words. Rage or not, I wasn't too worried about Goodhue jumping me. I'd put my Police Academy moves up against any he might have learned in an MBA program.

On the other hand, I wasn't a complete idiot. I compromised by lowering my .38, while grabbing his right wrist and yanking his arm high, behind his back. I made him bend down with me, as I disarmed the dead guard, sliding his pistol in my empty holster. I took his cuffs, keys, and cell phone as well. I was loaded down with all the extra artillery, but I wasn't going to complain.

I herded Goodhue toward the perimeter of the building.

"You sure you want to do it this way?" he muttered. "I could put a lot of money in your pocket. Just give me a number."

"The magic number is zero," I said.

We moved slowly around the perimeter in a counterclockwise direction. I didn't really know what I was looking for. Every time I saw a crack or an imperfection, I made Goodhue kneel next to me to inspect, but the walls and foundation, while blemished, were solid.

My phone vibrated in my pocket. I had service again.

But when I pulled it out, I was holding the guard's clunky flip phone in my hand.

"Don't move a muscle," I ordered Goodhue. He nodded.

I fished my phone out as well and brought up Gus's number. I called, using the guard's working phone. *Answer. Please answer.*

"Agent Gustafson. Who is this?"

"Gus," I said. "It's me, Tenzing."

A pause. Then, "What the fuck, Ten?"

I'd met official Gus and tipsy Gus. This was my first encounter with angry Gus.

"Sorry I couldn't call earlier, my . . ."

"Shut the hell up and start talking!" she yelled, illogically, to my mind.

"Is there a problem?" I kept my tone neutral, my eye on Goodhue.

Her voice rose. Soon Mark would be able to hear every word.

"Problem? I specifically told you not to go back there! I'm starting to think you're as full of crap as everybody else! Or maybe you're in on this whole thing!"

I said, "No. You've got it all wrong."

And then my phone went dead. Or maybe she hung up on me. Either way, the connection was lost.

We continued around the back and up the other side. Except for a single safety door—an obvious emergency exit from the building—nothing, nothing, a whole lot of nothing.

We arrived once again at the still body of the guard, his own patch of universe now darkened by a spreading stain of blood. I was running out of time.

Where was the underground entrance? The method of ingress?

I mentally riffled through last night's conversation with Gus and remembered her final piece of intelligence, the second anomaly: a reinforced foundation measuring slightly bigger than its building, a cut that extended a dozen meters beyond its cover.

I squinted at the sky to get my directional bearings. The angled sun, a god of hellfire, now hurled its hot rays at a slant. Mid-afternoon—Bets was halfway through her procedure. I hoped Kestrel's pill-fueled hands were holding steady.

I dragged Goodhue over to the west wall of the building, calculating. A dozen or so meters, that translated to about 16 yards.

"I'm dizzy," Goodhue whined. "I think I have heat stroke."

I ignored him. Using a grid formation, as if looking for a missing body in brush, I paced back and forth along the area perpendicular to the wall, scuffing at the loose topsoil, keeping Goodhue as close to me as my own hot breath.

Midway through my search, I found it—a flatter feel to the earth, something man-made camouflaged beneath the topsoil. Crude, but effective. Unless you were right on top of it and looking for it, you wouldn't know the change in terrain was there. I scraped away at the sandy soil, panting in the sweltering heat.

"Dig, you bastard," I snarled at Goodhue.

He applied his manicured hands to the task.

We slowly uncovered a wide plank, slightly recessed within a concrete frame. A triangle of small holes had been drilled into one corner of the thick wood.

"Any ideas?" I said.

"They look like finger-holds," Goodhue answered, grudgingly. "You know, like with bowling balls." He illustrated. So the man wasn't completely useless after all.

I met Goodhue's eyes.

"Okay. I'm going to lift this, and you're going to help me. Otherwise, and this is a promise, I'll cuff you to a cactus and leave you out here to roast. Understand?"

He nodded.

I squatted, fitting two fingers and a thumb into the holes.

"Brace me," I said.

He did. The wood didn't budge.

"Again."

I inhaled. Exhaled. Inhaled again, taking the scorched desert air deep into my lungs. I filled every cell and sinew of my body with intention. I pressed against Goodhue, while pulling upward with all my arm strength.

Move.

The cover yielded. Sweat poured down my face. I shifted the raised plank sideways and slipped one hand under it, then both. If Goodhue had been thinking, this would have been a good time to run. But his thrill of the hunt must have kicked in. My muscles were screaming as I lifted and shifted, lifted and shifted, enough to finally expose a set of steep concrete steps leading downward, straight into the shadowed bowels of Mother Earth.

I let the wooden covering drop to one side and fell against Goodhue. We stared at the opening, catching our breath.

"Now what?" Goodhue said.

"Now, I go look." I grabbed his arm. "We go look, I mean."

He shook his head.

"Not me," he said.

"Yes, you. You think I'm leaving you out here alone?"

He started to shake. "I can't," he said. "I can't do that." He was panting like a thirsty dog, and his eyes darted from side to side. He clutched at his throat.

"Claustrophobia," he gasped.

Great. Now what? It didn't seem like the right time or place for implementing exposure therapy. I looked around. My eyes lit on the EMS chopper, waiting patiently nearby on its helipad.

Five minutes later, Goodhue was cuffed and strapped tight to the helicopter gurney, Sam and the Heckler keeping watch, and I was feeling my way down, down, down into my first deeply buried facility.

This was like my recurring lucid dream about the tower, only in reverse. I descended a good dozen steps until I reached a concrete floor. The air was as dark and stale as you'd expect in a desert bunker, although at least 20 degrees cooler than the outside. That put the temperature in the 80s.

I couldn't see much, even after my eyes adjusted. My only flashlight was my iPhone app, but it was a whole lot better than nothing. I held the small square of light high and slowly turned, playing it over the hollow, cement-walled space. The room was maybe 1,200 square feet total. Big, for a tomb. I stepped to my right first.

Metal shelves again, a wall of them, holding thousands of handhelds, antennas, radios, repeaters, batteries, radio bases, and heavy flip phones like the one in my pocket—enough to connect a small city. I had found Chaco's personal Radio Shack: telecommunications central.

I moved to the next wall of shelving. Ah. The armaments department: AK-47s; belt-rounds of ammo; rifles, handguns, and more rounds of ammo; Barrett 99 Bolt Actions; Cugir semiautomatics; Romarm WASR-10s; Glocks, Berettas, and a dozen more submachine guns; night-vision goggles; heavy body armor—bulletproof vests and protective helmets. Even a row of fragmentation hand grenades, the size and shape of small melons but devastatingly deadly. This portion of the underground storehouse was a veritable Superstore of supplies for an army of survivalists. I wondered how much of this stash traced back to the Fast and Furious debacle.

The third area was the pharmaceutical section, mixing ten-gallon Ziplocs of prescription drugs with sealed blocks of cocaine and kilos of crystal meth. I didn't spend too much time there. I'd seen it all before.

I walked to the farthest wall and aimed my square of light.

Unbidden, an ancient chant of protection sprung up from my soul: *Palden Lhamo, Protectress who performs all pacifying deeds, pacify my illnesses, hindrances, and ghosts.*

I counted ten launchers—old but recently cleaned and oiled. Maybe a yard in length, and six inches in diameter, they were shaped like tubes, Army green, with two aiming sights on top, a narrow strap at one end, and a pair of black handles, one equipped with a trigger, jutting underneath like deadly fins. I carefully hefted one. It weighed about 20 pounds, unloaded.

I moved the light to read the stenciled information on the side of the launcher, but I already knew. I was looking at an RPO-A, a Russian Shmel, or rocket-propelled flame-thrower, launcher of thermobaric grenades. I had read about them around the time of the second Iraqi invasion. What stopped my heart were the grenades. Each rocket-shaped missile was silver, the front tipped with brass metal, the back sprouting bent wings. The payload was mustard yellow, striped with black. The colors of danger. The colors of death. The source of the heat.

With their enhanced, vacuum-packed blast, these weapons completely obliterated whatever they hit and were catastrophically lethal to any personnel caught within their radius—they literally sucked all the oxygen out of anyone unfortunate enough to live through the initial explosion. Short of nuclear warheads, no other weapons were as destructive, pound for pound, or as horrific.

And Chaco, aka Carnaté, had ten of them. No wonder his neighboring cartels wanted to make nice to him. I tried to place another call, but of course the combined concrete and earth blocked any signal. I tried to snap some pictures, but between the darkness and my shaking hands, I knew they would prove to be of little to no use.

But I had my answers. And so did Gus, once I could reach her and tell her what I'd seen. She finally had her boots on the ground, her eyewitness, her human intel.

And I was finally ready to land my killer whale.

Chapter 22

"You're familiar with firearms?" I pointed to the Heckler, steady in Sam's hand, Goodhue at the other end of the barrel. I'd returned to the chopper to implement the first step of my plan and had found Sam taking his guard duties very seriously.

Sam frowned. "Not really. We had a shooting range next to my college. I was pretty decent back then, but I'm out of practice."

"Better than Mark here, by a mile," I said.

Goodhue snorted. I'd freed him from the straps, and now he slumped, still cuffed and very sullen, on the edge of the gurney.

"What was in that hole, anyway?" Goodhue said. "What did you find?"

"Stuff," I answered. No need to set off a panic. "So here's what I need, Mark," I continued. "I'd like you to give Chaco a call."

His body jolted as if tasered.

"That idea scares you," I said.

"No shit, Sherlock. What am I supposed to say to him? 'Hey, Chaco, I fucked up. Can you come down here please, so the crazy Tibetan can arrest us both?' That'll go over well."

Who said anything about arrest? I thought. I motioned my gun at him, just to remind him who was armed.

"Tell him that you just discovered the Feds have been watching this building for months," I said. "That they're onto him. Tell him you found me here, nosing around, and you did what you had to do. Tell him he needs to get down here—*now*."

"You want me to set him up," Goodhue sneered.

"Hey," I said. "This is no time for you to suddenly grow a moral center."

He held up his cuffed hands. "Okay," he said. "I'll call. I'm screwed either way at this point. But take these off first."

I unlocked his cuffs. He rubbed his wrists, as I retrieved his phone from his pocket, unsurprised to see it was the same make and model as the guard's—and the arsenal of phones below. I powered it on and handed it over. "Put it on speaker."

He fidgeted, waiting for a signal. Then his phone let out three short squawks. He squinted at the screen. "Chaco just called, five minutes ago."

"Even better," I said. I waggled my gun. "Do it."

He punched the number. It rang twice before Chaco's voice shouted, *"Si? Si?"*

"Goodhue here. Can you hear me? Where are you?" Goodhue asked.

"Oh. You! Good. *Escúchame,* listen. I'm close!" Chaco's raised voice was barely audible over the choppy metallic whine in the background.

Sam widened his eyes and pointed up, rotating his index finger. So, another helicopter was on its way.

"My guy at Homeland contacted me!" Chaco yelled. "Is she still in surgery?"

Goodhue shot me a glance, and I nodded. He said, "Yes."

"Good!" Chaco said. "She'll be my bargaining chip, if necessary. Lemme speak to Fernando. He needs to send word. We have to move some product, and we can't do it alone."

That was going to be a challenge. Unless Fernando had nine lives like his boss, his current status made further communication difficult. Goodhue looked wildly in my direction for a cue. I mimicked puffing on a cigarette.

"He went out for a smoke."

"*Mierda*," Chaco said. "What about the Chink? Is he dead?"

So he knew I was here. Again, Goodhue looked to me for a cue. I nodded and mimed the throat-cutting gesture.

"Yes." Then Goodhue improvised—brilliantly, to my mind. "We dumped the body nearby, in the bushes." Goodhue was starting to get the hang of this. He'd given me a good idea.

"*Mierda*," Chaco repeated. "I wanted to kill that *hijo de puta* myself! Okay. I won't be long." Chaco disconnected.

As if on cue, the guard's phone buzzed in my other pocket. I checked the screen—it wasn't Chaco this time. It was Gus. Informative Gus, as it turned out. Clever girl, she'd used the only cell phone that worked here, the number I'd used to call her from earlier.

"Ten? Listen. You need to get out of there. We're staging a raid."

"Who?"

"ATF, plus FBI. Plus the local militia. Somebody from inside Homeland tipped us off. Said Carnaté, aka Chaco Morales, was on his way down there."

So Chaco was about to relearn a hard lesson: nobody's to be trusted; everybody lies.

"Gus, listen." I lowered my voice, glancing at Sam and Goodhue. "You were right. I found the underground facility. I got inside."

Her breath caught. "Tell me."

I stepped out onto the broiling landing pad. "Russian rocket launchers, ten of them. With thermobaric payloads. Plus enough arms and ammo to take down the entire Southwest."

"Flamethrowers? Mother of God," she said. "Homeland's sending two Hueys as backup. I have to warn them off!"

Two Hueys, one aeromedical transporter, and a chopper of unknown origin—at this rate, the sky was going to resemble the 405 at rush hour. Or a row of sitting ducks.

"Good idea," I said. "And while you're at it, can you tell your trigger-happy cohorts to hold off on doing anything crazy? We don't want another Waco. Tell them at least seven civilians are still here. And one of them is Bets McMurtry."

I grabbed Sam, and together we forced Goodhue to help us drag the guard's body a good 20 yards away from the entrance. We placed him in a thick scrub of desert chaparral. Now we had a body to go with Goodhue's story.

"Could you tell what kind of helicopter that was?" I asked Sam, as we tossed dirt and brittle creosote branches on top of the corpse until he was mostly obscured.

"Sounded lightweight. Single engine, probably," he said. "Probably two-passenger, max."

Good to know. That meant Chaco wasn't bringing his troops with him.

I hustled them back inside the building and ordered Sam to keep an eye on Goodhue and an ear to the sky, as I ran to the operating room at the opposite end.

I pushed inside, stopping at the doorway. Both doctors, as well as Nurse Delgado, were hunched over their patient. Three heads snapped up in unison. Kestrel's right hand held a bloodied instrument.

"Trouble coming," I said. "How soon can you finish?"

A muffled "Goddammit!" erupted from under Kestrel's surgical mask. He collected himself. "Half an hour," he said. "Now get lost."

"Is there another way out of here? For the patient, I mean?"

I spotted the emergency exit just as Gomez pointed it out.

"Good. The minute it's safe to move her, take her straight to the EMS chopper," I said. "Then get her to a real hospital, as fast as you can."

I ran back to Sam and Goodhue.

"Sam, get the chopper ready for liftoff," I said. "How many passengers are you licensed to carry?"

"Six," he said. "Including the pilot."

"Perfect," I said to Sam. Bets was going to need all the medical expertise she could get. The authorities could deal with the despicable Kestrel and his criminal cohorts later. "Keep the gun," I added. "Just in case. Now go."

Sam met my eyes. "Good luck," he said. He hurried outside.

"What about me?" Goodhue muttered.

"You made this mess," I answered. "And now you need to clean it up."

We waited, ears trained for the sound of approaching machines, airborne or otherwise. Goodhue fidgeted, scuffing the soles of his shoes on the floor in a rhythmic alternating pattern, as if his legs were already running.

I needed him calmer. I tried to distract him.

"You're a smart guy, Mark. I'm sure you could succeed anywhere. Why break the law?"

"I told you already," he said.

"Tell me again."

You wouldn't understand," he said.

"Try me."

"Fine. Here's what they don't teach you in B-school. Anyone can do okay. But there are only three ways to get rich—fuck-you rich—assuming you weren't born with a fuck-you rich daddy. One: be first—first to trade Bibles for land in Hawaii; first to find oil. Two: be better—find and keep the edge. Think Steve Jobs or Warren Buffett."

Or Chaco Morales.

"And the third way?"

"Cheat. Find the hole and dive in fast, before they plug it." His face twisted with rage. "Fuckin' Bets and her fuckin' housekeeper. We had the perfect win-win solution here, you know? Clara Fuentes was an illegal. Her presence was a huge political liability. So was McMurtry's suddenly failing health. So why not use the one to fix the other and make both problems disappear? But, no. Bets freaked out.

She was determined to find Clara, no matter what. I told her to drop it, but she wouldn't. Next thing you know, she gets a fuckin' private dick involved. For a fuckin' illegal alien!"

A distinctive rotary whine, distant but increasing in volume, chopped through the atmosphere. I moved Goodhue to the side window overlooking the helipads. I craned my neck. A lightweight, two-person helicopter was coming in low to land, green and spindly, like an insect. It circled over the guard's camouflaged body once. I was grateful we'd completely covered him.

I took two steps back, out of eyesight.

"Chaco," Goodhue nodded, peering through the glass.

"Meet him on the helipad and then bring him this way, through the front door," I said. "Tell him Fernando's inside, awaiting instructions."

Goodhue hesitated, then shrugged. "Okay."

He started out.

"Mark?"

"Yeah?"

"You're not going to tell Chaco I'm here, are you?"

He shook his head.

"Say no," I said.

"No."

"Then go."

He stepped outside and waded through the heat. I watched from the window. The helicopter touched down with the delicacy of a butterfly coming to rest.

A distant overlapping roar announced the imminent arrival of more helicopters.

Chaco jumped out of the chopper, and Goodhue ran to his side. Chaco clapped Goodhue on the back and started to walk in my direction. Then Goodhue made a huge mistake. He must have panicked, or thought he could save himself, because he took off running, waving his arms at the deeper throbbing noise in the sky.

Chaco spun, whipping a gun out of his pocket, a blur of metal. He took aim and dropped Goodhue with a single shot to the back. Goodhue pitched onto his face and lay twitching on the dry earth. Chaco walked over, nudged him with a boot toe, and delivered a second bullet into the base of Goodhue's neck. The twitching stopped.

Be first. Be better. Or cheat. Mark Goodhue chose to cheat, and for that he paid the price. You never know how long it will take for the wheel of karma to circle back around, only that it will. This time, the loop was lightning-quick, the death blow of karma from behind.

Chaco stood up, and I shuddered at the dead look in his eyes. No feeling. No remorse.

The thumping, pulsing noise above grew louder. Was this good news or bad? I couldn't see where these helicopters were, or if they belonged to friends or foes.

Either way, I needed to get Bets and her medical team out of there, ideally without Chaco knowing I was still alive. Whatever her politics, she was a human being with a beating heart, and she and the others didn't deserve to die a violent death. That was Chaco's form of justice, not mine.

I sprinted back to the operating room. Bets was lying on a narrow movable gurney now, tubes connecting her to a portable IV. Nurse Gonzalez was attaching a bag of clear fluid.

"It's done?" I said.

Kestrel nodded, peeling off his surgical gloves.

"We've got to get her out of here. I need scrubs and a mask," I told Gomez. "Now!"

He pointed to a metal cabinet.

In less than five minutes, two doctors, a nurse, and a Tibetan orderly were wheeling Bets McMurtry to the waiting EMS helicopter.

Chaco was slowly dragging Goodhue's body toward the same scrub that housed the guard. He straightened, and glared at us.

"Faster," I said. We ran the gurney to the open helicopter door. Sam was waiting.

Chaco dropped Goodhue and fumbled for his gun.

"Quick! The edge of the sheets!" Kestrel gasped. "One. Two. Three. Lift!"

Using the sheets as a sling, the four of us maneuvered Bets inside and placed her on the helicopter gurney, Nurse Delgado manning the IV behind us.

A bullet clanged off one side of the chopper. Bets's eyes were closed, her face ghost-pale. Kestrel and Gomez elbowed the rest of us away so they could minister to her. I wondered if she would make it. Either way, I had cleared my own karma, as far as she was concerned.

Chaco was a different story entirely. I ripped off my hospital mask and grabbed my gun. I moved to the helicopter door in a stoop, keeping out of sight, my .38 drawn, but Chaco had stopped shooting. I peered outside as the blades began to rotate.

"Ten! Buckle up!" Sam yelled.

Chaco's face had darkened to a murderous hue.

The engine whirred. "Ten!"

He was staring straight at the gap in the ground, where I'd pushed open the trap door leading to his hidden bunker of death. He started toward it.

I chose that moment to slip onto the tarmac and crouch-run my way horizontally toward the other chopper.

Sam lifted off, the roar sounding in my ears as my mouth filled with grit. I watched through stinging eyes as they banked steeply and flew away. A wash of relief flooded my heart area. I did a body count: two dead, five escaped, two still at large.

Plus me.

I reached Chaco's small helicopter and dove inside. I had my Wilson pressed to the pilot's temple before he had time to react.

"Take us up," I said. "UP!!!" I jabbed my finger at the sky, just in case he didn't speak English.

The distinctive hum started again, like a swarm of metallic mosquitoes.

"STOP!" I heard through the loud crackle of a bullhorn. "FEDERAL AGENTS!"

I located the source: several men standing on a slight incline about a football field's distance away. The shouter, a Feeb in sturdy shoes, lowered his horn. Behind him, armed ATF agents were scrambling for their guns. Behind them, a half dozen more suits were trying to get signals on their phones. They'd apparently all just arrived in a herd of black Range Rovers, any hubbub swallowed up by all the chopper noise. Now a bouncing black jeep materialized from behind the incline, and several heavily armed Mexican *federales* spilled out. I was witnessing the build-up to a potentially disastrous goat-rodeo, as Bill liked to put it.

Assess risk, my mind screamed. Which was worse, the fools on the hill or the maniac behind me?

Then we lifted off, and I realized that *this* was worse. In fact, this was my worst nightmare. I was flying straight up in a tiny helicopter, and the helicopter, as far as I could tell, had no doors.

Down below, the mix of Mexicans and Americans milled around chaotically, as if waiting for someone to tell them what to do. With no phone signals, that was tough. Finally, they formed a ragged line and started a slow, halting advance.

I couldn't find Chaco anywhere. I had a very bad feeling about that.

I fumbled for the guard's flip phone. I had a signal again. I called Gus.

"Ten!"

"All civilians are free and clear," I said. "Most of them are also criminals, so make sure you have a shit-load of handcuffs at the other end, along with an ambulance."

"Got it," she said.

"But Chaco's gone underground. I'm sure for a Shmel. Tell your guys to back off!"

"What about you?"

"I'm in the green bird. Make sure they don't kill me, okay? Tell them I'm going fishing."

I disconnected, moved to the pilot, and jabbed my thumb over and up. The pilot jerked the joystick and whipped us 50 feet to the right and up, and then stopped dead in the air to hover. My stomach lurched, and I swallowed back bile and terror. I got a visual fix on the scene below. The line of agents and Mexican soldiers was still advancing steadily, guns trained.

I crawled to the open doorway and waved at the men on the ground. "Get back!" I yelled. The wind threw my words back at me, "Get back!"

I turned to find the entrance to the underground facility.

A black helmet appeared, rising from below.

Now the two Hueys pulled closer and hovered like hungry buzzards, waiting for permission to dive.

The line kept advancing.

Can't they all see what he's holding?

And then it happened. Gus must have gotten through somehow. Or maybe somebody actually used their binoculars. The men on the ground started backing up swiftly, as a single unit, as if on command. They regrouped 10 yards farther back, then 10 more, repeating the motion until they were at least 60 yards back. The Hueys, too, backed off.

Advancing forward, slow and steady, was Chaco. He had donned a thick bulletproof vest, along with the protective helmet. Rounds of bullets, like deadly necklaces, were draped across his chest, and his wide leather belt holstered two automatic pistols. None of this mattered. What mattered was the heavy launcher balanced on one shoulder. What mattered was the thermobaric grenade, nestled in front. What mattered was the finger poised on the trigger, eager to annihilate all.

I motioned the pilot to drop down closer.

He looked at me askance, as if to say, *"Are you crazy?"*

Probably I was. But I, too, had made this mess, and now I needed to clean it up.

Chaco glanced up, and I ducked low, out of his line of vision. I could almost taste the rage spraying off his skin like sour spittle, as he realized his pilot had disobeyed his orders to stay put and was hovering overhead.

But if Chaco brought the copter down, he was destroying his only means of escape, guaranteeing at best a life behind bars.

He bared his teeth and swung his rocket launcher upwards. I so wanted to get a decent shot off but fell backward instead, when the panicked pilot launched the helicopter straight up. I closed my eyes and searched inside for an appropriate death chant, but instead my mouth curved into an ironic smile. I didn't have the heart to tell the poor pilot that there was no escape, no spot in the sky high enough. Bringing down choppers was what Shmel flamethrowers were built to do.

Suddenly my body flooded with pure adrenaline, astringent and tart. My five senses sharpened to a precise moment of knowing, like the deadly tip of a spear.

I was perfectly ready to kill or be killed.

I had never felt more alive.

And I finally understood Chaco's words, in the cabaña: *There is no other way to live but this—close to the flame that eventually must destroy me. In this way, you and I are alike.*

I belly-crawled to the open doorframe and sighted my Wilson, propping myself up on my elbows. I motioned the pilot to take me closer. He hesitated, and I swung my gun at his head. He saw from my eyes that hesitation was not an option.

I was hyper-alert. I knew I couldn't miss. Not him. Not Chaco.

As we descended, I saw the same conviction, the same

invincible certainty on Chaco's face, as he swung the launcher between the Feds, the hovering Hueys, the Mexican militia, and us.

We were both sure, but only one of us could be right. He had the bulletproof vest, the protective helmet, the rocket launcher. But I had the advantage, because he didn't know I was here.

My trigger finger itched. I was almost close enough.

Something winked at me. A flash of reflected light, near where we'd hidden the guard's body.

I found the source. A sniper, stretched behind the same chaparral that held the guard's corpse. His eye was pressed to the scope of a submachine gun, an MP5. He glanced up, then returned to sighting his target. Like me, he had a very tough kill shot. Too much body armor, too few points of access. But at least he was aiming from the ground.

And for one brief moment, I tasted the hot rage of a killer denied his kill.

I had a heart full of revenge and a soul full of bloodlust—my final terrible secret. I wanted to kill again.

Fucker! I'll take you down first!

I raised my Wilson. Darkness washed across my eyes. I blinked, but the shimmer of black remained, hampering my aim.

And then I heard Lobsang's quiet voice, reaching through my mind's shadows: *Whenever darkness draws you in, choose the* sangha. *Choose the light, my friend.*

The darkness ebbed, the adrenaline, too. I left that dark and hidden place, and returned to my body.

I took a moment to breathe, and then I told the pilot what I needed him to do.

I set my .38 aside, along with Goodhue's Beretta, still weighing down my pocket. I stripped off the orderly uniform, the windbreaker underneath, the shoulder holster. I took off my shoes and socks. Soon I was barefoot, in just my jeans and black T-shirt.

The helicopter lowered to about 50 yards above the rippling earth, and maybe 20 yards in front of Chaco. It hovered above him, like a hummingbird.

I inhaled, exhaled, and crawled to the edge of the helicopter. I pushed up onto my knees, centered my breath, and let my attention grow still, felt the delicate shifting of weight as my body danced with the seesaw motion caused by the hovering blades. Wind buffeted my face and body. One mistake, and I would tumble.

May I be safe and protected. May I be healthy and strong. May I be happy and full of ease. May I be free.

If I should fall to the ground and shatter, if my world should explode into metallic shards, if the same air I invite to help me should be sucked out of my body, turning my essence inside out, if I should die, I die knowing this:

I choose light over darkness.

I am not my secrets.

I am myself again.

"Chaco!" I called out. "Chaco Morales! Carnaté!"

He looked up, whether because he heard me or just sensed me, I'll never know.

His eyes darkened with shock when he realized who was riding shotgun in his helicopter.

I took another tiny move forward, so he could see me, all of me, balancing on the open lip of a flying machine. Placing my hands in prayer posture, I touched them to my forehead and then spread my palms outward, bowing slightly, an offering of loving-kindness and maybe even respect.

"Guess what?" I thought. "I came back to life, too." And I started to laugh.

Chaco squinted up at me, his face twisted, as if confused by this silent truth. His tipped head exposed a delicate, deadly target for the sniper, as I had known it would.

I saw the sniper's rifle buck. I saw Chaco's head snap back, as the bullet entered just under his chin and ripped upward into the dark matter of his brain, tearing it apart. I saw Chaco buckle to his knees and fall, and the grenade launcher bounce and roll to one side harmlessly, settling a yard or two from his still body.

Om mani padme hum. The words radiated through my body like sweet balm, before reaching outward, encouraging Chaco to transform from a state of impurity to purity, from ignorance to the exalted state of Buddhahood. I felt every syllable. I expanded the range of the chant, sent it on to his young daughter, to his beautiful wife. *Om mani padme hum.*

I returned to my seat and buckled in. I pointed my gun.

"*Vamonos*," I said.

I didn't have to say it twice.

CHAPTER 23

I straightened my tie, keeping one eye on the stone steps leading down to "our" table, the one where Heather and I had had our first date. The Inn of the Seventh Ray was only half full. It was a work night for most. I'd ordered myself a beer and a bottle of red wine for Heather and me to share. I'd chosen a 2006 Windward Pinot Noir, one of her favorites. It sat uncorked and breathing by her place setting. Heather had just texted me that she was running late. A late-breaking autopsy, another young celebrity dead of an overdose. This one was a former child actress, a star whose light burned way too bright, way too soon. That same light had been quenched before she'd reached the age of 30, her trajectory through life like a comet's, peaking early before crashing into the ocean.

I closed my eyes and wished her well. Expanded my heart's intention to include Heather. Expanded it further to reach the many others who had traversed my own sky these past few weeks.

The Baja raid proved to be one of the biggest hauls in law enforcement history. Everyone took credit. The DEA bragged about the accuracy of their intel. Homeland highlighted their heat-seeking drone. The FBI pointed to their sniper, and the Mexican Nationals held a celebratory press conference lauding the disruption of a rumored cartel of cartels, complete with table upon table displaying confiscated telecommunication devices for all to see. The ATF checked several hundred Fast and Furious weapons off their "missing" list, and the Department of Defense, after trumpeting the international quashing of a potential terrorist act, quietly removed the Shmels, final destination unknown. Even the San Diego border patrol got in on the Chaco act, after unearthing a highly sophisticated tunnel connecting a warehouse in San Diego with another in Tijuana.

As far as I knew, only one agent hit a home run, though. Within days of the raid, ATF Agent Gus Gustafson got a raise, a promotion, and a Cielo Lodero special interview during which Gus marched out of the closet smiling.

She had a bonafide girlfriend within 48 hours of airtime.

Chuy Dos joined Uno in prison. And GTG Services, Incorporated, named for a former Miss Tijuana, Gloria Teresa Garcia, was in the process of suffering an epic financial meltdown, after losing their CEO and all credibility.

Dr. Kestrel was fired, of course, and faced a slew of criminal charges, medical malpractice the least of them. Dr. Gomez, his Mexican counterpart, as well as Señora Delgado had been returned to Mexico, to face their own fates.

As for Bets McMurtry, I'd visited her in the hospital just yesterday.

Her body was shrunken and frail. The lipstick and pink powder couldn't hide the still-pale cast of her skin. "Well, look what the cat dragged in," she said, attempting a smile.

"Truer than you know," I answered. "How are you doing?"

"I'm alive," she answered. "For what it's worth."

"Did Detective Bohannon fill you in on everything?" Thanks to Bill's quick work, paramedics had found Clara Fuentes unconscious and bleeding, alone on a gurney inside the medical mobile unit. They'd raced her to County/USC, where a team of trauma surgeons cleaned up and reattached what remained of her liver, so the rest of it could eventually grow back.

Bets had struggled upright, wincing. "Tenzing, I swear to God, I had no idea about any of this. All Goodhue told me was there was a donor available. I didn't know it was . . ." Her eyes filled. "Clara's right down the hall, did you know that? She hates me. Never wants to lay eyes on me again, and I don't blame her. I can't stand to look at myself either." Her voice lowered. "This is all my fault. I wish I was dead."

I felt a twinge of compassion, despite myself. Her choice of Goodhue as go-to man, coupled with a sudden worsening of her health, had triggered an avalanche of consequences.

The slide began with Goodhue's decision to have Chuy's men kidnap Clara—a woman, as Bets herself had pointed out—so similar in size and shape they could share clothes, which also meant they could share a liver, if everything else checked out. A woman who presented a serious threat to Bets's political aspirations and was better off gone. A woman who would not be missed, because she was already invisible. But by veering from the gang-banger-donor model, Goodhue had overlooked two things: one, Bets's love for Clara and determination to find her, an attachment that overrode even her political ambitions (something Goodhue would not understand); two, the strange workings of karma that somehow threw Chaco and me back into the same ring.

"I'm done politically, of course," Bets now said, her voice weak. "And it's a goddamned relief, if you want to know the truth."

"You're leaving politics?"

"Already resigned my seat. It's time for Bets McMurtry to work for political change from behind the scenes for once." Her smile was wan. "I was so sure God was in charge that I ignored any red flags and refused to look at the men behind the money." She shrugged. "They say I probably won't be charged with anything, but if you ask me, I probably deserve jail, or worse, for goddamned willful ignorance and gross stupidity. Either way, I have to make amends. That woman is the reason I'm alive. I owe her."

The air in the hospital room seemed to roil with some sort of inner struggle. After a moment, her voice firmed up.

"Getting that close to evil changes a person, even a tough bird like me. Can I tell you a little secret?"

"Sure," I'd said.

"God works in mysterious ways, Ten. I still believe that. And so I'm questioning everything. Everything. Our policy on illegal immigrants, for example." She lay back down and closed her eyes. "Keep an eye on me. I might just surprise you."

I left her then and moved down the hall to look in on another patient.

Clara Fuentes was fast asleep in her hospital bed. It had been touch and go, but she turned out to be as resilient as her former employer. Even asleep, she looked kind. I nodded and smiled at the young man sitting by her bedside. Carlos was keeping vigil, as he had since I'd let him know where Clara was. A new little family unit was forming, forged by grief.

The waitress placed a basket of warm bread in front of me. I grabbed a whole-wheat roll, slathering it with butter. I'd dropped about six pounds over the past few months and lost some muscle mass besides. Too many skipped meals and workouts. Too many skipped everythings.

Not anymore. Yeshe and Lobsang had listened to my full confession and had assigned me a new regime of two visits a day to my meditation cushion, to which I'd added at least 45 minutes of sweaty exercise. This morning, I'd sat on the cushion after months of neglecting my inner world. My eyes had found the small statue of the Buddha.

You're still here, I thought.

Look inside: I never left, he seemed to reply.

I popped the final morsel of roll into my mouth. The diner at the table next to me, a very handsome man, nudged his companion, another very handsome man, and directed his attention across the restaurant. They were looking at a woman making her way down the stone steps. Both men gazed in awe, as if viewing a favorite work of art.

Heather was here, parting waves, as usual, with her beauty.

She had dressed up for the occasion as well, and her white silk halter dress managed to be demure and incredibly hot at the same time.

She pecked me on the cheek and sat.

"Hi," she said.

"Hi."

I poured her a glass of wine. She took the bottle from my hand, read the label, and hummed with appreciation.

We clinked glasses and drank.

"You look beautiful," I said. "How are you?"

She met my eyes. "Are you asking, or, you know, really asking?"

"I'm really asking," I said.

"Then the real answer is, I'm a bit of a wreck, but I'm going to be okay."

"Good," I said. "Me, too."

"Ten, I have to tell you something before I lose my nerve. I . . . I've been seeing this doctor . . ."

I reached across the table and touched her hand.

"I understand. And I'm really sorry things happened the way they did. I wish Kestrel hadn't turned out to be such a crook."

Heather blinked at me. "What?"

"He's under investigation. Didn't he tell you?"

"Ten, what are you talking about?"

"Your affair," I said. "With Kestrel. You know, the doctor you're seeing." I looked away, and then forced myself to meet her eyes. "I found the Post-it, Heather."

"The *Post-it*?"

"'Dr. K., 6 P.M.'?"

Heather's face cleared, and she started to laugh. Hard.

"What's so funny?"

"Oh, Ten, I do love you sometimes. The Post-it." She wiped her eyes. "Not *that* kind of doctor. Not *that* kind of seeing."

Now it was my turn to blink.

"Let's try this one again," she said. She took a deep breath and met my eyes. "I have an eating disorder, Tenzing. I've had it for years. It's called bulimia, but the name doesn't matter. I binge on food, and then I purge it. It's this big, horrible, secret thing I do, my most unfixable and shameful thing. But I'm finally getting help for it."

A series of moments flashed across my mind, like a sped-up slide show. The trips to the bathroom after every meal. The reddened eyes, when I thought she'd been crying. The breath mints, not quite successfully coating over something slightly sour when I kissed her. The missing . . .

I cleared my throat. "So the, uh, the peanut butter?"

She nodded. "Hopefully, my last binge," she said. "Oh, Ten, I'm so sorry. This thing has been like a wall between me and the rest of the world—between *us*, this whole time. I thought I was better. I mean, I was better for a little while after I met you, but it came back, got worse even, especially after you left and I was promoted to ME. I just felt so much pressure all the time."

"So Dr. K . . . ?"

She smiled. "Kirsten, Kirsten Lewis. Clinical psychologist, specializing in eating disorders. Dr. K.'s lovely. You'd like her. I'm seeing her three times a week for now. She says it's a long road back to healthy, but she's confident I can do it."

The waitress arrived with menus. "Would you like to hear our specials?"

I waved her off quickly. Heather cocked her head at me. "Sorry, but I mean, can you eat?"

Heather started to laugh again, before she started to cry. "I'm going to really miss this," she said. "You."

A warm wave of affection flowed through me. "You know what's weird?" I said. "I've never felt closer to you than right now."

It was true. We'd had our first heart-to-heart talk on

the phone last night, and I'd been the one doing most of the talking. I'd told Heather about how lost and angry I'd felt after my father died. I talked in detail about his death and the death of Julius Rosen. I shared everything—the money from Julius, my sudden craving for meat. How it felt to shoot two men. How it felt to almost be shot by another. I even told her about my one-night stand with Cielo.

"I knew it," Heather said. "That skank wasn't going to take no!"

Finally, hesitantly, I'd told Heather about what happened in Baja Mexico. How, when I'd thought I might die, I'd realized that there were two things I'd harbored in my own deeply buried facility, things that I needed to admit, because we both deserved to know the truth.

I'd hated a man enough to kill him, before I came to my senses.

And I'd let Julie, the woman I loved, get away, but I hadn't let her go. And until I did, I wasn't free inside to love anyone else.

Heather ordered buckwheat noodles with roasted mushrooms and tofu. I ordered angel hair with Parmesan, lemon, and chives. I was no longer a soldier at war. I couldn't imagine eating meat.

We spent the rest of our meal chatting about our day. I described my afternoon at Mac Gannon's estate, mostly watching Melissa and Tank fall in love. I'd finally kept my promise and brought the two of them together. Tank had immediately rolled onto his back and waved his four paws skyward, his highest salute of approval.

Mac joined us for the last half an hour, so I could bring him in on Lama Sonam's foolproof method for mindfully quitting nail biting—an early form of exposure therapy minus the actual nibbling

"With your mind, pick a nail, one you'd most love to bite," I told Mac and Melissa. "Now, take three deep in-and-out breaths and change your body position. Then pick another nail and do the same thing." I made them do it for ten minutes. Well, Melissa got bored and ran off, but Mac stuck with it. I explained how Lama Sonam claimed that interior breath and body shifts were the best tools we have for breaking old patterns. I think maybe it helped Mac a little bit.

I even paid a quick visit to Mac's wife, Penelope, who was holed up in her bedroom with another one of her chemically-induced "little headaches." I handed her my favorite waitress Jean's phone number, and told her Jean used to suffer from the same headaches and would be happy to talk to her about recovery any time. I did it for Melissa, more than anyone. The child needed her mother. Every child does.

She and Tank had been waiting for me outside her mother's bedroom door.

"We made you a tea party," she announced. She led me to her playhouse, Tank following on our heels. The tea was pretend, but karma came around deliciously for me anyway. I, who had served tea and cakes a thousand times to elder monks, now had my own cup of tea and pretend cake carefully handed to me by a nine-year-old *bodhisattva*.

As I told Heather the story, I was happy at how my heart softened.

We switched gears after that, as Heather filled me in on her busy day. Three autopsies: one accidental overdose and two drive-by gunshot deaths, gang-related.

Chaco was gone, but the senseless turf wars continued.

We skipped dessert. I was still catching up on sleep, and Heather had an early call. I walked her to her Prius.

"I'm proud of you," I said.

"I'm proud of us." She smiled, blinking back tears.

"I really hope we can be friends," I said. "You know, down the road. . . ." The lump in my throat made swallowing difficult.

"We'll get there," she said and climbed into her car.

I was about to make the turn into my driveway when

I changed my mind and kept going, continuing all the way to Pacific Coast Highway. I headed up the coast until I reached the turnoff to a favorite spot of mine, high on the cliffs overlooking the ocean. The lot was empty. I locked my car and carefully picked my way along the trail to the edge of the bluffs.

I sat. Closed my eyes and settled into an awareness of my heart area. I made myself reopen the "Is Heather the One?" folder. My inner cabinet was full of such files, starting with a beautiful young girl I'd met in India years ago, called Pema. "Is Pema the one?" "Is Charlotte the one?" "Is Julie?" "Is Cielo?" I even had a folder for Gus, a woman I should have sensed wasn't remotely interested in me romantically.

Jean once gave me sound relationship advice: "Put down the flashlight and pick up a mirror." In my case, the flashlight was more like a microscope. Now I picked up the mirror, and here's what I saw: the minute I appeared headed for a breakup, no matter the woman, my surveillance gear kicked in. I was like a heat-seeking drone, desperately surveying my surroundings for the next warm woman who would fix me. Complete me. Love me no matter what.

Now I drilled into my own deeply buried facility, the one I still wanted to keep invisible.

You claim to love your independence, but you're terrified of being alone. You need them to survive, but you hate them for making you so needy. You expect them to fix you, but you always end up more broken.

Admitting each truth cracked open more possibility for change, until an idea gusted in, like a cool, fresh breeze. Maybe it was time to take a break. Maybe I should make sure my own structure was solid for once. Maybe I needed to practice the microscopic truth with myself, before sharing it with, or expecting it from, someone else.

I watched the ocean waves break and retreat, break and retreat, in their own teasing dance with the shore. Then I shifted my eyes toward the dark horizon. Felt the tug of another unsettling thought, free to surface now that I was both quiet enough and open enough to let it.

Who was I but a living paradox—the embodiment of mixed blessings and a walking contradiction? I was born into a spiritual tradition that had been thriving in one form or another for thousands of years. In spite of that, or maybe because of it, now I seemed to be thriving in Los Angeles, the ephemera capital of the world. Did that make me the poster boy for the American Dream? Or the Buddha's worst nightmare?

I looked across the ocean's vastness, toward the place of my birth. I could feel within me a deep connection to Asia, both its exquisite mysteries and its relentless misery. For me, the very best of Asia was the Dharma, the teachings of the Awakened One. I carried the truth of those teachings in my bones. But now that my father was dead, I could also feel a new excitement building in me, a desire to plant myself more deeply right where I was. My divided youth, trucked as I was between parents and countries, had left me a perpetual nomad. I was finally starting to feel grounded, rooted in one place.

Allow. Allow.

A new sense of belonging sprouted like a seed inside. It felt good, natural even, but on the heels of it came a ripple of fear. Would I lose an essential part of me in the process?

I couldn't think of any way to find out without stepping fully into the present and seeing where it took me. I slipped off my shoes and pulled off my socks. My bare soles came in contact with the fine earth of my chosen land, letting my feet touch the truth of my commitment: *This is where I am. This is where I choose to be.*

I tasted the tangy salt-breeze and drew it into my lungs. I brought my hands to my heart and beamed a new prayer—my own words, my own deeply held mix of traditions—into the cosmic jet stream: *Wherever I go, may I learn and love as much as I can in every moment. Wherever I am, may I be open to inspiration and truth.*

I walked back up the path, shoes in hand. I climbed into the Shelby and headed for home. It was getting close to Tank's snack time, and there's a certain look he gives me if I'm late.

ACKNOWLEDGMENTS

GRATITUDE FROM
GAY HENDRICKS

I continue to be astonished by the skill, sensitivity, and beneficent vibes of my co-author, Tinker Lindsay. I've worked with her for years now, with never a blown deadline and never a cross word between us. Katie and I treasure her friendship as well as the gift of her talent in our lives.

To Katie, my beloved mate and co-creator for 34 years now, my gratitude is boundless. I read each new page of a Tenzing novel to her as soon as I've finished writing for the day. To try out my new words in the space of Katie's generous listening is one of the great delights of my life.

A deep bow of gratitude goes to Reid Tracy, Patty Gift, and the lovely people on the Hay House team. It's a writer's dream to have a publisher who really cares about the work and about making the world a better place. Thank you, Reid and team, for making that dream a reality.

I appreciate the detectives of the Santa Barbara Police Department, the Ventura County Sheriff's Department, and the guys at the Far West Gun Shop, all of whom are remarkably gracious when a harried writer calls in need of some obscure crime or gun detail. These folks see and hear things every day that no writer could possibly invent, and I appreciate them for passing along their juicy wisdom to me.

Thanks as always to Sandy Dijkstra, agent extraordinaire, for her dedication to my books through 25 amazing years. I can always count on Sandy and her staff to go the extra mile in making my life easy.

I'm grateful to all the readers who have posted the hundreds of great reviews of the Tenzing books on Amazon, Barnes and Noble, and other online venues. I've been moved to tears many times by reading the warm-hearted reviews by readers who have been touched by Ten and the world he lives in.

GRATITUDE FROM
TINKER LINDSAY

As our books continue to multiply and expand, so, too, does my gratitude for my co-author, Gay. His humor, generosity, openhearted affection, and extraordinary talent bring me daily joy, and I absolutely love working (playing) with him. He and his wife, Katie, are, quite simply, splendid, and I feel blessed to be a part of their lives.

Heartfelt thanks to the Hay House team: the brilliant editor Patty Gift, our first and biggest fan, to whom we owe this wonderful writing adventure; Reid Tracy for his insightful guidance; Quressa Robinson for her careful overseeing; Charles McStravick for his inspired artwork; Laura Gray for her expert editing; Erin Dupree and Darcy Duval for steering the marketing and publicity ship; and, of course, Louise Hay, for having the foresight to create the Hay House playground in the first place.

I am fortunate indeed to be represented by Sandy Djikstra and her accomplished literary agency, including Elise Capron, Jennifer Azantian, and Thao Le. I cannot thank them enough for their continuous care and expertise.

Where would I be without my beloved tribe of fellow scribes? Huge thanks to the people in my writers group, who read and responded to this manuscript in record time, and as always provided invaluable criticism, wrapped in warm support. They are my magnificent six: Bev Baz, Monique de Varennes, Kathryn Hagen, Emilie Small, Pat Stiles, and Barbara Sweeney. Thanks, also, to Tessa Chasteen for bringing her skills to bear on The Third Rule, helping fine-tune both plot points and character arcs.

Private Investigator Dana Champion sat and talked with me for hours, generously giving me a detailed inside peek at the specifics of a P.I.'s life in Los Angeles. She was both patient with the basics and unbelievably helpful with specifics. She also connected me with PI Ann LaJeunesse, whose wry humor and professional tales both inspired and impressed me to no end. I want to be them when I grow up.

Deep gratitude to Joan B., the inspiration for Ten's buddy Jean—I'm so fortunate to count her as a close friend. Thanks, too, to Katherine King for escorting me into, as well as under, the Santa Monica Pier while sharing her event-planning expertise. A shout-out to the friendly folks at Star Helicopters—they let me clamber inside their chopper and borrow their office décor, and to Chuck of Chuck's Auto Care for explaining the ins and outs of Shelby Mustang maintenance. A special bow to journalist Patrick Radden Keefe of the *New York Times*. His courageous, in-depth feature article "Cocaine Incorporated," covering Mexican Drug Cartels, was a tour-de-force, and beyond invaluable.

Finally, my whole-hearted love and appreciation to my fiancé, Cameron Keys. I wouldn't be successful, or sane, without your steadfast love and constant encouragement, much less your willingness to track down obscure BBC mysteries to cool my heated writer's brain after long days at the computer. I am in awe of your uncanny ability to make me laugh or allow me to cry, whatever I need, whenever I need it. I'm such a lucky woman.

ABOUT THE AUTHORS

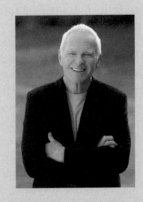

Gay Hendricks PhD has served for more than 35 years as one of the major contributors to the fields of relationship transformation and body-mind therapies. He is the author of 33 books, including *The Corporate Mystic*, *Conscious Living* and *The Big Leap*, and with his wife, Dr Kathlyn Hendricks, has written many bestsellers, including *Conscious Loving* and *Five Wishes*. Dr Hendricks received his PhD in counseling psychology from Stanford in 1974. After a 21-year career as a professor of Counseling Psychology at University of Colorado, he and Kathlyn founded The Hendricks Institute, based in Ojai, California, which offers seminars worldwide.

In recent years Dr Hendricks has also been active in creating new forms of conscious entertainment. In 2003, along with movie producer Stephen Simon, Dr Hendricks founded the Spiritual Cinema Circle, which distributes inspirational movies to subscribers in 70+ countries around the world (www.spiritualcinemacircle.com).

www.hendricks.com

338

ABOUT THE AUTHORS

Tinker Lindsay is an accomplished screenwriter, author and conceptual editor. A member of the Writers Guild of America (WGA), Independent Writers of Southern California (IWOSC), and Women in Film (WIF), she has worked in the Hollywood entertainment industry for over three decades. Lindsay has written screenplays for major studios such as Disney and Warner Bros, collaborating with award-winning film director Peter Chelsom. Their current screenplay, *Hector and the Search for Happiness*, with Egoli Tossell Film, stars Simon Pegg, Rosamund Pike and Christopher Plummer, among others, and will be released in 2014. She also co-wrote the spiritual epic *Buddha: The Inner Warrior* with acclaimed Indian director Pan Nalin, as well as the sci-fi remake of *The Crawling Eye*, and *Hoar Frost*, with Cameron Keys, the latter currently in pre-production.

Lindsay has written two books – *The Last Great Place* and a memoir, *My Hollywood Ending* – and worked with several noted transformational authors, including Peter Russell, Arjuna Ardagh and Dara Marks.

Lindsay studied and taught meditation for several years before moving to Los Angeles to live and work. She can usually be found writing in her home office, situated directly under the Hollywood sign.

www.tinkerlindsay.com

The Fouth Rule of Ten

Topanga Canyon, Calif.
July 5, Year of the Water Snake

*A vast herd of faceless children. Thick. Bound-
less. They slog forward, their pace slow and
strained, their arms outstretched, as if striv-
ing to get somewhere that's perpetually out of
reach. Their eyes are pools of yearning, of
faint hope mixed with despair.*

*Now I am in the midst of them, pushing
through the thick morass of mixed and sticky
emotions. I cast my eyes around, searching for
a tool, a magic wand maybe, to wave over these
struggling souls that I might ease their effort
and aid them in their journey.*

*Fear invades. Acrid and biting, it's sharp
enough to pucker my mouth. What if I'm one of
them? I'm in the middle of the herd, after all.
My own footsteps are labored and sluggish, as
if I'm wading through tar. My own heart is filled
with a nameless longing. Am I, too, trapped in
a futile journey?*

No. This is not real.

I bend my knees and drop into a crouch. With a burst of muscle and hope, I propel myself up, away from the throng, and out of the oppressive grip of the dream.

My heart thumped against the struts of my rib cage. I turned my head to check the red digits of the clock beside my bed. 3:43 A.M. and dead quiet except for a low rumble emitting from Tank. My cat, too, had been pulled from sleep. Now he sat upright next to my head, sphinxlike, purring, gazing at me with wide-eyed interest.

I slid my palm from the dome of his skull to the soft fur that surrounded his neck like a downy muffler.

"It's okay, big guy. Just another weird dream."

Tank lowered his head and placed it between his paws. His eyelids dropped like blinds, snuffing out a pair of glowing green orbs. Within seconds, he was sound asleep again. At 3:43 in the morning, this was a good skill to have. Unfortunately, only one of us had it.

I lay in the darkness as my pounding heart returned to a steady, slow beat. I consciously revisited the dimensions and images of the dream. There was something compelling about its emotional tone.

Allow.

I softened my awareness to feel into this particular flavor and found it buried in the borderland of belly and solar plexus: fear fueled by desperation.

Allow. Allow, Ten.

Inside the desperation two other distinct

feelings huddled close, like fraternal twins fed by the same womb: the deep anguish of a being trapped in a difficult journey leading nowhere good and the powerlessness of a fellow being who is unable to help.

I knew what the dream was about.

The clock had advanced an entire minute. 3:44 A.M. Woo-hoo. I surveyed my brain-space to determine if there was any possibility that I might get back to sleep. The answer was instantaneous: nope. I slipped out of bed without disturbing the rhythm of Tank's easy snores.

The wood floor felt cool and smooth against the soles of my feet. I reached my arms high, then bent to lay my palms flat against the hardwood. As I padded, barefoot, toward my meditation room, I declared the day officially underway. A new day, and my first opportunity to practice a new rule: let go of expectations, for expectations lead to suffering.

I sighed. No matter what events July 5th might bring, anticipated or not, I was fairly certain of one thing: it was bound to be less upsetting than July 4th had been.

CHAPTER 1

The long line of cars snaked up and over the hill. Grumpiness emanated from the family-filled vehicles like toxic gas. The July 4th traffic was brutal. Where was everybody going, anyway? Why weren't they at home cooking burgers?

My car crawled, too, all the way from Topanga to Bill and Martha Bohannon's home in Hancock Park, a two-hour drive that should have taken half that. I finally parked outside their house at 5:30. The smell of charred meat let me know Bill was already stationed at the outside grill. I was the first car there, so the bad traffic must be citywide. That fact made me feel a lot better, which tells you what kind of mood I was in.

I climbed out of my Shelby. Streaming slants of sunlight framed the Bohannons' bungalow in burnished gold. I tipped my head back, closed my eyes, and then inhaled and exhaled three times, deeply. Children's laughter floated from Bill's backyard. I smiled, grateful for the promise of frosty cold beer and friendship, and for the ability to reset my mood at any given time, if only I remembered to reach for that tool, the one that lets go of what was and accepts what is.

I have two favorite American holidays: July 4th and Thanksgiving, and for the past decade I've spent most of them at Bill and Martha's house. My ex-partner from the LAPD Burglary/Homicide division might be married to a woman of German descent, but Martha's commitment to celebration was decidedly un-Teutonic—sometimes I think she chose their house primarily because of the annual fireworks display visible from their backyard.

An American flag flapped merrily from its pole by their front stoop, and red, white, and blue ribbons were tied in bows on the branches of their magnolia tree. Some were tied more neatly than others, signaling that the twins must finally be old enough to participate in decorating.

I reached into the back of the Mustang for the six pack of Chimay White I'd set on the fiberglass shelf that stood in for the back seat on many '65 Shelby 350s. Life was good. I had a steady stream of clients in need of the services of a private investigator and willing to pay handsomely for them. The income was enough to support me, my newly licensed friend and co-worker, Clancy Williams, and even a recently hired personal assistant. Even more impressive, at least to me, is that I had made it for more than a year without getting entangled in any romantic relationships—a record.

Tank seemed to approve. I was a steadier, happier roommate without them.

For a brief moment, I allowed myself to wonder if Julie might be here, but I brushed away the thought lightly, and it floated off, the faint trace of longing I still harbored for her almost as insubstantial as a feather.

Besides, Martha would have told me if her sister was coming.

I smiled. I was looking forward to taking my place on a chaise lounge with a chilly bottle of Belgian ale in one hand and a specially made garden burger in the other. Biting into a burger topped with ketchup, mayo, and a slice of sweet onion was pretty close to a religious experience—even for a vegetarian. Fabulous food and drink, a slew of grimy kisses from a pair of twin redheads, the warm love of best friends, and fireworks: like Martha's red-white-and-blue bows in the branches, my expectations for the day were predictably elevated, jaunty, and filled with promise.

Yet even as those thoughts flickered through my mind, a whispered warning slithered into my reverie: *Take care, Tenzing. Remember what the Buddha taught: Expectation is the enemy of serenity and a root cause of suffering.* I recognized the voice's source—Lama Yeshe, one of my two best childhood friends. Yeshe and Lobsang had helped anchor me throughout the troublesome early years spent in my father's Buddhist monastery in Dharamshala, India. In those days my father had served first as monastic disciplinarian and then as head abbot. Whatever his role, he was none too pleased with his rebellious son. Time has a way of changing everything. Now my father had passed, Yeshe and Lobsang were themselves abbots, and I was living thousands of miles away in the City of Angels. But the Buddha's pearls of wisdom, it turns out, are valuable whenever and wherever you live.

Let go of expectations. Our Tibetan teachers at Dorje Yidam had urged us to practice this simple yet powerful step at every opportunity. According to legend, a monk once asked the Buddha (the *Bikkhu's* voice, in my imagination, plaintive): "But how can I actually live, as you suggest, without expectations?" The Buddha had answered with a question of his own: "How can you actually live if you *have* expectations?"

Never mind. Today was a good day, and my expectations were reasonable. Just in case, I dialed back the anticipation of Maude and Lola peppering me with kisses. They were almost three years old, and it had been a few months since we'd spent any extended time together. In toddler years, that's a long time, and I didn't know how they might now express affection. Either way, I was hot and grimy from Los Angeles traffic and smog, and aiming to have a good time.

Martha flung open the door, her smile wide. I stepped into her hug but not before noticing weary rings of gray crumpling the skin around her eyes. I chalked it up to an over-40 mother with twin preschoolers.

She accepted my six-pack with a quick thanks before calling over her shoulder, "Girls! Uncle Ten's here!"

Thundering hoof-beats approached at high speed. I squatted just in time, as Maude and Lola careened into me and wrapped their small, dense monkey-bodies around me.

I struggled to stand upright and hefted them, wiggling and squealing, through the foyer and living room and out the open French doors to the backyard.

"Bring me a brew!" I shouted back to Martha, laughing.

Bill, as I had guessed, presided over the grill, dressed in full suburban finery. A towering red chef's toque perched atop his head and a blue apron with the embroidered words "Best Dad in the World" hung around his neck. A bit over the top, but I was inclined to agree. As midlife parents, rewarded after years of IVF with the appearance of twins, Bill and Martha had showered their girls with the freely flowing love and joy reserved for unexpected gifts.

I set the girls down and looked them over. Lola was wearing black leggings, a puffy pink jacket, and sparkly shoes. She clutched a small blue stuffed monkey.

"I like your monkey," I said. "What's his name?" Lola studied her monkey for a full minute.

"Monkey," she finally said. Lola tended to be long on contemplation but short on words.

Maude was dancing from foot to foot. She had on the toddler version of a sports uniform, the bright blue shorts, long and baggy, the matching top emblazoned with the words *Property of the L.A. Dodgers*. Bill, a diehard Dodgers fan, had obviously started early with at least one of his girls.

"Nice uniform," I said.

"This isn't a uniform, Uncle Ten," Maude scolded. "This is my teamer outfit!"

"Ahh," I said, as Maude grabbed at my hand.

"Did you bring us a treat?" she went on, her eyes bright with hope.

"Not today," I admitted. Maude's face fell. Her eyes glittered with welling tears, and her lower lip started to tremble. A beer magically appeared in my hand as Martha stepped in, her mother-radar sensing imminent disaster. She knelt and cupped Maude's rapidly reddening face in her hands.

"Maude, sweetheart, we just talked about this, remember? How sometimes when Uncle Ten comes over he brings you girls a little something and sometimes he doesn't? How you love him either way, just like he loves you no matter what?"

"I know," Maude wailed, tears now streaming down her cheeks. "But in my mind, he bringed us something!"

The Buddha in me nodded and smiled with compassion.

"Get your butt over here, Ten!" Bill called, as Martha held Maude against her chest until the flash-storm passed.

I crossed the yard as Bill deftly flipped a burger. He stepped back from the grill and joined me for our ritual, awkward man-hug.

"Don't worry," Bill said. "I make Maude cry hourly. It rarely lasts more than two minutes. See?"

Sure enough, both girls scampered off, Maude no worse for wear.

"So," Bill teased. "Good to see you're still alive and well, Mr. Busy Private Detective-man."

"Look who's talking," I replied, "Mr. Canceled Lunch Last Week Because You Had to Meet with the Mayor."

"Right," he said, snorting. "Me, plus his personal army of network news reporters. God forbid he shows up when there aren't any cameras rolling." His voice was spiked with bitterness.

I studied my friend with concern. Martha's eyes may have been ringed with gray, but all Bill's gray had migrated to his hair. Call me crazy, but the last month alone had added a large swatch of silvery strands, turning his dark blond hair almost platinum. As a police administrator, Bill earned a lot more than he had during our days as lowly Homicide detectives, but the job came with a serious stressor: daily political wrestling matches between the City Administration and Police Headquarters.

I pointed to the wisps of gray poking out from under the chef's hat. "Very distinguished."

"Just call me George Clooney," he said. He looked over at Martha and half smiled. "What do you think, honey? Am I sexy, or is it time to break out that bottle of hair dye for men?" Martha was either out of earshot or chose to ignore Bill. As she disappeared into the house, I watched Bill's smile fade. I stepped in.

"Or you could get a job that doesn't bore the living crap out of you."

"Ouch." Bill clutched at his heart. "You really know what buttons to push, don't you?"

"I ought to," I said. "You're the guy who taught me how to push 'em."

That earned me a laugh, and for a moment Bill looked young again. I wanted to go a little deeper, but Martha and the girls reappeared with several more guests in tow. I tipped my bottle at Sully and Mack, still detectives with Burglary/Homicide and joined, as usual, at the hip. Another veteran detective, Marty Shumacher, trailed behind them, his cheeks ruddy and veined from a few too many happy hours. He spotted me and beelined to my side.

"Norbu! How the hell is civvy life treating you?"

"Not too bad," I said.

"You gettin' any these days? Or are you, you know, still going without?" Marty was obsessed with the notion of monastic celibacy and convinced I must be a staunch practitioner of sexual abstinence. For once, he was right, but no way was I giving him any satisfaction in that quarter.

"None of your business," I said, but he had glimpsed the cooler of beer and sped off. Conversation versus alcohol? No contest.

Two burgers, three ears of corn, and one soothing of a toddler's skinned knee later, the sky had grown dark. A few distant booms let us know that fireworks were starting to erupt across the city.

"Boomie-lights time! Boomie-lights time!" Maude shrieked. Bill slipped next to me.

"Can you get another bag of ice from the kitchen, Ten? In the freezer."

"Of course." I was glad to do it. I had tired a little of having the same conversation about two dozen times: "Work's fine. No, I don't miss the paperwork. Yes, I still carry a gun. No, nobody in my life right now . . . "

I took a moment to do a check-in with my self before pulling the freezer drawer open. I felt a little sad, but I wasn't sure why. Perhaps it had to do with the distance I sensed between Bill and Martha. Their adoration for the girls was still palpable, but the normally warm temperature they generated as a couple had cooled considerably.

A loud knock at the front door interrupted my musing. I crossed into the foyer to welcome the tardy arrivals. Before I opened the door my detective reflexes kicked in, so I glanced through the small barred window of the front door to see who stood outside.

Two women, neither of whom I knew. They definitely came from the same gene pool, though one was a good 20 years older than the other. Mother and daughter, if I had to guess. The younger woman rapped sharply on the door a second time. She was tall, maybe 40, with a wild mane of brown hair streaked with gray. Her snug jeans and man's button-down shirt tied into a knot around her waist complemented a strong, lithe body, fit as well as feminine. She was quite lovely. I glanced at her left hand. No tell-tale wedding band. The older woman stood next to her, also tall, also fit, but stockier. Her gray hair was roughly chopped so that it just brushed her shoulders and framed her high cheekbones, prominent nose, and clear, wide-set, brown eyes, characteristics shared by her companion. Her own faded beauty was further marred by the deep downturned creases bordering her mouth. She wore a loose T-shirt, sweatpants that bagged at the knees, and work boots. Her big-knuckled hands were chapped, as if she did manual labor of some kind. No wedding ring, either.

I opened the door.

"Hello," I said. The younger woman appraised me with steady eyes.

"I hope I am in the right place." Her accent sounded Eastern European.

"I'm sure you are. You here for the barbecue?"

The stockier woman barked a bitter little laugh. Her companion shot her a look. "Mama. Shush!" she said, abruptly silencing her mother.

So I was right. Mother and daughter.

"This is Bill Bohannon's house, yes?" she asked.

"It is," I said. "Bill's out in the backyard. There's a party going on right now. Would you like to come in?"

Her nod was curt. With her streaked mane of hair and flaring nostrils, she resembled a restless thoroughbred. I'm not a lover of horses, and I wasn't taking to her, either.

"Please to bring him to me here," she announced and crossed her arms. She was behaving as if giving commands and having them obeyed was normal. Was she military of some kind?

"Okay," I said slowly. My intuition was waving red flags right and left. Something wasn't right here. "Whom shall I—" She cut me off. "Mila," she snapped. "Mila Radovic."

I looked toward the other woman for her name. She glared.

Mila irritably rattled off something in a language I couldn't understand. The other woman shook her head, stolid and unmoved. "No," she stated, glaring at me. "My name not important."

This was shaping up to be a fairly unpleasant conversation, so I was happy to take a break. Still, my steps were slow as I retraced my way through the house and into the backyard. The noise of the gathering had risen in direct proportion to the percentage of alcohol in various bloodstreams. Adding to the racket was the tock-tock, tock-tock of four detectives playing drunken doubles ping-pong.

Bill had returned to the grill and was swabbing barbecue sauce on a couple of chickens.

I moved to his side, my pace still reluctant. The noise of revelers seemed to fade. My heart felt heavy in my chest, though specifically why I couldn't say. Sometimes I wish my gut wasn't wired like a Geiger counter, able to sense radioactive emotions invisible to the naked eye.

"Hey, Bill. You've got visitors."

"Hold on," he said. He maneuvered the sizzling chickens off the grill and onto a carving board. Sully and Mack fell upon them with carving knives. The aroma of caramelized barbecue sauce on chicken skin smelled intoxicating. When meat starts to smell that good to me, I know an altercation is looming.

Everything is about to change.

As I prepared to tell Bill more, Martha appeared. She glanced back and forth between us, eyes laser-sharp and antennae quivering. "What's up?"

I opened my mouth, closed it and then made a decision to tell the truth, though everything inside me wanted to lie. "Two women are at the front door. They're asking for you, Bill. They're not from around here."

A tight look swept over Martha's face, which rendered it unreadable, only her eyes expressing uncertainty. She turned to Bill. He patted her shoulder and immediately headed through the kitchen door into the house. Now Martha's entire body stiffened. Sensing trouble, I followed Bill, with Martha huffing along right behind me.

Bill stopped abruptly, just short of the doorway. Mila Radovic let out a sharp cry of anguish. She barreled inside and threw her arms around my frozen friend, not unlike Maude and Lola had done with me a few hours earlier, when the world was simpler. Bill tolerated the embrace, slack-jawed, his arms dangling at his sides.

His head swung helplessly from Mila to Martha, who had stepped around me.

Mila loosened her clutch and stared at Bill's dangling arms. Then she whipped up her right hand and cracked him across the face with an open palm. It was a mesmerizing moment—so much between them and nobody else. Neither Martha nor I could move a muscle. Then a satisfied cackle from "mama," still standing outside, broke the spell. It seemed at least that she had gotten what she came for.

But what was that, exactly?

Mila's mother now stepped inside and let fly another burst of foreign words, delivered to her daughter at high volume and with considerable passion. As she gabbled, she gestured at Martha and me. Mila replied in kind and moved to grip the woman's shoulders, giving her a little shake.

Mila turned, directing her words to Martha. "I am Mila. This is Irena. She is my mother." Then she wheeled toward Bill, her eyes flashing, willing him to complete the introductions. Bill remained stunned and motionless. Sweat glistened on his forehead and cheeks. He reached up with one hand to swipe at his brow, and the action seemed to return him to the world of the living. He swallowed.

"Yeah. Uh. This, this is my wife, Martha, and, uh, my best friend, Ten Norbu."

Bill's face roiled with a dire mixture new to me: grief, fear, helplessness, and confusion. I was rattled. He and I had encountered many dangerous situations through the years, some of them life threatening, but I'd never seen him jammed up the way he was at this moment in time.

Mila stepped forward and grabbed my hand. She was tall enough to look down at me. Her grip was muscular, her palm dry. I registered again the strong beauty of her face and the clear gaze of her brown eyes. Her mother observed us, arms crossed over her chest.

Mila moved on to Martha, her words meant to be placating. "Please. Forgive for the intrusion. I come only because I am desperate."

Martha's reluctance to engage did visible battle with her

natural kindheartedness. The latter won and she offered a weak, pained smile. "Of course. Tell me. How can we help?"

Mila shot a look at Bill, again waiting for him to say something, but he stood mute, once again sunk in a trance. She turned back to Martha, her voice firm. "Our son is missing."

Martha's smile wavered. "I'm sorry? Your . . . whose son?"

My stomach tightened, as Bill stared at the floor and his cheeks flushed scarlet.

Now Mila, too, looked down. Her mother rolled her eyes. "What I say?" she said to Mila and moved to take her arm. "Useless. We go."

Bill coughed and he reached toward Martha. "Martha. Mila and I were . . . we . . . we had a . . . we have a son."

Martha's knees buckled. She stumbled sideways, lurching into the living room and landing on the couch. The cushions whooshed, as if they, too, had just received a punch in the stomach. I crossed the room and sat next to my friend, offering a steadying hand on her back. Martha looked around wildly, as if hoping to find a different reality somewhere, anywhere. Finally she found Bill's eyes.

"How . . . how old is he?" Martha asked.

Something in Mila seemed to snap. "*He* has a name! His name is Sasha!"

Martha's eyes flared at the aggression, answering with a bolt of hate-energy, aimed at Mila.

Bill's voice was low. "Sasha is . . . " He appeared to be mentally adding up the years. "Nineteen?" he asked Mila. She nodded. "Nineteen," he stated more firmly.

"Nineteen," Martha whispered, defeated by the number. "Nineteen years old." Her breath grew labored, and I found myself taking several deep breaths, as if by doing so I could provide her with much-needed oxygen. The corded muscles in Martha's neck looked like tightly twisted ropes.

Bill said, "I'm sorry."

Martha gasped a sob-laugh and shook her head.

Mila made a curt, dismissive movement with her hand. "Please. Sasha is gone. Missing. You are father. I need help for finding him. No time for family drama."

Martha's spine straightened. "Excuse me? Family *drama*? Are you fucking kidding me?! We were doing just fine until about fifteen minutes ago!"

I knew that wasn't true—her family wasn't doing just fine. But I also knew she'd just received an unexpected gut-kick and would believe what she needed to.

Bill held up a hand. "Stop," he said, and I heard it in his voice: the Good Cop persona was taking over from the Errant Husband. "Martha, let her speak. Mila, why do you think he's . . . why do you think Sasha's in danger?"

Martha slumped, defeated. She clutched at my left arm, finding my wrist and gripping it tightly.

"Sasha very smart. Full of passion," Mila said. "Also, very stubborn. Like father," she added, and I felt Martha wince. "He study to be journalist," Mila continued, the pride in her voice unmistakable, "so he can change world. And . . . but . . . not a good world where we are. Terrible people. Gangsters."

"Where is that?" I asked.

"Bosnia," she said.

And the blurry, piecemeal images sharpened into focus. Bill had served briefly in Bosnia before he left the military to start his LAPD career. He had mentioned his participation in the bloody conflict once or twice. Me? I knew little about that war; I was young, and the conflict took place around the time of my mother's suicide, when my mind was preoccupied with other battles.

"Where we live, everything about the drugs for these men," Mila continued. "The drugs and also the sex, young girls. Terrible. Buying and selling like, like nothing more than toys for playing. Sasha decide on investigating them. He start writing about these bad men on computer, he write on his . . . how you say? Log . . . ?"

"Blog," I offered. Martha stiffened and pulled away, as if providing the word for Mila was a betrayal of some sort, and I regretted my impulse to speak.

"Yes," Mila said. "Blog, on Internet. Now I am scared these bad men take Sasha."

A tomblike silence filled the room. Random flashes of light and deep, distant booms provided a bizarre background—a mimicked bomb raid, an apt soundtrack to the drama unfolding in the living room. Martha started to sob. Mila and her mother ignored her, locked in on Bill.

He stroked his mustache. I'd seen him do it a thousand times while thinking through strategies.

"Okay," he said finally. "Go wait by your car. I'll join you in a little while."

Mila's nod was tight. She and Irena left.

"Ten," Bill said. "Can you keep an eye on them while I talk to Martha?"

I was already halfway to the front door. As I shut it behind me, the soft click of the latch had the sad finality of a coffin lid closing over what was, so very recently, a vibrant living thing.

We hope you enjoyed this Hay House book. If you'd like
to receive our online catalogue featuring additional
information on Hay House books and products,
or if you'd like to find out more about the
Hay Foundation, please contact:

Hay House UK, Ltd., Astley House, 33 Notting Hill Gate,
London W11 3JQ • *Phone:* 0-20-3675-2450
Fax: 0-20-3675-2451 • www.hayhouse.co.uk

Hay House, Inc., P.O. Box 5100, Carlsbad, CA 92018-5100
(760) 431-7695 or (800) 654-5126
(760) 431-6948 (fax) or (800) 650-5115 (fax)
www.hayhouse.com® • www.hayfoundation.org

Hay House Australia Pty. Ltd., 18/36 Ralph St.,
Alexandria NSW 2015 • *Phone:* 612-9669-4299
Fax: 612-9669-4144 • www.hayhouse.com.au

Hay House SA (Pty), Ltd., P.O. Box 990, Witkoppen 2068
Phone/Fax: 27-11-467-8904 • www.hayhouse.co.za

Hay House Publishers India, Muskaan Complex, Plot No. 3, B-2,
Vasant Kunj, New Delhi 110 070 • *Phone:* 91-11-4176-1620
Fax: 91-11-4176-1630 • www.hayhouse.co.in

Raincoast, 9050 Shaughnessy St., Vancouver, B.C. V6P 6E5
Phone: (604) 323-7100 • *Fax:* (604) 323-2600 • www.raincoast.com

Take Your Soul on a Vacation

Visit **www.HealYourLife.com**® to regroup,
recharge, and reconnect with your own magnificence.
Featuring blogs, mind-body-spirit news, and life-
changing wisdom from Louise Hay and friends.

Visit **www.HealYourLife.com** today!